The Bruce's Treasure

L.A. Kristiansen

Ringwood Publishing
Glasgow

Copyright L.A. Kristiansen © 2025
All rights reserved

The moral right of the author has been asserted

Issued in 2025
by
Ringwood Publishing AMC

www.ringwoodpublishing.com
e-mail: mail@ringwoodpublishing.com

ISBN: 978-1-917011-16-7

British Library Cataloguing-in-Publication Data
A catalogue record for this book is available from the
British Library

Printed and bound in the UK
by Lonsdale Direct Solutions

In Memory of
Margaret Kerr Irvine (1933-2024)

Dedicated to:

UMIST and The York Archaeological Trust
who made me better,

and

Emma and Hans who make everything worthwhile

The Bruce's Treasure

Book Three of the
Independence Chronicles

The Independence Chronicles: The Story So Far

Book 1: Raise Dragon

In 1291 John Wishart on orders from his brother the battling bishop Robert Wishart searches Acre for Geoffroi de Charnay just as the city is falling to the Mamluks. They escape Acre on a barge, full of dead sailors and knights brutally killed, the only person they find alive is an elderly monk Geoffrey, driven mad by the experience. The barge also contains unimaginable wealth, Alaric's treasure, and reason enough to kill.

John and Geoffroi decide to hide the treasure scared for their lives and the power the treasure could bring in the wrong hands. They travel to Italy and conceal it in Padua with the help of Reginaldo and Enrico Scrovegni. Its secret location scratched in code on separate amethyst rings, four in all owned by de Charnay, John, Enrico Scrovegni and the old monk Geoffrey.

John returns to Scotland with Geoffrey the monk and tells bishop Wishart what he found. They decide to leave the treasure until they can successfully recover it and wait for a time where it can be used for its greatest benefit for Scotland and the Templars.

The Scottish wars of independence ignite and Scotland is invaded by the English king Edward I. John leaves for France to seek King Phillip's help to fight the English with William Wallace and then disappears. The English king thinks he has subdued the Scots.

It's 1300. King Phillip's brother Charles de Valois is in Italy and close to finding the treasure. It is moved from its hiding place and concealed for many years. It is missing but not forgotten.

In Feb 1306 Robert the Bruce kills his rival for the Scottish throne John Comyn in Greyfriars Church. Bishop Wishart absolves him recognising without a Scottish king, Scotland will no longer exist as a kingdom but merely as a land with neither sovereignty nor an independent church. He crowns Robert de Bruce and the Scottish rebellion fully ignites.

Wishart confesses the secret of the treasure to Bruce. He then reveals a second secret that there is a rival for King Edward's throne. Edward I swears revenge on Wishart and Bruce for killing Comyn who is his cousin by marriage. He sends Aymer de Valence in pursuit of them, and the rival for the English throne.

Meanwhile in Constantinople, the joint emperors Andronikos and Michael scheme to capture Alaric's treasure. They send the head of their Norwegian Varangian guards called Axel Myhre known as Aurelian or 'the golden one' in pursuit.

In 1306, just when King Edward I believes Scotland to have been conquered, Bishop Wishart seeks the treasure's return, sending four Scottish knights to Geoffroi de Charnay to retrieve the rings and then the treasure.

The English, and French kings make several unsuccessful attempts to stop the Scottish knights reaching de Charnay in Paris. He reveals the treasure is hidden in Padua and Enrico Scrovegni can lead them to it. He also discovers that the Templar order is under threat from King Phillip of France and determines he will soon need the Templar portion of the treasure. King Phillip's is obsessed with capturing the treasure to further his own aims.

The Scots return to Paris seeking de Charnay who has tricked them to find out where the treasure is hidden. This time de Charnay joins with them to find it and return it to safekeeping in Scotland.

Book 2: Revenge of the Tyrants

The four Scottish knights find themselves in France guarding the treasure barge. Pursued by the agents of France, England, and Byzantium.

They fake their deaths and the loss of the treasure and hide in Chateau Gaillard whilst Geoffroi de Charnay makes preparation for them to escape France and return to Scotland tricking the French and the English with misleading letters and false trails.

Bruce suffers defeats at the Battles of Methven and Dalrigh and goes into hiding protected by his cousin Christina of the Isles. He loses his most precious relic of St Fillan at Dalrigh to his rival John Lorn MacDougall. The MacDougall's are kin of John Comyn.

Christina and the Bruce start a relationship. Whilst the slain John Comyn's brother-in-law Aymer de Valence pursues Bruce. Christina and the Bruce's location is betrayed by her duplicitous brothers Lachlann and Ruaidhri, and Valence attacks her at Castle Tioram.

Captued after the Battle of Methven, Bishop Wishart is arrested and taken to the Tower of London where he meets his agent Murdie MacBeith who spies on the English court. Bishop Wishart urges Murdie to find Jamie and tell him that he needs him to return from France. King Edward starves the bishop hoping he will die of neglect until the Pope's envoy Cardinal Orsini steps in as Wishart's protector.

MacBeith discovers that the English king had conspired to kill the Scottish heir Margaret the Maid of Norway. Now

Margaret is rumoured to be alive and hiding in Norway so king Edward sends Murdi under his alias Alain D'Orthez to find her accompanied by the Norwegian noble Gyrid Hugleikkson. Margaret is thought to be hiding in Gyrid's castle Audenborg. Edward has imprisoned her son Hugel and threatens his execution unless Margaret is brought to him. Gyrid and Murdie are forced to help Edward.

Murdie and Gyrid travel to Norway to find Margaret knowing they can't be left alive to reveal King Edward's complicity in the plot against his niece. They are also followed by the King of Norway's men to Audenborg Castle. He too wants Margaret who is a threat to his throne. King Haakon is made aware of the treasure and starts to make his own plans to capture it.

Christina discovers she is pregnant by King Robert. Christina and Domhnall MacBeith destroy Tioram with gunpowder and kill many of Valence's men. Then King Robert falls ill just before he escapes from Tioram. He believes the loss of the relic of St Finnian at Dalrigh has removed god's protection.

The Scots plan to take the treasure and head for Orkney and the protection of Lord Halcro but remain trapped in France by French and English spies. They call on Geoffrey de Charnay for help. He tricks King Phillip of France who sends his troops to La Rochelle to look for the treasure ship whilst it is still concealed within Chateau Gaillard.

Enrico Scrovegni discovers King Phillip's plans to destroy the Templars and sends men to warn de Charnay accompanied by a mysterious shroud created in his workshop by the enigmatic Brother Albertus. The Templars contact their Grand Master urging him to return to France.

*

A list of characters and their roles is provided at the end of the book.

Prologue

Thessaloniki, Byzantine Empire, May 1306:
The She-Wolf, Basilissa Eirene

'Out! Get out, all of you! And make sure Bishop Gregory and I are not disturbed,' Empress Eirene ordered as the numerous servants rushed out of the doors. She paused until the echo from their footsteps became so faint that she believed no one could eavesdrop.

'Old man, you are wearing away the mosaic with your pacing,' Eirene scowled at Bishop Gregory as he walked rapidly over the same ground, kicking the small wooden table blocking his way and swearing under his breath. 'You are in danger of collapse, and I am breaking into a sweat just watching you.'

The ex-Patriarch Gregory delivered an unconvincing nod as he continued swearing and murmuring. The great hall in the empress's palace echoed with the tones of fury as he wiped the beads of sweat that had popped out of his forehead with a silk neckerchief and stuffed it back in his sleeve.

It was unbearably hot, so the windows had been carelessly flung open, and wall tapestries had been repurposed as flimsy window shades. Every few seconds a variable breeze blew in from the sea that surrounded the palace.

The Bishop's wide-brimmed golden silk hat had almost blown away, and the empress struggled to suppress a snigger as it flapped like a winged bird in flight. She enjoyed pricking his inflated pomposity.

His neck had folds of fat that caught his sweat. He pulled

at the opening to his tunic like a bellow to cool himself.

'My husband, Andronikos, has sent you into exile and replaced you with the toadying Athanasius. Be thankful that at least you are alive. He normally gets his will delivered through the point of a Varangian's dagger. Think yourself lucky he didn't part with your services that way.' Eirene thought him malleable yet powerful – that was why she liked him.

'See how he treats me, his empress … sent into exile and constantly spied on. All my servants are in his pay, and I am one step from the dungeon or the convent.'

Bishop Gregory's body stiffened, and he made a mock bow.

'Indeed, Basilissa, I am constantly grateful and reminded that you saved my life by giving me sanctuary. Your husband may not have the appetite to order my death, because he is a patient man – my paranoia is warranted, don't you think? And as always, your concern is touching, heartfelt.' Eirene observed his sarcastic smile.

'We should both look to our safety,' he added. 'Your children are heirs to the throne. It is not beyond imagination, despite their royal lineage, that Michael will be forcing his way through the nursery door with a dagger the moment Andronikos is dead. He is standing between you and your children's death, so I would use my hate sparingly.'

The thought of her children being murdered occupied her mind – she always dreamed of undermining the rotting edifice in Constantinople and replacing the joint Emperors Andronikos and Michael with her own son John. That dream was now a plan, and its execution possessed her.

She clasped a feather fan in her right hand and gently wafted her heavily made-up face, which enhanced her considerable beauty. The thick powder, rouge, and eyeliner had started to crack and run, and she hated to look anything less than stunning. Empresses neither aged nor decayed.

She was a little over thirty years old. Her light auburn hair, inherited from her Spanish ancestors, betrayed her foreign origins. It was pulled back from her face and lay down her back in a tight plait. The hair was held in place by a gold coronet studded with multicoloured precious stones, and further covered with an almost luminous silk veil.

Her red dress was completely byzantine, tight to the neck, but as it moved down her body, the silk cloth enveloped her torso. Yet it was gently fitted to the contours of her frame and became more generous as it fell to the ground. Its lining was of cream silk, which was exposed within large open sleeves. The exterior was a dark red silk brocade that flowed towards jewelled cuffs, hung heavy with silk embroidery and edged with pearls. The folds of cloth were gathered in a jewelled girdle that fastened at the front. Around her neck was a decorated gold collar embedded with small icons and more precious jewels.

'Bishop, I have some interesting news that may stop your pacing. I had a visitor a week ago.' Eirene liked to play with her courtiers, and especially with Gregory.

'Lady, you have many visitors. What was special about this one?' His voice had the edge of offense; he needed to control all her actions.

'Raimund de Braose, the King of France's most loyal acolyte – and conversely, my cousin Edward Plantagenet's most fervent enemy. A good man to have dealings with – he is well connected.'

Gregory stared at the ground, silent, perplexed, and offended.

'You may remember that Raimund's ancestor William was starved to death by the English in a Corfe Castle dungeon. He has a considerable score to settle with the Plantagenets. It is not this unsavoury act I wish to discuss, but something else – something I wish to keep secret. It will help with my plan to weaken the emperors and replace them with my son, and Raimund de Braose has brought the means.'

Bishop Gregory nodded politely. 'How can Raimund de Braose help with that?'

'He is an embittered noble at the heart of the French court, hates the English King and has the ear of Pope Clement. Pope Clement wants what you and I want – the reunion of the Greek and Latin Churches. If I can move the Churches closer, that weakens Michael and Athanasius, who want the opposite. The pope will be more powerful with all those extra souls and the money they will bring. If I can bring the unification about, his gratitude will extend to providing soldiers and arms to move Michael out of his throne and move my son into it – and of course there is Alaric's treasure that will sweeten Clement even further.'

'Basilissa, you know about the treasure?' Gregory maintained his bitter tone. She knew he had deliberately withheld this information. She had spies too.

'I heard rumours years ago and now I am hearing increasingly in dispatches from my agents. Your voice suggests these rumours are more than that?' She scowled at her advisor and continued.

'This treasure is the same one the Latins stole from the empire in 1204 when they raided the city. The same one we stole from the Huns that lay buried with their leader Alaric, which he in turn had stolen from our Roman forefathers in antiquity. It has reappeared, and Emperor Andronikos is trying to retrieve it and buy an army so big no one will ever challenge him again. If we could get hold of it, and deny the emperors, combine that with the Pope's favour of a bigger Church for him to rule, it will make me so powerful I can crush any opposition.'

She couldn't suppress her smile.

'And de Braose, what was this valuable information?' Gregory asked.

'His news was initially bedroom gossip from the various

courts, but it didn't take him long to get to the point of his visit. He came with a tale that will ruin the English and their plans to weaken King Phillip and the papacy.'

Eirene paused and filled two ornate wine goblets. She handed a goblet to Gregory, who voraciously emptied it, the remnants dripping into his grey beard.

'Edward is obsessed with two things, firstly the Pope and his cosy relationship with the French King.'

'And secondly, Basilissa?' Gregory asked as Eirene finished her first goblet of wine.

'Scotland. He doesn't seem to have grasped the fact that every Scot fights for their country with the passion of ten Englishmen. He may win a battle here and there, but Scotland will defeat him in the end, he just hasn't realised it yet – but that's what obsession does, it blinds you to reality.'

'What exactly did Raimund tell you that weakens Edward – and the treasure, how can we get it under our control?' Gregory words were slurred, yet he stood taller, emboldened by the temporary power wine provides. Eirene observed that he had emptied the flagon.

'He recently visited the Palace of the Porphyrogenitus in Constantinople and by chance saw someone he knew very well, a man called Jean de Grailly – they grew up together. He also happens to be an assassin for King Phillip and vanished from Acre in 1291. De Braose was shocked to find him alive. Raimund was sure de Grailly recognised him and thought it strange that the man who he knew well would pretend not to know him. De Grailly was with another man who spoke with a very heavy German accent. Raimund believed that he was Konrad von Feuchtwangen who disappeared at the same time. Raimund made enquiries and found that Konrad and Jean had been prisoners together in the emperors' dungeons ever since 1291. More intriguing is that Jean de Grailly claims to be a presumed dead Templar called William de Beaujeau. Both men being assassins, have good reason to hide their identities.'

'They appear to have thrown in their lot together to survive,' Gregory remarked. 'In their place, I would have concealed my identity and done a deal with the devil.'

'Precisely. But that isn't the most interesting part of this tale. De Braose knew through King Phillip that de Grailly had also been tasked to find and bring back to him a competitor prince … the true king of England. He believes von Feuchtwangen was ordered by the English King to assassinate this prince, and that is why Phillip ordered Konrad's death. King Phillip wants the competitor under his control to weaken King Edward, and his heirs. A fight over the English throne and a civil war would make the unsmiling King Phillip grin at the very least.'

Eirene's mouth became dry and hoarse when she was stressed and drank the rest of her wine to conceal her emotions from Gregory.

'Basilissa, the tale sounds far-fetched. There have always been rumours about Geoffrey of Brittany leaving other children. Any living heirs would have to be his grandchildren, and, if they did exist, they would be at least sixty years old or more.'

Gregory was more familiar with the Plantagenet succession than she had thought.

'You have a great knowledge of the English King's family. Geoffrey of Brittany was also my great-uncle as well as King Edward's. You have no reasons to have such knowledge.' She emphasised the point with an accusing but mocking finger.

'How do you plan to use this information?' Gregory placed his wine goblet down and moved even closer. She could smell his wine-soaked beard and stale breath.

'Raimund de Braose will persuade the emperors to free these assassins so that they can complete their orders. They are fanatics who are renowned for finishing a job, so I will help them do that ... And there is this letter proving King Edward I ordered the murder of his own king. Once I tell the world, he will be disgraced and humiliated and will stop his plans to weaken Clement who will hold a debt of gratitude to me and make my son emperor.'

Eirene produced from her sleeves a torn, grubby piece of tightly wrapped parchment covered with patches of brown and red, which she handed to the now seated Bishop. He gingerly opened the parchment – which was difficult, as he unwrapped a tight tube and read the contents.

For the noble servant Konrad von Feuchtwangen, from Edward, by the Grace of God, King of England, Lord of Ireland, and Duke of Aquitaine, Overlord of Scotland, and Hereditary Duke of Normandy, Count of Maine and Anjou.

You are to eliminate the competitor prince for my throne without question or mercy. He is to be found hiding amongst the Crusader armies. He is rumoured to be guarded by the Templars, and around fifty years of age. He is an abomination, a threat to the proper order. His continued existence will create confusion, disorder, and chaos. His father is a Scot who seduced his mother, Eleanor, my royal cousin. Look for him amongst the garrison at Acre, hiding somewhere amongst the French as a knight, a servant, or a prisoner. His existence is a danger to the English realm and throne, and he must be killed quietly and his existence wiped from history. Report to Winchester once the deed has been done.

Sealed this day in Winchester, January 10, 1291.

Bishop Gregory examined the grubby green beeswax seal. On one side he saw a man 'in majesty' seated on a magnificent throne clutching orb and sceptre. On the reverse he was in an equestrian pose, seated on horseback.

'It's the seal of Edward I of England.'

Eirene could see his surprise.

'How did you get hold of this?' Gregory asked, holding his nose.

'It was stolen … stolen from Konrad by Jean and it has been kept hidden securely these last fifteen years until the moment when it would be useful.'

Bishop Gregory handed the parchment back and wiped his hands on his top.

'I know where that has been stored … for comfort, I expect.' He continued to try to eradicate the grease and smell from his hands.

'It is clear evidence, and in his own hand, that he intended to murder the true king. Any cause Edward supports will be so tainted it will demand a counter-position from his peers. A disgraced Edward is a weakened Michael, because they are both against Church unification. This will put my son with his father Andronikos as the new heir to the empire supported by the Pope.' Eirene was fired up with her intrigues and a sense of righteousness.

Gregory's wry smile acknowledged her shrewdness. 'And if you find the treasure that Andronikos is so desperate to find, you will be the new power in the empire. The Pope loves the acquisition of money more than any soul. You can buy even more favour from Pope Clement, the avaricious Byzantine court, and we can banish your husband to a monastery.'

'Exactly. Though the treasure is something I didn't initially anticipate, it is a considerable bonus. I know Andronikos has sent Aurelian in its pursuit, as I haven't heard of him in many months'. She paused as a smile forced itself onto her lips.

'I know just the man we need to counteract Aurelian and find the assassins. He is waiting in the adjoining room, and he is heading to Scotland where the treasure and our assassins are also heading. Information has become known that von Feuchtwangen's target hides amongst the Scottish king's men.'

'Scotland? Who is waiting?' Gregory's voice raised.

'Father Maccabi Tagaris. He will bring back the evidence of King Edward's foul act. He is just the man with the necessary talents to find this prince, these assassins and retrieve this treasure. Don't you think?'

'Tagaris?' he stammered. 'He … he has given up his former line of work. He has renounced the world, the sin of avarice and the pursuit of money. Killing Roger de Flor for Emperor Michael was his last assassination.'

'Yes … I believe they have *lost touch*.' Eirene emphasised the last two words.

'Not so much a rift as a chasm separates them. Maccabi is a changed man; his religious conversion is a genuine one. He has become a scholar of ancient Hebrew and Greek and curses the vile acts Michael ordered him to do. And I have offered him the one thing that could persuade him – the destruction of the fake relic trade. The integrity of the relics at Saint Catherine's and the return of those stolen are the one thing that Maccabi cares about more than his "retirement." He has a list of relics, including sacred objects from Solomon's temple, but top of the list is St Fillan, the Orthodox saint for healing – his bones were stolen from Saint Catherine's and are also in Scotland. An opportunity to get the relic back would be tantalising.'

Eirene opened the door to a small room only accessible through her bedroom.

Wooden shades had been brought down on the open windows to cool the room, making the light anaemic. The little sunlight that had passed through the slats edged the outline of a figure.

'Father Maccabi, come through,' Eirene ordered.

Into the large audience room stepped a tall, well-made hooded figure draped in a dark tunic. Only a simple gold enkolpion cross hung by a chain at his chest. His hair was black and shorn around the skull, and his face was chiselled but gaunt. Eirene could see how he had once been described as the most handsome man in the empire. His dark skin and green eyes held her gaze for longer than seemed right, and she could feel herself staring, trying to find a flaw which would make him just a little bit less than perfect. She understood that he had once had a temporal life with a wife and children, and had abandoned all in pursuit of his religious vocation. He had put away everything of his previous life – husband, father, and state enforcer. His current vocation was a waste of a man.

Maccabi bowed low first before Eirene and then Gregory.

'Father Maccabi, I have a job for you.' Eirene didn't want to waste time on pleasantries.

'Basilissa, if by "a job" you mean something that involves Saint Catherine's, then my answer is yes. If it is to do with my former life, I decline. I only work for God now,' Maccabi said with a surprisingly coy gaze, as if he had never been an assassin and had erased his past. She knew what he was capable of, and the change in him was incredible.

'You will be conflicted, because if you agree to help us, you can further the reputation of Saint Catherine's, yet it will also demand the use of your old skills. Sometimes we must sacrifice well-intentioned principles for a greater good. I want you to follow two old friends of yours and former guests of the emperors, known as William de Beaujeau and Otto de Grandison. Their real names are Jean de Grailly and Konrad von Feuchtwangen. Do you remember them?'

Eirene watched as Maccabi nodded in painful recognition.

'I remember them as Beaujeau and de Grandison. Aurelian tried to find out what they knew about Alaric's treasure – but that was many years ago. The other two I have never met, but their names are infamous as the best assassins in Europe. You could say we were in the same dirty business. De Grailly killed for the king of France and von Feuchtwangen for the king of England – what is the connection?'

His demeanour was less guarded, and Eirene recognised he was in familiar territory. Monastic life hadn't completely erased his memory. Regardless, she would help him remember further.

'Jean de Grailly has been hiding behind the name of Beaujeau, and Konrad von Feuchtwangen as de Grandison. My guess is that Jean de Grailly and von Feuchtwangen killed the two men and assumed their identities.'

Without invitation, Maccabi took over the conversation. 'Aurelian found them adrift in a small pilot boat which had come from a Templar ship. He was there hunting for Alaric's treasure. They were covered in blood and appeared to have been fighting with each other, and they blabbered tales of a ship crewed by devils. From what you are saying, it was all an act to fool Aurelian and stop him asking too many questions about their identities and why they were there … clever boys.'

Maccabi's confidence told Eirene his memories had not been buried too deeply beneath the religious veneer.

'It appears that although they were enemies, they had to appear to be friends, a pretence they kept up for fifteen years – an unholy pact if ever there was one,' Eirene added.

'How did you find out?'

Maccabi moved a step closer to Eirene, a little enticed by the intrigue.

'My old friend Raimund de Braose recognised them and reported this to me. They will be heading to Scotland. Von Feuchtwangen is there to murder a man under the Scottish King's protection on the order of King Edward, and de Grailly is there to stop him. Let von Feuchtwangen attempt to carry out his wicked plan and then bring me evidence of the deed. I want to know the identity of the man von Feuchtwangen tries to kill. Once you find out, bring me his name, and get a confession from von Feuchtwangen in writing if you can, by whatever means. After that, I don't care what happens to him.'

'And de Grailly?' Maccabi knew where she was going.

'Try and bring him back here to me alive. He will be my living evidence.' Her coldness was delivered without thought.

'Basilissa ... evidence of what? You can't ask me to follow these men without really knowing why. Who is the man von Feuchtwangen is out to kill? You can't be interested in an assassination in Scotland. What else aren't you telling me?'

Eirene gave a little more information – just enough on Edward's plan for the assassination and who she suspected von Feuchtwangen's target could be. She needed Maccabi to bring the evidence to confirm the story. She lured him further into her intrigue with the thought of recovering the lost relics of Saint Fillan, and Alaric's treasure that would transform the Monastery he zealously supported.

'Yes, such wealth would ensure St Catherine's future for a thousand years – a Monastery with unrivalled power and prestige,' Maccabi said. 'And the King of Scotland can definitely lead me to Alaric's treasure?'

Maccabi hands were clasped not in prayer, but as if they held a sword.

Gregory had been quiet, but Eirene knew he hated being left out of any intrigue and was itching to say something.

'De Grailly and von Feuchtwangen will lead you to the king of Scots, the competitor prince, and the treasure. Then Saint Catherine's can be restored and will be considered the one and only repository of original relics that supports true pilgrimage. Be aware that Aurelian is following the Scots too, and he is working for Michael. Bringing the treasure back to the Empress will not be easy, but you are a resourceful man, so I will leave the arrangements in your hands. Aurelian must not succeed.' Gregory had appeared reluctant to use Maccabi, but now he would willingly push him down the gangplank.

Maccabi had grasped Gregory's hand as if they were jointly taking a solemn oath.

'So, we are in agreement?' Eirene asked.

'When do I leave for Scotland?' Maccabi replied.

'The ship is waiting outside this palace. It is a trading ship, and it sails tonight. You will be there in about two weeks. The ship's captain will leave you on Scotland's west coast, where we believe the King of Scots will head. Now, both of you leave me.' She flicked her hand as if she was dismissing irritating flies.

Returning to the window overlooking the harbour, she watched as the clerics left the palace and headed out of the gates. She closed her eyes and put out her hand as if to touch the imperial throne. She was determined that the next emperor of Byzantium would be her son John.

Chapter One

Mariakirken, Bergen, Norway, Early September 1306: Queen Isabel's Secret Court

There was a soft mist dancing just above the roofs of the wooden houses stretching along the outer harbour. They were becoming more densely packed where the fjord narrowed. The boat glided through the dark blue water. The air above the fjord was cold and biting.

'I love the freshness of the air, it makes me feel alive.' Murdie wiggled his nose and drew in the chilly air.

Bergen was protected by a surrounding wall of high granite mountains to its back and the deep fjord which ran up to the front of the town. Murdie could see why such a formidable place had been the Norwegian capital for hundreds of years.

'I can't understand why Haakon would want to move from a capital so easily defended.'

Murdie was using the long oar to guide them around the point to Bergen's west. The town was laid out in front of him like a living map.

'It is not the place he objects to, but rather the people. They are no friends of Haakon, he wants to fight the Danes, and Oslo is nearer to Copenhagen. King Eric of Denmark is crazy, and Haakon believes that a victory against them will divert people's focus away from discussing his lack of a male heir. Danish land will shut them up.'

Gyrid's attention was concentrated on the oars, her back to the town. She made no effort to look over her shoulder.

Murdie sensed her unease.

Her face was concealed by a linen scarf, and only her pale blue eyes were visible.

'Is that necessary?' Murdie pointed at the scarf.

'There is always a chance that Haakon has word of the destruction of Audenborg. He has informants everywhere and his men will recognise me – but you are right, not here.' Gyrid pulled the scarf down and stuffed the ends down the nape of her neck.

The wooden houses were framed by the smoke emanating from the many chimneys and, combined with the mist, were partially concealing the activity of the numerous merchants conducting trade. It was noisy even as night approached, and a small rowing boat could slip unnoticed into the mouth of the Bryggen.

'Bergen is a thriving city. It doesn't appear to care about its demotion.'

Murdie had visited many years before and was reacquainting himself with a place that brought fond memories.

'The inhabitants of Bergen are people of business, enjoying the wealth their trade in stockfish brings. Add money to the freedom of an absent king, and you get very happy people.'

Gyrid might have been away for years, yet it was clear she still understood the local politics, even if the relationship had been fatally broken after the execution of her husband Audun.

As they got nearer, he saw chubby baskets overflowing with fish and fur stacked up against the harbour walls. The town was further announced by a range of dark, angry stones to both sides that marked the entrance to the close harbour.

'Why the smile?' Gyrid pulled her winter cloak tight around the collar of her threadbare gown.

'Just fond memories … of a time long since gone.'

Murdie tried not to smile.

On an outcrop of land, Murdie spotted some gallows. Several rotting corpses were still hanging from the uprights, and his joy immediately evaporated.

'You have spotted Nordnes.' Gyrid had seen his face move to something much darker.

'I didn't notice its gallows when I was here this morning.' Bergen was revealing itself to him, hiding its brutality through a veil of nostalgia.

'I don't think of this place with any fondness. My husband was executed here and his body left hanging until it rotted. It's called Nordnes. Haakon used to stare across from the Bergenhus just to check that my husband was still hanging there.'

Gyrid's eyes widened, and her brows joined. Murdie found her captivating.

As they rounded the coast, passing Bergenhus Fortress on the left, she turned to look at the town and pointed in front and to the right of them.

'Look for a free berth at the far end of the harbour – somewhere where there are few people and large ships that can conceal us.'

Murdie pulled the long oar to a ninety-degree angle, leaving the Bergenhus over his left shoulder.

'Move the oars gently but progressively to my right. There is a fine tavern nearby where I won a few coins.' Murdie pointed to Gyrid's left.

The harbour was a busy, untidy arrangement of masts and sails like intertwined twigs that could only be deciphered by the ships they supported below. The ships were of all sizes, their crews busily completing the day's tasks and preparing to leave on the high tide the following morning.

Murdie scoured the front of the harbour for anything suspicious.

Gyrid scowled. 'So, while I was freezing on that hellhole

island Hertia with nothing but seabirds as companions, you were supposed to be arranging an audience with Queen Isabel. Instead, it appears to have been an excuse to drink and play dice.'

Murdie found her directness reminded him of himself, except he had developed an ability to filter his thoughts. Gyrid's company was rewarding and compelling, and she demanded attention whenever she voiced an opinion. Unfortunately, she had an opinion on every subject. He could bear this flaw as she was also witty and charismatic.

'During the day I had to go alone – there are, as you pointed out, too many people that could recognise you.'

Murdie could see that Gyrid wouldn't concede the point, which she confirmed with a fixed scowl.

'There is a lot of intelligence to be found amongst the loose-tongued gamblers ... and I found out one important thing. There was very little gossip about Audenborg. We need everyone to think we are dead, as any rumours of our survival will not be helpful. No one seems to be waiting for us and the taverns will be filling, I can reach the church without being seen.'

'Murdie, you are right, but you could at least sound repentant ... although you did acquire this new red cloak for me.'

Gyrid's face softened as she pulled the cloak tighter around her neck. She tied it closed with red ribbon, and Murdie thought it made her even more beautiful.

Murdie stopped steering and gently wiped the seawater from her eyes.

'It's strange that she chose to meet at the Mariakirken after dark.' Murdie took her concerns seriously.

Gyrid grabbed the oars tightly as the waves shortened and gathered strength. Murdie steered around the boats moored in the centre of the narrowing harbour.

'I did not speak with the Queen. I found my way into her

apartments in the Bergenhus and met with her secretary, Sir Hector MacKeown, and showed him the seal – *Nemo me impune lacessit*. Sir Hector knew that I came on behalf of the Guardians of Scotland, and he made the arrangements. The meeting must be away from the court, because Isabel is watched. Anyone with any English loyalties is motivated to harm a sister of King Robert and force a breach in her relationship with Haakon.'

'That is the seal that Bishop Wishart gave you?' Gyrid asked.

She didn't fully understand its meaning and the strong bonds between those Scots loyal to the Guardians and independence.

'MacKeown asked to keep it to show to Isabel. I reluctantly agreed, but I must get it back. Bishop Wishart gave it to me, it's my protection.' Murdie treasured it.

Gyrid stopped rowing and the boat drifted into an empty berth. 'I didn't like you at all when I thought you were the English king's lackey. A part you played very well as Alain d'Orthez. I prefer Murdie MacBeith, and I admire a man that undermined King Edward for more than five years.'

They had only a few yards until they could tie up and rest.

'He sounds like an incredible man, this battling Bishop Wishart of Glasgow, to engender such loyalty.'

'You are right, Gyrid. He is a *most* remarkable man. I am always happy to talk about him.'

Gyrid's interest seemed genuine, and these conversations had pushed them closer together. For five years he had been unable to share his thoughts, and the weight of this silence was a burden he only realised he carried when it was lifted.

In Gyrid, he had found another soul who understood the torture of secrecy. She had carried the confidence of the Maid of Norway for over fifteen years. They had found each other and mutually mitigated that pain.

She also carried some deep unhappiness which he observed in moments when she thought he wasn't watching – her head bowed, her eyes closed. She overanalysed every situation and wanted to engineer outcomes when sometimes it was better to wait and let time do its work.

He trusted her, yet he hadn't told her everything. He wanted to tell her more, but he wondered if his darker experiences would make her question or think less of him, given that she had such a strong personality. Some things were buried so deep that he couldn't bring them easily into his thoughts and words. They gave him nightmares, and he didn't want to share these with someone who already had enough of their own. Their pasts were confused, and now they shared a future with a common purpose to save someone they cared about and then return to their homes.

Murdie was tasked to go to France and find Jamie Wishart. Once they had returned from there, he would join his brother Domhnall in Scotland, rescue Bishop Wishart and then continue fighting with King Robert. He had promised to help Gyrid free her son from the Tower. When it was time for him to finally say goodbye, he knew it would be hard, but for the moment they would remain together. That thought made him smile.

'Where is Bishop Wishart now?' Gyrid's forehead narrowed, it was her serious face. This question had been tearing at him for weeks.

'I don't know, other than some English dungeon. He was in the Tower the same day we met, and he won't stay there long. It is too near the papal legate, Cardinal Orsini. The Pope may be a duplicitous political device, but he won't allow King Edward to execute an archbishop. Edward was sending Wishart away from London, where he hopes he will quietly be forgotten. The bastards want him to die of neglect.'

Murdie could feel his rage surging.

'They must consider Wishart a great threat to their plans. He has many similarities to Audun, who was more scholar and lawmaker than rebel. He was sixty-two years old when Haakon hanged him. Age is no barrier to revenge.'

Gyrid gazed back towards Nordnes, she was remembering.

'Wishart offended Longshank's pride and made a mockery of his plans by crowning a king – a man who never hid behind his cowl. King Robert is the man we have been waiting for for twenty years, and Longshanks knows it.' Murdie did not have to dig deep to find his fire and passion.

'You still show such fervour and belief. I wonder if Queen Isabel has the same drive. She has been in Norway since 1297, a widow since 1299 and appears not to be inclined to return, despite her husband's death. Understandably – she has a daughter with a claim to the throne, and she needs to protect her.' Gyrid was suspicious of the motivations of anyone with a close connection to Haakon.

'There is no indication that her loyalties to King Robert are compromised. The Mariakirken is a normal place for her to take Mass and won't arouse any gossip.'

The boat rolled into the dock, and Murdie jumped onto the wooden quay, securing the boat to the wooden uprights.

'And I will keep out of sight like a good girl,' Gyrid added sarcastically. She was clearly frustrated at being left behind and her eyes looked to her feet. She had accepted with an ill-concealed level of resentment.

'You know it's the right thing to do.'

Murdie pulled down the small sail and secured the ropes and mast around them before fastening the sail to the iron fastenings that ran along the side. It provided a basic shelter.

'We can rest here a while until night.'

Murdie pulled a flagon of ale, bread with dried sausage, and fish from a small chest and handed these to Gyrid. He pulled down the open end of the shelter, just allowing in a small amount of the remaining daylight.

She tore into the food as Murdie took a handful of berries he had been concealing in his pocket and dropped them in front of her. Gyrid squealed in delight and hugged Murdie, her cheeks fully extended with the impromptu feast.

'At vespers I will leave and hide in the church and wait for compline. The church is only a few minutes' walk from the harbour. We will soon notice the activity of business decreasing as drink and gambling take hold. Increasing vulgarity will provide my cue to leave.'

Outside their boat, the noise of trade continued. Murdie felt safe for now, but his dagger was hidden in his left sleeve and his sword to his right.

Murdie grabbed at the food.

'Eat for the hunger to come,' Gyrid encouraged him.

'The hunger is already here!' Murdie felt his face, and even without a mirror knew he had lost his chubby appearance. Gyrid watched him before touching his lips with her finger.

'Murdie, you look good, we have been running since we left the Tower. We need our strength for the journeys ahead of us.'

Gyrid began talking of her son, and Murdie had accepted that long term he would always be her second priority.

'I have not forgotten about Hugleik. We will free him, you have my word, but we need Isabel's help to get out of Norway, and to find Jamie in France, Bishop Wishart is relying on me. I will need King Robert's help, and men, to stand any chance of freeing your son from the Tower.'

Murdie recognised the pain in her eyes.

'I said I will help you get to Rouen and back to your king, but after that I must return to England and free my son, with or without your help.'

Gyrid pushed the food aside and placed her head on Murdie's chest. They would enjoy these moments until the time came.

*

Murdie woke to hear the seventh hour designation of vespers. He gently rocked Gyrid, who quickly stirred.

He grabbed his sword and fastened his cape high to obscure his lower face. He pulled down the hood covering his hair and forehead. The night was chilled, and his efforts to be anonymous would not look out of place on such a cool evening.

'Stay within the shelter. The municipal guards are patrolling the harbour, so you should be safe. I will be back before the tide changes. We should leave immediately whether Queen Isabel helps us or not.' Murdie placed his hand on her shoulder.

'You know I can take care of myself. God protect you.' Her words were barely audible. She dropped her head and looked away.

'I survived five years at the heart of the English court. I am sure my wits can help me survive for a few hours in Bergen.'

Murdie looked again, but she did not face him.

'I have no intention of dying yet.'

Murdie jumped onto the dock. There were still many people around, some drifting between the taverns, others making final preparations for tomorrow's journey. The municipal guards who patrolled the harbour were questioning a German merchant. He had tried to leave without paying the harbour taxes. The man protested his innocence and claimed not to understand Norwegian.

The harbour was a mixture of everyone he would expect to see in such a place at such a time. No one took any notice of him.

The church was two streets across and three streets above the mooring. As he moved away from the heart of the harbour, the streets became quieter and darker. There were fewer taverns, warehouses, and bordellos, fewer traders to mingle amongst. This was an area on the fringes of trade, but not religion.

Two monks walked ahead. They were heading straight towards the Mariakirken.

I will follow them inside and hide in the portico.

Murdie soon found himself in a small courtyard in front of the stone church. It looked out of place amongst a sea of wooden buildings. The front had two large towers which shouted its location. The monks used the large main entrance, and Murdie crept up behind them. The door was open, and it was simple to be just another shadow. Inside was measurably darker.

The Mass had already begun, so the focus was the priest, and no one turned to see the late arrivals. Murdie crouched behind the last column of a set that ran down the entire length of the right-hand aisle adjacent to the main nave. The priest stood with his back to the congregation, and they in turn stood with their backs to Murdie.

This is a grand place fit for an audience with a queen.

The Mass continued with its ritual of chants and bells. Murdie closed his eyes, imagined his brother Domhnall, and thought of his home as he listened to the Kyrie, the Credo, the Sanctus, and the Agnus Dei. He hoped that the *Ite, missa est*, the dismissal of the congregation, would come soon. It was a rare hour of thinking time, and he wallowed in the luxury.

The ceremony was identical to any Mass he had attended. This was not a feast day, so it was the same mechanistic routine he had witnessed his whole life. He wasn't sure it brought him nearer to God, but it was expected, comforting, and the norm.

He hadn't really engaged in the church routines, even after collaborating with Bishop Wishart for many years. The Bishop was more interested in Murdie's temporal activities and had never really interfered with his relationship with God. He had concluded many years ago that the Bishop was more patriot than churchman.

He lowered himself onto the cold floor, tucking his cloak beneath him to function as some protection from the dampness, and waited.

After an hour the congregation departed, their voices drifting off into the night. The priest followed, shutting the main door behind him leaving Murdie alone. It was unusual to close the church door before the eighth hour or compline. The church should always be open for those in need.

That's strange, Queen Isabel must have asked the parish priest to leave. She is bringing her own chaplain. Cautious girl – she is taking no chances. She thinks like King Robert and is still a Bruce even after ten years in Norway.

On reflection, Murdie thought it better to stand. It would be difficult to defend himself sitting on the ground. The church was a labyrinth; it would be easy for someone to hide. On the right-hand side was another exit. If this was a trap, he would escape through there and disappear.

Suddenly the main door clanked, and he could hear the strain of a key turning. He focused on the side door and moved his sword out of its sheath and held it by his side. He had trained to fight with the blade and dagger like all nobility. If this was an ambush and it was the end, he would take many with him.

The side door was pushed open, and he stood back as far into the corner as he could. If he couldn't run, he would hide.

He couldn't see any faces. The forms were long and the voices deep. They were male and they had their swords drawn.

One of the men stepped forward holding a small lamp in his left hand, which he waved around him, searching for someone. He took several small steps and moved closer to where Murdie was hiding. Murdie's heart was pounding as he tried to hold his breath and the pressure on his chest was uncomfortable.

A third man came into the nave, and the lamp caught his face. Murdie recognised him.

'Sir Hector?'

Murdie stepped out of the shadow dropping his sword on the ground. The men with swords grabbed him and kicked his away.

'You can relax, gentlemen. This is Murdie MacBeith.'

Hector stood aside, and Murdie saw a slender figure clad in a full-length dark cloak. Hector spoke quietly but clearly,

'May I introduce Queen Isabel Bruce.'

Isabel removed her hood, revealing her face, and immediately Murdie dropped to his knees.

'Murdie, I am glad to meet you at last. Bishop Wishart and my brother talk about you with much fondness. My brother tells me you are 'a most able and talented man.'

Her voice was gentle and lilting, delightfully Scottish in tone. She had lost little of her accent after so many years in Norway.

'Gentlemen, there is no need for swords. I am safe in the company of a fellow patriot.' Isabel urged Murdie to rise.

'Well, if you are sure, Lady.' The two guards replaced their swords.

'They are Scottish?' Murdie pointed at the men. He was not expecting a Scottish escort.

'They are Scottish and ex-Varangian guards,' the Queen replied. 'I have many such men in my service.'

She waved the guards away. 'You can wait outside the side entrance. Sir Hector and I have some matters to discuss with Murdie.'

The men bowed and left them alone.

Sir Hector led the way towards the central nave before sitting on one of the backless stone benches built into the wall. He lit a small wooden candelabra left on the corner of the altar. The light framed the face of the Queen, and Murdie immediately saw the Bruce. She had the refinement of a woman without Robert's pugnacious features, except for the blue-green eyes which all the Bruces carried. She was striking like her brother.

'Sit by me, and we shall talk.'

Murdie and Sir Hector sat on either side of the Queen.

'Sir Hector arranged this meeting in this place for our safety. I am loved in my adopted country, but not by everyone. My brother-in-law, who is without a male heir, sees my nine-year-old daughter, Ingeborg, as a threat, all because her father was his older brother. Haakon sees plots everywhere, and it will remain so until he has a son. The jarls, spurred on by English gold, wish to drive a chasm between Scotland and Norway, make up a treachery that isn't there so that Haakon will withdraw his support. I can do much good for my brother, if I remain here and it is not without risk. If Haakon hears that I am meeting with the companion of Gyrid Hugleikkson, wife of the traitor Audun, he will condemn me without a hearing.'

Murdie was enchanted by her elegance and intelligence. She had long, slender hands, which she used as she talked. Her fingers weren't hidden by large, vulgar rings, but instead carried plain gold bands, engraved with animals and inlaid with enamel. Hector followed her lips as she spoke, like a lover. She reminded him of Gyrid – intelligence, strength and understated beauty. For a few seconds, he was astonished and didn't know what to say.

'Majesty, I came to ask for your help, not to endanger you or your daughter. Gyrid has no interest in Norwegian politics, only in rescuing her son, who is held prisoner by the English King. You know that I was at the English court, working for Bishop Wishart.'

'Queen Isabel knows about Audenborg. Her agents discovered what happened to Margaret of Norway,' Sir

Hector interrupted.

'It is a tragedy. You did the right thing in leaving her with Cnut Myhre. She would die again if she were to step back into the world and take her place in our war against the English. It will do no one any good, least of all Margaret, if Haakon finds out she is alive and hiding in Audenborg. He would use her for his own advantage and brandish her as an object to taunt King Edward. If he finds out we knew she was still alive, it will give him another reason to silence us all ... but I suspect that is not the reason you came to me.'

Isabel's voice was more stressed when she talked of Margaret. Murdie was sure she wiped a tear from her eye.

'I still work for Bishop Wishart, and he has asked me to find his nephew Jamie, who is somewhere in France. It has been several weeks since the Bishop ordered me so, and I need a ship and a crew to get there without delay. I gave Sir Hector the Bishop's seal to prove I come with his blessing.' Murdie looked towards Sir Hector, expecting the seal's return, but Hector appeared unmoved.

Queen Isabel removed a large velvet purse from around her waist and placed it in Murdie's hands.

Murdie opened the purse. Even in the dim light, he knew immediately that he had the seal back.

'*Nemo me impune lacessit.*' Normally he could only whisper these words.

'These words are sacred,' Queen Isabel said. 'I wouldn't be speaking to you if I had not received this proof. Many men ask for my patronage, and most are seeking personal advantage. When I saw this, I knew you were different – a patriot, working for the Bishop, King Robert, and Scotland. That isn't the only thing in the bag.' She pointed to the very bottom.

Murdie dug deeper into the velvet and could feel a large, cold stone. He placed it on the bench before carefully returning the seal to the purse and tying it to his belt.

Murdie held the stone to the candelabra, and it sparkled, but he couldn't fathom what it was.

'That stone is more valuable than anything in the world, it will protect you and give you an advantage in your journey to France, in seeking Jamie and in recovering Alaric's treasure,' Queen Isabel hesitated and asked. 'You do know about the treasure and its importance?'

'I was Aymer de Valence's steward, and he left me to deal with most of his correspondence – and those he kept hidden, I read anyway. He discussed it with King Edward, but I thought it was his usual boastful claims. I only gave it credibility when Bishop Wishart hinted wealth was heading to King Robert. I understand how it could help our struggle.'

Murdie paused, still fixated on the stone. It was a clear crystal, translucent, but at the corners where it caught the light from the candle, it sparkled, tinged with all the colours he could imagine. He had seen conjurors trick people, and he wondered why the Queen was giving this to him.

'Your Grace, what magic is this?' Murdie was perplexed.

The stone took the light from the candles and split it into a kaleidoscope of colours that streamed across the stone floor. He wondered if the stained glass had caught a beam of light from outside, but the street lighting was very dim.

'That is a rare crystal and a closely guarded secret. It will help you find your friends, rescue the treasure and get it back to Scotland. King Robert is waiting in Orkney and he informs me the treasure is likely in France with Jamie. I expect that is why Bishop Wishart sent you there to help rescue it for my brother and away from the clutches of King Phillip. The crystal is called a sunstone, and it allows you to travel at sea when others cannot. Can I show you? Murdie, please hand the crystal to Sir Hector.'

Sir Hector placed one of the candles behind the stone and hid most of its light with his hand. He placed a sheet of parchment before it, and the stone directed the small amount of light directly onto the paper. The stone seemed to have duplicated the light, as if there were two candles; it captured it and presented two beams, one slightly ahead of the other. Hector moved the candle, and the two bands of light moved across the parchment, following the light source. Hector adjusted the stone, and the bands joined one on top of the other. Two light bands had become one.

'The stone can still catch the beams of light even from a candle that is obscured. Consider the candle as the sun. This stone is used to find the sun even if it is concealed by clouds. When the bands of light join, the angle of the light through the stone shows you where the sun is located. When you know where the sun is, you are never lost. You can navigate the whole world.'

Sir Hector replaced the lit candle back in its holder and handed the crystal back to Murdie. The Queen continued.

'This stone will guide you to travel more quickly than any other ship. Once you have left France behind, you will have to travel up the length of England with the English in pursuit and then navigate around the Western Isles. Haakon may also know of the treasure and will have people waiting for you. Getting to Orkney and out of the grasp of those who would have the treasure for themselves will be a miracle unless you can sail away in conditions your pursuers fear. Haakon has the secret of the sunstone and guards the mines in Southern Norway, yet he is so afraid of his rebellious captains who owe their allegiance to the jarls that he hasn't shared the stone's capability with many – only a few very old men know how this works. Use it to get the treasure away to my brother before Haakon, or worse, Longshanks finds out.'

'I will need someone to guide me. Sir Hector has demonstrated that a stone can make light join, but I will need to know how to use it in the open sea. Otherwise, it is just a conjurer's trick.'

Murdie was not afraid to show his ignorance and didn't have time to learn. It was urgent that he travel to France.

'One of my men guarding us now has studied the manuscripts left by the old Vikings describing how the sunstones are used. He knows of a land to the west that only a few men long dead have visited called the "Land of Vines". I will send Adam de Irwyne with you.'

'I recognise that name, but from where?' Murdie asked.

'Adam is the older brother of Will de Irwyne, King Robert's armour bearer,' the Queen replied.

Voices could be heard outside, and Queen Isabel pulled her hood over her head.

'It is time for me to leave. Matins is approaching, and the priest has only been bribed until then. He was told I was holding a private vigil for my late husband. This church is also a favourite of King Haakon, and I don't want the priest to tell Haakon anything except that this time was used by a grieving widow to pray for the soul of her husband. He will be wanting to reopen the main doors. We must hurry.'

The Queen fastened her cloak and smoothed down the front, ready to leave.

'What would you have me do?' Murdie placed the sunstone in the purse.

'I will write to my brother and tell him we have met, and that you will soon be with him. Hector has prepared a ship that is ready to move on the tide. I will send six of my personal escorts that came over with me from Scotland to your berth near the taverns. They are loyal to the Bruce family and are known to King Robert.'

The Queen's words quickened, and Murdie sensed it was clearly time she left.

'Lastly, leave Bergen at first light and look for Jamie between Rouen and Honfleur. In Rouen there is a tavern, L'Auberge du Lion. Bishop Wishart used to have agents based there, and it's a good place to start. Be careful as I have reports from my agents in France that King Phillip is searching for them near Chateau Gaillard. I will send intelligence via a merchant in Honfleur – seek out the ivory merchant Jakob Dedekam. Trust him and know he will carry my words.'

'Bishop Wishart told me of this inn. And what about Gyrid?' Murdie would rather take Gyrid with the Queen's blessing, though she would be leaving with him even if he had to smuggle her on board.

'Make sure you leave with Gyrid. She will not last long if she remains here. Warn her that she must never come back to Norway as long as Haakon lives. She will suffer the same fate as her husband.'

The Queen's tone told Murdie this was a certainty rather than a threat and he took notice, yet he was also relieved she had given him a blessing of a sort. He wouldn't abandon Gyrid, and he suspected Isabel knew they were close.

Murdie hurriedly bowed, keen to return and make ready to leave.

'Murdie, give the Queen and I a few minutes to ride away before you return to the harbour. We will send the men we promised as soon as we reach the Bergenhus. It's nine o'clock, so you have eight or nine hours to prepare to leave on the next tide.'

Sir Hector grabbed the small lamp and walked ahead of the Queen towards the side entrance and left the church. The Queen turned and spoke for the last time.

'You can contact my brother via Lord MacDonald at Dunaverty Castle. Farewell, Murdie, God's blessing on you, and may he guide you safely to France and back to Scotland.' Queen Isabel left, and the side door gently closed behind her.

Murdie recognised the rhythmic sound of horses walking and then trotting away. He moved back into the smaller aisle and waited for the horses to distance themselves. Just then, the main door opened, and the priest strode up the nave, unaware of Murdie's presence, and started to prepare for matins.

Soon more of the faithful joined for the first of the canonical hours. The congregation was sparse, but it provided enough noise for Murdie to remain safely hidden, ignored in the shadows. He would leave through the main entrance and walk the short distance back to where Gyrid was waiting.

The reading of the scripture began, and Murdie took this as his cue to leave.

Outside, the courtyard was empty, and the stones were slippery with dew, and the air was barely above freezing. The Norwegian autumn was turning into an early winter. Only the homeless and the inebriated were scattered at the perimeter, using the few wooden houses that framed the yard as a source of free heating.

The walk was a short one, and Murdie was conscious of Queen Isabel's warning. He was carrying a sunstone and would take no chances of leading anyone to where Gyrid was hiding. He would meander and take a route only an idiot would follow.

He turned away from the church and the harbour. The area behind the church, heading towards the surrounding mountains, was not so densely packed with houses, more open with fewer dark lanes to hide in.

Echoes of feet would be amplified in an area where everyone was sleeping, even the vermin. The lighting was no stronger than a few near exhausted lamps providing just enough guidance to follow the gutters that ran down the middle of the streets. They were no grander than dirt tracks trodden hard by feet and held together by the near-freezing temperature.

Behind him he sensed a presence. The mice and their escort of cats started to wake up and move ahead of him.

Something has spooked them. I was right not to go

straight to the boat.

Murdie quickened his pace and walked east behind the harbour. He would turn south and then west, doubling back once he was sure he was not being followed.

Suddenly, he darted into a narrow ginnel between two ramshackle huts. He could only just fit. Turning himself towards the main street, he watched and waited. The rats trotted down the gutter and buried themselves in the rotting rubbish of fish bones and manure.

Clever. You are as cautious as I and in no rush. I am patient too.

Opposite his hiding place, he caught sight of feet gently shuffling along the perimeter of the street, stopping and searching between each hovel. He couldn't see any face or get a sense of proportion, but he was sure he recognised the outline of a blade in hand.

He carefully removed his dirk from his left sleeve, determined he would strike the first blow, by hand or steel. This nook would not hide him for long. The figure walked to his side of the street, and he could hear the breathing as it moved closer to him.

Someone was in front of him, and for a moment he hesitated. The figure was slight, and instead of stabbing them, he punched out, believing this would be enough to knock them to the ground. He wanted to know who was following him, not kill them.

The head flew back, and he could feel warm liquid spatter across his face and hands. It sprayed into his mouth, and he knew it was blood from the metallic taste on his tongue. A fragment of tooth was embedded in his knuckle, and he cried out, for at the last second he had recognised the face. The red ribbon shimmered in the low light, and he realised it was Gyrid.

'What are you doing here? I told you to wait for me at the boat.'

Murdie was shaking. He had punched Gyrid hard, and he could hear her spitting what he assumed to be blood out of her mouth.

He placed his arm around her and started to shake, angry with himself. He pulled her close and wiped her face with the corner of his cloak. Gyrid was standing, but she leaned into Murdie.

'Gyrid, forgive me,' he whispered.

She wiped the blood with her sleeve and started to wobble. Her hands fell to her side.

'Hold me, Murdie. You hit me like a man.' Gyrid collapsed as Murdie grabbed her by the waist.

'I will be all right in a minute,' she said. Murdie could feel her body go limp. Her eyes were closing, and she vomited.

Murdie carried her away towards the harbour, first walking, and then running faster and faster. His heart raced, and he could hear people's voices in the background, but he wasn't going to hang around to see if they were friendly or not. Gyrid had passed out, and it was not far to the wider streets nearer where their boat was berthed.

He was guided by the lanterns that hung from the numerous boats preparing themselves for the high tide. The voices behind him had dissipated, yet he ran harder.

He stepped carefully onto the deck and gently placed Gyrid inside the small, covered area still unconscious. He dipped a linen rag he had torn off his tunic in the water barrel and wiped the vomit and blood from her mouth and neck.

Her lips and left cheek were beginning to swell, so he tore more rags and saturated them in cold water before laying them on her cheek to stop the swelling.

'I am sorry, Gyrid. We will be away from this place in a few hours.' She did not move or answer, yet she was breathing, and he took comfort in that.

He hoped his voice would wake her, but she was out cold. He placed his cloak behind her head to make her more comfortable.

He didn't sleep but sat with her for several hours watching her and cursing his actions.

Lauds had been announced; it was still dark outside, but the dawn was a few hours away and that the Scots Varangians would be arriving soon.

He stuffed a couple of hessian sacks with what belongings they had and retied the velvet purse containing the seal of Scotland and the sunstone to his sword belt. They would need an hour to prepare to sail at dawn, and six o'clock was now only a couple of hours away.

Gyrid started to splutter and slowly came around.

'What happened?' Her speech was slurred, and she rubbed her swollen face.

'It was me – I hit you. It was an accident.' Murdie was embarrassed and had little time to say much more before he was interrupted by the sound of Scottish voices.

'I don't have time to explain everything, but we are leaving on a ship with an escort supplied by Queen Isabel. Those men outside are going to help us get to France and find Jamie.'

Gyrid carefully wrapped the scarf around her swollen face and pulled her cape over her head. Murdie then lifted Gyrid onto the dock.

'No one will recognise me now,' and pleaded. 'Once we have done with Scotland … then my son?' Murdie threw their belongings beside her.

'I promise we will get him back. Can you walk now?'

Murdie stepped onto the dock and lifted the sacks.

Gyrid nodded just as Adam de Irwyne strode towards them.

'I see you have exchanged the finery of a palace guard for the practicality of the open sea, but you retain the weapons of a soldier.'

Adam de Irwyne and his men were wearing woollen tunic

and hose, functional, thick with animal grease to keep out the wind and water. Their fine swords were hidden beneath the long tunics. Each man had a cloak loosely tied around his shoulders.

'Murdie, we will carry Gyrid to the ship and leave your boat here. Throw everything you have left on the boat over the side, leave no trace that you were here and join us. We must be quick, amongst the first away and not get caught up in the melee where the harbour narrows at Nordnes.'

Murdie noticed his resemblance to Will de Irwyne, his age about forty with a reputation for courage. Murdie couldn't have hoped for a better companion.

Adam headed towards the berth furthest away from the centre of the harbour. These berths were deep and supported the larger masted boats that spent longer at sea. They sat heavy in the water as their keels had been reinforced for the icy conditions where walrus ivory and skins were the cargo.

The crew and Gyrid climbed on board and prepared the ship to leave, shortly followed by Murdie who had quickly thrown their rubbish into the water.

On the deck below Murdie caught sight of the stores and sacks of what he assumed were weapons. The points of blades could be just discerned through the sacking. Adam pulled Murdie to one side.

'You have the stone stored safely? Sometimes the municipal guards search ships they suspect are smuggling arms or gold. We cannot be caught with the sunstone, so we will fight our way out if we are challenged.'

Adam's voice made a risk sound more like a certainty, which could explain his hurry to get away.

The crew removed the lids from barrels and quickly started to assemble arrows, placing them next to the bows. Small terracotta vessels had been stacked in the corner, and a large taper was already glowing and ready to make fire.

'We are at the furthest point from the municipal guards

and will see anyone coming. I would rather leave without the fanfare of a fight.' Adam jumped on board, and Murdie followed.

'Queen Isabel told me you know these waters, so you can help me. Can you prepare the sail and steer us through the narrow strait at Nordnes? You can use a rudder and a long oar, I believe? Men, get the oars ready and let's get out of here. We have enough arms for now. Distance from this place is our best weapon.'

Murdie sensed the looming danger in Adam's demeanour.

'My lady friend is Gyrid, and she is injured, so don't expect her to fight.' Gyrid was in no condition to help the crew.

The ropes tying the bow and keel were swiftly cut, and the boat started to drift away from its dock. In the distance, Murdie could see an assembly of men, swords drawn heading along the harbour front towards them. Voices became shouts, and the pursuers started running.

'I feared this. Row this bastard ship as fast as you can,' Adam shouted as he pushed the ship further away from the quay with a long oar.

There were three sets of two oars, and they dragged the heavy ship away, very slowly at first, yet each stroke moved the vessel further away from danger. The wind started to catch the sail and pull them into the centre of the harbour.

The voices onshore became a chorus. Hastily aimed arrows and bolts cut through the air and skimmed across the deck, but the guards had left it too late.

The ship creaked and cried like a beast before the tide and wind calmed it and carried it away from the shore.

'I couldn't have imagined a ship could move so quickly,' Murdie shouted as he clutched the rudder.

A few more arrows whistled through the air and struck the water behind them, but they were a token gesture fired more out of frustration than any possibility of harming the crew and stopping the boat.

'Could Queen Isabel be discovered?' Murdie asked.

'I don't think so. She is too clever to get caught up directly in the supply of this ship, the sunstone, or Gyrid's escape. If Haakon was involved, the guards chasing us would be his own Varangians, and they are far more competent than any municipal guards. They would have arrived in time to stop us and given us a proper fight.'

Adam grinned and playfully smacked Murdie on the shoulder.

'We are safe now. No vessel can catch us, and we will soon be past Nordnes with no other ships ahead of us. Relax and enjoy the journey. We have a healthy store of *uisge beatha*. Soon I fear we will be up against a more formidable foe in France.'

Murdie smiled. 'As soon as we are out at sea, I intend to drink my body weight.'

'A great idea,' Adam replied. 'And once we are past Nordnes, if you don't mind, I will join you.'

Chapter Two

Castle Tioram, Scotland, September 1306: Aftermath and Assassination

Aymer de Valence wiped the clotted blood from his forehead with his sleeve.

'Dam them.' The gash was deep, and floating particles clung to the sticky wound. He couldn't rise from the beach as he feared his legs would give way and was sitting wet-arsed and devoid of his dignity.

Esteem and nobility were everything to him. He didn't want people to see him so. He couldn't fathom what had just happened. He had more than lost his footing, he had been blown into the air.

'My lord, let me help you,' an equerry called out before jumping out of the boat and wading towards him through the reddened sea. Valence's hearing was muffled, and blood oozed from his right ear. He pushed away the hand of his equerry and staggered to his feet.

'I want any Scot you find alive brought to me!' he screamed with such anger that he struggled to get the words out without his teeth grinding.

The sky was grey, spotted with black soot, and the ground a pink mixture of blood and matter. He wiped brain from his face and spat the noxious black concoction from his mouth.

'My serjeant tells me there aren't any,' the equerry replied. 'There were a few in the forest that Lord Percy had killed. The rest have escaped.'

Valence slapped him hard in the mouth.

The equerry staggered and fell onto the ground grappling with the turf, he landed on all fours, just supporting his body and keeping it from hitting the ground. He crawled away from Valence on his knees and elbows.

'Look harder and find me one of the bastards I can hold responsible for this abomination. I don't care if it's man, woman, or child.' Valence kicked him in the ribs, and he fell, winded. Matter continued to trickle and glide like confetti onto anything and anybody.

Some boats were split in two, others blasted to smithereens on the rocks that surrounded the landing area. Body parts were spread liberally across the sand and floated eerily in the gentle waves, which foamed pink with blood and tissue. Some of the bodies were face down, some did not have a face, and others were floating upright and appeared to be asleep until the waves turned them over and their legs were missing.

Valence tried to make sense of what had happened. His men had been decimated, and his ships sunk or badly damaged.

'This is an abomination delivered by an unholy alliance of rebels inspired by the devil.'

He would never accept that they were cleverer than him. They had taken the fight to the English, and he would never forget or forgive.

Valence wiped the blood away from his eyes for the umpteenth time. Tioram was engulfed in fire, and he could feel the heat on his face and hands. Red-tinted sweat continued to pour down his forehead and dripped down onto his cloak and tunic.

The castle keep rocked and groaned as wooden supports gave way, crashing and fuelling the flames further. More explosions followed, and the ground trembled.

He stopped, but the world kept spinning and there were two of everything.

Am I dead, and is this hell? If it is, it is worse than I could have imagined.

Valence felt nauseous. Covering his face, he stood for a second and violently emptied his stomach.

Those who were still intact staggered around the beach, detached from what was happening around them. Order had broken down. Swords, daggers, and shields were strewn everywhere.

Lying moaning on the grass slope leading to Tioram, he could just make out a familiar figure. It was John Lorne MacDougall, surrounded by the remains of the castle and the men who had attacked it. If this was hell, Valence hoped that God had not sent him and MacDougall to the same place for companionship.

MacDougall was delirious and grabbed at his clothes with bloodied hands.

Nearby was Jean de Grailly, groaning and holding his head. His body was not bloodied and broken like so many others, yet his clothes had been shredded to a point where his modesty had been compromised. His tabard was still smoking from the inferno.

Valence watched as Jean moved in slow motion and ran his hands over his limbs, checking that they were still there.

'My lord.' The voice was muffled but familiar. Valence turned to find Konrad von Feuchtwangen standing directly behind him. He appeared unhurt, though his tabard was ripped and he was drenched. He came from the direction of the loch.

'I see the devil has preserved his own and you are unhurt.' Valence struggled to form his words.

'You could put it that way, Lord Valence, but it's more probable I was just lucky.' He thought he detected a grin on Konrad's face, and he was in no mood for smiles.

'I was beside Jean and was blown clear up into the air through a gap in the wall. I landed in the sea amongst some sailcloth, my fall broken by woollen bales. You were just on the shore and were bombarded with shrapnel – those in the keep stood no chance. Lord MacDougall and Jean had started to flee out of the keep but were caught in the maelstrom that followed. They didn't fare so well, I see.' Konrad nodded nonchalantly towards them.

'I saw this kind of destruction before in Acre. The mamluks used a black powder they captured from the Moghuls and enclosed it in barrels. In Acre it destroyed the walls and brought down the towers. The Scots have someone skilled in its use.'

Valence shook his head to try and clear his ears. He had heard Konrad, but the sound was muffled and his balance felt strange. He knew about black powder but had never seen its power. The alchemist at court had tried to interest him in this new weapon, and because he believed it to be sorcery, he had dismissed it. Now he saw it was wicked in the wrong hands, and he would embrace it.

'Bruce has added sorcery to his list of unholy acts. Killing John Comyn was not enough to have God condemn him. Only men in league with the devil would use this weapon in such a way. Men lured inside and then blown apart … Konrad, I will need you to find the Scot who helped Bruce set this trap and bring him to me.' Valence pulled Konrad closer to him. The people around him were paying no attention, but he would take no risk of being overheard.

'We need to talk about the other matter. The assassination King Edward and I have been waiting fifteen years for you to complete.'

Valence felt for his sword, which was still attached to his belt. It was hanging by a thread and had twisted upwards towards his side. He was lucky he had turned away and the sword had not become a spear, driven into his side by the explosion.

'I have never forgotten about the competitor prince – the

man who escaped me in Acre,' Konrad replied. Valence was so close he could see Konrad's breathing quicken.

'It isn't just Bruce we were after. I had word from the King this false prince is amongst Bruce's men. Find Lord Percy – his men may have seen the direction of anyone escaping. Also … check if there are any old men amongst the dead. I want any information on where Bruce is headed. He will have taken the traitor with him. Loosen tongues with daggers and gold. I don't care which you use, just find him – and then when we have found Bruce's whereabouts, we can turn our attention to that bitch Christina. Ranald tells me she is Bruce's whore – a relationship that shouldn't go without acknowledgement.'

Valence wouldn't stop. His tenacity was the trait that distinguished him from all the other gallants trying to impress the king.

Tonight, his battered and bloodied troops would sleep in the open air without the comforts or the booty expected from a captured castle. There wasn't a wall or a roof undamaged by the explosion. Even the outhouses were smoking shells of crumbling rock.

He wasn't a man who gave much consideration to those who served him, but as the rain started, his soldiers looked like they had been defeated for a second time by the weather and their grim surroundings. Beaten and injured men were no use to him, and in normal circumstances he would replace them, but so far away from the Glasgow garrison and fresh soldiers, he would be forced to let them rest for a few days. Then he would press them back into action. He wouldn't tolerate their malingering for long.

'Lord Valence, I am relentless and my obligation to King Edward is lifelong – and Christina Ranald could assist in this matter? She could be useful to you alive if we cannot discover Bruce's whereabouts through our normal means. It might bring out the hero in Bruce if we were to threaten her

– he is said to care for women. When she leads us to Bruce, she leads us to the competitor.'

Konrad was right, but Valence made it a policy to never take advice from anyone, decisions were his prerogative.

'I had considered how I might use her. The King would want her executed on the spot. The dragon banner is still in force; no quarter will be given to any man, woman, or child helping or harbouring Bruce. Yet, as you said she could be made useful, so we will keep her alive. Get her to drop her guard, make her believe we are not looking, and then she will lead us to them. We should explore all avenues in pursuing these men. I have an agent in her household, so I will send him a couple of men to capture her in her lair.'

What had been a cluttered beach covered in bodies and debris had started to be cleared. Valence had not completely lost the ringing in his ears, but his eyesight was no longer blurred.

'What is that Greek Maccabi doing here?' Valence pointed towards the Orthodox priest kneeling beside MacDougall. He had not noticed him before, and he was wiping blood from the injured man's face who was clinging to his cowl and seemed unable or unwilling to let him go.

Konrad rolled his eyes in surprise. 'MacDougall must have sent for him. He obviously arrived after the explosion. I thought he had gathered all the relics he could steal and headed east – he must have come back for Saint Fillan. MacDougall was wearing it and isn't now – I feel as if I have seen the Greek before, but I can't place him.'

'Not a scratch on the monk, I see – just like you, Konrad … you spent a lot of time out in the east. You must have met his like out there – the same merciful god must be protecting you,' Valence scoffed.

'MacDougall needs poppy water, and the Greek is giving him something to drink – the arrangement appears more temporal than spiritual. See!' Maccabi pulled a flask from deep within his vestment, and MacDougall, clutching the flask with both hands, drank greedily. Liquid rolled down his chin and onto his hands.

'MacDougall finds comfort in him,' Konrad said. 'The Greek has the manner of a schemer. Like most of his kind, he wants to appear enigmatic yet caring – most are charlatans. I lived amongst the Byzantines for fifteen years. Something strange about a monk who carries a dagger – see how he keeps checking his left sleeve. He has the gait and bearing of the Byzantine elite. They walk as if they have a cork up their ass.'

'Cowls don't protect monks anymore, and especially those that are a long way from home. I would carry a dagger in his position, too.'

Valence didn't think much about the monk, but he understood all about dealing with threats. The Greek was of no consequence.

'Once you have found Lord Percy and looked over the corpses, bring anything of interest to me – and do it alone. Bruce won't stay long on the Scottish mainland. He may head west to Ireland, where his father-in-law has lands. There is also evidence from my agents that Hugh Halcro in Orkney is expecting a visitor. I will send word ahead.'

Valence could see the damaged boats littering the beach and capsized in the bay. He didn't want to delay any longer than necessary in pursuing Bruce, and there was nothing to keep them in Tioram.

'We need to see what ships are salvageable and repair them. Some of the conscripted men are carpenters. Draft craftsmen from the surrounding area and search the villages surrounding the loch for fishing boats we can commandeer.'

'Yes, my lord,' Konrad replied. He walked past Jean de Graily and paused. Jean was sitting up, drinking from a leather pouch and washing the dirt from his eyes and face.

Konrad had not strayed far from Valence. Valence

watched Konrad studying Jean.

'Why are you still here? I want you to get on with identifying the dead.' Valence had issued his orders.

'Lord Valence, the soldiers can't go after Bruce because we don't have enough boats, but a couple of skilled mercenaries could find him in Orkney or Ireland and get the same outcome – capture or kill him and the competitor, but more discreetly.'

Valence had also considered sending in a small band of experienced men.

'By a couple of mercenaries, you mean yourself and Jean?'

Konrad nodded.

'My lord, you don't spend fifteen years chained together, without understanding what makes them tick. I controlled him for all that time, and I mastered him in the numerous disagreements we had. But he is clever, and our alliance then, as now, was one of convenience. I want to find out why he was in Acre and on that barge, and he wants to know the same about me. I am sure it wasn't the treasure – he was as surprised as I was when we found it. He may be of questionable loyalty and in the pay of the French, but he is a skilled assassin and just the type of man we need for such a job. He can help me get to Orkney, and I will find out his plans for me. When the time comes and he is of no more use he can be eliminated – in the meantime, there is no better man for getting me to Bruce and the competitor.'

The King trusted Konrad so he would let him go. If he was killed, there was nothing lost as Valence would pursue the Bruce regardless, but if he succeeded, then he would save effort he could devote to crushing Scotland.

'I need time to replace my ships – and you both survived the keep when others by them had not. God favours you and this adventure. I would prefer to get Bruce myself, but capturing a man guarded day and night would need many men and boats. I didn't plan a simple death for Bruce, something grander, more public at Smithfield yet the King wants them both dead. Achieve that and I will leave the time and place of Bruce's death with you … you need take no such considerations with the competitor – kill him and bring me his head.'

Konrad whispered in Valence's ear. 'And, my lord, if as a loyal and valued member of the French court, de Grailly was indeed to meet with an unfortunate accident whilst we are pursuing the Scots, we can blame Bruce and his rabble and isolate them further.'

Valence nodded and Konrad walked away shouting.

'Get the dead with heads lined up on the beach, I want to see if there are any Scots amongst them.'

Valence couldn't let Bruce or the competitor escape. He was indifferent to the assassins' fate. They were destined to die violently at some point. Konrad's and Jean's lives were a good investment if they killed both men. In any case he would still build ships, they were needed to pursue and destroy the rest of Bruce's men. One way or another the new King of Scots would only reign for a few more months.

*

King Robert studied the horizon, which flashed yellow and red, painting the sky like a powerful storm. Yet it was no tempest, only the death throes of Castle Tioram.

The noise of destruction was diminishing as they put distance between the flotilla and Tioram. It was a place where for a few short weeks he had lived a normal life.

The definition of normal now was different before he became king. It was sleeping in the same bed two nights in a row, eating at the same table, laughing, not mourning. Bruce had been in armies that had scorched lands and obliterated many buildings, including holy ones, yet the destruction of Tioram made him sad and thoughtful.

He remembered laughing until his sides hurt, sleeping without a dagger next to him and until the sun rose, rather than furtively leaving a forest at dusk – before dogs discovered his latest hiding place.

He had left Christina behind, and he felt guilty. Guilty for the pleasure he had found in her, guilty that he missed her, and guilty he had betrayed his wife.

He pondered whether a king could ever live a normal life.

'Some of the most wretched times are those lived in the wilderness. Don't you agree, Lord Sinclair?' Bruce was resting on a bench with his back to the bow, looking behind them. Lord Sinclair was adjacent to the King chewing on some dried meat. Geoffrey, the old monk, was asleep at Sinclair's feet.

'Sire, you must eat. Even in the most dangerous of confrontations, one must always take the opportunity to eat, and this dried venison from Lady Ranald's kitchen has been flavoured with juniper berries and steeped in *uisge beatha*. Hungry men make poor soldiers and weak leaders.'

'I never knew you were such a connoisseur in the kitchen. James will be watching you in case you are after his job. Isn't that true, James?' the King called to his steward, who was counting the stores on board.

'Yes, Sire,' James replied. 'I can use a good cook in the kitchen. The last one died at Dalrigh – something he ate.'

The King laughed aloud.

'During the siege of Acre, we lived on smoked rat,' Lord Sinclair said. 'After that, I got to appreciate the finer things in life.' He offered a slice of meat to the King who declined.

A light mist of cold water moistened Bruce's skin. It relieved the tingling in his skin and a weakness in his joints. The sea air offered some comfort.

Bruce had been light-headed, and Lord Hay, the king's bodyguard, had insisted he remain seated. He wondered if he had not fully recovered from the head injury he had received at Methven. He rubbed his forehead. The bump was still there, and it was still painful even after three months.

Hamish Campbell was working the mainsail, trying to catch as much wind and speed as possible to get them away from Tioram.

Bruce studied the four pairs of oarsmen working in unison. They were rowing backwards, guided by a helmsman. Their teamwork moved the oars effortlessly through the dark blue waters of Moidart Sound, and they were making excellent speed.

Tioram could be heard but not seen. Bruce couldn't help smiling as his left-hand shook. He held it down hoping no one would see it trembling lest they mistook it for fear.

'These are fine men, Hamish,' the King shouted.

'Indeed, they are, Sire,' Hamish replied enthusiastically. He was dancing along the keel as he manipulated and finessed the sail to maximise the speed. The boat was slicing through the top of the waves. Christina was right about placing trust in him.

'We are heading south now? I noticed Kilchoan Point to our left. We passed it on the right when we came south from Dalrigh. Any journey south towards England makes me uneasy.'

Bruce placed his trembling hand behind him.

'Yes, Sire. Lord MacDonald and your brothers are waiting with his men at Dunaverty Castle – Lady Christina sent them word. We will move past the Point and enter the Sound of Mull before we sneak behind the isles of Jura and Gigha. We'll follow the west coast of Kintyre and cling to the shallow waters, which only my men know well. Kintyre has a treacherous coast, and the English follow at their peril. They will only be able to navigate the waters if they have local help, and no one will offer that. Finding someone willing to help them, even with their gold, will cost them time.' Hamish's confidence and cheer were infectious.

'We are also heading towards the English border?' Lord Sinclair spoke the King's thoughts.

'Yes, my lord, but only for a short while to deceive the English. They will think we went north, not back towards danger. By the time they realise we have tricked them, we will be on the other side of Jura, resupplied with fresh men and in the open seas, on route to Lord Halcro and the Northern Isles. The English wouldn't dare follow us there. The King of Norway won't take kindly to the English hunting for you on his lands.'

Lord Sinclair nodded. 'Agreed, young Campbell, but let's get to Dunaverty. We need to be there before darkness.'

'Yes, my lord. It would be ill-advised to be out at sea at night. We will land unseen; the moon will give us enough light to pass into Dunaverty Bay. It has several rocks just below the water that have sunk many ships, but we are safe, those that follow are not. The castle is on a promontory between Dunaverty and Brunerican Bays. There is a steep path up to the keep. Once you are up there, you can see for miles in every direction.' Hamish tweaked the ropes guiding the sail, and Bruce sensed the boat speeding up even further.

Bruce recognised that Lord Sinclair was also impressed with Hamish. Sinclair was relaxed now and in a man who always had a slight edge to him this was telling. Sinclair claimed his anxiety was the reason he was still alive, and he had fought in the Crusades and survived Acre. He knew naval and military tactics better than any man alive. His support made their successful escape to Dunaverty and onto Orkney more likely.

'I have spread word and gold that we are heading to the Rathlin Islands under the protection of your father-in-law. The English will check there, and it will cost the English time, even if they suspect we are going elsewhere,' Hamish added.

'Into Richard de Burgh's lands?'

Bruce didn't know if his father-in-law had heard rumours of his infidelity with Christina; if so, he could be more inclined to hand him over to the English than hide him. Regardless, de Burgh was a political animal. He would wait to see if Bruce was winning before he offered any help, adultery would play no part in his loyalties. Robert knew his wife Elisabeth would not judge him so harshly and would understand he was a human being, not a saint.

He thought of Elisabeth at the shrine of St Duthac, and in the safety of sanctuary. He loved Elisabeth and Christina, and the conflict pressed heavily on him.

'Where is the Lady Christina going?' Bruce asked.

'She is behind us following the same route except that about halfway down the coast, she will be taking the inlet to the east that lands her at West Tarbert – heading to Tarbert Castle with Domhnall and the men who took the last boat. Most of her other men will join us later on foot. Father Domhnall will come by boat with more supplies. Sire, we are about to enter Sound of Mull.' Hamish pointed to a headland and the boat moved gently towards the southeast.

'Good. I cannot afford to lose men of Domhnall's calibre. Are we sure she will be safe there with only a few men to protect her?'

'She anticipated that you might be concerned and told me to tell you that she is well able to look after herself … Sire.' Hamish blushed.

'I can hear her saying it now – and don't be ashamed, young Campbell.' The King was amused, as he knew the message came unadulterated and she meant it.

Bruce understood Christina's bravery, but this was a rebellion in a barbaric world with a vindictive tyrant in the English King. There was no nobility or chivalry, for King Edward had raised the dragon banner no quarter, no mercy, no rules.

'Sire, Tarbert Castle is on the southern shore of East Loch

Tarbert on high ground with water on three sides,' Hamish said. 'Any attackers will need boats – lots of boats – to lay siege. It is also surrounded by strong currents as well as hidden rocks. The tides can keep you in the loch until they eject you like a catapult out to the open sea. The English think they rule our country, but they don't even know a fraction of it.'

In the moment Robert roared in approval, but reality was a short step away.

'I can only stay in Dunaverty for three days, or we risk the weather holding us there. The English will come eventually.' Lord Hay interrupted, he had been sitting at the stern watching for any sign of the English ships.

'Sire, you are right, we must leave once we are resupplied and the men rested. Our presence at Dunaverty won't remain a secret – it's not every day a flotilla of birlinns and eighty armed men turn up. Gossip travels quickly and you are more than a rebel – it's personal.'

Lord Hay never forgot his first duty was to protect the king's person.

'Valence will follow me to the ends of the earth, and we all know he won't stop until he has my head on a spike. I killed his cousin John Comyn and his family honour is at stake – yet I would do it again. Comyn would have sold our country to Longshanks just to be called a king and not act in the best interests of Scotland – the English will not make my countrymen slaves in their own country – that is the reason I raised this rebellion.'

'Sire, we need to keep running until we are strong again, unchivalrous as it looks and must keep you alive using any means we can. If you die, we *all* lose. Drink, Sire – the finest *uisge beatha* from the cellars of Tioram. Christina thrust this into my hand as I left and ordered I serve it to you at the first opportunity. I know you think I don't take orders from a woman easily, but in this case, it was a pleasure.' Lord

Hay carefully removed his flask hidden within his cloak and handed it to the King.

Bruce nodded as he sipped the warming spirit.

'Pass me some meat and a goblet for the monk.' The King handed the goblet to Brother Geoffrey. 'We will leave in three days – and let's drink to the power of women.'

The spirit relaxed the King and the pain and tingling didn't seem so pressing, yet he felt weak, detached from the brute strength that had kept him alive. He was thinking of the dreadful dreams he had been having ever since Dalrigh. He needed Domhnall, the priest and physician, to help him understand and recover.

'I will send a ship ahead under Lord Douglas's command to warn Sir Hugh Halcro of our imminent arrival. We can't leave it any longer to travel, as the sea to the Northern Isles in autumn are dangerous. We must be in Orkney as soon as possible – Bishop Wishart sent a letter to Halcro from Cupar Castle in the summer, so preparation will have been made, but there is always the chance the English are waiting for us, and we should find that out before King Robert arrives.'

'That is a sound plan, Sinclair. You know Orkney better than any of us. Aren't you the titular Earl of Orkney?' Hay asked.

'Indeed I am,' Sinclair replied. 'Know the waters like the back of my hand.'

The King was considering what he should do with the treasure when it arrived from France.

'And there is the other matter of Alaric.' The King's voice was just audible. The noise of the oars and creaking timbers prevented the information from reaching the crew.

'Orkney is remote but is it safe enough? The wealth would motivate my fellow monarchs to use the most herculean efforts to capture it. I have had thoughts of moving it west, beyond these most determined tyrants – lands you know equally well, Lord Sinclair.'

Sinclair continued. 'Halco Castle offers a unique protection we cannot find anywhere on the mainland. It sits on an island surrounded by an unforgiving sea. As young Hamish has said, attacks on Norwegian lands will not be taken lightly by King Haakon and in turn he wouldn't attack knowing the people's hearts and minds rest with Scotland. My time in my Orcadian lands was precious and prepared me for the adventures in the Holy Land. The people are stronger than oxen – Sire, the lands west are even wilder and the people mythical.'

Hay looked fleetingly at Brother Geoffrey, who could hear the King. His glance was scornful, as if Geoffrey was a threat, and the King noticed.

Bruce took a large gulp from the flask and sighed.

'Sire, are you displeased?' Lord Hay asked.

'When I see Geoffrey, I think of Wishart. I had not thought of him in days. Geoffrey was in the Bishop's care for fifteen years, and if the Bishop valued and *trusted* him, then so do I. We all need to take care of everyone involved in this rebellion, no matter what role they have played, or know the role God may have already laid out for them, or their age. Remember it was Bishop Wishart; a man of over sixty years who had me crowned and led our opposition when much younger nobles were resting on their fat arses risking nothing.'

Bruce drank some more, certain Lord Hay's face was flushed at the reprimand.

'It is to be hoped that the Pope will protect Wishart and see no harm is inflicted on him,' Sinclair replied.

'The Pope will be under pressure to punish him because he absolved me for Comyn, yet he is compelled to protect all clerics. No pope will survive long if he doesn't look after his own, and he won't want to be seen condoning executing clergy. An ugly precedent would be set. If I am a judge, Longshanks won't kill him – he is too cowardly – but he will neglect him. Sixty-five-year-old men have a habit of dying.'

Bruce hoped he was wrong, and Sinclair was right as he continued.

'Sire, Longshanks is ill and cares about his mortal soul a little more now, and if he neglects a Bishop, Clement will excommunicate him – and then where does his argument of moral superiority over Scotland go if he is also an excommunicate?'

'An excommunicated king? We will have something in common then. I hope you are right, Henry.' Bruce acknowledged Lord Sinclair's argument with a wry smile.

'Lords Sinclair and Hay, come closer.' Bruce beckoned them nearer. Lord Douglas was using his boundless energy on an oar and had ignored the whole conversation. The King had already confided in Lord Douglas.

'When we land at Dunaverty, let the crew disembark first and stay with me until no one is around.'

They both looked perplexed.

'Why, Sire?' Lord Hay asked. 'We need to get you off the ship first and secure your body. That is the normal protocol.'

'Because I can't move my legs. I won't be able to climb up the steep path to the keep. No one should see a king like this. People don't follow a weak king.'

The lords both quietly nodded and sat on either side of him.

'Hamish,' Lord Hay called.

Hamish was standing on the bow with his back to the King, taking measurements with a line, which he pulled up from the water. 'Yes, Lord Hay?'

'When we arrive at Dunaverty, leave the ship and take the men up to the castle. Ask the King's brothers, Edward, Alexander, and Thomas, to join us here on the boat – and tell them to come alone.'

Chapter Three

Kilchoan Sound, Argyle, Scotland, September 1306: Treachery at Tarbert

'The King should be well on the way to Dunaverty Castle – a couple of hours ahead of us. He used the channel of Riska, but we had to go around. That detour will cost us at least that time.' Christina had to concentrate as she steered whilst Domhnall managed the mainsail and the crew.

The wind was moderate, but Domhnall looked anxious as the strong current crashed waves onto the granite cliffs that guarded Moidart Sound, splitting boulders from the face. The sound was tumultuous – one powerful wave followed another, and the noise was unrelenting.

'I am wondering what those waves could do to us. I need to mind my work,' Domhnall paused, still holding the mainsail rope in his hand.

'I wonder if we will ever be able to harness the power of the sea or whether it will always be destructive. Each wave has the power to destroy ships and men, but once it has crashed, it is weak again.'

She could hear Domhnall's fear, yet she recognised and admired his strength. His knowledge of everything astounded her. He was curious about everything, and he had mastered many skills that could have made him a rich man, yet he had given it all up to follow God and King Robert.

'Don't look so worried. I know these waters as well as anyone. I grew up here. I could sail before I could ride.' The ship was swift and ideal for such conditions. She also knew that there were many dangers, so she studied the colour of the water.

Christina was acting master. The birlinn contained four pairs of oarsmen, plus Lady Eilidh, and they needed every man rowing if they were to keep ahead of the English.

'I am not sure how long the English will delay their pursuit. The mainsail is catching every whisp of wind and we will outrun the English for now, but for how long?'

'Why do you keep examining the water and dropping that line over the side?' Domhnall asked.

'If the water is blue and looks clearer, the channel is deep, and we are safe from running aground. If the water is brown and cloudy, we are in shallower waters and must be cautious.' Christina was also dropping lines over the side with wax on the end.

'The wax line tells me how far the bottom is from the keel and whether it is gravel or rock. Running into gravel doesn't hole the boat.' Christina wasn't just looking out for the boat; she was also searching the horizon for the King.

Domhnall looked out over the stern.

'I don't think they will be coming after us. We did a good job – We did a GREAT job,' Domhnall shouted.

His cassock and red hair were still covered with soot and tar. His face beamed despite the bloodied scratches.

Christina was also dishevelled. Her clothes were shabbier than the poorest of peasants, her face smeared with soot and mud.

'You do not appear the Lady of the Isles and chief of Clan Ranald,' Domhnall teased.

'At this moment, I do not worry about my appearance or the manner of convention. What I did today in keeping the King alive and free, I would gladly do again. That achievement matters more than finery. I sense I am amongst people who do not judge superficially. At Tarbert Castle there will be plenty of time for me to transform and emerge the lady once again.'

Christina purposely smeared the mud across her face.

'I think it will take more than a few days for the English to reorganise, and I suspect we destroyed more of their boats when the castle rocks fell into the loch. The roar of their displacement was frightening. Any ship connecting with those stone missiles would have been sunk, so they will need to repair, or better still, replace them. Trees need to be felled. Bet it's made them angry too. Good that my tenants took to the hills before they arrived.' She allowed herself to smile.

'Valence was born angry, like all of his ilk,' Domhnall scoffed. 'They have everything, and it's still not enough. He will be tearing Tioram apart looking for someone to take it out on – if there was any justice, we might have killed him.'

'We can but hope. We know that commanders like Valence wait until a castle is taken before they march in. He would have sent my stupid brothers in as the vanguard rather than risk his own neck.' Christina understood Valence better than she wanted to. 'Once we have reached Tarbert, I will get my steward, Harrison Deacon, to send out scouts to find out how the English fare and whether Valence is alive.'

'They will pursue the King and come for you, Christina.' She did not want to face Domhnall's concern, but she knew he was right.

'Yes, I know they will. They will be after you too, and your black powder.'

Domhnall nodded, still smiling as broadly as she had seen any man.

'So, after Tarbert and resupplying the King, I will go to my lands in Uist and hide out there until better times return before I risk joining the King. Robert believes Longshanks won't last long, and I doubt his foppish son will have ever heard of Uist, never mind be able to send someone to find me – then King Robert will return to take back our country. I can use the time to assemble more men, ships, and supplies.'

Christina was an outlaw too. She wouldn't survive if she stayed on the mainland, yet she was reluctant to leave.

'Yes, King Robert will return soon – but until then, Edward will make you an outlaw and your brothers will seize your land.' Domhnall's smile had disappeared.

'I am no different to the many who fight for King Robert in losing my lands and of course my brothers will use this opportunity – I would in their shoes. They can take a castle here and a manor there, but they won't hold them for long, because like the English King in Scotland, my brothers have no legitimacy, and the people who live on the land know that. They will be driven on a merry dance trying to get my people to pay their rent – I have always treated my tenants fairly, and I believe them to be loyal. Lachlann and Ruaidhri don't have the subtlety or the kindness to manage the estate by collaborating with the people.'

The current and the wind were pushing them faster.

'You can rest a while – eat and drink something. Even the currents and the wind are against the English.' She tossed a sack of bread and meat to the oarsmen.

Immediately, everyone pulled their oars up and out of the water. They were exhausted and slumped over their sculls. No one seemed to want to eat or drink, and Christina had forgotten the impact the sea had on the stomach. Though she wondered if her own sickness was entirely down to the sea.

Christina swung the square mainsail to catch the wind, pushing the keel southeast towards the Kintyre coast. The wind would have carried a woollen sack through these waters.

'I was hoping we would catch up with the King.'

Domhnall ignored her and opened a leather sack that had been placed carefully at the keel. She could see his face light up with anticipation.

'I will need these when I join the King and his men.'

Domhnall placed several bottles, pouches, and stone

vessels next to him, examining each one, checking the containers for cracks and examining their contents for water ingress.

'I fear I lost some of my valuable potions and balms as we escaped. Some were damaged when I waded out to this ship.' Domhnall poured water out of the pouch.

'You must join the King as soon as you can. He needs your apothecary skills for the trials to come ... he was unwell.' Christina had observed the King's exhaustion and feared worse. At times, his fatigue had seemed overwhelming, and he had struggled to rise from a chair. She believed his mental strength had compensated and kept his illness secret from everyone but not her.

She was fascinated by Domhnall and his skills as a priest, smith, and apothecary. Learning was a valuable commodity; she had been lucky, and her father Ailean had invested in his daughter's education.

'Where did you glean all this knowledge?' As they approached Kintyre, the boat was now steady, and Christina felt she could relax for a few minutes. 'Domhnall, tell me – why you do what you do? I inherited my lands from my father, so my life was already laid out for me. But you, Domhnall, are physician, philosopher, smith, and priest. How come?'

She always felt a little intimidated around him. His presence filled any room, and he seemed to know about things she didn't know existed. She wanted to know more about him, and this journey was the only time they could really talk – openly, honestly, without judgement.

'The MacBeith's are an old Celtic family who travelled widely and pursued knowledge. If legend is to be believed, we managed a king or two. My ancestors were great patrons of learning, and we made several pilgrimages, picking up ideas wherever we came across them and I am just a part of that legacy. When the English came, my father was murdered by Konrad von Feuchtwangen on their orders, our lands were seized, and my mother died of a broken heart. There was only my brother and I left alive. I avoided the situation, ran away to the Holy Land and became a monk in the Byzantine Church during the days when a pilgrimage to such lands was possible. My brother Murdie faced the situation; he was stronger than me then. Now I want to stay where I am needed – there is nowhere like Scotland, it's special, unique, and worth fighting for. All my hopes for the future are rooted here.' As he described his family his voice hesitated and then steadied as he described the passion of his belief in Scotland's future.

'You have a brother? You never mentioned him all the time you were in Tioram.' Christina was surprised – but then again, in what normal circumstances would a conversation occur? This was a discussion they could only have in moments when life wasn't immediately about survival.

'Murdie, or should I say Murdoch – I try not to mention him, as he works for Bishop Wishart. I don't want to know where he is or what he is doing in case I get caught – but I would be happy if I just knew he was alive.'

Domhnall turned away, but she thought she glimpsed a flush of deeper red in his face. It was clear he didn't want to speak further. He returned to his potions, and she knew to ask no more.

'We will arrive at Tarbert in about four hours if we maintain this speed,' Christina said. 'King Robert and Lord Aonghus MacDonald are waiting at Dunaverty. He is a kinsman of mine, and he brings with him much-needed reinforcements.'

Domhnall continued to press the water out of the sack, laying its contents on the deck.

'Found it!' he cried and playfully threw a rolled textile in front of her. She immediately recognised it.

Domhnall grinned. 'I thought this was too valuable to set

on fire and waste on any Englishmen.'

Christina shrieked with joy as she saw that Domhnall had saved the tapestry she had woven for the King. She picked up the wet fabric and embraced it, water still dripping from its edges.

'If I dry it quickly in the wind, it may not shrink or lose colour.' Christina carefully laid the tapestry out at the stern, fixing it down on one side with the anchor. The honours of Scotland danced in the wind behind the ship, and she felt an immense joy.

'I don't want to save this from the English only to lose it to the sea.' This was a good omen. 'Domhnall – you must take it to the King at Dunaverty. He will value it, and it will give hope to the men there. Such a banner will encourage more people to join him. Guard it carefully. Symbols are important when the real king must stay hidden. The people who fight for the king are ignorant about the man, but not about the crown and what it represents. They don't know about a king who weeps when he loses a man, who uses his strength to seek revenge and can also embrace his enemies when it means the security of his country.'

'I think I understand their power,' Domhnall said. 'I nearly drowned in bringing it here.' Christina detected a scowl; she hadn't meant her words as a reprimand.

Eilidh Robertson had been very quiet, and Christina could hear that she was struggling to hide her sickness. She had too much dignity to complain.

'We will soon be within the walls of Tarbert Castle,' she reassured Lady Eilidh.

The birlinn travelled south with the shore barely in sight. Everyone was quiet, reflective but not sad.

Christina recognised her life would never be the same, and she wondered whether everyone else was reconciling themselves with that decision and the challenges ahead. She had made her choice, and it wasn't one she regretted.

Everyone on the birlinn had lost much already.

Domhnall broke the silence.

'You are heading to your lands in Uist and the English won't find you there. How can you be sure you can avoid them for six months or more whilst you wait for the seas to calm?'

'The Gaels don't like strangers and that sentiment will be made at the point of a sword.' She suspected King Robert had tasked Domhnall to convince her to join him at Dunaverty.

She had a distraction, a reason to change the subject. The boat was drifting towards the Kintyre shore. She grabbed the rudder with her right hand and moved the birlinn further into the open sea.

'Tell me about Tarbert,' Domhnall said. 'I have heard about its location but never visited.'

'Tarbert was chosen with great care, and it is only a few hours by boat from Dunaverty Castle. Tarbert has clear views up Loch Fyne and the Firth of Clyde. We will dock at the east side, and you will take the boat and the men and join King Robert once his stores are loaded. My lead oarsman will take you to Dunaverty. He is the best guide for these waters. I will rest tonight with Eilidh before I resupply for the journey to Uist. My steward, Deacon, is always prepared for a crisis even when there isn't one. He is very efficient and will have ale stored in the cellar and the outbuildings bulging with produce for the King and for my stay in Uist.'

'Deacon sounds like the very man for the times. You seem to have thought of everything – and you tell me *I* am a man of many talents.' She was familiar with easy flattery, but Domhnall's praise was sincere.

'In this world, a woman with lands must be better than any man, or she will disappear. My ambition is not constrained to being the extension of a man and a mother of children.'

The boat jumped as the current dragged it directly east.

'Did you feel that?' she asked. Her heart began to race.

'Indeed, I did.'

Domhnall almost lost his footing as the boat cut across the waves that were moving away from the coast and out to sea, yet the boat seemed to want to go in the other direction. It moved violently from side to side, caught between where the current was moving and where the sail and rudder were pushing them.

'We are near the inlet to Tarbert. I will need to mind *my* work now.' Christina moved the sail to slow the boat down.

'Grab the rudder, Domhnall, and move it to your left. The current will make it easy for you, as it will push us away from the sea and towards the castle. Just steer between the gap in the cliffs that you will see very soon.'

The other sailors placed their oars into their fastenings.

'Stop,' Christina ordered. 'We don't need speed; we need to be canny. The access to the loch by Tarbert is full of narrows and hazards that will scupper us.'

Christina concentrated, as the wind was now picking up and the manoeuvre was complicated.

The birlinn swung to the left, and it was being pulled further and further into the shallows. Christina stood at the bow with her back to the stern, guiding Domhnall, who was now manoeuvring the rudder. He grunted as he struggled to hold the course. Every man in the crew was still and taut and no one spoke.

She moved her hands to the right and left as Domhnall finessed the course. 'Left a little … correct a bit to the right … we need to follow the dark blue water where the channel is deepest … follow my hands.'

'I am adding helmsman to my skills,' Domhnall added with a nervous laugh.

Christina didn't answer. She needed to follow the deep blue water, and the light had gone as clouds appeared.

'We need to pass through the gap in the cliffs, and then we can see the shape of Castle Tarbert in the distance.

Keep following my guidance, and it will show us the way to safety.' Christina's mouth was dry. She swallowed hard as her voice faltered. She tried to keep calm; everyone was relying on her.

The birlinn shifted further and further to the left on a direct course to run aground on the shore. Christina moved the sail to slow the vessel down. Mist had started to move down from the surrounding hills and had obscured what Christina knew was the gap in the cliffs. She thought she saw the gap and the shadow of Tarbert Castle in the distance, and she needed to be sure she had lined up to travel through the narrow channel. She needed to calibrate based on the tantalising glimpses of familiar spots, and she couldn't afford to be mistaken.

The wind picked up again and blew the wispy clouds away. Christina saw the strong sunlight beam down onto the gap in the shore as if it was pointing the way to safety.

'Domhnall, there is the entrance to the loch – steer straight ahead.' She tried to conceal her anxiety, but her voice was hoarse and shaky. She knew these waters, but there was always danger lurking amongst the primeval landscape of Kintyre.

'Keep steering straight ahead whilst I drop the mainsail and raise the lateen. It will allow us to sail into the wind rather than being pushed by it. Help me change the sail – and Domhnall, just keep steering.'

Christina and the lead oarsman quickly hoisted the triangular sail, which immediately steadied the ship. Domhnall was still wrestling with the rudder, his face ruddy, sweat dripping down his forehead. The ship started to respond.

'We will be safe in the castle by a quarter past the hour.' Christina had been scared, but her voice and heart had steadied. Domhnall's fingers were no longer locked on the rudder like a vice.

The crew thrust the oars into the water steadying the ship. The oars acted like a multitude of rudders, and the ship obediently sailed towards Tarbert.

As they approached in the distance, Christina could see a figure pacing down by the castle's entrance on the east side.

'That will be Deacon waiting for us.' She pointed at the figure.

Christina dropped the lateen sail as the oarsmen pulled the birlinn into its berth. A wooden harbour led up to an incline. An outer wall protected the drum tower, and there was a grassy embankment between the inner and outer walls. A small building narrowed the path and separated the tower from the harbour.

She dropped anchor, and the birlinn steadied. The lead oarsmen lowered a plank, allowing Christina to step off the deck.

'Secure the ship,' Christina ordered as ropes were thrown from the bow and stern.

'My Lady Christina,' Deacon said. 'It is always a pleasure – rumours reached us and we are prepared.' He bowed to Christina, but didn't even acknowledge Domhnall, as if he wasn't important.

'What rumours?' Domhnall was now at Christina's side. He reacted as if the steward was threatening her.

'Sir, and who might you be?' Deacon's tone was haughty. It was a foible she had learned to overlook, and with Domhnall, who dwarfed most men, an attitude she guessed he was unfamiliar. The steward normally meant no ill will; it was just his manner. She would talk with him tomorrow. For now, their duty to supply the king was more important. Domhnall would understand.

Domhnall continued to scowl and appeared more offended than he should be by the steward's slight. She valued them both, and unfairly, she was glad Domhnall was leaving so that she didn't have to deal with another conflict.

'Deacon, this is Domhnall MacBeith. He will be leaving very soon, as the tide is already turning, I see. We had a bit of excitement getting here.'

Christina's body was exhausted; she was functioning but barely. The entry into Tarbert Castle had drained her. 'Do you have news of King Robert?' she asked.

'King Robert Bruce? These are the rumours I indicated that he was in Argyll, but I didn't know he was coming here.' Deacon's face narrowed and his brows joined.

'He is not coming here. He is at Dunaverty. Send a rider immediately to the castle there and tell him we are safe, and Father MacBeith is on his way. He should get there before the King arrives.'

Christina realised that she hadn't informed her steward specifically about King Robert.

'I told you about important nobles in need of supplies. I couldn't write to you about the king. Paper trails must not be left for the English to intercept.'

'I have prepared stores and supplies for a hundred men as instructed and I am honoured they serve the king ... and I am glad to say all is ready. The grain stores are full, and the brewer and the butcher have been busy. I have men ready to load the provisions here onto your ship upon your order. More stores are in the warehouses in Tarbert.'

Deacon pointed to several carts lined up behind the sea wall. Christina could hear the oxen moaning as they waited.

Domhnall interrupted him. 'We must get these supplies at hand loaded as quickly as possible, or we will be stuck here for many hours. We can't lose another day waiting for the warehouses to be emptied.'

Deacon's face flushed red, his pride dented.

'Start the men loading this ship,' Christina ordered and pointed to the ship they had just arrived on. 'Domhnall will take these stores we have to Dunaverty. The ship should be able to carry most of it. Anything that can't be loaded now can be sent on later.'

'Lady, your apartments are ready if you would like to follow me.' The steward headed up the path towards the entrance.

'I will stay with Domhnall until he leaves. Lady Robertson can prepare my rooms.' She could only relax when Domhnall was on his way to the King.

Deacon continued towards the steep steps that hugged the ditch and led to the entrance of the main tower. At the edge of the inner ditch, he stopped.

'I don't much care for your steward,' Domhnall said. 'I have been a priest and taken confession from all occupations, and it has allowed me to measure men. Whatever he does for you, he is not a content man – he clenches his hands like a pugilist.'

'He can come across as arrogant, but he has been a servant for many years, overly educated for his position, and ambitious. I have had no reason to distrust or find him disloyal. My father brought him home from the wars in France where he was a novice whose monastery had been destroyed by English soldiers. In an hour or so you will be gone, and you never have to speak with him again.'

Christina thought Domhnall had judged her steward too quickly.

'I suppose I can put up with him until then, if he gets this ship loaded … I choose to be careful around him.' Christina acknowledged his warning but did not share his concerns.

A small army of men descended on the ship carrying sacks and rolling barrels and hand carts as Deacon ordered them out of the castle and down to the harbour to help load.

'The meat, barley, wheat, and oats from my estates will sustain King Robert's army until the spring.'

'They will be loaded within the hour,' Deacon called down to her. He continued to shout orders from above. A constant stream of men filled the ship, and she could see its keel drop deeper into the water.

'Deacon, be careful we don't miss the tide,' Christina called out. 'It's moving out, and the keel is moving down. We don't want to beach the birlinn. Make sure the loads are evenly distributed along the deck, and don't forget to leave space for the oarsmen and sails.'

The oarsmen were eating bread and meat that servants had laid out on the grass at the bottom of the embankment adjacent to the harbour. The leading oarsman looked anxiously at the keel.

'I will send what men I can from Argyle. I can get many more from the Isles. Tell the King I will find him when the weather improves in the spring. Tell him he needs to return soon and claim his kingdom and remind him of my loyalty.'

Christina found the separation agonising. They had been apart only a day, yet she feared for him and felt physically sick with the thought that she might never see him again. He had escaped from the English so many times that she feared his luck would run out at some point. That was a dark thought she couldn't dwell upon; she flushed it from her mind. Today she had much to do to help the King escape them again, and the thought of helping Robert confused these fears.

Domhnall kissed her softly on the forehead. 'It will be many months before we may see each other again. I am loathed to leave you to face the aftermath of Tioram alone.'

'The King needs you, and I know how to look after myself. I will be away from here within the week or sooner.'

'I will see you again, Domhnall, we are survivors and don't die easily, still that thought doesn't make parting easier – you make everyone around you stronger so don't get killed.'

Domhnall held her close to him, she could feel his heart beating and it gave her comfort.

Deacon returned from his vantage point above them and

was now on the ship. He avoided eye contact and busied himself moving the cargo before jumping back onto the land and reviewing the draft of the keel. He repeated this process several times as the crew ate and drank.

Other servants helped him lash the cargo to anything that would hold it steady. The tide was gaining strength, and the moon had started to shine as the sun decayed.

'The ship is heavy … but you will clear the rocks with a few feet to spare. The changing tide will help push you out from Loch Fyne towards the sea.' Christina was still fussing around the ship. Domhnall was close by, carefully repacking his potions for the journey.

Deacon did some last-minute rearrangements before he surveyed his work from the harbour wall.

Christina wanted the remaining minutes to last longer, but they flew by, and like all good moments in life, they left a briefer impression, as if time conspired with the devil to shorten life's pleasures.

'Lady, we are ready,' Deacon announced as he admired his work one last time.

The crew mobilised and climbed back onto the boat. Domhnall was last as the steward untied the restraining ropes, and the lead oarsman raised the anchor.

The tide pulled the ship away from the berth, and in a matter of a less than a minute the birlinn had turned to the left and the oarsmen pulled the vessel further into the channel leading from the dock. The mainsail was unfurled to accelerate the ship through the strait and out to sea.

She watched Domhnall pace the deck before turning away and heading back to the keep, her steward followed.

'I am going to my apartments where I can better see the ship, Eilidh will be waiting and I need to rest.'

It was only now that Christina could consider the day's events, and her body started to shake uncontrollably.

'Lady – are you ill?' Deacon was a few feet behind her.

She could hear his heavy breathing.

Almost immediately, Christina felt the blood rush from her head. Her eyes closed, and it was as if a black lens came down over her vision. Her legs wobbled, and she fell to the ground.

*

Christina collapsed backwards onto Deacon, and they stumbled onto the fringe of the grassy embankment. He scrambled onto his knees and lifted her eyelids, confirming she was unconscious. The sentries seemed to have observed the fall from the top of the tower and had warned the soldiers below.

'So, it appears to be true,' Deacon whispered.

He stepped backwards and trod on her outstretched hand as Eilidh, alerted by the sentries, scurried towards the prostrate Christina.

'What has happened?' Eilidh immediately knelt by Christina's side and tried to revive her. 'Get some men to carry her into her apartments.' Eilidh was frantic, stressed, and her voice trembled.

'You – over there.' The steward pointed to the brewer. He was broad and could pick up full kegs of beer, he could easily manage Christina's slender frame. The brewer carried her up the slope to the castle. Her body was limp, and she made no sound.

Deacon surveyed the harbour, hoping in vain that Valence would arrive, but he knew that was a fantasy, the English ships had been destroyed – they were weeks away. Until then, he would have to make things up. He had already sent a message about Christina's intended arrival at Tarbert and Valence would want to know Bruce was at Dunaverty.

'Good, the tradesman are finishing for the day.'

The men working inside the castle were leaving for the day, so he crossed the inner drawbridge and returned to the keep. Above him in the tower he could see the pale light coming from Christina's room.

The brewer returned to the courtyard and headed to his steaming vat of freshly fermenting ale. His apprentice had started to tap the contents of the large brewing vessel into smaller barrels.

Everyone was busy and no one was watching – a perfect opportunity for him to write his letters unnoticed. The news made him so excited he thought he would burst. He had never felt so important.

Now I need to write to Valence. I will also write to Edward Balliol; I have big news for them to justify the purses of gold they pay me each year. They will be keen to hear where they can find the traitor Bruce and the role of Christina in this tatty rebellion. This way I get gold from two parties.

It was a new chapter of intrigue, and he rubbed his hands in glee. He swept the random papers onto the floor, kicking them away from beneath his chair. He needed space and clean parchment to complete his work. The messages needed to leave Castle Tarbert as soon as possible so Valence could arrive in time to catch Bruce and Christina. Valence had men in the village who could carry his letters to him and Balliol.

He took a large goblet of wine and immediately emptied the contents. It rushed through his body, making him bolder.

He finished the first note quickly, then snatched another parchment and began scratching his second note for Balliol before hiding them within his shirt. He felt a rush of satisfaction and excitement, because he was no longer sending gossip about a minor Scottish noble in a forgotten part of King Edward's lands. He was at its heart, discussing kings, centre stage and a lead player.

Now I must plan to make sure she never leaves here and give Valence time to capture her. I don't have long, she leaves for Uist in a few days.

Outside, the night sentries were patrolling the castle

entrances and battlements. He opened the shutter and watched the soldiers in the courtyard, hoping for inspiration on how he could keep Christina in Tarbert.

It is easy to conspire; the complicated part is surviving any investigation. I must be above suspicion.

He heard footsteps outside his door. A small glimmer of light fought its way under his door before continuing into the courtyard.

And there's another obstacle to my plans – Robertson.

Lady Robertson was always careful around him, as if she could see into his soul. Her husband Hendor had always distrusted him, and he had shared that suspicion with his wife.

She was engaged in conversation with one of the guards. He couldn't hear or see clearly in the darkness.

These guards had families in the villages surrounding Tarbert and farmed the Ranald lands and were loyal to Christina. A pregnant Christina would be of even greater interest to Lord Valence and a rival for Edward Balliol if Bruce was the father. The king of Scots had an heir.

That's the herbalist's husband she is speaking with, I wonder if she is ordering a potion for Christina's possible condition. She was normally so strong, and her fainting was unusual. The rumours she is pregnant must be true.

He grabbed what remained of the flagon of wine and sat unsteadily on the wooden bed which took up the remainder of his small room.

The wine would help him sleep, for he had much to do tomorrow. He needed to be away on the first tide to meet with Valence's men. It wasn't every day that you were part of a plot to capture a king and his heir.

Chapter Four

The Temple, Paris, Early September 1306: Scrovegni's Warning and a Sacred Bribe

'They would have to get lodgings in this part of the city,' Geoffroi complained. 'I am not sure how you persuaded them to stay here, Hugh. Conversely, I am sure they will want to be away from this place and back in Padua – the place smells of the midden, and it's far too close to the river.'

Geoffroi de Charnay's boots squelched in the fermenting mud; he could sense it oozing between his toes. It was thirty minutes from dusk, and he couldn't gauge the depth of the slurry, so he kept stepping in deep piles of the obnoxious mixture.

'My hose is damp and the same colour as the street,' he complained.

'I told them to lodge here – out of the way from King Phillip's men and Pierre de Nogaret's attention,' Hugh de Verneuil said. 'De Nogaret has been asking every servant at the Temple where they are lodging, ever since Giordano appeared and told his clerk he was from Padua, and asking to see you. Why do you allow de Nogaret and his cronies to vet all the Templar visitors?' Geoffroi took Hugh's comment as a reprimand.

'Pierre is the most inquisitive man at the Temple – and those are exactly the skills we need when guests are disingenuous. I agreed reluctantly if that's any consolation.' Geoffroi knew Hugh was right Pierre was in most cases duplicitous, not diplomatic.

'Giordano should have been more discrete,' Hugh said. 'But he didn't know he was speaking to Pierre's servants. De Nogaret knows the connection between Padua and the Order, when others do not. It is safer that no one else links us with these men, as they are servants of Enrico Scrovegni, and he is too closely associated with the treasure. King Phillip would want to extract what he could from them. We are threatened if Phillip finds them so that is why I put them here. They would have a tale of treasure and templar involvement if tortured.'

'I bet Pierre's curiosity is killing him – doubly so since he can't find them,' Geoffroi said. 'It will be eating him up not knowing where they are. We must expect that King Phillip will eventually discover why they are here. I hope they are cautious and handy with a sword. What do you know about them apart from the fact that Enrico Scrovegni sent them?'

Geoffroi had covered his mouth with a loose scarf in a vain attempt to reduce the pungent odour that had made his eyes and throat sting.

'I saw them briefly, and Pierre's servant wasn't keen on me hanging around them. Giordano is in his mid-thirties and claims to be the head of Scrovegni's guard, and there is a younger servant, Geraldo Procacci, who only came to the Temple once – seems overly young to be sent here.'

Hugh found a route above the water table where there was little mud but the same lingering smell. He pulled Geoffroi with him.

'Scrovegni is a shrewd man so I can only assume he trusts young Procacci who embraced the adventure only to end up here in the unwelcoming Marais. Are their rooms much further?' Geoffroi was walking with considerable care. He didn't want to add the indignity of a fall with visiting such a place on foot without servants.

'At the corner of the street – over to the left. We should wait here a while just in case we were followed.' Hugh pointed to a row of houses where the end of the terrace consisted of first-floor rooms looking out towards the river, with a stable block below. They huddled below another terrace facing the lodgings. Brown-tinted water dripped from the level above down onto their cloaks.

'You can't walk the streets in this area without a dozen curs following you. It's quiet today – probably because the river has flooded. The vulgarity will deter Pierre's delicate sensibilities. I hope the servants left the horses behind the building over there as instructed, as I don't want to return to the Temple on foot. After we have come all this way, you are sure they will be home?'

Geoffroi smiled despite his complaining, amused by the thought of the pompous de Nogaret having to visit such a place. Hugh was right to hide the Paduans here.

'Master, Pierre watches your comings and goings. If you had asked for your horse, we would be followed for sure. Their Lombard contacts delivered the message that we were coming. I also warned them to be alert – look, Master, which is Geraldo Procacci. He was wearing those clothes when he came to the Temple,' Hugh whispered as he pointed to a small balcony, stretching across the top of the stable, joining together two sets of rooms. The fine livery was recognisable. Geraldo stopped briefly, staring out towards the river, but he didn't dwell there. He hurried back to the rooms on the left-hand side.

'We should approach with care. The way he ran inside, you would think he was being held hostage,' Geoffroi quipped.

'Master, more likely he is looking out for us, but I do wish he wasn't so conspicuous. They have been waiting to speak with you since the riots. The Lombards also informed me that Scrovegni's letter is urgent and that they have brought with them a shroud.'

Geoffroi's face broke into a very broad smile.

'If I had known they had the shroud with them, I wouldn't have delayed this meeting. The Scots and the treasure took all my time. I have been waiting for it for over a year.' De Charnay was delighted.

'What is so thrilling about a linen cloth that it generates such a grin?' Hugh looked perplexed.

'I kept the shroud a secret until I was sure I could use it. The timing of their arrival is perfect. It's a bribe for King Phillip and just the item that would appeal to his piety. It will only work if he believes it is genuine, so its provenance had to be carefully crafted – that took a while for Scrovegni to create. It is the burial cloth that held the body of our Lord after he was crucified – or so I will tell King Phillip. In truth, it is one of Brother Albertus's creations. Many years ago, the Order sold the King's grandfather an old thorn bush rebadged as the Crown of Thorns. Why shouldn't such a deception work a second time with Christ's shroud? King Phillip would see the acquisition of the shroud as equalling if not bettering Saint Louis's purchase of the Crown of Thorns. He is vain enough to want to outshine a saint. The King's weaknesses are so human in a man so devoid of humanity.'

'I know we are under threat,' Hugh said. 'A shroud is a powerful symbol and could buy a king … but King Phillip is also duplicitous, and it isn't beyond consideration that he takes the bribe and destroys us anyway.'

'That is a real possibility, but we need to try. The key to our survival is keeping Clement on our side. If we hand such a relic to the King, he will be assured of our devotion and loyalty to Church and realm … is it safe to meet them now? My cloak is getting saturated here.' Geoffroi casually wrung out the bottom.

'The street has been deserted for several minutes, I think it is safe now master' Hugh set off across the street and he followed, hugging the shadows the overhanging terraces gave to anyone walking below.

The stable entrance was to the right and went directly from the street into a small courtyard. There were four or five horses stabled, and the extra manure provided an even more attractive place for the numerous flies and biting insects to settle.

'I see the horses the servants left for us are over there.' Hugh pointed to a gap in the back of the stables. Just fifty yards away, four horses were patiently waiting, tied to the back of a dishevelled wagon missing three of its four wheels.

'They sound like there are only the two of them but let's take no chances.' Geoffroi removed his sword from its sheath on his left hip, ready for the unexpected.

Hugh's sword was at his side as they climbed the steps to the upper floors. The steps were white from age and neglect, yet didn't betray them with cracks and squeaks as they cautiously took one step and then another.

No one else seemed to be around, which Geoffroi considered a little unusual.

'Hugh, there are more than the Italians' mounts here – where are the riders of the other horses?' he whispered.

He gripped his sword tighter.

They stood on either side of the door listening, trying to confirm that only Procacci and Giordano were inside. If there was a fight, it would be easier to escape if they remained outside the room on the stairs rather than inside, trapped within a confined space.

Geoffroi listened for the sound of steps approaching the door and the snib being lifted. He stood still daring not to breathe, but the flies continued their onslaught of biting.

Suddenly, the voices stopped. Soft footsteps cautiously walked towards the door. Those inside the room were alarmed by something.

Geoffroi heard distant voices below, and he could feel the cautious movement of the door latch being lifted upwards. The door moved slightly inwards, and the metal fastening let out a faint squeak as it was released. He would remain still until it was fully opened.

The door creaked open inwards, and a sword was thrust into the gap. Hugh kicked the sword to the ground. A dagger was thrown through the gap, but Geoffroi parried it away, and it crashed down the stairs. The door was now fully open, the lower bracket was loose, and the door hung off its mount.

Another sword appeared, which Hugh tried to knock away, but this blade was resolute; the grip was not going to be broken. The point came forward towards Geoffroi and Hugh; they were both still outside the room and were being pushed backwards towards the steps they had just climbed.

'Gentlemen, put away your swords. I think you are expecting me, Geoffroi de Charnay.'

'Geoffroi de Charnay, you said. I am Giovanni Giordano and the man on the floor is Geraldo Procacci. Friendly visitors knock on the door rather than break it. We were warned that people were looking for us, and we saw shadows, heard voices in the street and feared the worst. Our master, Enrico Scrovegni, ordered us to find you at the Temple, not in this shithole Marais.'

Giordano had a sword in one hand and a dagger in the other, and his bulk kept Hugh and Geoffroi outside.

'I arranged for your lodgings here and got the warning message to you via your Lombard cousins. We had to get you away from the Temple as your presence brought you to the attention of people who would do you great harm.' Hugh's face was flushed with exertion. His sword hung loosely in his hand.

Geoffroi cautiously lowered his sword. Procacci didn't move from the floor as he looked at de Charnay for the first time.

'Gentlemen, we should talk inside.' Geoffroi placed his sword back in its sheath, followed by Hugh. Giordano hesitated before allowing them inside.

There was a small table with a bench on either side. Giordano pointed to the bench furthest from the door.

'Take a seat. How do we know you are de Charnay?'

De Charnay produced an engraved amethyst from his purse and slid it towards Giordano.

'Enrico had one identical to this.'

Giordano gave it a cursory examination and nodded.

'I remember Master Enrico owned such a stone.'

Procacci was now sitting opposite. He had been hit in the face when Hugh had kicked the door inside. His face was reddened, his lip and tongue swelling and he wiped the blood away which was now gathering at the edge of his mouth.

'Ever since we arrived at the Temple, we have been ignored and disrespected. It has been like dealing with a ghost.'

Procacci's breathing was quick and shallow, he was trying to control it and not appear frightened. Geoffroi remembered the pride he'd had at the same age.

'You are right to be cautious. I wouldn't expect anything less from a servant of my good friend Enrico Scrovegni. I was told you met with servants of Pierre de Nogaret' Geoffroi tried to sound calm, measured and not like he was accusing them or implying some treachery, but Giordano leaned across the table clearly irritated by his questions.

'We met a young squire who we only know as Guy – as I am sure you already know,' Giordano replied curtly.

'You were talking to Guy de Nogaret and a step away from the King himself – Guillaume de Nogaret is his uncle and the King's chief advisor. He would want to interrogate you himself if he found out your connection with Enrico and some treasure he believes belongs to him.'

Giordano and Geraldo's expressions darkened, and they looked anxiously at each other.

'Guillaume de Nogaret – is he also related to a Pierre de Nogaret?' Giordano had obviously heard the names before.

'They are brothers – how do you know Pierre de Nogaret?' Geoffroi moved towards Giordano and needed to know more. The proof of Pierre's treachery may be in reach.

'He is mentioned in a message from a Hubert de Lacy we found in Padua, hidden in a dead man's shoe. The same message also discussed Alaric's treasure and indicated that Pierre de Nogaret is helping the English capture it – and *we* have unwittingly been in dialogue with him.' Giovanni eyes looked downwards as if he was ashamed to have been deceived.

'How much did you tell Guy about why you are here?' Hugh asked nervously.

'Only that we needed to speak with the Templar Geoffroi de Charnay, and we had travelled from Padua.'

It wouldn't take Pierre long to make the connections between them and the treasure.

Geoffroi cast his mind back to the spring day he had spotted Gaston de Bezier leaving the Temple, following the Scots to Padua. He had been working for Pierre de Nogaret then and had not returned to the Temple.

'I think I know who the dead man was, Gaston de Bezier – and he is Pierre de Nogaret's man.'

It was too much of a coincidence that Bezier was missing. Now the English ambassador Hubert de Lacy had revealed Pierre's treachery.

'You have brought me the evidence I had suspected for so long – that he was working for the English. Support for his beloved Cathars might be behind his duplicity and his newfound alliance. Your presentation of irrefutable proof of deceit gives me no pleasure, only permission to act.'

Geoffroi felt angry and nauseous.

'The same note also carried news about an Innes de Mayon searching for the treasure and said that the English king himself had ordered his elimination. The dead man's note is still with Master Scrovegni – but he sent this.'

Giordano removed a small, rolled document from the seam of his shirt collar.

'Here …' Giordano thrust the parchment into Geoffroi's hand. He was surprised he knew Innes by name. Giordano's knowledge confirmed Scrovegni trusted him. In Padua, Enrico had proved his care for the Scots and had helped them return to France to help him move the treasure.

Geoffroi unfurled the parchment and started to read.

My dear friend Geoffroi,

King Phillip is well advanced in his plans to suppress the Templar Order and steal the 'room full of gold' which he claims exists below the Temple towers. He has obviously turned his envious eyes towards stealing our treasure. My acquaintance, the greedy yet knowledgeable Bishop Torre, has confirmed that Pope Clement is of a mind to help King Phillip destroy you – a corroboration that cost me ten thousand gold florins, but it is money well spent. Torre believes the Pope will not protect you, and I am forced to concur. King Phillip, urged on by the serpent Guillaume de Nogaret, has told Pope Clement a fanciful tale, embellished by a multitude of lies – lies that include heresy and unspeakable acts of depravity. The King never did skimp on the fanciful, and he has laid the Order's crimes with a heavy emphasis on the entrenched level of heresy and the threat it poses to Christendom. The King is taking a viciousness in approach that I didn't imagine even he could conjure up. This is a most grave threat, and you must act. I cannot advise when he will strike, other than that Torre suggested the plan is mature. I also must warn you that Pierre de Nogaret is a traitor. We discovered a letter that proves he is working for the English, written in the hand of the English ambassador, Hubert de Lacy. Pierre's desire is to see our treasure in the hands of King Edward. He also describes how Innes de Mayon is to be eliminated on direct order of King Edward. De Mayon is a known agent of Bishop Wishart and suspected to be in pursuit of the treasure. Aymer de Valence has agents in France looking for him. Lastly, I am sending the shroud you tasked Brother Albertus to make. It has been a long wait, but a worthwhile one. I hope it proves useful in your current predicament.

With warm greetings,
Messer Scrovegni

Geoffroi was aware of the threats to the Order, but not the role Pope Clement was now taking. The shroud would help as he had anticipated. Now no Scottish agent was safe from the English, and the threat to Innes was specific. He had to warn Innes, and he would task Hugh to carry that message to Gaillard.

Soon Geoffroi would travel to Italy to see his good friend Scrovegni. The relic trade was at the heart of the Order's wealth, and in these chaotic times, it needed his protection.

'Did you *read* the letter?' Geoffroi asked. He couldn't soften his concern, and it came out more like an accusation.

'Not the letter – in case I was caught but Messer Scrovegni keeps few secrets from Geraldo and myself.'

'You must thank my dear friend Enrico when you meet him again, and that will be very soon. Where is the shroud?'

Procacci pointed to a saddlebag hiding in the corner.

'Brother Albertus made us swear not to let it out of our sight. It must never be wet, so we have covered it with sheepskin with the hide on the outside to repel moisture. Take care of it and only unwrap it when you have a long table available. Place a candle behind it and observe the magic. It is one of Albertus's finest illusions.'

Procacci carefully lifted the large leather satchel and placed it at Geoffroi's feet.

'You both risked your lives to get this letter and shroud to me, and I will protect your lives by getting you safely out of here. Hugh, please lead them to the waiting horses?'

'Yes, Master,' Hugh replied, standing and ready to leave.

'Collect what belongings you can carry. Hugh will take you out of Marais to the road south towards Padua. Ride hard out of France; don't dwell or dawdle. Soon many men will arrive here to torture then kill you. Tell your master that Innes de Mayon is in Rouen and that his warning will be delivered personally as he would have wanted.'

Procacci and Giordano bowed with respect.

'Leave everything you don't require or value, because it's all about to go up in smoke. We will leave nothing for these men to find; they will spend time looking allowing us to escape.'

Procacci and Giordan appeared to have already packed and took moments to make ready.

'I will take this.' De Charnay placed the saddlebag containing the shroud over his shoulder.

'We must go now.' Hugh handed Geoffroi a large flask of what smelled like *uisge beatha*, and after taking one gulp, started to spread it over the straw mattresses and rushes on the floor. It smelled like warm burnt sugar and honey, with the associated power of an eye-watering level of alcohol.

'A shame, but necessary,' Geoffroi complained as Hugh pushed Procacci and Giordano out of the room, leaving him alone.

Quickly, to catch the fumes, he threw a fuse onto the mattresses. Almost immediately, smoke billowed from the room, and he could hear the crackling and whoosh of a fire taking hold.

Procacci, Giordano, and Hugh ran towards the horses, de Charnay was a few yards behind. They acted on his instructions and galloped away without looking back.

De Charnay attached the saddlebag carefully to either side of the horse's back and pulled his cloak over his head before climbing on. He would not gallop but meander away.

Behind him in the street, he could hear many raised voices, the clanking of armour, weapons, and horses.

'Find them and bring them to me,' the voice was aggressive.

He didn't look round to see whose soldiers they were – his escape covered in a thickening blanket of *uisge beatha* flavoured smoke. He turned his mount away from the commotion and headed back to the safety of the Temple.

On the ride back, he had time to consider what he would do with Pierre de Nogaret.

Chapter Five

The Seine, September 1306:
Madame Discovers the Truth

The morning had just broken through, its light barely strong enough to provide guidance, yet the banks of the Seine were full of furtive shadows digging and picking away at the bank. Small lamps could be seen dancing between the rocks and rough flora.

Madame watched the scavengers picking up coins and debris from the explosion. Valuables were still being discovered, but these finds were diminishing.

'I hope you have searched the river thoroughly for the remains of the barge?' She paced a few feet, studying the river, and then her gaze focused on Chateau Gaillard.

'The riverbed is still disturbed from the explosion, and there is much silt in the water. We have sent down free divers to try and feel their way around with sticks and nets, but they can't find any remains of a vessel the size and shape that was reported because it was blown into many pieces.'

Madame was increasingly irritated 'You need to work smarter, harder Baldwin, and I thought we had cleared the river of these scavengers. The more evidence we lose and the longer our search takes, the more likely our prize will escape us.'

Baldwin's brother Bertrand gestured towards the half dozen guards that Charles de Valois had provided from his personal escort and shrugged.

'Talk to *them* over there. They are supposed to do that.'

Betrand made sure they could hear him.

'If you catch any of this rabble, string one up from a tree. That should send out the proper message and scare them off,' Baldwin added, as the guards reluctantly moved away from the shore where they had been standing.

'Madame, they are hardly dressed for such work in their blue velvet House of Valois livery with its golden *fleur de lis* and the leopards of Aquitaine edged in velvet. They look – and I presume, feel – out of place, mincing around the shoreline avoiding the muck. They are more used to waiting in the splendour of the royal palaces than sleeping out in makeshift shelters, stopping peasants from stealing.'

Bertrand was right as she observed each guard gingerly tiptoeing along the muddy shore in a vain attempt to avoid adding more mud to their vestments. Not even the peasants took them seriously.

They are dressed more sumptuously than the king's men. You are indeed a man of considerable vanity, Uncle Charles.

Her thoughts only drifted for a few seconds.

'We don't want another riot on our hands. Just stop them coming down from the bank where it is narrow and less steep whilst I complete my investigations.'

With the end of her dagger, Madame pointed to a small copse clinging to the bank where treasure hunters had used the branches and roots to climb down the treacherous muddy banks to the shore. Next to the fresh path was an untidy collection of cloth which she recognised as a body.

'I see your handywork from last night.' She nodded towards the corpse. 'I heard the man scream, but it hasn't put the scavengers off.'

'Our methods work, and we have loosened some tongues. They have supplied some useful information which might be of some help in finding the treasure.'

She disliked Baldwin even more when he was being smug. She wouldn't indulge him in conversation unless it was on her terms.

'I hope you collected *all* the litter thrown out from the explosion?'

She didn't wait for an answer as she walked purposefully towards a collection of detritus that had been left on the bank. An assortment of objects were laid horizontally along twenty feet of bank. They had been ordered by colour as much as the fragments could be. Piles of disordered wood fringed the larger pieces.

Baldwin followed quickly behind, pecking information into her ear like a bird.

'Yes, Madame. We have collected everything that has washed up or blown onto the shore. We will look for more once the light is better. There is no value in any of it. The peasants offered up a collection of broken pails and these iron chains – nothing that looks precious. What else were you expecting? What could anyone want with this rubbish? We are here for treasure, not this junk, and we have found only a handful of coins!'

He picked up a short, thick chain, and Madame watched him throw it theatrically with all his brutish strength towards what remained of the barge. He then kicked a holed pail into the air.

'I am not interested in a coin here or there; I want to know what happened to the barge,' she snapped.

She studied the wood mounds and picked up several of the smaller pieces, carefully brushing away the mud from the surfaces and throwing pieces on different piles. The brothers watched her in silence, perplexed, as she scrambled over each pile of objects, throwing items to the left and right of her.

'We found most of this rubbish together and laid out each as they were found, as you instructed,' Baldwin added. Bertrand aimlessly threw his dagger repeatedly into the soft ground as if he was pointing at an imaginary target.

'And the metal objects – were they all found on the shore?' She ignored Bertrand's disinterest; he was like a child that couldn't keep still. He was not a thinker.

The chains were only part of the numerous, mostly iron, shrapnel that had been placed next to the shattered wood mounds. There was also a large, isolated heap of metal grouped together.

'Yes, Madame. We have placed any iron or metal we found with the wood attached. We found that pile of metal on the roads on the left side of the river. Is there a problem?'

Bertrand could be as argumentative as he liked if he did what he was told and recognised she was in charge.

His eyes followed her as she climbed over all the mounds, still curious, but he didn't ask any more questions and feigned disinterest. He was like many brutes – adept at following orders, but unlike a leader, he had little interest in why.

'Madame, let us know if you need us to join you.' Madame could tell this was what he thought he should say rather than what he wanted to say.

She shook her head and continued to wade through each pile, throwing pieces to either side.

'Did you find any sign of the keel when you were scouring the river?' She continued rummaging.

'No, whoever sent the fireship set the explosion where the river is deepest, and the water is still full of a devil's mixture of soot, mud, and charcoal. You can only see a few feet down from the side of any ship.'

'Send more free divers to take a look?' Madame continued to scrutinise each mound.

'Madame, there are no more to be found in these parts. The peasants consider it a mistake to learn to swim, and we would have to send south for the Persian divers. And in any case, you can't see your hand in front of your eyes.'

Baldwin cleared his throat, spat on the ground, and placed

his hands directly in front of his eyes to illustrate his point.

Bertrand pulled a small chest which had miraculously survived almost intact from one of the piles and sat on the lid, followed quickly by Baldwin. He then produced a small flask from inside his tabard and seemed to drink most of the contents before he handed the flask to Baldwin.

She was now covered in more filth as she progressed deeper into each mound. Blackened sweat started to drip into her eyes, stinging them, rendering her vision blurred. As she attempted to wipe the moisture away, she only made things worse, but it was of no consequence, as she had found what she was looking for deep in one of the mounds.

Her exertion had aggravated her wound, the pain was excruciating so whilst her companions drank, she removed a leather pouch from her tunic which was filled with poppy juice that Olivier de Pau had provided. She felt underneath her woollen shirt and recognised the sticky, warm sensation of fresh blood.

'Madame, did you find anything in those piles of rubbish?' Bertrand mocked, emboldened by the contents of the flask.

She could see both men grinning. 'Indeed, I have.'

She kicked the chest onto its side, surprising the brothers, who fell onto the muddy ground.

'What have you found?' Bertrand struggled to get up from his backside.

She pulled the chest upright. 'Sit, and I will explain.'

The brothers sat down, and Bertrand produced another flask.

'Some people will tell you lies. Others will tell you what they believe to be the truth and mislead, despite genuine intent. Evidence has no voice. It cannot lie, and it tells me a lot without any concerns about truth or the perception of truth. The trick is interpreting what it is shouting out. What are you looking like and what is it telling you?'

Madame pointed at the largest heap and drew a frame in

the air around the detritus with her hands.

'Isn't it obvious? It tells me everything was destroyed, and the barge is at the bottom of the Seine.' Baldwin delivered his conclusion with the ignorance she had come to expect. Bertrand simply nodded and continued drinking.

'That is partially true. The wood I threw to the right is covered in soot and a black resin, which is tar mixed with the magical black powder that created such carnage. The explosion has blinded your senses. You are ignoring what is in plain sight and what is missing from these remnants.'

'You are sounding like a sorceress. Be careful.' Bertrand's torso swelled, and he placed his dagger on the chest. His comment was mocking, but managed to sound like a threat.

Madame had already marked them both down for death. Bertrand's continued ignorance had simply made that outcome more certain. Stupidity combined with drunkenness, even if there was a brutal efficiency about them, it was something King Phillip could do without amongst servants trusted with such serious state business.

'Look again. We believe both the fireship and the barge were destroyed in the explosion. Several other ships were damaged but not sunk, including our own. The large heap on the right is what remains of the fireship. The grain and texture of the wood is the same, and it smells the same, because it came from the same ship.'

'Fascinating, but as you have said, we already knew that ship had sunk. Hundreds of witnesses saw it completely alight before it sank.' Bertrand added impertinence to ignorance.

'Now look at the tiny pile on the left. I am sure these wooden chests and the one you now sit on came from the barge. The pieces don't look damaged – they look like they were jettisoned overboard. There is no sign of fire, because the barge survived the explosion.'

Bertrand interrupted, 'Or it sits at the bottom of the Seine, as my brother told you.'

Madame ignored him.

'We have clear evidence that the fireship could blow large, heavy lumps of metal several hundred yards onto the shore. Heavy metal like gold … and I am sure the chain you brandished came from the barge. It wasn't French in construction; the metal looked different and the quality finer. Why wasn't more of the treasure blown onto the shore? Each day the tide exposes a handful of coins here and there, but there should be more on the bank.'

'It sank quickly because it was so heavy,' Bertrand said. 'You have seen the coins washed up. They were buried in sand as they were blown into the banks. Who would jettison all that wealth if they didn't have to?'

'No gold is worth dying for, a shroud has no pockets … consider the possibility that the barge didn't sink. Doesn't wood float, regardless of which boat it came from? And even if it did sink, there should be more evidence of its existence and more wood detritus for us to find. As for the coins, they are but a small portion of what was on that barge. I would give up a small part to ensure my safety.'

'So, you think it escaped and you ask us to consider the evidence. Well, I am doing that now. We have placed guards and spies all along the river, and there are no sightings of the barge, its cargo, or the Scots. If it was still afloat, we would have heard something.' Baldwin was now slurring his words.

'What are the other possibilities? Think about the Templars and what they did to keep the treasure a secret for so many years.' Madame's face brightened; she knew she was right. 'It was hidden once, and it can be again,' she shouted, hoping that the message would land with the brothers.

'Yes, hidden in hundreds of feet of river and silt. We will never recover it.' Bertrand was intransigent. Baldwin was now quieter.

'There are few places for hiding such a barge and keeping it quiet,' Bertrand said. 'It is a waste of time looking for something that is destroyed.'

'It is a possibility that the treasure is still in France and still on *that* barge. We must start looking for hiding places, no matter what you think. We cannot allow it to escape us by giving up the chase. I tell you it didn't sink, but we are all meant to think it did. The Scots are ingenious, because that's the only way they were ever going to get out of here.'

Madame removed her scarf and immersed it in a small pool of water that had remained from the last tide. She wiped the black soot away from her face, then washed her hands and brushed her filthy hair down, framing her face.

Bertrand snorted and looked away.

'So, gentlemen, get off your arses. I want you to send word to the men on either side of the river to search every possible hiding place. Bribe anyone who might know something, elicit any rumour or unusual event that might point to where it is concealed, and investigate it.'

Madame started up the shore towards the path leading up the bank. She spotted the corpse and turned back; the brothers were trailing about ten feet behind her.

'Baldwin, you were telling me about the man you tortured. Valuable information, I believe. I am always sceptical about any information got under torture. People will say anything to get their tormentors to stop, and as skilled as you think you are I find it hard to find any credibility in information obtained in such a way.'

'It is pertinent, Madame – strange activities in Rouen,' Baldwin slurred.

'Rouen would be the obvious place for the barge to wait for people to stop looking for it. It could be hidden in plain sight.'

Madame's instincts told her that this was a real possibility that the barge could be concealed amongst the multitude of other vessels that traded on the river.

'Go on, Baldwin. The tortured man told you a tale?' She sensed that this could be important.

'A local innkeeper, Bernard du Gascon, was absent for over a week. He was given up for dead; his wife believed he had been killed in the explosion and had started mourning before he suddenly reappeared. He claimed to have been injured by flying debris and returned unaffected by his experience. He is a popular man, and his death was widely reported. His return is being seen as a genuine miracle. Should I investigate this further? It gives me an excuse to ask questions and look around Rouen, assuming discretion is still important where the treasure is concerned.'

Baldwin wasn't clever, but he was cunning and had a certain brutish intuition. He could be onto something.

Madame nodded reluctantly. She wasn't certain this Bernard was involved, but she was looking for anything unusual.

'Yes, investigate this, and be discreet. Other parties are pursuing the barge. Remember, we know that the English covet it and the Byzantines claim ownership and want it back. We don't want the King's interest in this matter to be known and the location of the treasure to leak out. You must act with caution.'

Several screams tore through the air. Madame couldn't see what was happening, but she didn't have to. The terror in the man's screams told her he was being attacked. The scavengers on the shore collected whatever they could and scrambled up over the sandy banks, disappearing in seconds.

'Valois's soldiers are adopting your form of persuasion, Bertrand. Not something we want to repeat in Rouen – as you can see that sort of behaviour drives people away, and we want them to talk. Spread some of the king's gold if necessary.'

Madame threw a purse towards the brothers as she hurried away. She needed to rest and did not want the brothers to see her pain and vulnerability. These men were vultures and preyed on anything they perceived as in distress.

She needed to be away from them and write to the King, because she needed ships now. The barge had to head out of France and if she couldn't capture it on the Seine, she needed to seize it at sea.

She could feel the blood seeping down her side. Her shirt was now sticking to the wound, held fast by a clot but her efforts today were worth the pain. She was now convinced that the barge was out there. There was still hope, and she would write her letter to the King as soon as she had rested. The treasure was within her grasp – and she could feel its presence.

Beyond the copse, she saw another body face down in the mud. Valois's guards appeared to have cleared the riverbank as they had been instructed, but these methods were unhelpful.

'Make sure you go to Rouen today,' she shouted back towards Bertrand and Baldwin. 'Take riders with you that can bring word to me. I will remain here beside Gaillard. If you find out where the barge is, real or suspected, do not act alone – fetch me and the king's guard, and we will recover it together. We know the Scots are getting help from someone, and we can't be sure how extensive that help is. They are tricky and resourceful, perhaps sorcery, as you suggested, Bertrand.'

Madame would send some of her men to watch them and make sure they did as she told them. They did not readily accept orders from anyone and taking them from a woman stuck even further in their craws.

'But before you go, get someone to clean up this mess!'

She pointed to the two corpses and climbed to where her horse was waiting.

The brothers grunted a response before following her to their horses.

She started to ride away but looked back again. The brothers were talking to one of the senior palace guards.

'And lose the wolfskins if you are trying to enter Rouen without being noticed – though I doubt you can lose the smell. Your reputation and trademark are known to many people in our line of work.'

Madame hoped they followed her advice, but she also recognised that their arrogance was biblical in size, like their egos. If they weren't careful, it would be their undoing.

*

Aurelian remained hidden in the thick grass and bushes that shabbily covered the bank. A nosey guard had come too close, so he had slit the man's throat before he had time to shout and was dressed in his uniform. Luckily, the guard had been of a similar width, but the man's arms and legs were several inches too short. He lowered his trousers down as far as he dared to cover his ankles. He would use this camouflage to escape the beach, but he doubted it would fool anyone for any other purposes. He pulled the tabard down to conceal his axe and ornate sword. Even Valois's guards were not fashioned with such weapons.

He sniffed the tabard.

I do believe that is perfume.

Further down the beach, Valois's guards had become immersed in a fight with some of the local peasants, and daggers had been drawn. The noise had concealed his own brief melee.

Madame strutted up and down the beach, followed by her loyal apes. He had been watching her for weeks now, ever since he had sent the fireship that almost killed her and her crew. Their ship had been holed and had barely survived. He had watched them struggle to the shore and ground the vessel.

Next time I will kill you.

His actions had allowed the treasure barge to escape. Her death had been part of his plan, but her survival could work to his advantage. Madame had been studying the scene like a surgeon looking for a tumour.

He too was perplexed. He didn't know where the barge was hiding, and he was sure he wasn't alone.

You think the barge is still around. Why else would you remain here and conduct this theatre, scurrying over the burnt and shattered remnants of the ships? You are looking for something, and I think the flotsam on the beach told you what you wanted to know. You rode away a happy woman.

She would lead him to the treasure. The Scots would again need him to escape France, and it was clear Madame was a formidable opponent – but then, so was he.

But where to find you, boys? Where are you hiding?

He marvelled at how a slight woman managed to instil the fear of God into so many men. He admired her spirit, skill, and intelligence. He had seen her fight like a man, think like a scholar, and lead like a king.

He had seen the wolf-men ride off in the direction of Rouen. They had heard something, and it was worth his pursuit. He had the measure of these beasts and would find out what they knew.

The tide was now moving swiftly in, and the guards were removing the bodies, slinging them over mules.

I will follow your henchmen – but for now, I really need to get off this shore.

Chapter Six

Chateau Gaillard, The Seine, Late September 1306: Plans and Suspicions

Jamie knelt on the cold, damp sandstone floor and observed through a narrow chink in the exterior stone wall.

'Our accommodation is less chateau and more prison. I long to see normal light through something bigger than a two-by-eight-inch crack. It hurts my eyes squinting like this.'

'You shouldn't be so nosey,' Hendor replied.

Jamie had passed a lot of the last few weeks watching and judging the people scouring the shore for treasure. Each night Bernard had spread coins across the shore and in the shallow pools that emerged as the Seine's tide revealed the shoreline. Everyone needed to believe the barge had sunk and the treasure lost.

'I enjoy watching the scavengers dance with excitement and scream with joy as they first spot and then pick up their piece of Alaric's treasure. A gold coin is life-changing for a peasant, and I can't blame their avarice. It's *real* life being played out before me. There's an old man sat on a stool, a spade in each hand and picks at his feet. He's guiding newcomers to the best spots and pocketing for his advice. He will become the richest man.' Jamie's voice resonated within the chamber.

'What do you mean, the richest man?' Hendor was diligently sharpening a sword, preparing for the next part of their journey. 'And speak softer, Jamie. This cave vibrates like a bell tower. Who is he?'

'There's an old man making a large profit advising the treasure hunters and lending them his tatty old farm implements. He is the cleverest man out there. He's not relying on luck and the unpredictable shifting of the tide. He gets paid by everyone who has hope and needs a spade. He will be a wealthy man with truly little effort, because he seized the opportunity. He has the best spot on the shoreline – the place where the tide is strongest, trapping Bernard's discarded coins. I have seen his purse grow each day. He has taken to burying it beside him because it is too heavy to have on his belt. It almost pulled his hose down today.' Jamie thought about it again and sniggered.

'So, he sits on his arse all day whilst everyone else grafts,' Hendor scoffed. It was obvious he disapproved of the man's opportunism.

'You may sneer, but he is wise, and I admire his intelligence despite your cynicism. While everyone else wades through the cold water and tries to dig their way through the river silt, he sits there getting rich. That's clever thinking. Who is the one who makes the most without risk? It's the man on his arse, Hendor.'

Jamie watched Hendor prepare, check and recheck everything they would need each day as they prepared for their journey back to Scotland. Everyone understood the passage from the Chateau through Rouen would be the most dangerous.

'I find it better to work hard for myself and not rely on other people.'

Hendor was sharpening everything: swords, dirks, and arrowheads. Replacing feathers, tensing each bow, greasing each longbow mechanism, and finally testing each weapon by firing into the narrow water-filled channel. Jamie was sure Hendor was now starting the process over again.

They had been here for several weeks, filling their time

with repetitive activities. He yearned to be back home.

The Scots and the unobtrusive leper Jean had been kept like prisoners because the explosion was still attracting crowds, even after several weeks. Bernard had been placing fewer and fewer coins each day, hoping the treasure hunters would disappear, but it just encouraged even more to try even harder.

Jamie wanted to be away. His appetite for risk had increased and he passed the remainder of the time honing his skills with his responses to Hendor's gentle teasing.

'Jamie's right, Hendor. Hard work and effort are to be admired. But it also needs to be channelled correctly and mixed with a dollop of acumen to make a difference, don't you think? The old man has done both and that's why he is old and alive.'

Innes's voice was unsteady, and he shivered as if from cold. Then Jamie noticed he was soaking. He was drying himself by the brazier, but his dark hair was saturated and dripped incessantly onto the floor. The leper was adding charcoal to the fire and supplied the drying linen.

Like Hendor, Innes had been preparing – patching the bow of the barge and renewing the caulk.

'The keel has a narrow but deep crack just above the waterline – damaged by the explosion and a steady flow of river water is leaking into the hold with every wave. It's a good job the channel lifted the barge above the river's waterline. I can make the repairs without too much underwater work.' Innes enjoyed such work and Jamie knew it was best not to interrupt but encourage.

'I see you have created a contraption for underwater work'.

'Indeed, young Wishart, I have glued a number of hollow reeds together and sealed them with sticky tar that has hardened but still flexible so I can move underwater as I work.'

Innes had punched a hole in the bucket just wide enough for a hollow reed to be pushed through and sealed the hole with pitch. The bucket floated upright filled with air, and an empty glass bottle stopped the bucket overturning allowing him time to work under the waterline whilst still breathing, the reeds followed him like a snake stalking its prey.

'The fire ship must have been packed with metal and our keel was holed by a piece of iron travelling at considerable speed.' Innes dropped shards which clattered on the floor. 'It is strange that powder explosions have happened twice to help us escape. They are unlikely to be a coincidence. Is Bishop Wishart behind this?'

'Possibly,' Will said. 'Bishop Wishart is resourceful and will find some means to help us. Our guardian chooses to remain anonymous, but they are certainly connected to the Holy Land. The Chinese have had black powder for centuries … and the Crusaders used it for years. They stole its secret from the Mamluks before Acre fell.'

Jamie noticed the leper had stopped loading the brazier to listen in, and he wondered why the man would take an interest after so many weeks of ignoring what was happening around him.

'Bishop Wishart even said the monks of Drumziel made secret hiding places using its magic. Mark my words, it will soon make sword and armour outdated. Why kill someone up close, risking your own life, when you can kill from a distance?'

Will was the most learned amongst the many diversely skilled men. Jamie thought Innes was right, and the coincidence didn't sit easily with him.

'You are right, Will, it must be the Bishop,' Innes said. 'One thing is for sure – we need to be away from here and back to Scotland. It's only then we can see events straight on. I hope Bernard returns with some more pitch. We can do with some to spare. This keel was more damaged than I thought.'

'I hope he managed to get the dispatches back to Scotland,' Will added. 'With Bishop Wishart missing, it is vital our king knows of our progress. I wrote to Lord MacDonald at Dunaverty Castle, telling him we are coming home. King Robert told me to send word of our progress there.'

Jamie considered Bernard supremely competent and intelligent. He had brought in pitch, oakum, and nails whilst Innes had used some of the wooden planks de Charnay had had the foresight to add to the barge's cargo, and with the Gascon's typical comedy, he had remarked that the wood had turned out to be far more valuable than any treasure.

Innes climbed back into the water to continue his work, despite the shivering that had worked its way into his voice. 'My repairs to the bow will also make her go faster and help us get away from this place. Just like the old man on the bank, we are opportunistic, taking advantage of an unusual set of circumstances. Who would have thought we could be hidden in hostile territory with the luxury of making repairs undisturbed?'

Innes sneezed and coughed.

'I think you should stop getting in and out of the freezing water,' Hendor said. 'We can't navigate our way out of here without you, Innes. These weapons are useless without a guide.' He sent two bolts in quick succession thudding into the water.

'The air has the aroma of warm stew with a soupçon of tar and burnt hemp. It's time we moved out of here. I yearn for daylight and fresh air. When will you finish the repairs, Innes?'

Jamie's face scrunched up as he kicked a small rock across the cave floor in disgust. He was brimming with energy, ready to fight or make an escape towards the sea – anything but sit in this darkened cavern for another day.

'The caulking was forced inwards by the strong waves

brought about by the explosion.' Innes was now standing under the torches that burned continuously above the barges, smearing tar on with a heavy brush. Jamie could see the thick, sticky substance on his face and hands.

'If we leave here now, we are all dead men. Hugh was sure he spotted Madame on the shore, and if she is around, we must remain hidden, so I suggest we are patient and enjoy the calm – and Jean is cooking something delicious.'

Will pointed from his chair on the deck as Jean stirred the cauldron set over the brazier. The stew was gurgling and spitting, and bread rested on the lip of the vessel, expanding as the yeast warmed.

Besides cooking, the leper kept himself busy lighting torches, renewing their pitch, and ensuring the braziers were well fed with charcoal. His threadbare bandages had become even more dishevelled, and his hands tanned black with his work. Each time they threatened to reveal more than his eyes, Jean pulled the bandages around his face. Jamie did not want to contemplate what lay beneath.

'Bernard should be back with some more supplies soon. I have asked him to bring some of that delicious Gascony wine he liberated from the English.' Hendor was still surveying the supplies on deck. He held a long blade up to a candle he was holding, and the sharp edge caught the light. He nodded, pleased with his work.

'I hope he is being careful, Hendor,' Will added. 'We all suspect Jean de Bretagne tipped off the men who ambushed us in the tavern. He is working for the English, maybe the French too and for himself.'

'Bernard is aware of his duplicity and will use it to help us,' Hendor replied. 'The greater danger is in not knowing.'

The leper continued to prepare the food adding ingredients that layered one delicious smell on top of another, overwhelming the smell of warm pitch, and Jamie grudgingly appreciated his efforts.

Yet he was unnerved by him and would catch him staring when he awoke and just before he fell asleep. The leper watched him sleep and his eyes would follow him around the cave. When Jamie caught him staring, he would turn his head away like some sneak thief. Bernard had vouched for him, but he behaved suspiciously like a spy, watching and planning when to strike.

'When will Raoul return from La Rochelle?' Jamie asked without waiting for a response. 'I am going to learn French once I return to Scotland, when we have peace and learning replaces fighting. After all, the Wishart or *Guichard's* were Normans.'

Jamie had related more to Raoul because they were of a similar age. While they came from different backgrounds, they shared a love for politics, learning, and swordsmanship.

'Soon I hope,' Will replied. 'The French will need ships if they are going to chase us in the open sea, and the Templars are the only ones with a fleet and an appetite to lend it to King Phillip. You could join me, Jamie, in looking at some of these documents. Many are written in French, and I can teach you so you can chat with Raoul.'

Whilst Innes worked on the bow and Hendor saw to the weapons, Will had been sitting in the stern amongst a pile of neatly stacked papers and documents that he had found in one of the crates. He had been studying them for days.

'It was quite fortuitous that Bernard happened to break into this crate for the gold he needed. Someone went to some trouble to hide these documents in a concealed compartment. These documents are more valuable than the treasure?'

Will's eyes never looked away from the scroll. His face distorted as he deciphered and then wrote down what Jamie assumed to be a translation.

'You are the scholar, Will. I looked at those old texts when you started studying them. I want to help more, but some are written in a script I can't even read. My uncle schooled me in Latin, not whatever that is.' Jamie pointed scornfully at the unfurled scrolls, frustrated he couldn't understand them.

'It's called Archaic Latin. This is a script much older than I have ever seen before, and it's written in the ancient form. This is a challenge I won't let defeat me.'

Will pulled his lamp nearer. For weeks they had been working at all hours, and discarded beeswax candles were piled in an untidy pillar beside him.

'There are some other Latin parchments I want you to look at. They have the Templar seals attached ... and I spotted a few English seals amongst them. They came from Acre, stored in a library or vault. I even noticed a few with the seal of Scotland – Alexander II or perhaps Alexander III.'

Will had carefully placed several scrolls next to him, and patted the bench, urging Jamie to sit.

Jamie's stomach started to groan and rumble in anticipation of the cooking that was now filling his nostrils and occupying his mind. Hendor had often laughed about the fact that Jamie seemed to need feeding every hour on the hour.

'It's incredible that the last people to read these scrolls were the kings of Scotland and Longshanks himself. You can interpret what's inside these recent ones whilst I delve into these ancient Latin parchments.'

Will pointed to a second collection of discoloured parchment next to him that Jamie assumed must be the ancient texts he was referring to.

'We have been looking at these for weeks now and the opportunity to read the letters from the Alexanders is just the encouragement I need.' Jamie felt his energy returning.

'If I had a choice between a book or a sword, I would take books every time. Some of these Latin scrolls are early Christian. There's a lot about Saint Helena and the relics she discovered in Jerusalem. There must be something important in these recent documents – important enough for someone to want to save them and then smuggle them away from Acre. Why bother with paper when you have gold, unless the paper is worth more?'

'The answer is in there somewhere,' Jamie replied.

Will meticulously smoothed the read document out before picking up the next. Jamie noticed the care with which Will handled each document, as if the words were precious, and he remembered that Bishop Wishart treated every book in the cathedral library in the same manner. Will kicked the gold-filled sacks to one side as if they were nothing and treated the papers as if they were treasure. He was sure he detected a squeal when Will retrieved another ancient scroll, like a small child discovering a new toy.

Jamie thought he understood why documents were important to Will, but he would test his theory. 'My uncle often talked about building a university in Glasgow to rival the one where he studied in Bologna. When I was twelve or thirteen, I helped him hide many books and documents out of English hands in the cathedral crypt. We made an archive of our ancient texts and sent them to Baldred Bisset. He used them in making the case for Scottish independence when he visited the Holy Father … must have been 1301. My uncle called them the foundational principles of the Scottish people.'

'I have read those principles too,' Will said. 'If you destroy a country's ancient texts, you destroy its culture, and no one remembers it a country soon after. Longshanks had one of his rages when he found out Bisset escaped with them and presented them to the curia and Pope Boniface. If I remember correctly, Bisset wrote: *Nothing of the Scots or Scotland is of concern to the King of England. The English can display no more right to the kingdom of Scotland than the Egyptians.* Isn't that statement more powerful than any sword?'

Will continued, 'Those words didn't do Bisset much

good – I hear he is in hiding in Paris somewhere, avoiding English assassins. Words and ideas can also be incredibly dangerous if someone powerful considers them the wrong ones, even if they are the truth.'

Jamie nodded as Will continued.

'The preservation of Bisset's letters is one of the many reasons the English despise the Bishop. They wanted them in a fire. Love of learning, as you have shown yourself, doesn't necessarily mean that your head is perennially stuck in a book or a document. It's also preserving and sharing the contents for others. Bisset knows that, to his cost.'

'Will, you are appealing to my curiosity, but I can't concentrate when I am hungry.'

On cue, Jamie's stomach let out a large roar that echoed loud enough for everyone to hear.

After four weeks, Jamie was certainly looking for distraction and stimulation, and Will was doing his best to motivate him.

Jamie stepped onto the barge and Will dragged the document beneath his nose as if he could smell the contents.

'English and Scottish seals you said, Will?' Jamie pulled up a barrel adjacent to Will. Jamie was curious. He took out his dirk and, using the fine point, carefully started to loosen the Crusader seals that had been reattached next to the original court seals.

'Acre had an ancient library that had been removed from Byzantium,' Will said. 'Saving ancient texts feels noble, and if the tales are true, there were more cowardly acts during the fall of Acre than noble ones.'

'My father was there.' Jamie found it hard mentioning John Wishart.

'Please forgive me, Jamie. I meant no disrespect. We wouldn't be here with this treasure if it wasn't for the sacrifice he made. Never think I have forgotten, and I mourn his loss every day.'

Will's apology was genuine and gracious.

'We all remember him and honour his memory,' Innes said. He was inspecting the side of the barge but had been listening to the entire conversation.

Will was animated. 'John Wishart would want us to find out everything these documents can tell us and how they fit together. Why such a mixture of the old and new, Latin and French, as well as some Greek and even Hebrew? It is a collection with no clear connection, with some documents even older than the times of our Lord.'

'Sounds like a personal archive, or maybe it was from one of the Orders,' Hendor said. 'The Templars were there – and de Charnay, of course. There were lots of powerful and influential people in Acre and throughout the Crusades, on the make or hiding their sins amidst a noble cause.'

'They are fascinating, especially the early documents – and I have only scratched the surface,' Will said. 'Lots about the Romans' sacking of Jerusalem, the destruction of Solomon's temple, and a hefty amount of gossip about Saint Catherine's monastery and that avaricious Saint Helena stealing for the Byzantines. They also call themselves the inheritors of Rome and the followers of true religion. Never ones for the understatement,' he sneered.

'Who can ever claim to own knowledge and inherit grace?' Jamie said. 'They are arrogant fuckers, if nothing else.'

'The mother of Constantine appears to have spent heavily in her pursuit of holy artefacts,' Will pointed out.

'Very noble of her – but that's no secret,' Hendor scoffed.

'True … and not worth risking your life to remove from a besieged city. There are hundreds of scrolls to read. Here are some more to read on top of those English and Scottish documents.'

Will placed one of the neat piles of vellum directly on Jamie's lap, which was already untidy and full of scrolls.

Some fell onto the deck.

Jamie picked them up and stuffed one with the seal of King Alexander II untidily into his shirt. He thought he noticed the name Knox de Mayon written on the top on the outside, and he wanted to take it away for closer examination before showing it to Innes.

Out of the shadows the leper appeared, enveloped in an invisible cloud of venison stew and juniper berries.

'Perfect timing,' Jamie mumbled.

Jean placed two wooden bowls filled with hot stew and topped with a large flatbread on the raised ledge that ran along the deck.

'I will take these with me and waste no time.' Jamie carefully placed a further handful of scrolls into his woollen shirt and one into his left sleeve.

'Careful with them.' Will looked at him as if he had committed a significant act of sacrilege.

Innes was warming himself by the brazier. He acknowledged the well-timed meal with a casual bow and was about to say more when Jean scurried away towards Hendor, who was still preoccupied with his weaponry.

Jean placed the final bowl with a goblet of wine next to Hendor before disappearing back into the shadows and his own silent corner.

'Perhaps Bernard will bring his son Guillaume. They aren't expected until tomorrow. I know Bernard can look after himself, yet he is outside without any support, and with Madame around and the traitorous Jean de Bretagne, he must be cautious.'

Innes was speaking for everyone. They had come to enjoy Bernard's strength, wit, and reliability. Like all the best innkeepers, he had an incredible ability to listen without judgement and the skill to say just the right thing. Jamie understood why Bernard was such a successful merchant.

'Bretagne and Madame aren't normal adversaries,'

Hendor said. 'They are much more adept.'

'Bernard can look after himself,' Will said. 'He was a soldier, and when we arrived in Rouen to find Innes and the riot broke out, I saw him smash the heads of sword-wielding soldiers with a simple wooden club. He was more than a match for them. For many years he hid in plain sight whilst working for Bishop Wishart and de Charnay.'

The food took over their thoughts, and they concentrated on eating and drinking as their day began to close.

Jamie sensed an increasing chill in the surroundings. The stones were weeping, losing the heat of the day. They told the story of time better than any clock; the sun was weakening.

'It feels like night is approaching.'

No one was listening to Jamie as they ate.

'I am hoping everyone returns tomorrow. This stew would be better with some rich Gascon wine, and it will numb the pain from my injured limbs.' Hendor was sensitive to the cold, and he stretched his fingers.

Jamie knew the scars of his old injuries turned pale and then blue when the air cooled. Hendor was beginning to struggle with tying bows and fitting new feathers to the arrows. His remaining fingers locked and resembled a claw.

Jamie took the bowl and returned to the small gap in the wall, where he confirmed the approaching darkness. The shore that had been so busy with treasure hunters was now empty. Jamie could see that the water was cooling, and a light mist was dancing skittishly across its surface. He ate greedily, and the gravy ran down his chin which he caught with his finger.

'It's overcast but not dark. It will be misty tonight.'

He scanned the area but could only see directly in front of the stone unless he moved his position.

Immediately the door to the secret chamber started to grumble and groan. Jamie dropped the bowl in surprise and everyone grabbed their swords.

'No one is expected now,' Hendor shouted. It was a statement not a question.

Whilst the entrance was concealed from the river, the noise of the door sliding into the river would attract investigation. Jamie saw the leper pick up a meat cleaver and leap to his feet like a man who was no stranger to defending himself.

I see you want to save your skin too. There is more of a man behind those bandages than I imagined.

The lights and brazier had been placed at the side of the entrance. The walls hid this light, and it couldn't guide any intruder unless they were already across the threshold of the entrance. It was a clever optical illusion aimed to protect the hiding space from anyone looking from the outside. The space would look like an empty void for anyone who didn't know about the cavern and the channel that ran inside.

The Scots hid in the shadows. There was only one way into the cave, and Jamie was ready to fight whoever came through the gap.

The wall dropped into the river, and the entrance was now fully open. A sudden strong draft blew out the concealed torches and candles, and the cave darkened immediately. The brazier was the only light remaining as two shadows rowed stealthily into the channel and stopped behind the barge.

'Put your swords down! It is me, Bernard – and I have brought Guillaume.' Their small riverboat's momentum urged it into the barge, and with a gentle groan and crack, the barge in turn lunged forward, pushing its bow into the side of the narrow stone channel.

'For fuck's sake, Bernard. I have only just fixed the keel.' Innes rarely swore. He rushed towards them.

'Grab this, Innes.' Bernard threw him a rope which he tied to a wooden capstan. The rope pulled the small boat away from the stern of the barge.

'Let me help.' Jamie hurried towards Innes.

Guillaume leapt onto the edge of the channel. He was taller than his father, though his body had yet to fit into his height, which made him look skinny. Jamie recognised how similar he had been in frame and stature just six months ago. Jamie estimated that there could be no more than a year between them.

The leper hurriedly began to relight the lamps that had tumbled over.

'I have brought some wine for you all.'

Bernard rolled a small barrel of wine to the edge of the deck, then placed it on its bottom and tried to lift it off the boat.

'I am going to need some help – it's full to the top with the best Gascony wine, donated by the King of England himself,' Bernard chortled.

'I will volunteer as long as I get to open it first.' Hendor didn't have to be invited twice. He jumped onto the deck, and together they heaved the barrel the several feet up from the deck and onto the cave floor.

'Where is Hugh? I thought he was with you.' Will scoured the boat.

'He is the connection to Geoffroi de Charnay and our journey to the sea,' Innes added.

'He is with de Charnay – I think.' Bernard struggled to find the right words.

'What has happened that you return hours earlier, and why is Hugh with de Charnay?' Hendor spoke the questions that were on Jamie's mind.

'Four days ago, some of Valois's personal palace guards came into the inn – unusual to see them so far from Paris. Couldn't control their tongues after a few glasses of wine. They talked about two men dressed in wolfskins and a beautiful blue-eyed girl who was ordering all the men to search the banks for the wreckage of the barge.' Bernard sounded worried.

'Their drunken indiscretion confirms what Hugh saw. Madame is here in Rouen looking for us, supported by those heathen brothers. She can carry a wound better than any man.' Will knew Madame from the Moor's Head Tavern on the Ile de la Cité and described how she hadn't flinched as the innkeeper stitched her up.

Hendor's face flushed. 'I hope the Wolf Brothers are here, as I have a dagger for each of them.'

'It couldn't be anyone else, and she has been tearing the surrounding area apart looking for you and the barge,' Bernard continued. 'She now thinks you are near Rouen and has a camp on the left bank about a mile south of here. Hugh rode out to check the information to confirm it was her.'

'How does she know we are here?' Hendor asked as he removed a wooden tap from his pocket and started to work on the barrel's wax seal, intent on liberating its contents.

'She hasn't moved her camp in over a week and has combed the area south of us, collecting wood and searching the river for signs of the barge and the treasure,' Bernard said. 'She hasn't narrowed down where we are yet, otherwise Gaillard would be dismantled stone by stone until she had us. It is only a matter of time and the risk grows greater the longer we remain here. Hugh has left to see de Charnay's advice on our next move.'

Bernard paused. 'She is still looking for us south of Gaillard where the explosion happened. Hugh left as soon as he heard – hurry and open that barrel,' he urged Hendor.

Innes gathered more caulk, his work unfinished. 'It's a good day's work that I patched her up, but the barge is not going to outrun a riverboat.'

'Hugh knows what Madame is capable of more than any of us. He will not delay his return. I will drink some wine and drop off these other supplies. Guillaume, unload those sacks.' Bernard stepped back onto their riverboat and slung the sacks out of the boat. The leper dragged each one away.

He had organised a store of the food and supplies at the back of the cave away from the water where it was dry.

'I will return to Rouen with Guillaume. We will wait for Hugh there. There is a reason he hasn't returned here first; he wouldn't want to lead them to you.'

'On the basis that if he saw Madame, maybe she saw him?' Innes asked.

Bernard nodded. 'We must wait for him, and for no more than a couple of days. It is getting too dangerous, and Madame is not going away. De Charnay has confidantes amongst the King's and Valois's guards, and if anyone can find out the King's plans and a safe way out for us, it's him.'

'I wondered how much longer we would have to hide here and how much longer our luck would hold out,' Hendor added. He drank most when he was worried, he took out his whisky flask and swallowed half the contents.

'Innes, the barge took quite a battering on the river. You have patched her up. Is she seaworthy?' Bernard asked. He stepped out of the boat, leaving Guillaume to move the last sack.

'Seaworthy, yes, but the barge is no match for a galley. It was touch and go, but she is a strong old bird, and well-constructed. The pitch and oakum you got and the wood de Charnay left are holding her together. She is blessed – after all, this vessel has escaped Acre, Padua, Paris, and crossed the Mediterranean Sea. She is lucky, but I am not sure she can take much more excitement.'

Innes smiled, clearly attached to the vessel, as though it were something greater than simply a means of escape and more like a faithful servant.

'You speak like she is a woman,' Bernard laughed.

'I never thought of it like that, but I believe you are right.' Innes raised a rare smile.

'And before Guillaume and I leave, I deserve to share some of this barrel of fine wine, which I carried most diligently from my tavern for you to enjoy. Fetch more goblets, Jean.'

Bernard had only just spoken before the leper appeared with a tray of goblets, as if he had already anticipated the request.

Hendor had finished tapping the barrel and was now filling each goblet in turn.

'May I have *uisge beatha* instead?' Jamie held his hand out, and Hendor handed him his flask. He removed the cork and took a single hearty swig. The spirit hit his stomach and instantly raised his mood. Jamie realised its healing and therapeutic qualities. It was indeed the water of life.

'You are a true Scotsman,' Guillaume spoke fondly as he toasted Jamie.

'I just needed something a bit stronger … to fortify my disposition, as Will has given me some documents to read.' Jamie finished the rest of the flask.

'You mean those tatty vellum scrolls, Will?' Bernard was teasing them both. The wine was relaxing everyone.

Will feigned a scowl. 'Don't mock his desire to learn. Education is a fragile commodity and should be preserved.'

'Drink up, Guillaume.' Bernard emptied his goblet, and the dregs dripped down his chin and onto his shirt. Guillaume followed.

'We will return with Hugh and will soon be away from this place.' Bernard jumped back on the boat as Guillaume unhooked the heavy rope, assisted by Innes.

'Jamie, check that there is no one watching outside,' Will ordered.

Jamie moved the loose stone to the left and scanned the shore opposite. It looked and sounded quiet outside, not even an animal was stirring. There was a gentle mist obscuring the right and left of the entrance, so Jamie assumed if that was hindering his view, then it would be an equal obstacle for anyone scrutinising Gaillard and the entrance to the cave.

'It looks clear, Will,' Jamie replied.

As Jamie returned the loose stone to its regular position, the scroll that had been hidden in his left sleeve fell out. He picked it up and placed it into the leather purse attached to his belt.

'I will read you later,' he murmured.

Innes pushed the small boat back down the channel as Hendor grabbed the rope, and together they pushed and pulled the boat towards the emerging gap in the wall.

Bernard and Guillaume left in silence, and Jamie returned to his scrolls. Will looked on approvingly as Innes and Hendor returned to their preparations.

'Jamie, you will be a happy man – it looks like we will be leaving this place soon.' Hendor took some more wine as he sharpened an axe.

'And get working on those scrolls. I need you to review them – unless you have something better to do?' Will was back to studying the parchments.

Jamie knew he wouldn't stop until the candle had been exhausted, and Hugh was unlikely to return for a few days, so he started to unfurl the scrunched parchments he had in his shirt. He placed them beside him, lit his small lamp, and started to read the scroll with Alexander II's seal.

It told a tale about an affair between Knox de Mayon and Eleanor of Brittany more than sixty years ago and how they had produced a child who was a prince of England. He couldn't decide if it was a rumour written down or a true report.

The child was hidden in Acre by his mother to save him from assassination by the English king, and his identity had been forgotten, as his mother and later his father had died. This man was a prince, and no normal one. He was the rightful king of England.

Jamie saw the letter was anonymous. It was deliberately mischievous to stir up a world that was already disorganised by making up rumours about Longshanks. He despised the English King, but he didn't believe there was a challenge to King Edward's right to be king. It was intriguing, but he would dig deeper into these documents before he raised it with the others.

Everyone was busy working except Hendor, who was resting. Even the leper was sweeping the area where he prepared food. That gave him more time to validate what he had read.

If this is true, I will have to put this to Innes's but only after we have left France. I don't want to upset him – I remember the words of Geoffroi de Charnay when we left the Temple regarding Geoffrey de Mayon, and Innes's reaction. He must have known he has a brother, and this parchment proves it – or maybe Innes needs this proof, and the prince could still be alive. I will find the right moment, but not yet.

*

Aurelian had been scouting the edges of the river for days. The barge had neither sunk nor escaped past Honfleur, so he had concluded that it must be hiding in Rouen or close by the town. He had followed the gold and had bribed an old man who was sure that this spot was the best for finding evidence of the treasure ship.

If the locals had known the barge's location, he would know by now, as he had been discreetly spreading his interest in the barge in the form of gold, opening his purse for intelligence, but none of the leads had come to anything.

Now he had fallen back on his own experience, and he waited. Following the old man's advice, he was hiding amongst the tall river reed beds that stretching along the north side of the Seine opposite Gaillard.

I can wait for the barge to reappear.

There was nothing remarkable about this side of the fortress. It was featureless, unscalable, a sheer climb of a hundred feet or more before its face dropped directly into the deepest part of the river. As a result, the garrison rarely patrolled the rampart above. There was no rope or siege equipment big enough to breech the castle using this route.

He could be wasting his time, but he was running out of options, and he needed to get word to the Byzantine navy that was assembling west of the Cherbourg Peninsula.

These men are clever, but I am cleverer. I have more patience than Job.

The navy was waiting for his word that the barge had reached Honfleur where the Byzantine Captain's ships were less than a day's sail away. They would have no problem capturing the treasure as the Scots attempted to cross the Narrow Sea.

The Byzantine's navy is the only one that can navigate the treacherous open sea weather and currents. Ships by the Genovese and captained by the best admiral Ferran d'Aunes. Our fleet is small, yet experienced. The French and English fleets are inexperienced, manned by fishermen who had yet to travel far from the coast and were intimidated by the unknown and believed in tales of sea monsters.

He smiled.

Only the Norwegian fleet is a threat to my plan.

The weather was cooling, and Aurelian wrapped his cloak tightly around him. The reeds and scrub around the shore concealed him from Gaillard, but the mist had made it damp, and the cold was seeping through his clothing. He had brought some food and wine to give him some distraction.

Even the river was unusually quiet, as the normal traffic was to the south of the fortress. The presence of the garrison guards was sufficient reason to avoid this place, and he knew they still skulked around the perimeter of the outer walls – but not tonight. The fog was above the river, and any sentry would see nothing below.

He drank the wine straight from the flagon as he peered

through the grass. The pot was emptying more quickly than he had planned.

His eyes swivelled as he heard the clatter of small rocks; some were no bigger than gravel. Unexpectedly, they started to fall into the water. A soft grinding noise like an axe being sharpened on a stone emanated gently from the north face across from him.

In normal circumstances, the sounds would be enveloped by the raucous river traffic. He looked to the south to see if a boat was approaching, but his attention quickly moved back to Gaillard. He dropped the flagon onto the sand and stared into the clear gap between the river's surface and the mist fifteen or twenty feet above it.

What is that beneath Gaillard's walls? Whatever it is, it's moving, and it's appeared from nowhere. Is the wine making my mind play tricks?

He was sure the river was empty, and he couldn't have missed a boat's approach.

Aurelian could just make out the shape of a small riverboat with two oarsmen. The boat moved out from a small beach that was on the far left-hand side of the tower and turned right, heading downstream towards Rouen. The oars were covered with cloth, and they cut through the water in near silence.

Where did you come from? You aren't the barge, but that doesn't mean you aren't interesting.

He tried to think of options that weren't inexplicable, but there weren't any.

You came from within Gaillard. There must be a place to hide underneath the north wall. I will see where you are heading.

Aurelian buried the flask to remove any evidence that he had been there. Madame and her henchman were around, and she was collecting evidence. They had been following each other and the Scots for months.

Where is that boat? I moored it nearby.

He climbed into the boat, slipped off the rope tying it to a tree stump, and followed the men who could lead him to the treasure.

Chapter Seven

The Temple, Paris, September 1306:
Geoffroi and Hugh Plan an Escape

Geoffroi de Charnay studied the courtyard as he waited for Hugh de Verneuil to return. He had led the Paduans away from Marais and then headed to Gaillard, and he was hoping for good news.

Men were drilling below and watching them kept his mind active without requiring concentration. Hugh would not enter via the courtyard, but through the chapel entrance from the river. Geoffroi was never sure who was taking an interest. The only certainty was Pierre de Nogaret would be watching him even more closely now that he knew about Giordano and Procacci, and Geoffroi had to make sure he learned nothing more.

It was dusk, and he read the unsigned note in his hand.
Master, expect me.

Esquieu de Floyran was still spying for Valois, and Geoffroi used him to feed Valois information that would end up with King Phillip. This had helped the Order and allowed the Scots to avoid capture. He had risked Raoul du Bec and had sent him away to La Rochelle until he was sure that Esquieu didn't believe Raoul was part of his conspiracy in feeding false information on the treasure. Esquieu was brutal, but not very smart. Still, Geoffroi couldn't risk harm to Raoul. He was a novice and he was sworn to protect him.

He saw Pierre de Nogaret for the duplicitous charlatan that he was, yet he wasn't sure about all his motivations apart from his Cathar obsession. He now suspected that de Nogaret's next move was to oust Geoffroi as the Templar's next Grand Master. The Order was de Nogaret's instrument to help the Cathars. Their support would strengthen any cause, including that of Prince Edward, a vulnerable heir whose father was doing everything he could to ensure his unquestioned succession.

I wonder just how close Guillaume and Pierre de Nogaret are. Pierre wouldn't help the French King, because Phillip persecutes Cathars, but blood ties can create the most unlikely alliances. If Pierre captured the treasure, any old resentments would disappear, and he would be the new Grand Master – are his loyalties shared only between the Order and the English?

Pierre had been keeping himself away from the Temple councils for many days now. Normally he was all-seeing and all-knowing when it came to Temple affairs.

'You can tell a lot of what is going on in the Temple, not from those you see, but from those who are hidden,' Geoffroi muttered.

The Temple guards had resumed their normal routine since King Phillip had returned to the Louvre. Stone and wood were still stacked against the inner walls, ready to fully restore the outer walls and portcullis that had been damaged by the Paris riots in mid-August.

'And what are you up to, de Nogaret? I am more suspicious when you aren't around.' He was still deciding how to deal with him, when your brother was the chief counsellor to the king Pierre couldn't simply disappear.

He had been in touch with his confidants at court and was monitoring the actions of Valois and the King. It was clear the King believed the treasure was in France, and he hated to admit that he was right.

That was where the consensus ended, because he wanted the Scots out of France just as much as the King wanted to keep them here.

Gerard de Villiers, who was the most charming Templar, had made a point of being friends with the new head of Valois's guards, the veteran Adam de Valencourt. Adam had left the Templars, joined the Dominicans and then repurposed himself at court in Valois's guards. This connection had allowed de Charnay to hear many of Valois's plans as quickly as the King. Gerard and Adam were old friends who liked to gossip and share confidences.

'Now I must see what young Raoul's report from La Rochelle.' He removed a tiny scroll from his sleeve.

Master,

Valois's men are still stationed along the roads and rivers as we required and he has not abandoned his pursuit of the prize, though some of his men have been drifting away from the West of France towards Rouen and the Seine. I suspect the young lady is behind these actions. We are running out of time before this drifting becomes an avalanche. We need to act now before the prize is discovered.

Your faithful servant,
Raoul

He believed Raoul's letter and Hugh's return today were related, and he needed to act quickly before the King moved his entire force back to Rouen. There were also rumours King Phillip was looking for ships and he didn't believe in all these coincidences. Plans were being made to capture the treasure at sea if Madame failed at Rouen and he would make sure the Scots escaped.

He placed Raoul's letter next to him to show to Hugh.

De Charnay heard the tapestry move to one side. A stale odour and dust crept into his room, and he recognised the welcome voice of Hugh de Verneuil.

Hugh smiled as he brushed the cobwebs from his hair and cloak.

'You are a welcome sight for my aged eyes even if it's for a short while. I assume you need to get back to Gaillard as soon as possible?'

De Charnay pulled a chair towards Hugh. His old friend looked exhausted, and the marks of the horse reins were clear on his hands.

'I have ridden through the night.' Hugh slumped onto the chair as de Charnay sat down next to him and pulled over a table with wine. Some meats, cheese, and bread sat on a wooden platter, and despite his obvious exhaustion Hugh stuffed his cheeks with large slices he cut hastily with his dagger.

'I have received more informative letters. Only three words, yet its cryptic nature serves its purpose – I expect you will need this.' De Charnay handed Hugh some wine.

'I led the Paduans on their way and went to Gaillard. The roads between Gaillard and Paris are full of nosey soldiers stopping everyone.' Hugh downed the wine in seconds.

'It isn't only the king's guards we need to be wary of,' Geoffroi said. 'I suspect everyone and trust no one. Unimagined wealth changes even honest men into liars, thieves, and murderers. You were right to be cautious entering the Temple. Word of this treasure is deep in the minds of the European royalty. They are chasing after it like the thieves they all are. I am beginning to think they would eat their young to possess it – the English, the Byzantine's or even King Haakon,' Geoffroi paused.

He could see the strain on Hugh's face. He was tough and resilient, yet the weight of the burden had aged him – the treasure had to leave Gaillard immediately.

'How are my Scottish friends? Quite an explosion, I hear. Pity we don't know who did it. I wonder if they are helping the Scots because they are working for King Robert – more likely a competitor who sees getting out of France with the treasure as compatible with their own objectives – I don't like not knowing who they are but I am determined to find out. I will make more enquiries after you leave.'

Hugh nodded.

'The explosion allowed us to escape Madame's ship – bought us time, nothing else.' Hugh's throat tightened and his voice started to break. 'Excuse me master my voice is weak. I have ridden many miles in a few days, consuming particles of road dust and mud.'

Geoffroi poured him some more wine.

'Our plan was that people would stop looking for us. Greed would overtake our pursuers, and they would focus on finding the wreck, allowing the barge to slip away, but…' Hugh's voice was fortified by the wine. 'But Madame remains close by Gaillard, and we watched her henchmen dressed in wolfskins patrol the shoreline, and heard they have threatened anyone in Rouen who they think is involved or knows something. We kept well-hidden, hoping she would give up – and there must be more than the French pursuing us.'

Geoffroi interrupted. 'There is certainly someone determined that King Phillip will not succeed, and we know Madame never gives up. These two opposing parties may cancel each other out. You are right, Hugh – we need to take command and finally resolve this situation.'

Hugh was more animated, but Geoffroi shared his worry. 'Now we have been hiding in Gaillard for four weeks. I came to see you for guidance. How best do we make our escape surrounded by enemies?'

'We can try to divert attention away from Gaillard, the Scots, and the barge – but we have already tried that, and it was only partially successful, and I doubt the tenacious Madame or even that idiot Valois will fall for that ruse again.'

'I would agree with you, master – they will not be fooled again.' There was a tinge of hopelessness in Hugh's voice that Geoffroi had never heard before. He was normally so resilient, but he had been pushed to exhaustion.

'Then we must give the barge to those who pursue it,' Geoffroi said.

Hugh held his hand up with the palm towards him, as if trying to stop the words. 'So, you mean to give up the treasure after all this time, after all we have been through … when you have taken such measures to preserve it? The Scots need it now, and it won't be long before the Order may need the power it brings. Do you want to give it up to those who would use it for the worst possible purposes? I will take my chances with Madame and make a run for it.' The pallor of exhaustion had been replaced with the colour of anger and frustration. He stood up and appeared ready to leave.

'Sit, Hugh. You are tired and misunderstand what I am saying.' Geoffroi placed his hand on Hugh's shoulder and gently pushed him back into his seat. 'I don't intend to give the treasure up to anyone. The people chasing this fortune know about the barge, and more importantly, know what it looks like, so we must give it to them – but only once we have emptied it of its contents.'

De Charnay would need Hugh at his side in the battle to save the Order but that was for another day after they had made the treasure safe.

'What do you mean? How can we do that and survive?' Hugh leaned towards Geoffroi.

'When I heard about the explosion, I thought the worst. I feared you had all been killed or captured and the treasure was swallowed up by the river. When there was no word of the treasure, I knew you had made it to Gaillard. But how would I get you out of there and past Rouen? I have been using the last few weeks wisely.'

Hugh's face lightened. 'You have my attention.'

'Laurent d'Aumale is moored in Rouen with an empty, inconspicuous seagoing cog. It looks just like the rows of merchant ships berthed at Rouen harbour. In a few hours it will be in Gaillard. Under the fortress's protection, he can safely remove the treasure from the barge and transfer it onto the cog. The ship is quicker than the barge. It's high-sided, which makes it hard to board if any hostile ship attacks it – and it can carry more than the barge, navigate rivers as well as the sea. It is fit for the dangerous journey between France and Scotland, and it can outrun anything sent after it.'

Geoffroi couldn't think of anyone better to sound a plan through than Hugh. 'You are smiling, Hugh.'

'Master, our pursuers will have more ships – bigger ships?'

'You are correct, Hugh, but Laurent has made some adaptations. The cog is quite remarkable.'

'What type of adaptations? Hugh asked.

'The cog has a single mast that can be dismantled, so we can transfer the treasure underneath Gaillard unnoticed and undisturbed. Its current cargo of sand ballast will replace the treasure, put on the barge and will find its way to Rouen and into the hands of King Phillip.'

'On the barge?' Hugh's question was rhetorical.

'Exactly, and we will make sure anyone in pursuit follows the barge with its sand cargo, crewed by loyal Templars as far as Honfleur – but you will not be among them. You will leave the Scots and the cog at Rouen, as I need you back here. I need you to work on saving the Order – Innes can manage such a ship. I will be sure to leak the barge's escape plan into the nest of spies in Rouen, and I have just the man who will unknowingly help us. He is working for our enemies and will lead them into the trap I set.'

'A Templar perhaps?'

Geoffroi didn't answer. 'We will hide the sand under the thinnest veneer of gold, so anyone careless in its inspection will not immediately know they have been fooled. Whilst we make for Honfleur and the sea, they will be scrambling around for answers, and we will be out of reach.'

'Master, that may get us past Rouen and Honfleur, yet there is a long and dangerous course between the French and Scottish coasts. There could be ships waiting for us anywhere between leaving France and getting to safety.'

'The cog's keel is angled to cut through waves faster than similar vessels. I have used such ships to transport valuables in the past, so it is fortuitous we have them in our fleet. We will run away faster than they can catch us!'

'What do you need me to do?' Hugh had emptied the platter and finished more than his fair share of wine.

'I will send a message to Bernard, so he will know about the switch. You will be needed in Rouen in case there is any trouble and a sword is needed. Laurent is crewing the barge with his own men and will make sure Madame follows him.'

Hugh nodded. 'I was to meet Bernard at his tavern with your instructions. We were then going back to Gaillard to make the barge seaworthy and escape.'

'Now there will be no need. The barge has served its purpose and your escape rests with the cog. Meet Bernard as planned and make the necessary preparations to get past Rouen. I will make things hard for Madame when she realises she has been tricked, to resume the chase she'll need ships, and I am making sure she doesn't find any. There will be no ships at La Rochelle for her because they are putting to sea as we speak.'

Geoffroi could see the realisation in Hugh's face.

'She will not follow to the open sea in her ship – it was badly damaged in the explosion and doesn't want to perish in a rash act.' Geoffroi considered Hugh's judgement correct.

Hugh nodded. 'Aumale must be as cunning as she is – think as she does. Whatever tactics you use to deceive Madame and leak the plans to our enemies, they must be convincing.'

'I will always use whatever skills I have to protect everyone involved. We are all placing our lives in danger to achieve great ambitions. These are not adversaries with romantic notions, and I can't fail in such an important task. Even after all that, I will not sacrifice Aumale or you for anything.'

Geoffroi was serious. He was ruthless with his enemies and compassionate with his friends. Hugh's life was worth more than any treasure.

'May I rest a while before I return to Rouen?' Hugh picked up the flagon of wine and poured the last drops into his goblet.

'A fine proposal. I have dismissed my servants, so you can sleep undisturbed. It is better that no one knows you are here. Rest and remember to warn Innes about Scrovegni's letter. Valence is making Innes's death a very personal matter.' De Charnay pointed to the bedroom that was at the end of his L-shaped quarters.

Hugh did not need any encouragement. He yawned. 'I arrived unseen, and I will leave in the same manner.'

'And there is some more wine to be found adjacent to my bed.' De Charnay grabbed parchment and pen and began to write.

Hugh shuffled towards the bedroom, and within seconds de Charnay could hear his snores. He had peace to write to Bernard and would send this letter immediately.

Bernard,

I have secured alternative means to transport our prize and ensure it doesn't fall into the wrong hands. Laurent d'Aumale has all the details and he will contact you. He will need your help to transfer the goods from the barge to a cog I have waiting in Rouen. Raoul is maintaining a watch in the west, but the longer Valois's men find nothing, the lesser the reason to remain there, and the focus will return to Rouen and the route out of France via Honfleur. We need to act immediately and get out to sea. Our English and French friends must believe that the prize remains on the barge and are encouraged to follow it to just within the Narrow Sea, where their navy can capture it. Jean de Bretagne is the route to the English. I am relying on you to help Laurent and make the French believe the same. Use Les Frères Loups – they are the weakest link in the French plans. With the French and English fighting it out, there should be enough confusion to slip away. The finer details I will leave to you both.

He would let Hugh sleep for an hour, but no longer, as he recognised that time was running out and he needed to be on the road to Rouen.

He would create a similar letter for Pierre de Nogaret to discover, confirming the barge with its treasure would be in Rouen in three days but omitting to tell him that the cog would leave in two. Pierre de Nogaret would pass it on to the English. The cog would be gone a day before the English knew they had been tricked.

He would leave it on his table for Guy de Nogaret to find. He had learned to stick anything he wanted Pierre to pay particular attention to at the bottom of the pile. Guy regularly picked the locks to his offices on Pierre's orders and copied everything he found. The news would be with Pierre within hours.

He started to write the second letter.

*

Pierre de Nogaret had watched Hugh surreptitiously enter the Temple and leave. That was several hours ago and he had used the time wisely to plot.

'You arrived like a thief and left like one – and you think no one knows about your furtive meetings and the wealth you seek to keep for yourself. I know about Procacci and Giordano. They only just escaped my men.'

Pierre had been frustrated that the English appeared no closer to securing the treasure for themselves. That had now changed. Guy had picked the locks to de Charnay's offices.

That evening, whilst Hugh slept and de Charnay ate, Guy had copied the letters he found and discovered that the barge was hiding in a tributary to the south of Rouen and would be travelling past Gaillard in three days.

'De Charnay, there is so much I despise about you but I must admit you are a fine administrator. You order your letters meticulously, the most sensitive you keep at the bottom – I know where you are hiding the treasure and soon Jean de Bretagne would also know.' He couldn't stop himself from grinning.

Hugh had left in darkness, but he had not left alone. Pierre had someone follow him – someone whose loyalties and motivations were no different from his, a man whose skills he had been nurturing these few years and his nephew.

He was to gather Jean de Bretagne's help and get the barge out of France.

Guy was evolving into another avenger for the Cathar massacres, and that pleased Pierre. His drive for revenge wouldn't die with him.

'This time the treasure will be mine, and the English heir is mine already.'

He was in correspondence with Prince Edward. He rummaged through his desk, pulled out a large drawer, and flicked a latch on the underside. The front of the drawer detached, revealing a compartment where a letter was hidden. The letter carried the seal of the English heir.

My loyal friend,

Hubert de Lacy has brought to my attention your most wonderful endeavour, which brings me more joy than you can imagine. My rule will soon be upon us, and I will remember those that have helped me with such a generous pledge. Faithful lords are already assembling, and traitors fleeing. Those that have been my silent supporters are now vocal and working in my favour. Your friends are my friends and your enemies mine. There will be nothing we cannot achieve together. I await your confirmation when the gold is on its way.

There would be no misunderstanding – and just in case Edward dithered in the role he was to play in restoring the Cathars, Pierre would hold back a substantial portion for the cause. Prince Edward knew what his terms were and needed friends with money.

'Some don't want Prince Edward to be king for no other reason than that he was not his father, others because he prefers art to war. Some even claimed he is a sodomite. His future wife Isabella is more like a man than her brothers. That will be to his liking.' He laughed admiringly at his crude logic.

Pierre did not care about Prince Edward's morality. He only cared about restoring Catharism.

He imagined the fury of the French King once he found out the English had acquired the treasure. There would be plenty of blame to allocate around, and it wouldn't matter if anyone was guilty or not. Pierre would make sure de Charnay took personal responsibility, and he knew just the man to inform if events necessitated: his brother.

*

Guy de Nogaret had just met with Guillaume, and he measured the meeting's importance with the weight of his purse, which was straining his belt. It told him that Guillaume firmly believed he was working for him now and not Pierre.

Guillaume had even shown him a copy of Madame de France's letter demanding ships to be sent to Honfleur harbour and further demanding Phillip to coerce the

Templars to help her. That was a secret Guillaume would not have easily shared with someone he didn't trust, especially a Templar squire. He was to report back to Guillaume on any information regarding the barge.

Guy had a unique skill of memorising letters and considered Madame's words.

Sire,

I undertook investigations, and it is clear to me we were following the treasure. Solid gold coins have been found on the shores of the Seine. They have been placed there to trick us into thinking the barge is sunk. Whilst our ship was badly damaged, we lost only a couple of men, and following intelligence, I am convinced we will find evidence of the treasure's whereabouts in Rouen. I have sent Les Frères Loups in pursuit and expect nothing but positive news. I advise all secrecy, as we are not the only parties in pursuit. Should we be unsuccessful in Rouen, the barge will travel to the sea via Honfleur. We should intercept it there or in the Seine Basin. For this, I will require two or three stout ships, as mine is not fit for a chase on the open sea. I await your advice.

Valois had been sent to Honfleur to press any ships into her service in case the Templar fleet did not arrive. King Phillip always wanted a fallback plan.

Guy was in no hurry especially when he looked at his purse, swelled by two greedy uncles. He enjoyed watching them scheme against each other.

They had treated him like a chattel all his short life and he was getting his revenge in the most satisfying way. He wanted his mother to see from heaven how he had honoured her name and the Cathar cause she died for. He had no loyalty to either of her brothers.

Pierre spoke like a Cathar zealot but hid behind the Order that he had joined in the persecution. He talked like a politician, words that veiled inaction – *if*, *when*, *wait*, *not the right time*, *but* – a plethora of excuses and platitudes. If only Pierre knew what Guy knew – that his beloved Order was truly doomed, and Guillaume was planning its destruction.

Guy wanted direct action, swords and blood, not ideology and rationalisation. He would not stay hidden much longer once he got hold of the treasure.

There would be no sharing with Prince Edward of England, no masters to cheat and persecute them.

In his saddlebag he had a letter from Uncle Guillaume to be handed to Madame detailing their plans for the ships. From Uncle Pierre, he had a letter for Jean de Bretagne, and he was to follow Hugh de Verneuil. The first would help the French, the second the English. The first would never arrive, the second would. Bretagne would provide his third purse.

He would stage a robbery in Rouen. There were so many desperate treasure hunters that a rogue or two could be bribed and he was just a Templar novice.

Today he would enjoy the early autumn sunshine on the road to Rouen and dream of his glorious future.

Chapter Eight

Wisbech Castle, September 1306:
Two Old Men in Chains

Water dripped incessantly, rhythmically, from the roof and down the walls, creating shimmering pools between the straw and filth that lined the pitted floor.

Bishop Wishart found the squalid surroundings strangely attractive.

'I wonder how this works. When the sun was high, the light split into different colours reflected by the stones. God's wonders even reach this grim place. Reminds me of the stained glass in Glasgow Cathedral, just to the right of the nave – this place is growing on me already. The remains of the day however are not so pleasant – but I will get used to it.'

Wishart pulled his woollen cloak around him as he sat in the corner on his thin straw mattress. He mumbled.

'I thank Cardinal Orsini for providing a few crumbs of comfort. This cloak was one such act of kindness and will protect my bones from the cutting cold of the forthcoming winter and away from the toads and rats that kept me company at night – I have a chair, a desk, and a small lamp. Orsini has sent me some dried meat, fish, and fruit – I will store these in a dent in the stone walls to protect my small larder from the vermin – up there I think.'

Wishart wrapped his larder in a piece of cloth that had conveniently fallen from his shirt. He stood on the simple chair and concealed it far away from any thieves.

There was a large crack running down the inner wall to the floor, and vermin squeezed between the stones in their constant pursuit of food, water, shelter, and sex.

'I have fooled you,' he scoffed as they searched.

Longshanks wouldn't execute him, and it was clear his intention was that the Bishop would die of neglect or by his own hand.

'If he thought for a minute I would allow despair to take over my mind, he really doesn't know me.'

His thoughts turned to Murdie and the Maid of Norway. He remembered Wallace's hidden message in the Tower – the single word *Margaret* scratched onto a stone. Now the English had forced Murdie to find her. He shuddered when he thought of the danger.

Wishart had known about Longshank's plan to kill her in 1290. Even in such a brutal world, killing his great-niece would make King Edward an excommunicate.

'If anyone could survive, it would be Murdie, and with the grace of God he would find his way to Rouen and find Jamie, Will, and Hendor. I will make sure people don't forget our cause.'

He had taken to speaking most of his thoughts. There had been no one to hear his voice, and he knew the damage solitude could do to a man's sanity, so he chose to speak to God and share his mind. He intended to hold back little, but now he would need to be more measured and silent. He had a neighbour – one whose snoring had penetrated the walls like the mice.

Last night he had heard the dragging of chains and the clunking of keys, accompanied by the harsh, unkind tones men used when addressing prisoners. He hoped his neighbour was agreeable, but he would also be alert to the possibility of a spy.

Apart from the snoring, which had now stopped, the dungeon had been quiet since last evening. Wishart examined the walls, looking for a convenient crack in the decaying stonework where he could sit and observe. The insignificant became the significant when there was nothing to do. He would petition the cardinal for books, but his eyes were becoming weary when he read.

The last time they had met, Longshanks had promised Wishart that William Lamberton, the Bishop of St. Andrews, would join him.

Two traitorous clerics decaying alongside the dilapidated walls. Longshanks had cursed them both.

He was hoping that Longshanks, a habitual liar, was telling the truth. He might have thought keeping the Scottish rebel leaders together allowed the English to isolate them and keep them from rescue so far from the Scottish border. Wisbech was in the See of Ely, East Anglia, about as remote from Scotland as possible, however if Lamberton was housed next to him, they would use the time wisely and make plans for even greater insurrection.

Wishart had first seen Lamberton as a talented young cleric in the scriptorium and had sent him to France for his education. He would recognise him immediately, and with a glad heart.

He lifted his ankle chains off the floor and shuffled as quietly as he could towards a small chink in the wall, dragging his small chair with his other hand.

He could see the back of a sleeping figure on a straw mattress. The body was motionless, yet he could hear the rhythmic cadence of heavy breathing, the deepness you would expect from an exhausted man. He thought the long woollen vestments were those of a priest and could just glimpse the pale cassock contrasting with the darker and much heavier outer chimere.

Some opportunistic rodents dined on a piece of bread next to a bowl the jailers had left. He admired the animals' ingenuity and drive to survive.

Wishart had also slept for several days when he had arrived.

'Turn around,' he muttered.

He took his spoon from his sleeve and pushed some loose stones through the gaps. They were obscuring his vision. He hoped that the sound would stir the figure from its sleep. He pushed harder at the mortar.

'William … Bishop Lamberton, wake up.' Wishart raised his voice slightly but dared not shout any louder lest he alerted the guards. The figure didn't move.

A large rat had been startled and backed into the pottery bowl, upending its contents onto the stone floor. The rat immediately ran away as the bowl resonated and rattled.

'For goodness' sake, Robert … can't you let a man sleep?' The figure turned around, rubbed his eyes, and for a few moments tried to locate the Bishop's voice. The light was coming from the left and framed Lamberton as he sat upright. Wishart could see bruising and deep cuts around his face, no doubt a welcoming gift from the jailors.

'Over here. Turn around and look for the gravel on the floor. I am directly above it looking at you.' Wishart's voice was just above a whisper.

Lamberton lifted his chains and crawled along the floor. Even in the daylight, the edges of the walls were in shadow. He was feeling for the gravel to lead him to Wishart.

Wishart recognised his old friend, and for a few seconds he just smiled. It reminded him about how the simple things in life, seeing an old friend made you forget all the cruelty. Robert could see that his face was gaunt and grey, but his eyes still had the sparkle of defiance.

'Over here, William. Forty years old and you look marvellous.' Lamberton followed Wishart's voice and sat on the ground next to the chink in the stones. Wishart was sitting on the chair; the irons draped around him on the ground. They weighed heavily on his emaciated arms.

Wishart started to cry, but these were tears of joy, not sorrow. For a couple of minutes they cried and laughed, saying nothing.

'We shouldn't weep, for we have much to be grateful for because we are together now. Two old friends in chains. God has brought us to meet in this place.'

Wishart heard the relief and anxiety in Lamberton's voice. He was ashamed of his tears but thankful he was sharing his weakness with another proud man who wouldn't judge.

He recovered his composure.

'We have so much to talk about. Where did they seize you? Do you have word of King Robert? Is he safe? Did he reach Argyle?' There was so much Wishart wanted to know. He tripped over his words in his excitement.

'Robert … so many questions.' Lamberton sighed and placed his hands on his face.

'King Robert is taken? Your face is telling me much, and it doesn't look like good news.' Wishart feared the worst.

'I have been travelling for many days. My appearance is a temporary fatigue. I was initially taken to Winchelsea Castle, but that was too near the French, so they moved me here, further away from King Phillip and rescue, but nearer to you. Importantly, the king is still free.' Lamberton wiped the grit from his eyes before continuing.

'I was captured in Stirling. After we crowned King Robert, the English tore Fife apart hunting me. They killed my clergy and tenants before I let them catch me, armour-clad and enjoying my last decent meal courtesy of King Edward's deer. I am a bit thinner now.' Lamberton's voice was fragile.

'It was hard after Methven,' Wishart said. 'I was captured by Valence, and as he couldn't hang me, he starved me. Then Cardinal Orsini offered me his protection.'

'Longshanks wants us to rot. However, King Phillip has intervened on my behalf and has asked for my release. After my study in Paris and my many diplomatic missions, the French King took a shine to me. This truce between France and England might help us. King Phillip can negotiate with an ally, not an enemy, and Longshanks needs friends. It is rumoured his son has an uneasy road to the soon-to-be-vacant throne.' William's face brightened.

'King Phillip would have your head on a spike if it suited him. He cares for no one, and he does nothing out of mere attachment. However, you are favoured now, and it is an indication of your diplomatic skills that he has interceded on your behalf. I have no one to speak up for me, and that's why we must use this time to plan before you are released. There is much I must share with you. When your freedom comes, you must use it to help King Robert. He needs the Church's support – it was a good day when I sent you to France – I wanted you to get the right education. That investment may just pay off.'

'Indeed, it did – that's why I am here in a dungeon in chains.' Lamberton laughed and rattled his chains. Wishart laughed too.

'I never imagined we would end up here in adjoining dungeons discussing rebellion,' Lamberton said. 'Yet I wouldn't change anything.'

'Apart from being caught,' Wishart said.

'Indeed ... I have missed your humour, Robert – but it doesn't conceal your suffering. The gap in these stones may be small, but I can still see how you have aged.'

'I am over sixty – and I am determined to outlive Longshanks. I want to be alive when they cry out, "The king is dead" – and I don't think we will be waiting long.'

'Have you seen him?' Lamberton asked.

'He brought me to the Tower to boast and intimidate. He wanted to see me before him, humbled, but instead he emboldened me. He is declining and will be lucky to last the year ... and with his death, we are presented with an opportunity.'

'What do you mean? Just because that old bastard passes into hell doesn't mean it will be the end of the English in Scotland. There is always another tyrant to take his place.'

Robert recognised that the unwavering fighting spirit was still strong in Lamberton, and it strengthened him. His spirit felt nourished.

'The English nobility are curbed under Longshanks. They feel beaten, broken, and downtrodden, and his death gives them the opening to flex their muscle against a feebler, more malleable character. Prince Edward is more interested in finery than the battlefield. He won't fight for anything, unless it's one of his lithe courtiers – William, Longshanks is in terminal decline. He will never lead an army again. When I saw him at the Tower, he could barely sit on a chair without sliding off it. He shivered so that a roaring fire was lit in the middle of summer. Whilst the English fight amongst themselves, we take our country back.' Wishart could feel his strength fully restored.

'I recognise that they will never let me go free, as I gave absolution to King Robert for Comyn. Comyn was married to Valence's sister and is part of the Plantagenet dynasty. My crime is more than just crowning a king. The Plantagenets have taken it very personally.'

Lamberton interrupted. 'They executed Sir Christopher Seton. He suffered a traitor's death. It bodes ill for what they will do to King Robert if they catch him.'

'Seton was at Comyn's slaying and was married to Bruce's sister. The English will take their revenge on anyone associated with Comyn's death. We are only spared because we are clerics.'

Wishart kicked the wall in frustration.

'And what do you want me to do?' Lamberton shuffled closer.

'I need you to speak to King Phillip and King Haakon

and urge them to support King Robert. Buy their support if you must.'

'Buy their support with what? The Scottish treasury is no more. The English take the taxes raised in Scotland and spend them in England.'

Wishart was happy that the treasure had remained a secret from Lamberton.

'There is a treasure, and it is heading to Scotland. It is more wealth than you can imagine, and I have arranged for it to come to Scotland with my nephew Jamie Wishart. Innes de Mayon, my servant Hendor Robertson, and King Robert's armour bearer, Will de Irwyne, they are all working for me now. I have asked Murdie MacBeith to join them in France. Try and get word to the King about where Murdie is. I am sure that Domhnall will want to know.'

'Of course I will, Robert.'

'William, I couldn't think of better men to send, and they will succeed. When they are in Scotland, you must guide them and help the King. He will need to conceal the treasure from our enemies and will need advice on spending it wisely.'

'Heading to Scotland from where? What treasure? Where did the wealth come from?' It was Lamberton now tripping on his words. 'Where is the King?' Lamberton asked.

'The treasure is one we acquired by right saved from Acre by my brother John Wishart and kept safe by my old friend Geoffroi de Charnay. I needed to make sure the treasure was out of the hands of tyrant kings. They would do much harm with it, whereas we can use it to ensure our freedom, and in keeping it from Longshanks, we will achieve that. King Robert knows about it, and if he has gone to where he has, he will be able to keep it away from King Edward and King Phillip – but it may still fall into the hands of King Haakon.' Wishart removed a small flask from his pocket and gulped the whisky inside.

'Where is King Robert heading?' Lamberton asked again.

'I am not sure. All I know is that he planned to go west. I advised him to hide with Lord Halcro. One of the gloating guards told me he was attacked in Argyle on MacDougall land, shortly after Methven. Once he leaves the Scottish mainland, it will be much harder for the English to capture him. If he was taken, Longshanks himself would have come here to tell me. He is heading to the Northern Isles and the lands of King Haakon, the lords of Orkney, and most of all the barbarous sea. The English won't begin hunting King Robert again until the spring, despite their protestations otherwise …' Wishart drank from the flask again. 'William, your presence gives me strength, but we must be careful the English don't discover our plotting, so we must seal up this gap in the wall.'

'We are like Pyramus and Thisbe,' Lamberton said.

'Their end was not a pleasant one. Take some ale and mix it with the grout. Grind it with your spoon and smear it over the gap between us. It will seal and harden but will still be weak enough to poke through. You have slept through most of the day, and the shadow is widening. The guards will be around to check on us and deliver food.'

Wishart could hear Lamberton scraping the fallen grout off the floor and mixing it with ale. Wishart pushed the filler into the gap between the stones, and Lamberton's face slowly disappeared.

He returned to his bed as the guards opened his cell, scraping the floor with its uneven door. The wooden bottom had swelled in the damp conditions, making the door fit tight to the frame and difficult to open. It took two men to free it from the grip of the floor.

Wishart lay on his straw mattress and did not look up.

'Sit up, traitor. Cardinal Orsini wants us to trim that beard.'

Two guards appeared with the jailor and pulled him

upright whilst holding Wishart's chained arms.

The jailor brandished a small axe and a leather strap. He proceeded to strop the blade against the leather strap, removing clumps of a dirty white beard.

'What are you smiling at? If it was up to me, I would be cutting more than your hair.'

The jailor moved the blade down to just below Wishart's right ear before moving it back to the straggly beard.

'Wouldn't you be happy if someone was shaving your beard?' Wishart beamed.

'Don't be flattered. We can't let a traitorous dog like you have a razor to slit our throats. We have all the dregs of Scotland under one roof now. Once I have finished with you, I will be trimming the beard of another Scottish cur, and I might not be so careful.'

The jailor nicked Wishart's cheek, and blood trickled into his mouth.

'That should take the grin away.'

'I am sure he will be as appreciative as me.' Wishart wiped the blood away with his sleeve as the jailor left, followed by the two guards.

He was no longer alone. Lamberton would leave, but not yet. There would be more time to finesse their plans for rebellion, and King Robert was alive and free.

He removed his whisky flask from his pocket and daintily placed a small amount on his finger, dabbing it onto the wound on his face.

He winced, then started to grin. His smile became broader, as he knew now he would survive until Murdie and Jamie returned.

Chapter Nine

The Tower of London, September 1306: Balliol, the Rival King

King Edward drew his chair closer to the fire. It was September, yet he couldn't keep warm. His hands could barely close, and he flexed his fingers whenever he was alone to help his joints warm. The warmth helped them move and seemed to stop them from sticking in place, neither straight nor entirely bent.

He stretched his hands out in front of him, framing his fingers with the fire before clenching them tight like a pugilist, then extending them again. They cracked like embers.

The previous week he had dropped his dagger, unable to grip it to cut his meat. He didn't want a public repeat of this weakness, so he had chosen to eat in private. He had been king for over thirty years, and he didn't need any vulnerability that his enemies could exploit. He knew the court was alight with rumours of his fragile health.

Baron Clifford had returned from Norway without Gyrid Hugleikkson and Alain d'Orthez. Clifford had told him that Orthez and Hugleikkson had perished, but he needed that confirmed in person. Clifford was ignorant of Margaret and his plotting to replace Bruce with her. The plot had failed, Margaret was dead and Longshanks had moved on in his scheming.

He pulled a parchment from his sleeve; the Clifford seal was still hanging by a tatty ribbon.

Sire,

We return without any cargo. Orthez and Hugleikkson are dead. Castle Audenborg was obliterated in a cataclysm only the devil could have created, and no one could have survived.

Our ship was nearly destroyed in the aftermath. We were lucky to survive, but God protected us so that we may return to serve.

I await your summons and pledge you my loyalty as your most humble servant.

Edward read Clifford's note again before throwing it into the heart of the fire.

He had not entirely wasted his time, because he was fermenting another plan to weaken Bruce and his ally King Haakon. He had an alternative king, the son of his puppet King of Scots, young Edward Balliol.

Edward Balliol was ambitious, stupid, and easily manipulated – the right profile for this role. Longshanks had put his father, John Balliol, on the Scottish throne in 1292, only to have to remove and exile him. Edward Balliol appeared more malleable. His principles could be bought for a gold circlet, ermine robes, and a purple cushion to place his arse on.

He understood that attraction as he sat back in his chair, upholstered in lavish silks embroidered in vivid colours, and for a moment he contemplated his achievements.

I am king, near seventy years old, and still in control. People were waiting for me to die but they were still scared of my power. It is only when I think of what comes after me that I regret not teaching my son to be a stronger man and a better king in waiting. I fear for the future, a future that must continue the fight in Scotland.

This space doubled as his bedchamber and audience room. He had risen only an hour before and heard mass the first of a five times a day ritual. He had an intense and direct relationship with God as an anointed king, and he needed to keep him close. Edward talked directly with God as a king and not through any priest. He believed God had approved of his rule and wouldn't allow him to act as he had in Scotland without his blessing. Mass was the conduit where God absolved him of any sense of guilt.

He heard the door open and the wood floors creak.

'Come in – I will eat now. I am hungry.'

Servants entered the room, bowing as they approached him. They placed linen cloths on the trestle table next to silver plates and goblets. Four places were set.

Platters of bread, cheese, and meat arrived. Stuffed chicken, a haunch of venison, and a loin of veal joined them, covered with pomegranate seeds, sugar plums, and sauce. Cheese and fruit were placed at the end of the table. The sweet and sour aroma filled the chamber.

He had fasted before the first Mass of the day. Now that he had gratified his soul, he would quench his thirst and satisfy his stomach as much as he could, and he hoped his bowels wouldn't grumble. He had lost weight, and his long, lithe frame was becoming frailer. He needed his strength to lead his army for one last campaign completing his conquest of Scotland.

Today he had asked for all his favourite foods, hoping that for one day he could be a glutton.

'Constable!' he cried out towards the antechamber where he knew his small collection of close advisors would be waiting.

Ralph de Sandwich bowed in front of the King. The King liked having a man even older than himself around. There were a handful of years between them, yet he was concerned that whilst he was visibly aging, Sandwich appeared more robust. The King's hair was white, his skin dry and wrinkled. Sandwich's hair still contained a hint of colour, and his skin was plump and pink.

'Lord Sandwich, I put down your indomitable good health to your days as a lawyer lifting nothing heavier than a quill. At the same time, I was fighting the heathens in the Holy Land deprived of food, warmth, and kingly comforts.'

'Your Grace and, as a result, I are destined to pay for my sins with many more years in purgatory.'

The King laughed at his wit hoping it was true.

'Constable, tell Baron Clifford and Edward Balliol I will see them now, and when you return, join us for prandial.'

'Yes, Sire.' De Sandwich hurried out the room.

He moved hesitantly the short distance from the fire to the carver chair at the near end of the trestle table. It was but a few steps, his legs were still supple from all the years of riding, but there was a creeping stiffness, and he groaned each time he stood up and sat down.

'Leave plenty of wine,' he shouted, and a servant darted towards the small wooden dresser where several silver pitchers of wine had been assembled.

The servant filled the King's goblet carefully, wiping down the side before the King raised it to his lips.

'Stay,' the King commanded.

The sweetened wine tasted wonderful. He rapidly drank the first goblet and then a second as Baron Clifford, Balliol, and de Sandwich arrived. Clifford looked as tired and troubled as any man whose ship had so nearly foundered.

'Sit. We have much to talk about.' The King pointed to the three empty seats. The English nobles sat on either side of the table closest to the King, outmanoeuvring Balliol, who was forced to sit furthest away.

Balliol was desperate to catch his king's attention. His relative rank meant he couldn't speak first, and he was most desperate to speak. He leaned forward to catch the King's eye. It was unnecessary as Longshanks knew what he wanted – the restoration of the Scottish throne to his family.

Longshanks were minded never to allow Scotland to be a kingdom again. It would be known as the Lands of Scotland; therefore, it had no need for a king. But that was only once he captured Bruce. Until then, Balliol could be useful. He had a reasonable following amongst the Scottish nobles who couldn't stomach a Bruce on the throne.

He would promise Balliol a crown, then remove the offer as soon as he didn't need him. For now, he would fuel the young man's ambition.

'Leave us after you have poured the wine.' The servants nervously filled each goblet and scurried away.

'Baron Clifford, I am glad to see you returned from the northern seas. However, we have come not to talk of your adventure, but of the Scottish throne and young Balliol.'

'Yes, Sire,' Clifford responded without hesitation. Edward didn't expect any other answer because he had no principles of his own.

The King was contemplating moving the baron into his inner circle. He had already rewarded him with James Douglas's lands in Scotland and was considering further reward.

'Eat, my lords,' the King ordered as he leaned forward and sliced a piece of veal. Delicately, he placed the meat on the end of his knife. The sauce dripped onto his plate. He then pulled off a leg of chicken glistening with fat and spiced fruit filling. He placed a piece of wheat bread next to it and started to soak up the juices.

The nobles hesitated, allowing the King to eat first, then quickly followed.

'Baron Clifford – I see you have lost some weight on your travels.' De Clifford nodded as he lifted bread and a rare slice of venison, still dripping with blood and covered with juniper berries, verjuice, and honey.

'And you have a healthy appetite, Constable,' the King added.

De Sandwich was already cutting a third slice of veal while at the same time pulling off the second chicken leg.

Balliol did not appear hungry, and the King suspected his nervousness had removed his appetite.

'How is your father's health? I hear he has retired to his chateau in Helicourt under the Pope's protection.'

'My father is content and wishes to live a quiet life now.' Balliol's face flushed. He had not been expecting the King's question about a man he had imprisoned and then exiled.

'Your father was crowned king of Scots. There is no grander station in life than to be crowned a king – God's anointed. Everything and everyone else pales in comparison. He didn't handle his responsibilities to me in the right manner and threw it all away in a fit of petulance.' The King was goading Balliol.

Balliol nodded. 'Many still regret his absence in the light of more recent events and the traitor Bruce. I will show better judgement and unswerving fealty.'

'You are right. No man should gain a throne through murder and keep it whilst an excommunicate.' Baron Clifford and de Sandwich banged the handles of their knives on the table in agreement.

'Even the grand traitor Wallace supported your father, and if there are a few disgruntled Wallace supporters still willing to support an alternative king, they could turn the nobility away from Bruce's cause and back to the Balliol's. What would you say about that?'

The King had a piece of meat on the tip of his knife and pointed it towards him.

'I would say that any Scot who believes in a just cause and the proper order would want a Balliol on the throne rather than a Bruce. I would deliver an obedient land and remove any challenges to your overlordship. Scotland would blossom in the peace English guardianship would bring.'

The King smiled; the young man's unctuous manner was

perfectly pitched.

Balliol was pushing the food around his plate – he had rehearsed this speech. It proved one thing – his ambition would make him greedy for the crown.

'Why should the King help you when your father failed?' Clifford interrupted.

'Because I am not my father. I am twenty-three years old, yet I am here asking for the King of England's faith and support. I am a fighter.'

'Courage, blood, and ancient right are a powerful trinity, and with my support you could turn this rebellion against Bruce.'

The King thought Balliol a better man than his father, but that was a relative measure.

'If I was King of Scots, you would always have a loyal and obedient friend in your Northern lands.' Balliol was saying what he wanted to hear, and he believed him.

Balliol could beat Bruce *and* turn sufficient wavering members of the Scottish nobility – especially now, whilst Bruce was weak. Then his rebellion would fade away, and his support would disappear like spring snow. What Longshanks wouldn't do was make the Balliol's hereditary kings. Edward Balliol would never be crowned; there would be no more Scotland, just lands to enrich his English realm.

'What support do you require from your king?' de Sandwich asked. He knew the King was using Balliol.

De Sandwich was clever and politically experienced. He had been an administrator to Longshank's father, Henry III, as well as Lord Chief Justice, Lord Mayor of London, and Constable of the Tower. At seventy-one, he still had ambition. He had not fought in a battle since Evesham in 1265, yet his insight was useful in enabling the King's plans.

'My constable, Ralph de Sandwich, can support any plan you might have with men and supplies.'

'Sire, I have stayed connected with my father's supporters.

There are many who are not prepared to follow Bruce. I have used them to keep close to the ill-informed who are helping him. I have people in many of the noble houses who will share important information on Bruce's plans and the whereabouts of his allies, including Christina of the Isles. She is Bruce's cousin. I have had reports she hid Bruce from the MacDougall's after the Battle of Dalrigh. They are now lovers and that she may be carrying his child.'

'You have good judgement, Balliol. The best informed of Bruce's whereabouts are his family. I recently had his brother-in-law Seton executed when he wouldn't talk. He is on display at Dumfries Castle.'

'Yes, Sire, and you generously joined Bruce's lands with mine.' Baron Clifford was greedily clearing the banquet, filling his cheeks with slivers of meat and chunks of bread that he had used to wipe the sauce away from his plate.

'My troops are pursuing his wife and brother,' the King said. 'I want no family left for him – no one to turn to for a desperate man, friendless and heirless. It is to be regretted that he may have a child with Christina Ranald. I would hear more of that, and if it proves correct, we must make sure she doesn't deliver any child to confuse the succession. Even bastards can inherit thrones.'

King Edward remembered he was a direct descendant of William the Bastard. Illegitimacy could be made legitimate.

'Christina has servants in my pay at her castles at Tarbert. She will join Bruce at some point, and then we can deal with them all.'

Balliol emptied his goblet, and the wine was making him confident. 'I have reports that Lords Percy and Valence have driven her away from Tioram and the castle is a ruin. Bruce was certainly hiding there. There is no word where he is now, but we will know soon. He will try and leave the mainland, as there is no place he can hide there. I also received news that only Ruaidhri Ranald survived Tioram.

Lachlann is dead.'

'I received dispatches from Lord Valence telling me this news. Lachlann had proved loyal, but there is a question surrounding his brother.'

'Sire, that is why our best course is to find Christina, and then we can use her to trap Bruce,' Balliol declared pleased with his proposal, but the King had already ordered Valence to capture her.

The King pushed away his platter and slammed his goblet down on the table, startling the gluttonous Baron de Clifford. He was fatigued, and he had heard enough. It was time for Mass, and he had made his decision.

'Baron Clifford, I want you to take young Balliol to your castle in Appleby and await my instructions. The constable will arrange men and arms, and you are to join with Valence and capture Christina – but only once your informant has located her. I want this done quietly and clinically. She must not know our intentions, and she must not escape. Once Bruce finds out we have her and she carries his child, he will find us or reveal where he is hiding. Now, all of you, leave me.'

They all bowed and moved towards the door before the King called them back.

'Balliol and Clifford, be prepared to leave tomorrow. Constable, send riders in advance and arrange for fresh horses every twenty miles. Time is critical. If the Bruce escapes the mainland before the first week of the autumn storms, he will have all winter to plot, and his survival will embolden more to rebellion.'

'Of course, Sire.' They all bowed and left the King. He returned to his place by the fire. He looked around and made sure no one was watching before collapsing into the seat.

The fire was glowing, but the fuel had been exhausted. His body felt chilled, but his mind was fired. He felt young again, like he had in the Holy Land before he had become king. When his beloved Queen Eleanor had been alive.

He had found a young rival for Bruce, determined to be king. He would hammer the Scots and their king. He would never give up.

'Boy, fix this fire.'

Chapter Ten

Akershus Fortress, Oslo, September 1306: Haakon Seeks the Treasure

Wamrok Skjelden knew this day had to come and yet had hoped it would not. His encounter at Audenborg Castle and the explosion that had followed were reported swiftly to King Haakon. The jarls of Western Norway were known for their ambivalence to the King, yet news of this event had been expedited to him. It was another sign of the uneasy peace between them. The nobles assumed it was the act of one amongst them, but it was none of them, and only Wamrok knew the truth.

He would not voluntarily speak of Audenborg. If it was known that he had betrayed the King on the matter of the Maid of Norway, he would face a traitor's death.

Now the countryside around Foerde was alight with theories that Audun Hugleikkson was alive and was returning to remove Haakon from his throne. The jarls had delighted in forwarding this treasonous gossip unfiltered to the King but had not gone as far as validating the rumours by exploring the castle.

Haakon would not be truly safe from dissent until he had fathered a legitimate son.

Wamrok was sitting in the courtyard, alone with these thoughts amidst the chaos of construction, surrounded by masons from England along with the odd smattering of French, Breton, and Gascon.

'Haakon's cautiousness around the English doesn't

extend to castle builders,' he mused as he studied the human interactions before him.

He scuffed his heels in the ground, wondering how today was going to end.

A Scottish master mason was in charge and had caught his eye. He was solidly built; his face baked with years in the sun and dust from the stones. He commanded the workforce with a gesture and a glance. Wamrok appreciated such presence, and his curiosity killed some time whilst he waited.

He had observed the dark-robed Dominicans wandering around, so he expected that despite Haakon's irregular arrangement with the Church, Rolf Steen would be with the king. Steen had been a fighting man before he took the cowl. One of Wamrok's captains, Olav Nielsen had once been a friend of his but no longer.

The main tower of crenelated granite and brick had a ground floor and two upper stories and overlooked the Oslofjord.

A perimeter wall ran around the tower and the main outbuildings; kitchens, stables, storerooms, and a small chapel were in the last stages of construction. The king's rooms were on the top floor of the tower.

A small harbour sat below this wall, and a heavy iron portcullis was set within the stone to allow the castle to be provisioned from the sea.

The two outer walls were each five yards high and three yards thick, pitted with holes to fire bolts and arrows from small towers at twenty-five-yard intervals. Two stout iron portcullises allowed access through the walls and spanned the gaps across the killing zones between each. Wamrok realised he had seen this design before.

Haakon was taking no chances, and the Akershus Fortress was based on the layout of the walls surrounding Constantinople. Wamrok had been in the Byzantine

Varangian Guard and had spent twenty years as a bodyguard for the Emperor Andronikos. Haakon had taken good advice.

The defences emphasised the permanency of Akershus. It was clear the King intended to make Oslo the centre of his realm, and it was no whim; this was forever.

He heard voices from below the wall, where three ships were docked. They were the king's ships, war galleys, and each deck had places for more than a dozen paired oars. The massive woollen sails were being waterproofed for their journey, and finally, on top of each mast, the king's colours flew.

These vessels were ready to sail, and the crews were examining the ropes and pulleys. The keels sat low in the water, heavy from the provisions stacked on the single deck.

His thoughts were interrupted when he heard his name.

'Commander Wamrok, the King is waiting.'

A servant wearing the king's livery of a golden crowned lion on a red field brandishing a silver axe was running from the perimeter wall and the entrance to the tower. The ditches were so steep that he tumbled over in his haste.

Wamrok climbed up the ditch and joined the increasingly impatient servant.

'Hurry up. Brother Steen is also with the King.'

He followed Wamrok to the second floor where the audience room was. It was filled with numerous carved chairs upholstered in sumptuous dark red velvet; cushions embroidered in heavy gold thread with the same House of Sverre emblem he had seen on the ships. The King sat on the other side of a large, dark oak table carved with mythical figures from the Norsk sagas.

The tall figure of Rolf Steen sat beside him. The seat was too small for his frame and broad stomach.

Steen, you are a devout man, but your devotion obviously didn't extend to depriving yourself of a very full diet.

Neither man greeted him with the usual pleasantries.

Steen and the King were studying a dispatch. The King mumbled as he read the dispatch a second and third time.

'All of you, leave us,' the King dismissed the servants and guards.

Wamrok was uneasy. This felt different, and he wondered if the King already knew. *Was the dispatch telling Haakon that Margaret was alive and Wamrok had deliberately left her in Audenborg?*

The King pointed to an empty seat, and Wamrok sat uncomfortably, waiting for someone to say something.

'Is my throne unsafe?' Haakon asked. 'I need some explanations.'

This was not how he expected the self-assured Haakon to behave.

'Sire, we didn't find any princess – only that old servant of Hugleikkson, the infirm Cnut Myhre, and several English masons. These foreigners were drunkards, and as we searched the castle, the keep exploded with such force that no one could have survived. The masons were English agents tasked to kill your guards, and my men were lucky to survive. Now not a stone of Audenborg remains on top of another. It is destroyed.'

Wamrok had rehearsed this statement, and in his mind it was true. He was sure he was convincing, because he believed what he was saying.

'Did you find any evidence that she had been there? We heard Audenborg burned for days. Olav Nilsen wouldn't build a castle that was easily destroyed.' Brother Steen shuffled in his chair, the oak squeaking under his weight.

Wamrok recognised there had been a discussion before his arrival. He had returned without Margaret, and they knew that. Were they giving him time to confess?

'It was obliterated, and we found nothing to suggest Margaret was there. The masons used the magic of black powder. Hugleikkson had several Templars and Crusaders amongst his men, and they stored barrels in the castle basement. Cnut Myhre had been at Acre and fought against the Mongols – and he would have learned of its power from them. It was the masons or Myhre behind the explosion. There is nothing else that can explain what happened.'

Wamrok didn't want to say anymore. He believed the best lies were those told simply.

'I also heard the story that Hugleikkson had stored up barrels in his cellars, intending to raise a rebellion against my authority before I had him hanged. The explosion certainly scared the local people – so much that they are refusing to work the land nearby.'

Wamrok couldn't control the palpitations in his heart and chest. He was sure his nervousness would give him away; he felt a slight tremor in his legs. He tried to control his breathing, but he felt his face flush. His chest felt like it was about to burst when the King looked up and nodded.

Haakon's manner changed, his shoulders relaxed, and he placed the scrolls to one side. Haakon believed him, and the superstitions of the local people had substantiated his story.

'Sire, will that be all?' Wamrok asked as he motioned to stand. He wanted to get away.

'Stay seated. I needed you to confirm what I had already heard about Margaret, but that was not all. Now I want to talk to you about a very important task. If you are successful, you could change the future of Norway forever.'

The King pushed the parchment he had been reading across the table to Wamrok. Wamrok lifted the document and started to read.

'The message is from my agent in Honfleur, Jakob Dedekam. He gathers all the news in the area, and he confirms other intelligence I have received over the past few months regarding Alaric's treasure. The treasure was in France, and I am guessing it is heading north away from France and England, possibly to the Scottish Western Isles or Norway. I requested confirmation and received that note a week ago. Since then, I have been preparing. You will have seen the three ships below this tower?'

'Alaric's treasure? That's a fable, like the sagas.'

Wamrok had heard of a legend involving a barbarian rebel who had sacked Rome in the fifth century and looted all its wealth.

'No myth. It is very real!'

Brother Steen had been quiet, and Wamrok knew he wasn't a reticent man, and shouted in his excitement.

Steen wasn't just here to dissect his time in Audenborg, he could smell the money. He was in desperate need of funds to build his churches and increase his profile with the Curia. He wanted to be pope and acquiring that crown took lots of money. This was his true intent, hidden beneath a thin veneer of humility. Olav had warned him about Steen's lofty ambitions and determination to succeed.

'It is a treasure of such magnificence that it could change the fortunes of our nation forever. We will no longer have to fight the English or the Danes to maintain our independence. With the treasure under my control, I won't have to concede any of my power to the traitorous jarls. My lack of a son will be of no matter, because the treasure will be my heir.'

Wamrok was loyal but hadn't had time to consider the treasure's power or even accept its existence.

'Sire, I had heard the legend, but I never expected it was true. It states here that the ship carrying the treasure is thought to be in Rouen, heading out of France to Scotland. It's sought by an ambitious trinity of competitors. The Byzantines have even hired a navy from the Genoese and are headed for France. The French King won't take kindly to losing such wealth to anyone else and considers it his by right of location.'

Wamrok read the note again, as there was a lot of information. It had been written in some haste, and the handwriting was difficult to decipher.

'You are right, Wamrok. Trying to capture the treasure in France wouldn't achieve anything except get a lot of good people killed. King Phillip can't be allowed to have the pope in one pocket and unimaginable wealth in the other. Why should it always be the French or the English that believe they are exceptional and that they should dictate how things should be? Why shouldn't the King of Norway own a pope and this wealth? I am determined power should shift away from these men who masquerade as noble rulers. We will use cunning and espionage, and I have Jakob Dedekam. He is guiding our actions, and I want you to work with him.'

Wamrok was not well connected after twenty years in Byzantium.

'Sire, Dedekam recommends we be patient and wait for the ship to travel out at Honfleur. It will sail through the Narrow Sea and northwards by the east coast of Ireland, as it is headed for Orkney. He has a plan to confuse and trick the pursuers, allowing the treasure to escape France and reach the open sea where we can intercept it.'

'Dedekam is following the Byzantine agent feeding information to these foreign ships. This agent is also tasked with recovering the treasure, but for the emperors. You know him – Axel Myhre, sometimes called Aurelian.'

Wamrok's eyes widened. 'I knew Myhre for many years in the Varangian Guard. The emperors trusted him, and he took on the state's most confidential dirty work, assassination. He is skilled at what he does and with the favour of the emperors, he was always one to be wary of.'

'Yes, I have heard the same. I have advised Dedekam to keep close to Myhre and exploit any discord,' Haakon was quick to acknowledge.

Steen nodded. 'Dedekam discovered the barge was heading to Orkney to Halcro in South Ronaldsay. His information is usually correct; he is an excellent agent.'

'And when the treasure reaches these islands, it will be on my lands,' Haakon said. 'I will assert my claim of ownership and rights of seizure. The Earls of Orkney are all Scots, and they have sworn allegiance to me as their overlord. You *will* seize it, and in this case, brute force will be required. To guarantee success, not only have I prepared three of my fastest and most robust warships, but I have also selected the best men to crew them. These are seagoing vessels and can travel to every corner of the world.'

The King was making it clear failure wouldn't be tolerated.

'I don't suppose you have persuaded Nilsen to come on this journey?'

Olav's estrangement with Steen had poisoned his relationship with the King, but the mission would be considered more important than a flawed association.

'Olav will command the second boat in your flotilla, and Jonas Fjelstad will lead the third. I have also secured most of your men from the former Varangian Guard. The ones with sea legs.' As the King discussed Olav, Steen looked away. Wamrok took this as a sign he didn't support his inclusion. The schism appeared as deep as ever. Wamrok was relieved that Olav would be with him.

'Sire, who is Jonas Fjelstad?'

'He is your navigator and can guide you to places where only the reckless would venture. Those that possess the treasure will be desperate to keep it and if they run, we must follow. Orkney is full of travelled men whose knowledge of the world is considerable. Where King Robert runs, the English follow. Neither the English nor the Scots can be allowed to get in the way. Amongst Bruce's men is Lord Henry Sinclair. It is said he has been further west than Groenland to a land of vines and honey. If Bruce runs with the money, he will use Lord Sinclair to lead that expedition, so Sinclair must be eliminated. It is also clear Bruce's men are currently controlling this treasure, since it is heading to Scotland. I am an ally of King Robert, so use restraint in any direct action with him, but show no mercy to his men, specifically Sinclair – and if it comes to the treasure, no alliance is worth it. The treasure will buy so many more.'

'I have heard of Henry Sinclair – his background and his reputation as a soldier and explorer was unrivalled outside the sagas. I know Halcro castle, it's on Ronaldsay,' Wamrok said. 'They called it Halcro's fortress, and I visited it with my father twenty years ago. I still remember the layout of the island. The castle stands overlooking the bay at the south end. It is a formidable structure with a tower, one of the highest on any island and not an easy prospect for a land attack. To capture a castle, you need siege weapons and overwhelming manpower, sometimes as many as ten attackers for every defender. It won't succeed with less than two hundred men, and starving them out would be impossible, would take years. We must capture the treasure at sea.'

Haakon appeared impatient, and Halcro's castle could be supplied from the land. Wamrok didn't have enough men to surround it.

'I agree, and I picked you because you have experience with these waters. Your knowledge combined with Fjelstad's is to our advantage. Fjelstad is one of the few men who understands the magic of the sunstone. His skills are of such value that he works only for me.' The King placed a purse on the table and removed a long clear crystal about the length of his fist. It was resting on a velvet cloth.

'Be careful when handling it. It fractures and splinters like a fingernail.' The King pushed the stone towards Wamrok.

'I have heard of these stones and how they allowed our ancestors to conquer the world, but I assumed the knowledge of how to travel without the sun's guidance had been lost.'

Wamrok picked the stone up and noticed that two small black circles were etched into the crystal close together on one side.

'Place it on top of the letter you still hold. When you place it on top of a word, you will see that the crystal duplicates the word.' The King pointed to Myhre's note.

Wamrok placed the stone directly over a word and saw a duplicate slightly below the original.

'Indeed, it does. How marvellous – but I don't understand how we can use it to navigate.'

Wamrok moved the crystal around the paper and saw that for every sentence, a second identical sentence appeared below.

'If you can find the sun, you know where you are. Look at those black circles. When you point them to the brightest point in the sky and the circles merge, there is the position of the sun. Fjelstad knows the finer points of its use, and he will need to educate so you should be on your way. Put it in this and take it to Fjelstad. He is waiting for it.'

The King slid the velvet purse over to him. Wamrok carefully placed the stone in the purse and tucked it inside his leather jerkin.

Steen passed a note to Wamrok. 'I have written your orders and provided safe passage. Many of the islanders are our subjects, but they don't take kindly to strangers, no matter who they might be. Read it on the ship and pass only the necessary information to your commanders not the crews.'

'You must not miss the tide,' the King added.

There were three goblets on the table nesting around a flagon of what Wamrok assumed was sweetened wine. He knew Haakon was particularly fond of this drink. The King had finished his instructions and poured two goblets of wine. Wamrok's goblet remained unfilled.

The audience was concluded, and it was time for Wamrok to leave.

Wamrok bowed before descending the steep steps of

the fortress tower past the ground floor and into the cellar. Outside he could hear the noise of the crew as they were making their preparations.

He walked the fifty yards to the ships, which were tied in a neat row to iron rings driven into the ground. Their bows pointed directly into the fjord, facing south.

The ships were bursting with provisions, and the decks were busy with men making everything ready for the open sea. The sails had been proofed for the winter journey with a foul-smelling wax to protect them from seawater. The ropes were rewound and ready for the next tide. The oars were resting in their fittings, ready to be plunged into the dark blue water lapping gently against the base of the fortress. The tide was turning, and within an hour, the waves would be taking them away from Akershus and northwest to Orkney.

Wamrok spotted Olav checking the stockfish which would provide them with the strength they needed to row across the sea.

He thought there were four or five hours before dark, then remembered Steen's note and opened it. Its contents were confidential, but everyone else was preoccupied.

Wamrok,

Fjelstad has the guile and experience to get you to Orkney as secretly as possible. He will avoid sailing too close to land once you leave the Norwegian coast. Remain in friendly waters as long as possible and hug the coast of Norway. You will move southwest and turn north. Then you will cross the open sea out of sight of land as far north as the weather allows to avoid detection. The sunstone will allow you to sail where others cannot follow. Avoid the mainland of Scotland until you get to Hjalsmdal on the east coast. Fjelstad knows routes in the open sea where enemy vessels will not venture. The fishermen at Hjalsmdal will have word if any ships have passed through the Pentland Firth towards Orkney. Your crew has been selected for its strength and loyalty, and they will not ask questions yet will give their lives for their king. Many have been selected from your own guard. Keep your own counsel. Only your commanders know the purpose of your mission is treasure. Men and supplies will be offered if you show this seal, as well as assurance of safe conduct. May the gods grant you grace and speed.

Embedded into the second parchment was the great seal of the House of Sverre. It was the same emblem of the crowned lion carrying an axe. Below, it read:

By the order of King Haakon, you must offer the bearer all assistance as may be requested and will be handsomely rewarded. Anyone hindering the bearer will be subject to the full consequences of the king's law and retribution.

'We have the sunstone and the king's advocacy. How can we fail?' He smiled. He had arrived at Akershus not knowing if he would leave alive, and now he was in command of three magnificent ships under the king's orders.

Wamrok carefully replaced the order back inside his jerkin.

Olav had his back to the quay as Wamrok stepped on board. The boat was new and smelt of resin, fresh-cut wood, and dried fish. The deck planks creaked directly behind Olav, and he turned around.

'Master Skjelden, I was wondering when you would join us,' Olav scoffed. 'Have Steen and the King offered us a new opportunity to die in his service?'

'Have you spoken with Steen?' Wamrok asked.

'He knows I am here.' Olav's reply was flat and intended to shut down this line of conversation.

'He is with the King, and they are deep in discussion. Their intrigues and plotting filled the room. Did you know the King wants to make him pope?' Wamrok wasn't allowing

Olav to divert the conversation. If he was going to risk his life, he wanted to know more about the man giving him orders.

'Steen wants to be pope. I told you he was ambitious. The humble churchman with a weak constitution is an act. He thrives on power and will live forever, and he doesn't hide what he wants. His relationship with the King is a practical one. Haakon wants to be the most powerful ruler in the world and Steen will help him do that, even if he believes our king is not of a pious nature, Haakon needs to make him pope to do that. Then he will be powerful in his own right and can control men's faith. They could achieve much together with all that money. Haakon is brave and Steen intelligent and sly.'

'So, you have heard about the treasure?' Wamrok was surprised by Olav's insight, but then he remembered they had spent twenty years in the Byzantine court where intrigue accompanied every meal.

'I was guessing based on gossip and a sprinkling of facts. There are still Varangians in Constantinople who hear things and write letters home. Axel Myhre has left the Byzantine court. Andronikos wouldn't send Myhre away unless it was something extraordinary. Andronikos was obsessed with getting back the treasure that was stolen from his family, and Myhre is the only man that old bastard trusts, so I made some assumptions.'

Olav was looking for a response, and Wamrok had no need to deny it.

Wamrok nodded. 'I have orders to seize it. It's heading to Orkney, but only the two of us and Fjelstad will know what is in the ship we are to capture. Are we well prepared?'

Wamrok would need to have a man in his company who wouldn't be compromised by the possession of such incredible wealth. He would rely on him and his loyal Varangians to control the crew once they realised what was in the cargo.

Olav was the luckiest man he knew, and his presence amongst his men gave him confidence.

'Indeed, we are – or at least, I think we are. I have enough chests of food and wine to keep us supplied for months, and I even managed to smuggle a couple of barrels of that marvellous black powder we used to demolish Castle Audenborg. I thought it might come in handy – and it's our secret.' Olav pressed his finger to his lips.

'I missed the sea when we were in Constantinople. We became full-time soldiers and recreational sailors. Not to worry, though – on board are many men who are equally at home on the sea and the land. They will help us – and of course, there is Fjelstad.' Olav grinned as if he knew something Wamrok didn't, an unwelcome surprise.

'What Norwegian doesn't know how to sail a boat?' Wamrok said. 'I could before I could walk. We build the best boats in the world, and we have the men to sail them. I assume that man over there is Jonas Fjelstad. I have something for him.' He pointed to the ship furthest away from them. The man was not engaging with the rest of the crew and stared at the horizon.

'He is known to a few of the men, and they speak highly of him but comment on his eccentricity. He is a man who thrives with a fixed routine. He eats and drinks at the same time, and always the same meal: stew and bread. Bread at the bottom and stew on top, spoon on the right-hand side. He gets upset if it is any other way, but he is a good sort.'

Wamrok saw that Fjelstad ignored the noise and bustle around him as the men loaded the ship and avoided eye contact. He had met people like this before and understood their value. They had a fixation, a skill, and little interest in anything outside that narrow area.

Olav continued, still grinning. 'He has been asking repeatedly about a sunstone as if I knew what it was. I showed him my looking glass to shut him up, and he wouldn't give it back.'

'The one we used for seeing faraway objects close up?' Wamrok asked.

'Yes, that one. I told him not to point it at the sun or spend too long squinting through the lens. He listened to me about the sun but spent hours watching across the fjord. I had to insist. It wasn't that he was a thief; he was fascinated, like a child with a new toy. He kept mentioning some heathen called Ibn al-Haytham and his *Book of Optics* … look.'

Olav pointed at Fjelstad.

'He always carries a copy with him. Squinting with my prism made him dizzy, and he nearly fell over the side. Likes to count things and makes notes. Don't get him talking about Bologna University – he never shuts up about his time with Brother Albertus. I like him, but he is certainly different.'

Next to Olav, resting on a barrel, was a skin stretched to its limit with liquid. Two tankards were conveniently hanging above it. Wamrok was hoping it was ale or sweetened wine.

'I assume you prepared refreshment knowing I was coming on board?' Wamrok pointed at the skin.

'After twenty years, you can read my mind. A chest full of skins arrived this morning, a gift from the King – sweetened wine, and from his personal cellar. You are favoured.'

Olav clumsily poured the liquid into each flagon and handed one to him.

'Apparently Fjelstad will lead in the first ship, and you and I will follow in the other two under my overall command. Does he know I am in command?' Wamrok asked.

'Yes. He doesn't seem to have directed many men, but he really understands boats. He prepared and checked everything whilst I was still sleeping and made no complaint. It's good to have a thinking man on board. He is not a Varangian, though.'

Olav was dismissive.

'Give him time, it will take men of many skills coming together to make this mission successful – there are more than enough of the old guard here,' Wamrok added, as he recognised a few of the palace guards. Many had served at the Palace of Blachernae, carving out a little oasis of Norwegian culture in the heart of Constantinople and spent many years together. These men had made enduring friendships that extended over many years, and that level of allegiance was hard to create in any army.

'He hasn't fully explained his role yet. Have you got his damn sunstone?' Olav asked as Fjelstad approached them.

'It's in a safe place, next to my orders.' Wamrok reached inside his jerkin, retrieved the velvet purse, and held it out by his side.

Fjelstad was neither young nor old, and dressed in the tatty clothes of a peasant: a long woollen tunic, hose, and a cape. The remarkable thing was their state of repair. It was clear that he had little interest in his appearance. Unusually, on the left of his tunic he had a top pocket, and Wamrok could just see a lens.

'Sirs, good day.' Fjelstad bowed.

'I am Wamrok Skjelden, and I believe you have already met Olav Nilsen.'

Fjelstad caught Wamrok staring at his pocket.

'I see you are looking at my eyeglasses. They allow me to see small things much more clearly. They are a gift from my friend Alessandro della Spina. He is a Dominican friar like me. I found reading stones useless on ships, and as these are fixed on my nose, I can see even in the stormiest weather.'

Fjelstad fixed the lenses on either side of his nose. An ivory mount and bridge held the glasses in place.

'I find lenses so interesting. Your crystal for bringing distant items close I found fascinating, incredible.' Fjelstad's enthusiasm was palpable as he placed it back in Olav's outstretched hand.

Wamrok had not been told Dedekam was a cleric, only that he was a navigator. He wondered why Steen had not told him that Fjelstad was a Dominican. He would have known that Wamrok would have questioned him further. Their loyalty to their order was taken as an oath when they accepted the cowl. He wondered if the self-absorbed demeanour and eccentricity were an act to make him seem like less of a threat. In Wamrok's experience, Dominicans were calculating and ruthless. Now he had another risk to consider. Who was Fjelstad working for, the king or the Church? He would watch him closely from now on. He squinted at Olav, who appeared unconcerned by the confession.

'Is that my sunstone in the purse?' Fjelstad pointed to the purse by his side, which Wamrok handed him. He jumped with joy and then sat on the deck and delicately opened the purse, cupping the stone in his hands.

'It takes time and luck to find a crystal of this quality.' Fjelstad's voice had dropped to a whisper, as if sound itself could shatter it into pieces.

'I heard these crystals are fragile.' Wamrok lowered his voice too, Fjelstad treated the stone like a holy relic.

'They are useless rocks if they fracture. Their power is in their clarity. Only whole can they read the power of the sun and tell me where we are positioned.' Fjelstad held the stone up to the sun. 'The stones are only of use when we can't see the sun, and on such a fine day they are valueless, but come the approaching months when the sun is obscured for weeks on end, they are more valuable than gold.'

He placed the stone back in the pouch and into his top pocket.

'Master Wamrok … what are our orders?' Fjelstad asked.

'We are to leave on the next tide, hug the Norwegian coast as long as we can, and head for Orkney stopping at Hjalsmdal for supplies and the local gossip. We are to capture a ship and return with its cargo to King Haakon. You will lead, Fjelstad, so we will need to keep close and use horns and lamps to keep in touch.'

Wamrok noticed several large iron lamps had been secured to the masts of every ship.

'The ships are all well stocked with oil lamps and candles,' Fjelstad said. 'I have provided a Gjallarhorn on each ship to allow us to keep in contact when we are fogbound. I have selected a man from each ship to calculate our positions, and now I know the route, I can instruct them accordingly. Orkney is made up of many islands, and they are spread over a considerable distance. Do we know where this ship is hiding?'

'Halcro Castle is the destination, on South Ronaldsay.'

'Commander, the tide is turning, so we should be onboarding our ships, ready to cast off. I will lead, and we will head south out of the fjord. We can anchor off the coast and head north tomorrow with a full day's light to guide us.'

Fjelstad did not wait for Wamrok to answer, but turned and headed off to Wamrok's ship, which was the last of the three moored and furthest away from the exit at Akershus.

'Olav, you should join your men. They are waiting.'

Olav's vessel was berthed second, and the crew were already in position to start rowing. Fjelstad's ship was untied, and the huge square sail had been unfurled, ready to catch the first wind, which was conveniently blowing off the land, southwards towards the open sea.

Wamrok was now alone.

'Untie the ropes and get ready to leave, men. We have many miles to travel.'

The crew cheered, settled back, and made themselves ready to row.

Chapter Eleven

Rouen Cathedral, September 1306: Henry the Young King's Tomb

Jean de Bretagne scoured the streets for anyone suspicious. He stopped frequently amongst the small houses which crowded the area, snaking up the small hill from the harbour to the cathedral, looking for any unwelcome company. His eyesight was limited from a dead eye, but he compensated for it with an experienced sense of the unusual and the dangers that lurked behind any strange event.

He liked to spy on people, so between the cracks of the wood frames, he stared into people's houses and watched as they ate, drank, slept, and had sex. His voyeurism unnecessarily diverted him, but he couldn't stop himself from being distracted.

Bretagne didn't fear attack – he could handle the boldest of assailants – but he didn't want to be seen because it would risk exposing a part of his life he wished to remain secret. He struggled to hide who he really was because he knew that despite his nobility, he would always be a rogue, and that part of him helped fool people. No one really knew him, and he was happy in that state, because he had to remain hidden until his position could be revealed. The time was not right. He needed the treasure to take up the station he deserved.

There were about six rows of densely packed wooden houses, stables, middens, and workshops. Each building almost touched the ones opposite before they eventually cleared to reveal Rouen Cathedral.

Every time I stand in front of you I am overwhelmed by your magnificence. You dominate the town in every way. I have come to see the chapel dedicated to Our Lady and seek counsel.

The west front portal door was open, ready for the evening worshippers. The area was gloomy, and the rain was heavy. He wrung the bottom of his woollen cape, which had become saturated by the downpour, and looked around again for any spectators. This was his secret devotion, and he didn't want to share it.

'Only the most fervent will be attending Mass tonight, only a zealot would go out on a night like this – or a scoundrel.'

Standing beneath the upright of the baker's shop, he had a little protection from the rain. He stared admiringly at the decorated portal and smiled as water dripped off his nose. The Virgin was bathed in a sea of light as the brightly coloured stones beneath her depicted the Tree of Jesse.

'I am in pursuit of my family. Holy mother, protect me, as I seek guidance from them.' His actions wouldn't normally attract the intercedence of the saints, but he had rationalised that God would value him more as a sinner than a pious man who had nothing to repent.

The area was quiet thanks to the weather, so he pulled his cloak over his head and walked purposefully towards the door. Candles guided him into the nave, as the priests busied themselves preparing for the Mass.

He had removed his gaudy red boots, replacing them with something less ostentatious, because they were for show, and a hallmark of the man he pretended to be. Beggars and those seeking shelter from the weather were gathering in the nave.

He hurried towards the choir, which was in the east at the opposite side from the entrance. The choir was separated from the nave by a screen, but the masons had left rubble, and he could move inside unseen.

The priests had almost finished their preparation. Soon the mass would start.

The priests won't look for me in the choir. They are only looking for the congregation in the main nave.

The choir was darker, because the windows had been covered with cloth to protect them from the work beneath, but there was a little light to guide him diffusing from the nave. He trod slowly through the random rubble, which extended to the far end of the choir. Discarded shards of stone were covered with the dark, silty soil that indicated their proximity to the river.

He was careful, he didn't want to alarm anyone by falling over. The rocks and shards looked sharp, which was why they had been stored here, away from the congregation.

He could see a faint candle ahead, and as he approached, he fell to his knees. He had been here before, but the presence of this tomb overwhelmed him.

'I have missed being in your presence, dear Uncle Henry,' Bretagne whispered as he placed his hands on the tomb.

The figure lying horizontally on the tomb was that of a young knight, long-limbed, wearing splendid armour and a golden coronet. This was the final resting place of Henry, the young King of England. Crowned whilst his father Henry II still lived but then died six years before him.

Offerings surrounded the sculpture. It was a place of pilgrimage for those that hoped for blessed intercedence in heaven. Numerous candles had been lit, and pilgrim badges had been placed carefully around the carved figure. The face still showed the original painted features, which were handsome, framed by cascades of long yellow-gold hair.

Bretagne closed his eyes and mouthed a prayer but was interrupted; he heard an echo as if a candle or lamp had fallen from its mountings. He drew his sword, ready to abandon his prayer, when he saw the shadow of a scurrying rat running underneath the rood screen towards the central choir. It navigated around the tomb as he knelt.

'You were lucky tonight.'

He lifted his sword and then thought better of the screams the animal would make if he ran it through. He pushed his sword back into its sheath and took several mouthfuls of poppy water. Since his injury he had relied on it to relieve the pain in his head.

His voice was a whisper, his eyes closed, and his thoughts moved into another state.

'Dear Henry, you have guided me these past few years in my thoughts and prayers, and now I must ask for your help. How can I restore our fortunes in France and seize the English crown that should be ours. Edward Plantagenet occupies a throne that isn't his.'

The choir lit up in golden rays, and he could see Henry in his shroud, his crown in place and his face surrounded in a halo like the icons and holy depictions that were in every window of the cathedral. The young king had stepped out from the past and was speaking to him like the Archangel Michael.

The years had not aged him, and he was still twenty-eight, his age at death.

'You are the rightful heir to my crown, and to that end you must seize Alaric's treasure and use its power to restore the proper order, the true heirs to England and Brittany. Your ancestor, Geoffrey of Brittany, my brother, comes before John and his line. I have guided you into the heart of the English court. They trust you and believe you are working for them. Now you must trust me again – work for yourself. King John betrayed us all in seizing your birthright and doesn't deserve your loyalty.'

The vision became more powerful, and he sensed Henry's breath on his face. Bretagne felt that if he stretched out his arms, he could embrace Henry's body.

This was indeed a message from God and could not be

ignored.

The voice sounded so loud and clear he was sure the priests could hear it, yet he didn't want it to stop. He wouldn't open his eyes and let it disappear; he wanted to stay close, as the vision gave him confidence and purpose. Now the treasure was nearby he needed to know what God's will was.

'What must I do?' Bretagne pleaded.

'Retrieving the treasure is the key to your restoration. Once you have it, you can continue our work – beware there is another heir to my brother Geoffrey that lives amongst the Scots, who must be removed. King Edward and his heir are weak, and you are strong. They must all be eliminated and God's will is that you rule alone. Reestablish the rightful line of the Plantagenets and finally take your place amongst our glorious ancestors.'

Suddenly the vision imploded. Henry's presence and the light vanished, and Bretagne was alone, kneeling on the cold stone.

'Don't leave, Henry, there is so much more I need to know about the family and Geoffrey.'

He held his eyes closed, expecting that at any moment an angry congregation would arrive, demanding to know about the voice of a long-dead king and the sorcerer that had brought him to life.

He opened them slowly and discovered he was alone apart from the near exhausted candles that burned on Henry's tomb.

Henry's voice was now replaced by the chanting of the Mass. It would end soon, and instead of the uncertain man who had entered the cathedral, he was leaving more confident than ever. He was motivated each time he visited the tomb, whenever his spirit was weakened, being next to his sainted uncle's bones gave him strength.

He would return to L'Auberge du Lion and the duplicitous Bernard du Gascon. Bretagne had studied him these past months and had observed his furtive behaviour. He had been reported dead just after the explosion on the Seine and then had miraculously reappeared. Bretagne was sure he was the key to the treasure; he always was involved in events – he was in contact with the Scottish rebels, he knew Wallace and John de Wishart. Will de Irwyne and Jamie Wishart, the men he had transported so many months ago had disappeared from his tavern. The sailors Bretagne had sent to follow them had died at the inn. He didn't believe these were coincidences.

'It is all beginning to fit together, and Bernard du Gascon is at the heart of this conspiracy. Always in the thick of it with Rouen's villains, whilst pretending he is nothing more than an amiable host. He is working for Bishop Wishart or Geoffroi de Charnay, probably both.'

He was convinced Bernard had helped the Scots escape from the men he had sent to the tavern to kill them. If Hugh de Verneuil had been involved, it would explain much about how the Scots had escaped him last March.

'Bernard, how could you believe that I would not see you meeting with Hugh de Verneuil, the creature of Geoffroi de Charnay, and understand your connection with the Scots, the Templars, and the treasure? And why would the preceptor of the Templars, one of the most powerful men in the land, be communicating with an innkeeper in Rouen?'

Hubert de Lacy's messages had told him that Scottish agents were active in the town and that Geoffroi de Charnay was helping them and had hidden Alaric's treasure within the Temple. He had seen the Templar seal amongst Bernard's papers.

Bernard had neither realised that he had searched his private rooms nor understood that Bretagne would recognise the seal's importance. He had carefully cultivated the impression of a careless rogue who worked only for himself, but he was far more calculating, and Bretagne kept that side for himself.

He had been right to follow Bernard when he had left in the dead of night, headed towards Chateau Gaillard, and then disappeared, only to reappear outside Gaillard. Now he knew for certain the treasure barge was hiding in a tributary to the south of Rouen. Pierre Nogaret's note had cost him a purse of gold, but Guy had never let him down even if his information was expensive. He would gather his men once Madame and her henchmen had left Rouen and then seize the treasure for himself. The English had outstayed their usefulness. It was his opportunity now, and he would keep close to the Gascons. They will know its precise location.

'I will watch you and your son Guillaume even more closely. If the treasure is to head to Scotland, you will have to make a run for it very soon. The sea won't forgive a later departure, and then it will be mine.' His voice was soft but his intent hard and he knew what he must do.

The last section of the Mass was underway, and Bretagne decided he would leave with the other pilgrims.

The priest's resonant voice spoke the *Benedicamus Domino*, and the congregation started to head out the main entrance on the west side.

Bretagne snuck out the way he had come in and joined the small group that was escaping into the sombre night. No one looked at their neighbours; the devout were more interested in remaining dry and rushing back to their homes and once outside, they scattered in all directions, and he was alone.

He was keen to rush away, not because of the rain, but to get back to the inn. He would look for anything to indicate where the Scots were hiding.

He pulled his cloak over his head, wrapped his scarf around his face, and started to run through the puddles that were filling the streets.

*

A figure watched Bretagne hurry past the front of the

cathedral before disappearing down towards the harbour.

Bretagne's immediate destination was hidden by the narrow gap between the rows of wooden houses. Even shadows were concealed amongst these lanes. No one bothered with lighting such places at night, and as a result they were a haven for violence, robbery, and clandestine activity.

'With a bit of luck, he will be robbed.'

The rats took the opportunity to dine on whatever had been thrown into the open sewer running down the middle of the street. Street dogs hid underneath the houses, eyeing the rats and their feast before grabbing those fattened rodents that ventured too close.

'So, you are back at the cathedral, praying or plotting,' Bernard whispered, his face hidden by his hood. 'I know it is the latter. John de Wishart was right about your callous nature. I heard it from your own mouth. Even the rats don't kill their kin.'

The rain was coming down harder, bouncing off the roofs and cascading into the hard-packed roads, which now resembled small rivers. The detritus was starting to float, following Bretagne down the small hill where the cathedral sat towards the harbour.

Not everyone had been listening to the priest and now Bernard knew everything. Bretagne was heading back to L'Auberge to find a treasure and kill anyone that got in his way. The worst charlatans always believe they are guided by God because that fits into their foolish sense of entitlement. I know it is nothing but your own twisted imagination, and I will stop you.

A rat ran across Bernard's boots and out from under the protection of the overhanging building. It was unafraid as it cleaned its face of all traces of its meal. Bernard wondered if it could be the same one that had saved him as he hid behind the tomb adjacent to the young king and had heard everything.

'Thank you. If it hadn't been for your intervention in the cathedral, I would surely have been discovered.'

The rat acknowledged the praise before running under the nearest building.

Bernard remained silent, waiting until he was confident that Bretagne would be back at his tavern. He knew how careful he had been to cover his regular visits to the young king's tomb. Bretagne had layers of arrogance woven into his soul and had forgotten that there were many good agents in Rouen, better soldiers that could follow any man without being observed.

Bernard had learned his craft in Gascony while searching for those who had harmed his Cathar brothers, hiding in plain sight and quietly eliminating those who would do harm. He would use these skills again when the time came to deal with Jean de Bretagne.

Chapter Twelve

Rouen, September 1306:
The Wolf Hunters

Murdie was overjoyed and relieved to meet with Bernard du Gascon. He had shown him the Seal of the Guardians of Scotland which he recognised, and they bonded immediately.

'You are like all good landlords, a layer of geniality hiding a torso of iron.'

Bernard acknowledged the compliment, but Murdie wasn't here to praise the ambience.

'I work for Bishop Wishart – I am here to find Jamie Wishart, and the men he sent here.'

Bernard pointed to an empty table at the far end of the open public room. It was early evening, and the tavern was filling rapidly.

'I know the Bishop well and I know where they are, and the treasure – I just can't tell with all these people around. I feel like I am being watched all the time.' Murdie understood the need for secrecy.

'Half the rulers in Europe are looking for them, and there are spies everywhere.'

Bernard pointed towards the customers nearby. 'There is a free drink and stew waiting for you at the bar.' Free was the magic word and everyone cleared from their immediate area.

Murdie had met Will de Irwyne, and Innes de Mayon in the past with Wallace at Stirling Bridge and Falkirk, though it had been many years ago. Hendor was a good friend and they had both been part of the Bishop's household.

Murdie couldn't deliver on his promise to Gyrid without men, and they in turn needed help to get the treasure out of France. He now realised why Bishop Wishart had sent him to Bernard.

'Bishop Wishart spoke fondly of you and he was no fool, you are the right man to help me. Returning the treasure to Scotland is vital – it can't fall into the hands of the English and King Robert needs it more than ever after Methven and Dalrigh, to buy weapons and men.' Murdie knew from Valence's letters the efforts Edward was making to retrieve the treasure.

'Where is your ship, Murdie?' Bernard asked anxiously.

'Waiting at Honfleur – we made it in eight days from Bergen. Our navigator steered the ship through early autumn storms with a mixture of calmness and sheer determination – Gyrid and I travelled the last miles from Honfleur on horse. We left the crew preparing the ship for Scotland – be reassured it is unobtrusive. The harbour is busy this time of the year with the spoils of furs and ivory from the north. We arrived like any other Norwegian merchants, hidden in plain sight.' Murdie was confident that they remained undiscovered.

'Good, the treasure will have to pass through Honfleur to escape France. Out at sea, the French King's forces count for nothing but here he has a garrison. King Phillip has no standing navy, and your ship can help Jamie; two ships are two more than the French have.'

Bernard was right but Murdie needed to see the men he had travelled so far to see. Bishop Wishart had sent the seal to Jamie, it had meaning for every Scot and he had to deliver it.

'Gyrid is waiting in the room above the stable block – she isn't a patient woman and is just as interested in knowing where Jamie is hiding.'

Murdie could see Bernard's hesitation.

'I have put this secret so far back in my mind I fear I may forget – Jamie and his companions are in a cave below Chateau Gaillard and are currently moving the treasure from the barge to a cog supplied by Geoffroi de Charnay. His captain Laurent d'Aumale is helping load the treasure right now – I don't want to take you there, as I may be under investigation by Guillaume du Nogaret, I received this information from his nephew Guy, so I am taking it seriously. The risk is so great that I can't stay in Rouen under his eye and I can't risk leading someone to their hiding place.' Bernard paused. His body was tense, and his fist started to clench.

'I will be leaving here with them.'

That wasn't everything Bernard wanted to share, and his voice dropped to a whisper.

'The cog will dock in a berth just below the tavern, and we will make our escape. I will need extra swords in case Jean de Bretagne or Madame and her henchmen, Les Frères Loups, try to stop us.'

'Madame, I have heard of her – she works for King Phillip?' Murdie remembered her from Valence's correspondence.

'A slip of a girl, but don't underestimate her – she is more ruthless than any man. We have a plan to get her to follow the barge, which is filled with rocks and sand, but that won't fool her for long. We need to be far from here when they discover the truth. I am waiting for Geoffroi de Charnay's captain Hugh de Verneuil to join us. I am worried that he may have been arrested. The roads are filled with Valois's guards stopping everyone as well as gold hunters who will slit a throat for a coin.'

Murdie nodded. He had kept Gyrid away from the tavern's public room for her safety. He understood the fervour gold could create amongst people who had nothing and therefore nothing to lose. For them, killing was often a consequence of greed or desperation.

'Today the talk in the tavern was nothing but gold and arrests. There was an old man who came in this morning with a purse full of pure coins. I later heard he had been murdered and his eviscerated corpse washed up on the shore. He had signs of torture on his face – branded with an iron. I have been exposed to violence for many years, yet I am still surprised that people will kill for money.'

'It sounds like the work of Les Frères Loups,' Bernard said. 'Anyone indiscreet enough to wear a weighty purse, or suspected of a connection with the barge, the gold, or the Scots will be targeted by these men. People are disappearing from the streets. There are rumours of dead bodies in gutters. In a realm so starved of money and compassion, death doesn't seem to put anyone off. Hendor Robertson warned me about these men – they tortured him and removed some of his fingers.'

'I know about Hendor, he is a close friend – being such beasts disqualifies them from living amongst us.'

Murdie was not violent, but now that he had found out the names of the men who had so injured his friend, he would make a point of seeking them out. After the mutilation, Hendor had hidden away and isolated himself from his wife and son, consumed with shame. Some churchmen blamed mutilation on the victims, as if it was some form of judgement, when Hendor had simply been on the receiving end of vile cruelty.

'Murdie, I saw them, just minutes away from here, on the streets by the cathedral. They are beasts indeed except animals don't kill for fun,' Bernard replied.

Earlier, Murdie had rested and then explored Rouen, looking at the escape routes and assessing the numbers of guards, so he had studied that area of town.

'I walked around Rouen earlier whilst Gyrid slept, even went to Mass at the cathedral. The talk in the streets nearby was less about God and more about the gold washing up on the shore,' Murdie said. 'I listened to many of the clerics as wine loosened their tongues; their discussions more commercial than spiritual. I was gathering information, seeing if anyone had heard about the barge. The belief is that the ships involved in the explosion were destroyed.'

Bernard interrupted, 'As for the chattering clerics, they may have stopped searching. The French agent Madame believes otherwise, which is why we have swapped the cargo to another ship. She is looking for a barge and whilst she follows that, we will escape in a seaworthy cog that will take us to Scotland – Geoffroi de Charnay has made all the arrangements.'

Murdie had heard gossip in the town that there were underground caves full of goods and money on route to the pope. The Church was just concerned with making money and keeping their taxes away from the king.

'I overhead a couple of monks describing two men who were hiding in a church house on the Rue de Faulx – they had left and were seen heading south out of Rouen. They also let slip that Charles de Valois owns this house.'

Murdie ran his right hand up his left sleeve, feeling for the outline of the blade, and nodded, satisfied that it was secure and in place.

Guillaume appeared at his father's side. The noise in the tavern was becoming so loud it was difficult to hear.

'People are forcing themselves through the door. Should I bring more wine and beer from the stores?' Guillaume was competing to be heard as even more people piled into the crowded tavern, pushing each other out of the way. Bernard's wife and two other servers were coping, but only just. 'Word of the gold has brought people from distant counties – I have heard every dialect in France.'

Murdie liked Guillaume, he had charisma like his father and hoped he wouldn't be caught up in any violence.

'Now you would be hard pressed to hear anything, son

– yes, go fetch some barrels. I have stored them in Jean's room. We should not assume everyone hanging around here is necessarily after food and wine. Alcohol loosens tongues quicker than torture.'

Guillaume nodded and smiled.

'Go quickly,' Bernard called after him.

'Jean's room is on the ground floor below your room, but no one goes there in case they are afflicted – he is a leper.'

Guillaume left through the rear of the tavern and headed for the lane that led to the stables.

Murdie's senses were heightened, and he looked for any indications of trouble, the mismatched signs of people pretending to be something else. Overly tatty clothes and a smart sword, oversized clothes that covered mail. The stance of the soldier rather than the stoop of a peasant or fisherman. He could spot their awkwardness at a distance, but it was hard to identify anyone in this crowd. All he could see were disjointed arms and legs and the fleeting appearances of the red-booted Jean de Bretagne. Bernard had told him that the English agent stayed in the Inn.

Bishop Wishart had played Bretagne over the years but had always known he was working for himself. The English were the best means to get what he wanted – money, position, and power.

'Bretagne is holding court as usual with his slimy sidekick Nicolo,' Bernard said. 'I see you were looking at Bretagne. He appears drunk but misses nothing. I put up with his arrogance as he rented rooms and spent readily in the tavern on himself and his cronies because I knew who he was. He thinks he was using me, but all the time I was using him. Wallace and John de Wishart used him to feed information to the English.'

Murdie wondered what was taking Guillaume so long. Then he felt a hand on his shoulder and turned, keeping his right hand near his left sleeve.

'Murdie, Father, can you come with me?' Murdie could see the seriousness in Guillaume's face. His youthfulness had vanished.

'Go where? What is it, boy?' Bernard replied.

Guillaume pulled them towards the side door and the stables.

'Just follow me, the others can manage for a few minutes … Hugh is here.'

Murdie stepped into the narrow lane and could see a small shack below the stable. The door was ajar.

Guillaume and Bernard went inside, followed by Murdie, and the door slammed behind them. A lamp lit up Hugh's face.

'Apologies for all the secrecy. I recognised Jean de Bretagne's back as I passed the front door … Who are you?' Hugh embraced the others whilst keeping an eye on Murdie.

'This is Murdoch MacBeith,' Bernard interjected before Murdie could answer. 'He works for Bishop Wishart.'

'Just call me Murdie. Only my mother ever called me Murdoch.' Murdie extended his hand, which Hugh gripped strongly.

'I have been travelling many miles over the past few days between Paris and Rouen, so I rested a while in Jean's hovel. I assumed that with its associations with leprosy, I would be undisturbed.' Hugh dropped onto the ramshackle bed and sighed. Murdie was looking at a man relieved to be seeking refuge in a leper's shack.

'That's the same reason we keep the stores here. Even thieves value their life. Geoffroi wrote to me about the switch. Laurent should have moved all the cargo to the cog. I hope it will dock in the berth below the tavern this evening.' Bernard pulled up a stool, and Murdie followed. Hugh didn't answer as his gaze fixed on Murdie.

'I assume you are here to help us get this treasure back to Scotland?' Hugh asked.

'In part, I am also here to fetch Jamie. His uncle, Bishop Wishart, is in an English dungeon, and I need all the men guarding the treasure to rescue him. Wishart is considered a great traitor by the English King.' Murdie was reticent. Whilst he trusted Guillaume, knowing about their intentions to rescue the Bishop would put the boy in danger. He scowled at Bernard, who took the hint.

'Guillaume, I think you should return and help your mother. Take another barrel of ale and wine with you. Return and bring some food for us, and some goblets – and keep an eye out for anyone coming down the lane.'

Guillaume nodded and rolled two barrels through the door, one in each hand, before closing the door tight. The latch held fast as it snapped shut. Murdie listened at the door for voices and footsteps.

'You said a leper lived here?' Murdie asked.

'Jean, lived here for many years and retained a modest degree of dignity. The Church encourages charity to the sick on the one hand whilst also preaching that the diseased are forsaken by God on the other. That is why I left the Church many years ago.'

Hugh raised an eyebrow. 'Bernard, that's a dangerous thing to say in such times. The Inquisition hunts for people with no religion.'

'I have religion, Hugh; I just don't care much for the Church. One of their own tried to kill me – a young English monk when I was fighting in Gascony. My issue with the Church is primarily a personal one, yet the hypocrisy is breathtaking. Most lepers live outside and are shunned wherever they go. I took the New Testament approach of kindness and let him stay here. "He who is without sin," and all that. Look behind you.' Bernard pointed to a long, flat linen cloth lying on a shelf.

'Lift it down, but be careful as you unwind it,' Bernard warned.

Hugh took the bundle from the shelf and placed it on his lap. He started to unwind the cloth, exposing a sword.

There was only a small lamp illuminating the room, but the blade caught the light and sparkled. The finely enamelled pommel held a dark green quartz stone with a gold fault running through it.

'Jean appears to have had an interesting life before disease changed him, he will come with me and return to the Temple where we have an infirmary. He can spend what remains of his time in relative comfort,' Hugh commented as he gently rewound the sword and placed it back on the shelf.

'Where is he now?' Murdie recognised the sword. The dark green stone proclaimed the owner as a Scottish noble, and he had seen such a decoration amongst the Crusader knights who had served in the Holy Land.

'He is at Gaillard with your friends and the treasure,' Bernard said. 'I can see you recognise the sword as Scottish. One should never judge. He was a soldier and did unchristian acts. The Church would say he has been punished by God with leprosy. Yet he has many skills and speaks many languages and obviously has an education. I found him almost dead, covered in blood … clutching that sword, which was his only possession. He had been in a fight and became delirious, babbling about a past in the Holy Land. The rest he chooses to conceal through his reticence. The sword only hints about the man behind the bandages.

Bernard gently pushed Hugh down on his seat as he attempted to place the bundle back on the shelf.

'Take the sword to Jean – for we have no idea how today will end and Jean was willing to die to keep it as a reminder of the life he had – we can't let it fall into the hands of the likes of Jean de Bretagne or worse the Wolf brothers.'

Murdie thought he knew who the sword belonged to, but it was a distraction. He wondered how a leper would own John Wishart's sword.

'Laurent sent word that Jean will stay at Gaillard and dispose of any traces of the Scots – he waits for you there Hugh'.

Hugh nodded.

Murdie would tell Bishop Wishart about the sword and that his brother could still be alive but that could wait. He would find out later, the leper would be at the Temple, and he knew where to find him. Now was the time to escape France.

'Do you have news of Raoul?' Bernard asked.

'Raoul has the easier task watching Valois's men in La Rochelle,' Hugh said. 'Getting to Honfleur will be hard enough – but then getting from there to Scotland will require all our strength and cunning. Les Frères Loups followed me here – they must have been waiting on the road from Paris that passes Gaillard. We can finish these fiends, and you can make your way to the sea – and another Scot with a sword is always useful. Madame I suspect will be waiting for the barge.' Hugh nodded towards Murdie; he now accepted him after his initial coldness.

'I saw Bretagne as I arrived, I wonder what his plans are. Geoffroi has written a letter telling of the barge's location, which will find its way to Bretagne. I wonder who he is working for now. If it's the English he will make sure the treasure leaves France, if it's himself he will try to capture and hide it here. The Wolf Brothers want the treasure to remain in France and to get the glory of finding it. Whatever happens one of them will be disappointed and they won't give up without a fight.' Murdie, who had spent hours reading Valence's intelligence, knew all about Bretagne's double dealing and thought Hugh was right.

'Jean de Bretagne has loyalty to only himself. If they try to stop us, we can finish them all,' Bernard added, with an edge that surprised Murdie. Bernard was a soldier, and had always displayed an element of joviality which he didn't want to extend to Bretagne or the Wolf Brothers.

'The cog looks like a sleepy merchant ship, but it has been modified for the seas. It's fast – very fast. I would have your swords and daggers at the ready when it does arrive.'

Hugh stood to leave as Bernard grabbed his arm.

'Listen, something's not right.'

The door rattled and then burst open. It was dusk and the light was almost gone.

Bernard reached inside his left sleeve for his dagger as Guillaume appeared, red-faced. Rising voices filled the small shack and Murdie unfastened his sword and grabbed his dagger.

'I found Jamie, Innes, Hendor, and Will standing just outside the front entrance. Jamie had me come fetch you all. He thinks Nicolo saw him and then more men appeared. A fight broke out.'

'They recognised Jamie?' Murdie asked. 'Seems so – Bretagne may be a scoundrel, but he is no idiot, and he wouldn't employ men who were,' Guillaume replied.

Murdie sensed a surge of energy. He held his dagger fast.

'Is Bretagne outside with his men?' Bernard asked, sword in hand. Murdie followed him outside. He didn't want to start a fight, but he had no reluctance in joining one. If the Wolf Brothers were around he wouldn't be able to resist the melee.

Bernard, Murdie and the others ran the short distance down the adjoining lane leading from the stables. It was a few minutes past dusk, dark enough to conceal faces. Murdie heard familiar accents amidst the sound of metal striking metal, and the grunts associated with physical exertion.

The side door was closed, so Murdie and Hugh kicked it open, and it fell inside. They pushed indide standing on people held fast beneath the door. People spilled out, stopping Bernard and Guillaume from following. Murdie pulled people to one side and cleared the way in.

Blades flashed and crashed before him, and blood from close by spurted across his face and into his mouth. He felt a crossbow bolt cut through the air, impaling a man and fixing his chest to the wall. The candles lighting the room had been scattered across the floor, but the lamps hanging above him still etched out the faces of anyone standing.

Hugh was fighting beside him.

'Murdie, look over there,' Hugh shouted.

'I wondered how long it would take you to arrive.' Hendor was beating a man with a table leg, the man was thrashing with his dagger, but Hendor was too skilled and he swept the man away with a heavy strike to his chest.

Jean de Bretagne was in the centre of the fight, but there were many unfamiliar heads surrounding him. Murdie didn't know who was friend or fiend.

'That's Wishart … I am seeing Bishop Wishart in his youth.' The face was familiar, and his voice had the same nuance and character as his uncle.

This had to be Jamie. Jamie was wrestling with a man who was heavier than he was and was pushing Jamie's hand to one side. Jamie had a broken flagon which he was using as a dagger.

'Jamie, I have your back.' Murdie cried as he punched the man hard in the ribs. They cracked loudly, shattering and burst through his woollen tunic, then he smashed his sword across his chest. Jamie followed and stabbed him in the head with the makeshift dagger. This forced blood and brain across Murdie and Jamie. Neither stopped to wipe it away before more assailants thrust swords and daggers at them.

As soon as one man was finished, others seemed to appear from the side. The Scots were surrounded by what felt like twice their number. Bolts screamed through the air just as Hugh cut the crossbowman a crunching blow across his skull with his sword. He fell to the ground as his final bolt flew across the room, crashing into the bar and shattering several goblets. The shards exploded across the room like sharpened missiles.

'Kill them all and seize their ship. Quickly before the garrison guards arrive!' Bretagne was slashing aimlessly at anything near him, but Murdie could see that he was surrounded by his men and was in danger of striking them.

Bernard had now joined Murdie and Hugh. Guillaume was close by, brandishing his dagger in his left hand, his sword in his right. He killed two of Bretagne's men before Bernard could stop him.

'Son, this is not your fight.' But Guillaume ignored him and without hesitation headed towards Bretagne at the heart of the melee. Bernard fought towards his son but bodies and fighting got in his path, and he lost sight of his son.

'Where have they gone – have Guillaume and Bernard fallen?' Murdie couldn't follow as he was attacked again.

Will and Innes were fighting with two, three – no, it was four of Bretagne's men, two on one. Will had his sword in his right hand and his long dagger in his left. Innes was at his back, fighting in the same manner. Murdie saw Will fall to the ground, crashing through a table.

Will got back on his feet and turned quickly, slashing one of his attackers across the stomach, and he fell. Innes ran both his attackers through with his sword before joining Will in finishing off the last of the four with a thrust to his groin. Blood sprayed across the room and hit the wall just beyond where Hendor was standing, picking men off with his crossbow.

People were fleeing out of the door in panic – parts of chairs and tables were being thrown about like sticks.

The room was in chaos: bodies, chairs and broken crockery. People were stumbling and slipping in pools of blood mixed with food and wine. The room suddenly cleared as Murdie fought off his attacker, striking him to the ground. He then saw Guillaume.

'No.' Guillaume fell as Bretagne plunged a long dagger into his chest, its point piercing through to his back. Murdie heard Bernard's cry as he realised his son was down.

Bernard picked up an axe and swung it from side to side clearing everyone away between him, Jean de Bretagne and Guillaume's body.

'I enjoyed killing your son. Come for me,' Bretagne mocked.

Bernard pushed Bretagne towards the wall, slashing with the axe and then his dagger. Bretagne was forced towards the door.

'Watch out, he will flee if he gets the chance.' Hendor followed his warning with more bolts. Bretagne pulled a man in front of him as a human shield, and the bolts thudded into his back.

Murdie could see Innes pushing men away to get to Bretagne. But Bretagne's men didn't give up – they fought bravely. Innes wasn't going to get to Bretagne first; Bernard was in front of him.

Bretagne threw his dagger like a spear at Bernard, catching him in his gut. Bernard pulled it out exposing a huge gash but still strode forward. Bretagne looked around for a way to escape, but he slipped on the blood-soaked reeds and tried to scramble out of the door on his hands and knees. Bernard looked ashen, his blood pooled on the floor. He lifted his axe high into the air.

'Mercy, mercy, mercy!' Bretagne shouted.

'This is for Guillaume, you bastard.' His axe cut through the air crushing his head like a soft apple.

Murdie saw people streaming out into the street in front of the tavern to escape the fight. The authorities would be alerted, and they needed to be away from here.

'Over there, Murdie, in the shadows those bastard Wolf Brothers. I am going to finish Bertrand,' Hugh screamed as he charged towards him.

The inn had only one large room with a small space at the far end from the bar. The Wolf brothers looked like they were hiding.

'Cowards,' Murdie cried as Bertrand smashed Hugh back against the table, producing an axe from his back. Hugh was on the floor as Betrand prepared to strike.

Then Murdie caught sight of Hendor, who calmly placed a bolt between Bertrand's eyes. His axe fell heavily, and he lunged forward landing on top of the blade, which stuck into his chest.

'Brother!' a voice screamed. Seeing his brother go down, Baldwin's rage got in the way of his senses. Will, who had been fighting with another of Bretagne's men had carefully moved towards Baldwin pushing several dead men away before he stabbed him between the shoulders. He fell onto his brother's eviscerated corpse.

Murdie felt a stabbing pain in his arm. Blood spurted out and ran down his right hand, and his sword became difficult to hold. He sensed a second blow, but it swung past his head, followed by his attacker, who slumped forward. The back of the man's skull was now missing.

Gyrid appeared with a wooden club in her hand, the end now smashed and covered with blood and brain. She collapsed, and Murdie realised she had been stabbed in the back.

The room emptied as Bretagne's remaining men ran away. There was no winning here and Murdie found himself alone in the room with the Scots. They were exhausted.

Bernard was sitting on the ground next to Guillaume, holding his hand – he turned to Hugh, who was barricading the doors as best he could to stop anyone else from coming back.

'Honour me and Guillaume and get out of here,' Bernard cried as he clutched his stomach. A growing pool of blood oozed from the wound. He pushed his intestine back inside the deep gash.

Murdie looked at the other men. They were all strangely quiet. There was nothing they could say, and no one wanted to move. Bernard's pain was overwhelming.

'You heard me. Get the cog out of here. Don't let my son's sacrifice be for nothing.' Bernard fell onto Guillaume's body.

'You heard him,' Hugh cried. 'There is no dishonour in leaving us. Go!'

The Scots waited for a few seconds before they left through the harbour entrance that led directly to the cog, Murdie carrying Gyrid.

In the street, the young red-haired man Murdie had thought to be Jamie turned towards him.

'Follow me, Murdie. Our ship is berthed a few hundred yards from here. My uncle Robert has told me a lot about you. I am Jamie Wishart.'

Chapter Thirteen

Dunaverty Castle, Scotland, Mid-September 1306: The Bruce's Dream

The flotilla of ships had waited off the southeastern shore for darkness to fall. The night was calm, the moon was full, and its reflection was at its maximum. It looked like a circle of gold was covering Dunaverty Bay.

Dunaverty was situated on the point of the Mull of Kintyre. It commanded the landscape, conspicuous on the headland projecting into the Sound of Sanda.

Bruce was resting alone on a stout chair, surrounded by lords and common men busying themselves with their assigned tasks. He found such hours of quiet contemplation more valuable than the deepest of sleeps. They allowed him to plan his next steps.

I will never be drawn into open battles; engagement will be on my terms. Small victories like Castle Tioram will take back my land castle by castle, kill the English man by man, and erode their spirit.

'Let them gain nothing from their victories,' he mumbled.

'Did you say something, Sire?' Lord Douglas asked.

'No, James, just thinking out loud,' the King replied.

'What about?'

'About planning and controlling this war, my mind is full, heavy with the responsibilities of my position. I keep my head full to avoid having to think about my queen and daughter – about the battles we have fought and the cries of men like Sir Christopher Seton – he saved my life and now his head is rotting on a spike at Dumfries Castle – about my friend Bishop Wishart.'

'Sire, you are the man for the times. You will prevail and you wouldn't be the man you are if you didn't carry such burdens – it's the price of being a king, and you know that,' Lord Douglas nodded.

The hours travelling to Dunaverty gave him more time to think uninterrupted, a respite with no rest. His mind darted around, and he didn't know where it would land.

The golden moon reminded him of Alaric's treasure, and the men Bishop Wishart had sent to retrieve it. He had heard nothing of his armour bearer, Will de Irwyne, since he had left him at Glasgow Cathedral several months ago.

If anyone survives all of this, it will be Will.

Bruce considered the impact the treasure would make. He hadn't considered it seriously at first, but now he couldn't ignore the difference it would make. Those plans were for a time when it was in his hands.

Will was self-reliant and cunning, and the English had placed an ever-increasing price on his head, which told Bruce he was still alive.

Today was also a day for reality. He was looking forward to seeing his brothers Edward, Alexander, and Thomas. They were all younger and looked to him as king, lord of Carrick, and brother. Edward and Thomas were soldiers, and Alexander, the youngest, was the scholar. Importantly, any personal ambition was secondary to keeping him on the throne.

There was a rumour that his brother Niall had been captured, and English soldiers were in pursuit of his sisters, wife and daughter.

He hoped that his message to Davie Munro would get through, and he would find them first and send them to his sister Isabel in Norway. He was anxious for news.

'You were right, Hamish; the English will need many

ships to attack us here. Christina chose wisely.'

Bruce liked Hamish and recognised his intelligence. Intelligence was in many ways better than raw courage, and Hamish had that, too. Bruce could see why Christina had put him in command of her guard.

'Sire, we sank more than a few of their ships at Tioram. We have a little time here before the English will follow and we will see them coming, Men, row his majesty to a hundred feet behind the other ships. They are to berth first.'

Hamish raised the anchor as the oarsmen carefully rowed Bruce's ship towards the north of the castle and behind the other birlinns.

There was a narrow path cut into the sea cliff. Small torches scattered along the beach were being lit to guide the ships to their berths. Timbers had been driven into the shore to prevent them from running into any rocks.

'Pass the word around. Carry your weapons and keep the noise to a minimum. Seventy soldiers arriving is big news around here – Sire, your ship will land last. I need to send Lord Hay ahead with your guard to make sure the English aren't lying in wait. Once everything is safe, he will return with your brothers.'

With Will de Irwyne missing, Bruce would ask Christina for Hamish to be his armour bearer once he was able to return to his castle at Turnberry. Hamish was just the sort of captain he needed if he was to get his kingdom back.

Dunaverty was set on top of a huge rock that was two or three hundred feet higher than the sea around it. The keep looked small but was protected by an inner wall surrounding the main building and an outer wall running along the top of the rock. A steep embankment separated both walls, and the castle was protected by the sea on three sides. The only entrance was from the north, where a narrow causeway linked it to the mainland.

The other birlinns anchored and their men disembarked

directly onto the beach below the keep. Any garrison above could wipe out a much larger force below. The castle entrance was narrow, and no more than one man could climb the path towards it. The entire north side was a killing zone.

'Sire, I have asked one of the archers to send up a flaming arrow if the garrison is friendly. If we don't see that signal in ten minutes, we will cut the anchors and get out of here.'

Hamish took a marine sandglass from his pocket and turned it upside down. He placed a lamp behind it, and Bruce watched as the sand rushed through.

'When it has emptied one-third, we will have to leave.' Hamish was right; Valence could have sent men here. It was a MacDonald stronghold, and they were Bruce's allies.

'Hamish, my safety is in your hands.'

Bruce watched anxiously as the succession of torches wound their way towards the keep before disappearing behind the outer wall. He didn't hear any sounds that suggested an ambush.

'Sire, we need to make sure they aren't luring us into a trap. Remember, it is you they are after. They may be waiting until they are sure you have landed before they attack.'

The minutes dragged by, and the glass approached a third. Hamish started to lift the anchor.

'Look, Hamish.' The King pointed as a flame dashed across the night sky.

'Sire, a ship is leaving the castle and it's travelling too quickly for my liking.' Hamish was agitated and ran from one side of the boat to the other looking for other boats.

'Let's just be prepared. Arm yourselves, my lords, and the rest of you, prepare to row hard if there are any tricks.'

Hamish took his longbow from his back, locked an arrow to it, and followed the approaching birlinn, ready to fire. Boarding the king's ship wasn't going to be easy.

Bruce couldn't make out the men in the ship. They were too far away.

They approached quickly at first and then slowed. Bruce removed his sword from its sheath and felt for his helmet and shield. If they did attack, he would die before he would let himself be captured. He was more used to preparing for battle than most men, yet he still felt the tension. His heart raced, and he wiped the sweat from his palm.

'Sire, we don't fight today, we run. Strike oars.' The anchor chain started to race into the ship.

'Hamish, you are right, this is not the place to make a stand. It would achieve nothing.'

Voices carried from the other ship. It was difficult to hear them clearly, but the accents were pure Ayrshire. Even with the moonlight, it was difficult to recognise faces.

'Sire! It's me, Lord Hay, with your brothers.'

A collective sigh took hold of the boat as the men returned their swords to their sheaths and set their crossbows on the deck.

Hamish guided their birlinn next to the king's ship. He threw ropes from the bow and the stern to the approaching ship.

'Tie these to your bow and stern and this to your mast – securely. Drop your anchor. The sea is calm, but we would do well in avoiding a collision and sending both our crafts to the bottom.'

The ships brushed gently against each other as a third rope was attached to the mast.

'Lord Hay and the Lords Bruce, swing over onto the deck.'

Hamish and his crew steadied the adjacent boats with grappling irons. The four men used the rope from the mast to swing a few feet from their deck to the king's ship.

'Untie the ropes and return to Dunaverty. Quickly, now,' Hamish ordered as he lit a larger lamp, which he hung onto the mast. Its light was concentrated towards the King.

The ropes landed on the deck, and the birlinn manoeuvred

quickly and carefully away before heading back to its berth on the north side of Dunaverty.

Then Hamish fully lifted the anchor of the King's ship, and they made for the shore.

'My dear brothers. I am so glad to see you again. I wish the circumstances were more pleasant.' Bruce tried to stand, but his brothers crowded around him, kissing him on each cheek.

'Sit, brother.'

Alexander Bruce gently pushed the King back into his chair. He wore the clothes of a cleric – a dark tunic and cape with a loose-fitting dalmatic beneath – and sported the tonsure. A large, heavy cross hung around his neck. His clothes were ruffled and untidy, and a sword was hanging from his left side.

'Alexander, I hear you are following in the footsteps of Bishop Wishart,' Bruce said. 'King Edward has banished you from Glasgow Cathedral and put a price on your head.' The King was fond of his serious youngest brother.

'He took umbrage at me repurposing the wood he supplied for the cathedral towards helping Bishop Wishart build siege weapons. I am still learning when I can, but the English are hunting us all. I don't think any Bruce can live in peace now.'

Alexander had combined a sharp theological mind with that of a soldier. Bruce was proud of the man he was becoming.

'Our father may not have made the right choice in sending you into the Church. I see you are becoming a soldier.' Robert pointed to the sword.

Alexander quickly covered the sword with his cape.

'Circumstances have dictated a move away from the pen to the sword. Though I am still convinced that I can do better as a cleric than a soldier – Thomas, Edward, I hear that our lands in Galloway were confiscated?'

Bruce noticed that both sported scars and gashes on their cheeks.

'We had a small reckoning and managed to escape to Islay,' Thomas said. 'It's a fine place, and Lord MacDonald looked after us well. We laid low until we were sure you could join us in Dunaverty … Christina kept us informed. We did what we could protecting our Galloway lands from MacDougall. With English support, they overwhelmed us, and our lands were overrun. They were ordered to kill any Bruce they captured.'

Thomas was fast becoming another commander like his older brother Edward. Robert would soon rely on them both to lead the rebellion.

'Sire, we are proud to serve you,' Edward declared.

Robert could see a scar running across his forehead down towards his right eye. It had been a serious wound, and whatever had happened had almost cost Edward his life. It was no small reckoning.

'I am only glad you are all alive. Remember, I need men, not ghosts. I don't want to lose any of you. Remember, bravery is sometime a kinder word for stupidity. Don't fight when the English and their allies are too many.'

Robert could feel his stomach tighten at the thought. He needed men who he would never doubt and who would stand by him unconditionally in these times of adversity. Their courage was a testament to their family bonds.

'Have you fresh news of Niall?' Robert asked, hoping for good news but fearing the worst.

'We think he is still at Kildrummy,' Thomas answered. 'Davie Munro got word to us that Queen Elisabeth, Princess Marjorie, our sisters, and Lady MacDuff are in sanctuary. There was no word of Niall being with them. That is all we know.'

The King felt the ship veer to the left. Their ship wasn't heading towards the other birlinns moored at the north side of the castle, but towards the south side, which was open to the sea.

'Hamish ... where are we going?' The King tried to stand to see what was happening.

'Sire, there is a concealed entrance that leads directly under the keep. Only a few people know of its existence. The ship can anchor there and we can get you inside unseen. Lord MacDonald is waiting for us there. The route is still steep, and we have prepared a room for your rest and recovery, and there are enough of us to carry you.'

Hamish extinguished the mast light and directed the birlinn towards the open sea and the cliffs beneath the castle.

'Christina Ranald sent word from Tarbert confirming you were headed to Dunaverty, and that Father MacBeith was on his way,' Alexander added.

The King could feel that Alexander had eyes on him, and he looked concerned. Robert wondered if his current frailty was obvious. Was he displaying fear, or did he look sicker than he felt? He didn't want to ask what concerned Alexander, because he feared the response.

'The news about Christina and Domhnall pleases me. They left behind us and we heard the Castle fall. I feared they may not have made it.'

Alexander's mannerisms reminded the King of Bishop Wishart, and he was indeed the Bishop's creation. Wishart not only wanted a Bruce on the throne but also in his cathedral in Glasgow.

'Alexander, I had forgotten that you studied under Domhnall at the cathedral scriptorium. Look – he made this sword for me after I lost mine at Dalrigh – every time I touch the sword, I think of the man who made it. Domhnall always said he put a portion of his soul into every sword he ever made – every sword is a testament to the man that made it rather than the one who uses it.'

The birlinn slowed, and the entrance seemed to open

before them. It was extremely well hidden. Bruce observed sentries in the keep above watching and covering the King with their bows. The birlinn slid through the entrance and travelled a short distance to where he spotted Lord Aonghus MacDonald lighting a half circle of torches that guided them the last few yards.

The quay was sharp-edged and uneven, and Hamish had to use all his skills to stop the birlinn from crashing into them.

The keel twisted before neatly slotting into a small gap between the dangerous outcrops of rocks on either side of the deck.

Hamish grabbed the grappling irons and threw Lord MacDonald a rope, which he carefully tied to a heavy iron ring fixed to the cave wall.

'Sire, we can't stay here long,' Lord MacDonald shouted. 'The tide is constantly shifting and will push the ship onto the rocks or even aground.'

Aonghus og MacDonald was from the Western Isles, rough as the rocks, with hair as red as the sand and deep blue eyes as threatening as the sea. Bruce admired his tenacity and uncompromising spirit.

'My dear Aonghus, it has been too long since I was last at Islay. You are still stronger than an ox and twice as belligerent.'

Aonghas grunted and then laughed. 'When we meet it always raises my spirits; been the same since we were boys. You are most welcome, Sire, I only wish the circumstances were better. You have bruised Valence's very fragile ego and he will only be able to mention your name through gritted teeth.'

The three Bruce brothers jumped down from the deck onto the berth. MacDonald stood about three or four feet away from the ship. They tightened the ropes, but just enough to prevent the gap from closing and the ship striking the rocks.

'Pick up the King and lower him down onto the quay. Be careful that he stays above the gap and doesn't slip between the keel and the quay. He will be crushed for certain – I will steady the ship with the long oar.' Hamish looked more anxious than Robert.

One man held his legs, another his arms, and a third supported his torso.

He felt weak, and the pain was agonising, but he would not cry out. He had to hope that his incapacity was temporary, he had aged many years in the six months since he was crowned. His mind felt ten years younger than his thirty-two years and his body ten years older.

The men held him carefully, tenderly, he felt precious, as they lifted him towards the open arms of his three brothers, Aonghus, and a waiting chair.

Then they moved back to the seats and picked up the oars. Hamish untied the rope and pushed the birlinn away from the rocks.

'Sire, we will anchor beside all the other ships and attend you presently.'

The King watched as Hamish negotiated the tight exit back towards Dunaverty harbour.

MacDonald led them up the winding staircase towards the cellar directly below the ground floor of the keep.

'You are heavier than I thought you would be, Brother. Are you still wearing your crown?' Edward teased.

The ground floor door was ajar, and the reception room was empty of people.

'I hear relief – they are laughing. It has been a hard few months since Methven. They are right to enjoy a few days of peace – we dealt the English a humiliation. I won't forget how winning feels.' They were experienced soldiers and would take time to eat, sleep and prepare for the battles to come starting with the journey to Orkney.

'Sire, we have arranged rooms on the first floor.' Aonghus lit the remaining torches as they climbed up the steep staircase to the next floor.

There were two doors on the first floor. One was tantalisingly open, and the King was greeted with a roaring fire. His brothers carefully laid him on the bed.

'Lord MacDonald, the men did well these last few days. See that they are well fed and you open a few casks of *the water of life*. Tioram was only the start of fighting back, a small step in the return of the king. I have a huge duty of care to all of them!'

'Sire, you also must take care of yourself and rest. The cooks are preparing bread and stew to be washed down with honey-sweetened ale and *uisge beatha*. Everyone will rest well tonight – Drink this, Sire, it will help you sleep, and you need that more than anything right now. There are some dispatches from France that require your attention. I put them near the top, but for later.' MacDonald lit the lamp next to the king's bed and handed him a goblet.

The parchments were compacted into a tight bundle. On the top, there was a letter from his sister. He recognised the seal of the Norwegian royal house of Sverre. He was hoping for news of Will and Jamie from France, and word of Bishops Wishart and Lamberton. His eyes were tired and blurry so he would read them tomorrow. He had waited many months for news and one more day wouldn't make any difference.

He took a large gulp of what he thought was sweetened wine, wincing as he put the goblet down.

'Sire, the wine includes poppy water, so it will taste slightly bitter. We sweetened it with honey, but obviously not enough. It was brought back during the Crusades and will take away the pain. Treat it with caution, as it can also bring out the devil.'

MacDonald picked up the empty goblet and wiped it clean with his sleeve.

'Bishop Wishart introduced me to its miraculous healing powers at Methven.'

The King felt a surge of calm rush through his body.

'James Stewart, my high steward, will be itching to help make the feast for the men a night to remember.'

The King could hear Stewart below ordering the cooks around him. He wanted to say more but his eyes became heavy, and much as he tried he couldn't keep them open.

His brothers removed his sword, boots, and cloak, leaving him in only his shirt and hose before closing the heavy door behind them.

He knew he was alone, his body started to close and his reserves were gone. He could just hear faint voices outside, and he wondered if they were real or if he had started to dream.

'Thomas and I will watch our brother tonight; he must be guarded day and night.'

A bench or chair was being dragged across the wooden floor, and he could hear Edward and Thomas chatting, but it was becoming more indistinct.

His mind was still fighting sleep.

'I will organise Lords Hay, Sinclair, and Douglas and Hamish Campbell to take watch in turns until Domhnall arrives. The King will need to recover and be away from Dunaverty before the English soldiers find out we are here. Their ships may have been damaged, but they can attack us from the land, and we have limited supplies for a siege. It is better that we are away soon – Christina sent a note with her messenger'.

MacDonald was reading out a dispatch.

'She is sending supplies for a hundred men for six months. Domhnall is expected with his few men before nightfall. He knows he is needed and is the only one allowed to see the King. Come, my lords. We need to make our preparations for we have only three days.'

He heard the voices of Lords MacDonald, Douglas, Hay, and Alexander Bruce disappearing down the narrow staircase, leaving Thomas and Edward Bruce, who continued to chatter.

'I will send up some wine,' Lord MacDonald's voice echoed.

Finally, the King fell into a deep sleep.

*

The King had woken in the early hours and had read his dispatches, but his eyes became tired again and he had fallen back to sleep with the help of more poppy water.

'Robert, wake up – are you all right?' Alexander shook his brother hard.

'What's happened?' The King lifted his head: his words were slurred, and for a few seconds he wasn't sure if this was part of his vivid dream.

'You called out as if you were being attacked. Lord Douglas flew into a panic and kicked the door down trying to get in here.'

'I can see.' The King saw what remained; the door was splintered and twisted, hanging in two parts. The frame was shattered, the lock smashed, and the mechanism strewn on the floor.

Alexander was standing over him.

'There is no one here.' Douglas returned his sword to its sheath.

The King was still groggy, but he found the strength to speak. 'There is only one way in here, and that's up those stairs – unless they flew through the window or scaled a seventy-foot sea wall. It was nothing but a dream.'

'It sounded like much more than a dream.' Douglas's concern sounded genuine.

'How long have I been asleep? A couple of hours, at least?'

The King pulled himself up onto the bolster that ran the whole breadth of the bed.

'Or over a day,' Douglas replied as he opened the shutters completely and surveyed the surrounding land.

'The poppy water had the desired effect.'

The King's mind was becoming clearer, and whilst he was still weak, a little of his inner strength had returned.

'Your Majesty, Lord MacDonald has sent me.'

A servant appeared at the door, a tray containing food in one hand and a wine flagon in the other.

'There is no one more welcome.' The King beamed and the servant appeared perplexed.

The King was not looking at him but at the large figure behind him. The servant hurriedly placed the wine and food next to the King as Domhnall, clad in the robes of a cleric with a large leather satchel over his shoulder, knelt beside Robert's bed.

'My dear Domhnall, rise.' The King extended his hand.

Alexander Bruce stepped out of the shadow and embraced Domhnall.

'Dear MacBeith, we meet under different circumstances than we did last time. We were arguing over a translation of Aristotle's *Meteorologica*, and we disagreed on the four prime contraries and their relationship with the four elements of fire, air, water, and earth. I didn't accept that this was Aristotle's work, and you firmly believed it was.' Alexander's face had broken into a broad smile.

'Alexander, my work as a smith confirms the view that hot and cold are the active factors driving construction and destruction. No other man could have come up with this except the great Aristotle. I use his theories every time I make a sword or heal a man. It is a combination of the contraries and the elements at work in healing the sick or making a sword good enough for a king.'

Domhnall pointed to the sword he had made for the King,

which was hanging next to his bed. Just as he did so, the fine jewel on the handle caught the light of the sun, as if he had ordered the sun to single out its splendour.

'Domhnall, I doubt we will ever discuss Aristotle again – I miss my time at the scriptorium. Taking up the sword has been a difficult choice for both of us.' Alexander's smile disappeared.

'We will when this war is over. That's what we are fighting for – to be able to read and think what we want without fear or requiring anyone's permission. Neither of us wants to be here a moment longer, but freedom is the right to an education that covers all perspectives under the guardianship of a Scottish Church. I know we are doing this for the same reasons.' Domhnall was passionate as always, and Alexander nodded.

'Lord Douglas and Alexander, I would like to be alone with Domhnall.' The King filled two goblets adjacent to his bed as the two men left.

'You will excuse me if I don't get out of bed. You see, I am quite unwell. Please sit by me.' The King pointed to a large carver chair. 'How is Christina? – the English will have a price on both your heads by now.'

'Sire, we set the sky on fire.' Domhnall let out a roar.

'I heard the explosion miles away. You did a great job and gave Valence an even greater surprise. The English will paint us as sorcerers.'

'It wouldn't have worked if I hadn't had help – Christina set the fuses with Lady Eilidh Robertson whilst I spread the Chinese snow all over the castle. We are lucky to have someone so young with such talents willing to sacrifice for our cause. She emptied her food and weapon stores – I brought enough with me to last months, and she is arranging to send the rest by boat before we leave – I nearly drowned, and she dragged me from the water. I was carrying this at the time.'

Domhnall unfurled the tapestry with the House of Bruce coat of arms.

'It wasn't worth drowning for, but it is a wonderful sight, and a great omen.' The King clapped his hands in delight. 'She is right to transport the supplies by sea. She has boats at Tarbert, and it would be too dangerous by wagon. The food and weapons will allow me to feed and arm the men whilst we wait for more to join us. What are her plans?' Robert hoped she would soon follow Domhnall.

'She is planning to leave for her estate in Uist and will join you in the spring as soon as the winter storms are over. Reluctantly I left her with her steward, Harrison Deacon.' Domhnall's voice trailed off as if he didn't want to talk anymore about Christina.

'Is there something you are not telling me?' The King sensed there was something wrong.

'I didn't take to Harrison Deacon. There was something not right about him – I couldn't put my finger on it, just a feeling. I watched him carefully, and when he thought no one was watching him, he looked at her as if he hated her. I have seen that look before. You recognise the genuine from the fake when you are a priest. What came out of his mouth was the usual platitudes – he couldn't wait to see me gone. His words and his demeanour are at odds. I don't know what he stands for, and I don't trust him. I am worried about her.'

Domhnall was always measured and did not raise matters unnecessarily.

'Deacon was in her father Ailean's service as a steward, an English novate rescued from a monastery and rumoured to be a Cathar,' the King said. 'Been in the Ranald family service for many years. There may be nothing in it, but we should check on her anyway. Send Hamish Campbell back to Tarbert. It will put our minds at rest. Aonghus will arrange it, and he can be there by tomorrow. Did anyone see you arrive?'

'Sire, I left as soon as the tide allowed me to get out of Loch Fyne. It was near dusk when we left, and we sailed around the Isle of Arran to avoid being seen. We didn't see any ships as we passed, but that doesn't mean we weren't spotted by people on shore. Times are hard, and English gold is in abundance if it concerns the King of Scots. There is no love for the English in Argyle, but we are near MacDougall country. The men we didn't kill at Tioram are hunting for you with a fire in their belly. They will have certainly sent scouts throughout Kintyre to seek word of the Bruce or his men.'

'And they will be looking for Christina?' Bruce knew the answer.

'Certainly, Sire.'

The English would know the role she had played at Tioram and would pursue her with the same vigour as himself.

'Was there talk of my ill health?' the King asked, hoping that his incapacity was secret.

'No, Sire. The only word in the area is the destruction at Tioram. They are scavenging what boats they can from the local people, and many are hiding what boats they can to avoid Valence and MacDougall stealing them. Explains why there were so few on Loch Fyne. Reasonable conditions, and the fishermen were nowhere to be seen. Sire, is there anything going on apart from fatigue – which, given the circumstances, is understandable?'

Domhnall was now playing the role of a physician.

'I had to be carried up here – I can barely stand, and I have a weakness that is overtaking my body. I have had little time to rest since Methven, where my horse rolled onto me. I damaged my leg and took a knock to the head. Sir Christopher Seton led me from the field … but my illness is not the main reason I have called you here.'

'Sire, I am not entitled to lecture a king on how to rule, but I can advise you as a physician, a priest, and a friend.

Scotland only survives if you survive – it is my duty to keep you alive, so listen to your body and rest a while. Valence won't send an army to Orkney. That would mean conflict with the Norwegians – I beg you to take the opportunity for quiet whilst you make plans for your return. Then we will take this land back stone by stone. Your health is always my concern – but if you haven't called me because of that, how else may I serve you?'

'Domhnall, I can always rely upon you to give objective advice, and kings must be physically and mentally strong. Longshank's ill health has started conspiracies and plots, his once loyal courtiers are scheming, a dying king has no future even after thirty-four years on the English throne and I have been king just six months. The stakes are high – and I find it hard to explain this other matter even to my confessor.'

He wondered if his mind had been impacted and if he had lost God's favour. Domhnall was the only one with whom he could discuss his spiritual anxiety.

'I have been having vivid, frightening dreams since Dalrigh. I wake up sweating, my heart racing like I have only known in battle. The visions are as real to me as you are sitting here drinking wine. They are messages I dare not ignore, and I couldn't discuss them with anyone. You are a physician who knows the mind and a priest who understands the soul. No one else has the skills to interpret these dreams without thinking me mad, neither the lords that surround me nor my brothers – I need you to interpret, tell me what they mean and what I must do.'

The King was seeing the dreams again and could feel sweat on his forehead and see it on his palms.

'Sire, describe them, tell me why these dreams disturb you? Do you believe God sent them, or that they are directing you away from him?'

'They are not from the devil, if that is what you are suggesting. They are wonderous, fabulous, overwhelming, repetitive, and in the morning I remember everything about them as if they are from God – Saint Fillan has come to me every night since Dalrigh to comfort me, and he talks to me as I am talking to you now.'

The King handed a goblet to Domhnall before drinking his empty.

'The same saint whose relic you lost at Dalrigh?' Domhnall asked.

'Yes, his finger bones are contained within the brooch torn off by one of MacDougall's men – I stopped anyone from repairing the tear in my cloak. It didn't feel right, like I had accepted its loss.'

The King pointed to his cloak, and the fastening was missing.

'Sire, you were never a man for the frippery and trappings of nobility, except for this. I remember its loss very well. Tell me more.'

'I see images of my men in battles. The images are so real that I can smell the blood in the air and taste the acrid smoke of burning wood and metal. All these battles are won, and the English lose castle after castle, except one. No matter how many men I send against its walls, they are never breached. The English build the walls back up as quickly as I knock them down. Wave after wave of men die, and I cannot break through. I lose heart, yet I neither give up nor succeed. Each night the scenario repeats itself. In these dreams I don't believe I can win, but I don't lose. I am king and I am incomplete, because the English are never fully routed. I have always felt Fillan's presence, but since I lost the brooch reliquary, I only hear him in my dreams. I am sure God guides me through him. In these dreams he is there, but whilst he speaks, his voice is silent. He is the only one who can plead with God on my behalf. To reconnect with God, to hear his voice, I need to get the reliquary back. I can't beat the English unless his relic is returned to me. I fear I will never breach the wall of the last castle and achieve final victory unless Fillan is with me. You are the only one I have told. A belief in dreams is for mystics or heretics. Men have been burnt for less. Am I going mad, Domhnall?'

Domhnall nodded, leaving the silence for the King to fill, knowing the King wanted to talk.

'Domhnall, am I possessed, or mad?' He wanted a sane voice to tell him he wasn't mad.

'There is something irrational in believing in dreams?' the King continued. 'Yet these visions are genuine – the men who follow me would understandably lose faith in an irrational and fearful king. They must believe that I believe I can win, and without hesitation – otherwise, they are risking their lives for nothing – if I lose the faith of my soldiers, that will finish my crown more surely than any defeat on the battlefield. I cannot keep quiet and ignore these visions. I am convinced there is something in them and that I must get the relic back – how else should I interpret these dreams – what should I do?'

He had not been able to fully function, and he was convinced it was the source of his illness. Today he would act in whatever way Domhnall advised.

'Sire, you are the sanest man I know, so put aside your thoughts of madness. You are the man to lead us and a worthy king. It is human to have doubt and fear – it would be greater madness if you didn't. Our Lord had such misgivings when he wandered in the desert before his mission started. Remember that God works in mysterious ways and his messages are not only delivered through clerics. We don't decide when God speaks to us. It is for him to decide the moment – you are a king, and no one stands between you and God, and he has chosen to speak to you now because he can see you need his guidance.'

The King was reassured. Domhnall had brought his own fragmented thoughts together and had made them whole in a way he couldn't.

Domhnall started to rummage in his satchel. He placed a small, plain pottery flask and a handful of smooth stones on the King's bed.

'What are they?' the King was curious.

'Saint Fillan is the patron of ill health, and before he died, he blessed these healing stones. This flask contains water from a small pool near his cave where he spent the last few years of his life. The Augustinian monks immerse the sick in this pool – the water's healing powers are considerable. You must sip this water when you are melancholy – Sire, your wounds are not physical, so we need to look at what ails you elsewhere. These stones will give you comfort. Keep them by you and believe in them, as they are blessed by a saint. Rest, Lord MacDonald's poppy water remedy are easy to come by – getting the relic back from the field in Dalrigh may prove more challenging.'

Domhnall placed the stones and flask into the King's hand, and he grasped them tightly.

'Challenging to retrieve, certainly,' the King said. 'I have information that the brooch reliquary is not in Dalrigh but was stolen off John MacDougall as he lay injured at Tioram by an Orthodox monk called Maccabi. He is a monk at Saint Catherine's monastery and will return there at some point.' He removed a tatty parchment from his left sleeve and pushed it towards Domhnall, who read the note.

'So, the duplicitous Ruaidhri Ranald has written to you. Sire, can we trust a man who tried to kill you, and Christina. He is in Valence's pocket?' Domhnall's doubt was contempt.

'I understand your caution. The handwriting is scratchy, and the seal is crusted and dark red, sealed more with blood than wax. He must have written it whilst Tioram was still smoking. His message got here almost as quickly as we did, so he is clearly having doubts about allying himself with Valence. Valence is sending assassins after me and wanted

Ruaidhri to help. I knew Ruaidhri in better times, and he was a good man. His judgement was blind when it came to his brother Lachlann, who is dead, killed at Tioram. As you can see, he wants to work for me now. He could have stayed with the English without risk and with a better chance of getting the lands he craves – Christina's lands. He knows I will never give him her lands, so his motivation to join me must be more altruistic. He has developed some integrity, and I will have to learn to welcome many men who started off on the wrong side if we are to win this war. I may accept them, Domhnall, but I will never trust them. However, I believe I can rely on his information about Saint Fillan.'

Domhnall would understand the need for pragmatism, even if it was flavoured with his rational cynicism. The king's army was too small to turn away even one man.

'Sire, I am aware how important Saint Fillan is to the Orthodox Church. He is venerated as a healer just as he is within our Catholic world. The relic was removed from Saint Catherine's by the Byzantines and disappeared, so I can see his desire to return it to what he considers its rightful place. There have been reports that the Byzantines have many agents tasked with returning what was stolen from them in the Crusades, their relics and treasure.'

'Who would blame them? But Fillan died here in Scotland many years before the Crusades. We have a duty to return these relics to the rest of his body at Inchaffray Abbey. A soul can be tormented if it isn't offered back to God whole. Once the English are gone for good, I will return his relics to the abbey.'

The King wasn't a particularly pious man, yet he wanted Fillan to receive respect.

'The Byzantines are Orthodox and see themselves as the inheritors of Rome. Saint Helena was an empress of the Eastern Roman Empire, and she paid for the relics with Roman money, bringing them back to Saint Catherine's so they could be venerated. The Crusaders stole them away to sell them to anyone with the cash. The Orthodox Church consider these stolen goods that they are legitimately taking back, and they have a strong argument. However, Saint Fillan is speaking to you, Sire. He wants to come home and help unite our country.'

The King nodded.

'Domhnall, you are the right man to bring Saint Fillan back. You are uniquely placed to find Maccabi. You studied, lived with the monks, and learned the science of healing. You understand the Orthodox practices, and your family has a connection with the monastery that goes back several generations to the time of William the Lion. That patronage may help you persuade this monk Maccabi to return the relic.'

The King wanted Domhnall to go willingly, conviction was a stronger driver than compulsion.

'Sire, I understand the power of St Fillan but there is an immediate need here, I am still tending to men injured after Dalrigh and Methven however I have sworn my allegiance to your kingship,' Domhnall fidgeted with his beard, and, for someone who was normally so decisive appeared to be in a dilemma. Domhnall wanted the Bruce to make the decision for him.

'The men are recovering, and none will die thanks to your skill. I don't intend to fight the English army any time soon. That will only happen when we have thousands of men, and now we only have hundreds. I will avoid a battle until I am sure we can win, and I don't think I can win the country unless you bring the relic back to Scotland.'

Robert was convinced this was true.

'Sire, I am a priest, a man of learning. I have had to acquire new skills in your service which I never imagined. But I am not an agent that can roam undetected across borders. My brother Murdie is the man for this work. He has survived in Longshank's court undetected for five years, so he has polished political skills a rough-hewn priest like me will never have. He is your man – if I only knew how to contact him.'

The King could not conceal what he knew.

'I have been looking for the right time to tell you, the dispatches from France and Norway had been in Lord MacDonald's care and they have word of Murdie.'

Domhnall smiled, 'Sire, please tell me how it is. It has been so long that I had almost lost hope of hearing good news of him – I had prepared myself for the worst whilst hoping for the best.' Domhnall's struggled to keep his voice controlled.

'You *are* the most practical man I know and yes, you are right that Murdie could also find Maccabi, but he is already working in my service. Murdie is alive and in France. I received word from my sister Queen Isabel. She met with Murdie a couple of weeks ago and was helping him reach France, following orders from Bishop Wishart to meet up with his agents there. He is doing important work to help the rebellion.'

Domhnall's face lifted. His eyes were wide and his smile broad.

'This is wonderful news. I did not think in coming here I would hear his name and learn that my brother was not only alive but away from the English court. I have prayed for this moment for years.' Domhnall grinned.

The King thought for a second. Should he tell Domhnall about a treasure whose knowledge would place him in great danger?

Valence would put a reward to capture the 'sorcerer priest' responsible for the explosion at Castle Tioram and it wouldn't be too long before Valence knew his name. If he was caught, he would be tortured before he was executed. The treasure couldn't fall into Valence's hands. Bruce was learning that he couldn't share all his secrets with everyone. Camaraderie had its boundaries, even with one of his confessors.

'Murdie is a fine man, but I know you are the right man. You stopped Valence with some black powder and a whole heap of intelligence. I think you can use that cunning to recover a relic. When Murdie returns, I have another task for him. I need him to take care of the cargo he is transporting from France – I cannot tell you anymore.'

'Sire, I am at your command.' Domhnall bowed.

The King was again tired, and Domhnall recognised his fatigue.

'Sire, I fear this audience has taken your energy. Drink some of the water blessed by Saint Fillan.'

The King sipped a little from the flask, and almost immediately he felt strengthened. He believed and recognised the healing powers of faith.

'Lord MacDonald has prepared a birlinn which is waiting for the next tide to take you to Bergen.'

'Bergen, Sire?' Domhnall was surprised.

'It would be too dangerous to send you back via the Irish and Narrow Seas. The English have hired merchant ships to look for any Scot that might lead them to me. If you are caught, you will not survive. The English will immediately understand the seal's meaning.'

The King pushed a folded parchment bearing his seal to Domhnall. The seal showed Bruce mounted on a horse, armed and ready for combat.

'Here is a letter for Queen Isabel. I have asked her to give you her protection and help in finding Maccabi. She has amongst her guards Scots who served in the Varangians. They can help navigate the seas and rivers better than anyone – MacDonald's men will only take you as far as Bergen. I can't risk you travelling from Scottish ports. The English are guarding them. I have no option but to send you directly from

Dunaverty, such is the importance of recovering this relic. Speak to no one before you leave except Lord MacDonald, who has a purse of gold to help you.'

'Sire, I will not disappoint you.' Domhnall bowed and turned to leave.

The King grabbed Domhnall's sleeve.

'Maccabi won't give in without a fight.'

'We aren't that much different. That is a description of me – we just have different causes.'

The King nodded. The war for independence had confused the established order. It compelled changes in roles that in normal circumstances were unimaginable. Soldiers had become priests, and priests had become soldiers. He called out to his servants.

'Help Domhnall to the boat and send Hamish Campbell to me.'

Domhnall bowed and left.

It was a difficult decision to send Domhnall. He was vital to the king's army for his healing skills and his spiritual guidance, but most of all, he was clever and resourceful.

This year Bruce's attacks would be gradual and effective, each one a small victory, designed to erode English confidence. At some point he would have to fight the English in battle, but he would wait until he was stronger and could pick the ground where he had the advantage. He would engineer that fight when everything pointed to victory.

Now was not that time. He needed Saint Fillan more.

The King held the healing stones tightly, willing God to look favourably upon him – his mind was no longer frantic. The energy within him could focus elsewhere, and his whole body was relaxing and healing. The room was peaceful and comfortable, and he was drifting off to sleep.

'Your Majesty … Your Majesty!'

He could see a blurred figure in front of him.

'Sire … you summoned me.' The voice was familiar.

He woke suddenly and recognised Hamish Campbell.

'Yes, young Campbell. I have a task for you. You must leave immediately for Tarbert Castle.'

Chapter Fourteen

**Tarbert Castle, Mull of Kintyre, September 1306:
New Life and Betrayal**

'How did I get to my chamber?'

Christina woke early with only faint memories of the previous day after she had kissed Domhnall goodbye. She liked being in control and yesterday unnerved her. She couldn't appear weak, unable to fight, as this would be a signal to the rivals to seize her lands and the clan leadership.

Eilidh watched Christina like the attentive companion she was. 'Madame, you fainted, and the guards brought you here. You must not be too harsh on yourself. It is only a few days since the English attack on Tioram. Even the castle guards are still recuperating in the cellar. We are all exhausted after the battle and know the English will come again. It is preying on everyone's mind.'

She handed Christina a goblet of ewe's milk. 'Drink this. It will give you strength. I have arranged for the herbalist to visit. She has tonics for all ailments.'

Christina did not want to eat but hadn't eaten in over a day. Her stomach growled and twisted, and she emptied the goblet.

'That feels good – ouch' Immediately she felt a twinge just above her groin on the right side.

She didn't know much about sex, but enough to understand the consequences. She didn't regret anything, and she felt no shame. Deep down, she knew she was carrying King Robert's child – her feelings were a mixture of pure joy and fear. The fear was not for herself but for the child. Its innocence wouldn't protect it if it were known that it was the child of an outlaw king.

The joy was because she had been loved by a fine man, and this child would be born out of affection and respect. If it inherited the traits of either party, it would be courageous, intelligent, noble, and kind – a child that had the potential to make a difference. If being a ruler was its destiny it would be a fine one with the advantage of being descended from a worthy man, a king, and a mother who ruled vast lands and even if it was not yet born, she was already devoted to it. This child would also protect her, as she would have an heir to inherit Clan Ranald lands and strengthen her hold against her brothers, who were both childless.

Robert had told her that Valence wouldn't achieve Longshank's goals until he had killed him, destroyed his family and his allies, and eradicated his name. Her brothers would also have another common cause; they would now have two incumbents to unseat. They would need to remove her child, just as they needed to remove her.

Her child would be hunted just like Bruce's family. There was news that Prince Edward had captured them. Fishermen had brought word that Niall had already met a traitor's death at Berwick Castle and that Elisabeth and Marjorie were incarcerated somewhere in Yorkshire. She hoped that they were rumours to demoralise the King and his supporters.

Now that Robert's daughter and heir, Marjorie, was in the hands of the English, her child would be an even greater threat to the English King's ambitions.

I will keep this child a secret until the time is right, but not for long. Soon I will start to show so I will hide in the Uists and my condition. It will be born before I meet Robert again.

She counted the months in her head and believed her child would come in May or June next year.

'Madame, you are pale. Are you still unwell? Apart from the ewe's milk, I haven't seen you eat much in days.' Eilidh reminded her of her childhood scoldings. Eilidh's voice was strict, direct as she stood over Christina with one hand firmly on her hip.

'As you said, Eilidh, we have had more than enough excitement. This rebellion has only just started, and the English want to snuff it out before it flares into something bigger. I never intended to play a part in this, but now that I am involved, the cause is intoxicating as well as exhausting. The King needs the supplies Domhnall took with him. I must get what remains over to King Robert at Dunaverty. Wagons rolling through the narrow paths between Tarbert and Dunaverty will be noticed, so we will send them by boat. The remaining supplies are in a barn outside Tarbert village.'

Eilidh frowned. 'Madame, you have servants to organise this.'

Christina shook her head.

'I think I should see to the supplies myself – Deacon can help me. Then I need to see to my own departure. My part in the destruction of Tioram and Valence's humiliation has made me a fugitive.'

Christina was resting by the fire on the top floor of Tarbert Castle. She felt dizzy and weak as well as fatigued, yet she needed to pull herself together.

'Leaving here will be as hard as Tioram, and if I remain, Tarbert Castle will be under siege, and this time Domhnall and his black powder can't be called on. I will have to tear down this castle too. There are cellars beneath the main tower that extended under the walls. I will fill them with wood, and light fires under the foundations, and leave the walls to crumble away under the heat.'

She remembered her words to King Robert.

'Let your enemy benefit nothing from their victory. Let them celebrate amongst the charnel and charcoal of devastation.' She found herself talking aloud.

'Madame, did you say something more?' Eilidh asked.

'Yes, no, sort of. I was just listening to my own advice. There is another reason for me to leave. Valence and his men can travel here by horse not boat. I have sent some of our men to watch the routes from Tioram to Tarbert. I can't let my birlinns fall into his hands so he can attack the King.'

'They will still need boats to cross Loch Linnhe and Loch Fyne,' Eilidh replied as she nervously looked out at the courtyard.

'What are you looking at?' Christina asked.

'Our men. They are loyal and brave, but we have only twenty – and when Valence comes, he will come in force.'

'Eilidh, I had forgotten that you grew up in Argyle and know the land better than most. I realise that I have placed you in great danger and neither discussed nor asked your permission. I have made assumptions about your loyalty and forgotten how much you have lost already.'

Her son Hamish Campbell was Christina's captain and a known rebel in King Robert's army. If he was caught, would be summarily executed as a traitor. Her husband Hendor had left the family, shut himself away after being mutilated by French agents working for Valence. Theirs had been a great love, and she could sense the hurt of being apart. Now Eilidh had channelled that devotion to Christina, and Christina would be more careful not to take advantage of her in the future.

'I was hoping Tarbert could be different. Hamish was born here. Hendor and I weren't married then and he was fighting with John Balliol, yet your father gave me rooms here to have my son and provided me with a father for the child, Alexander Campbell. I kept my child and my respectability. Tioram was your home and Tarbert was mine. I will never forget that time. I associate this castle with my happiest years.'

'Eilidh, this conversation is long overdue but there was never the right moment during peace time. It's a side of war I didn't expect to see, during chaos you make the time to talk because you never know when it will be your final opportunity. You are my eyes and ears, and you keep my feet on the ground with little complaint. Never underestimate the esteem in which I hold you and your family. I never meant to get you so involved. If you are ever captured, you must say you were coerced and had no choice – you and Hamish.'

Eilidh nodded and smiled as the door shook, and Harrison Deacon strode inside. Christina observed that Eilidh always looked pained when Deacon arrived. She never greeted him or tried to build any sort of rapport. Christina put it down to a generational chasm and the fact that Hendor had never trusted Deacon. Eilidh followed Hendor's lead in the company she kept.

'You must have read my mind.' Christina needed to speak with Deacon and plan for King Robert's supplies and then Uist. 'We will need to ride out later today.' Christina was ordering him, not asking.

'Is that wise, my lady, given you fainted yesterday?' Deacon asked.

'King Robert requires the surplus food and weapons we have stored outside the village … and I need you to organise their transport onto a birlinn and take them immediately to Dunaverty before the King leaves.'

'When does the King leave, and where is he heading?' Christina felt he was asking more questions than he should.

'I am not party to his plans, and they are not our business. We should also make plans to leave for the Uists.' Christina was irritated.

'Where were you this morning? I was looking for you.' Eilidh was curt.

'I went with the brewer to Tarbert. I had some questions regarding game being delivered.'

'You went alone to the village to do the work of a cook. All that effort for some grouse and partridges, when you should have been here to help Lady Christina.'

It was clear from her tone that Eilidh did not believe Deacon, but Christina had learned that their relationship was one that was unlikely to sweeten. They just didn't like each other.

Christina hadn't noticed his absence. And Eilidh was right – it was the cook's job to take care of the kitchen and its provisions.

'We can travel to the stores more quickly if it's just the pair of us. We can take the remote road and avoid the village. Please get my horse ready.'

'I will be ready on your command.' Deacon bowed and left.

He had barely left the room when Eilidh asked, 'Don't you think I should accompany you, given that you are sick? Or at least take a couple of the guards who can bring you back should you faint again.'

'I will be fine,' Christina said. 'It was just a reaction to the escape from Tioram. I am rested now.'

'Deacon is an administrator, not a soldier. He wouldn't put up much of a fight if Valence's men turn up.'

Eilidh was right, but Christina wanted to move fast, and there were men at the barns that could protect her and load the supplies.

'I can more than look after myself, and we will only be alone as far as the village.'

'Well, eat and drink a little. It will help prevent fatigue. The route to the barn is down that narrow path, and you don't want to faint again.' Eilidh presented Christina with more ewe's milk and a bowl of autumn berries. 'Eat, my lady,' she ordered.

'All right.' Christina started to eat the sweet fruit, and despite her initial reluctance, her appetite started to return, and she ate more, emptying the bowl.

'I wonder where Deacon is? He has been gone an hour, and I am anxious to be away.'

Christina finished her meal and was well prepared for the ride. In addition to a thick cloak to guard against the weather, she secured her sword around her waist, concealed a dagger in her left sleeve, and slung a crossbow over her back.

'I know you can take care of yourself. That's what worries me.' Eilidh smiled.

'Don't worry. I will be back in a half a day. Find out where Deacon is?'

*

It was lucky Deacon had rushed back from Tarbert. He had met Valence's men there, and they had returned with him to the castle to plan how they could capture Christina. They had hidden in the cellar below his rooms and had stabled their horses away from the castle on the road to the village, which was a convenient coincidence, as they would be able to wait for Deacon and Christina on the way to the barn.

'I had not expected such good fortune to fall into our laps. Christina is leaving the castle without her escort, and she is waiting for me so I can't talk for long – this is an easy opportunity for you to grab her. Take two horses from the stables. You don't have time to walk.'

They grunted an acknowledgement.

The men were well armed and fitted the part Deacon needed them to play. They had strong arms and were conditioned to following orders. Valence was good at instilling unquestioned obedience.

He would make up some story about how they had been attacked and would still be able to maintain his cover.

'She is walking into a trap, and we didn't even need to bait it.' He squeaked with delight and tingled with pleasure as the men left. He needed to delay Christina long enough for the men to reach their horses.

Valence's men would seize her on the way to the barn. He had pointed out a suitably quiet spot for her abduction and she would be taken in chains to London for King Edward to judge. He would execute her for Tioram, and there were other reasons. She was also a cousin and ally of Bruce.

King Edward would heap rewards upon him for her capture, and her death would further demoralise the Scots. He was already imagining how grateful Edward would be.

The barn was near the shore, and they could bundle her into a boat more easily from there. He had several moored nearby for transporting goods around the Ranald estates.

Finally, Eilidh appeared, and she was in a temper.

'The mistress has been calling for you. It doesn't take an hour to saddle two horses. Get to your business.' Eilidh was red-faced.

'I have a bad stomach and have been visiting the latrine,' he replied holding his belly.

Eilidh looked at him with distain as a groom led two horses into the courtyard.

'I sent word to prepare the horses, as you can see.' Deacon pointed to the groom.

'I will fetch Lady Christina.' Eilidh turned on her heels and lost no time in climbing the stairs to Christina's apartment.

Within a minute, Christina appeared and mounted her horse.

'Get a move on, Deacon – you will have to catch up with me.' She quickly kicked the horse on and galloped out of the courtyard and under the raised portcullis towards the coastal path. She didn't look around to wait for him.

As she left, he noticed the crossbow over her back. Valence's men were experienced soldiers, but he could be injured if it came to a confrontation.

'I love gold, yet I draw a line at dying for it and she is

handy with a crossbow.'

He had set up this capture, but that didn't include taking an active part in any fighting.

Deacon kicked his horse multiple times and whipped it out of the courtyard. The beast reared in pain, but he pushed its head forward and headed after Christina. He spotted the ever-inquisitive Eilidh at the window above, watching him as he left.

For the next half hour, he would make polite small talk until they were away from the castle and he could execute his plan, far away from prying eyes.

Christina had ridden hard, but the path was narrow and steep, and she had slowed.

'The King showed the English how we Scots can fight.' He was trying flattery, but Christina looked tired and only nodded when he tried to engage. They'd had conversations, and their discussions were normally limited to matters of the estate and included little small talk.

'I am sure he will welcome the supplies and weapons.' Deacon rode behind Christina in case she tried to double back. He was looking at the crossbow and thinking about how he could disarm this weapon. He decided he would rely on the English soldiers to do any dying today.

They had ridden across the causeway and turned down a narrow, heavily forested track. It was the only route towards Tarbert village, but was used infrequently. Many preferred to use the rivers and lochs to travel and transport valuables where the vagabonds taking advantage of the disordered time were less able to rob people of their goods and purses.

The trees were thick on either side of the path. The season had just slipped towards autumn, and the green pine trees were peppered with birch and maple that were turning brown, gold, and crimson. The lush ferns were at their peak and acted like great feathery blankets, covering everything where space allowed. The track was slippery with the decaying leaves and mud churned up by hooves and feet.

This was the only land route to the town from the castle.

Deacon hoped that the English soldiers would be waiting for them. They should have had enough time to arrive and hide. He had picked the perfect place for an ambush. The trees overhung that path, making it dark like the night. He would feign injury and let them pounce.

Christina stopped frequently to sip from her flask, which frustrated him.

'Madame, we need to be back at the castle before night. At this pace, we won't have time to complete the loading of the ships and return.'

'Excuse me, Deacon. I am still fatigued from Tioram.'

He rode closer, prodding her horse with his toe, hoping it would speed up. He kicked harder and the horse kicked out.

After a half hour, he was becoming anxious. They were at the spot he had picked out, he could hear noises, the breaking of branches and the snorting of horses. People preparing an ambush required the element of surprise. This couldn't be them, or if it was, they had blown any advantage they had. Christina was alarmed as she pulled the crossbow off her back. It was already loaded, and she was ready to fire.

What have they done? She will have them dead before they raise their swords.

Ahead were two figures, one following the other. With the light struggling to cut through the trees, it was difficult to recognise the lead figure apart from the shape of a horse and rider. The horses struggled to keep their footing and climbed slowly, slipping as they nimbly tried to negotiate the slope.

'Don't move. This bolt is aimed at your heart.' Christina held the crossbow directly in front of her. Her aim was steady, and her tone gave no doubt that she would carry out her threat. Deacon knew if the figure moved, it would be dead.

He started to panic; this wasn't the plan. Valance's men

were to ambush her – creep up, surprise her, and carry her away without a fight.

The lead figure remained still. Even the horse stood fixed to the spot.

'Lady Christina, it is Hamish. The King sent me. Can I move now?'

Christina lowered the crossbow, and Hamish rode towards her.

'Hamish!' Christina shouted, obviously pleased to see her captain. He was with one other man, who Deacon assumed was one of Bruce's men.

Just as they were about to embrace, the trees at the side of the path parted and branches splintered as two horses climbed from either side. Two men were leading them, and as they came up behind Hamish, they mounted and charged him from behind, forcing him and his guard off their horses. Christina's horse was startled; it threw her off its back, and she tumbled off the path and down the embankment. As she fell, Christina managed to lose her bolt. It flew past Hamish and into a tree, just missing one of the assailants.

Deacon's horse stepped backwards; the overhanging branches covered his retreat. He would melt away if it looked like the soldiers were going to lose, but they had caught Hamish, his guard, and Christina unprepared. They stabbed through the foliage, trying to run them through. They swung their swords repeatedly, slicing through bushes and ferns. What had protected the soldiers from discovery was now protecting the Scots.

Deacon slid off his horse and hid behind a tree where he could watch the fight at a safe distance.

Past the English soldiers, he could see the three Scots. Hamish was standing in front of Christina, parrying blows, as the guard fought hand to hand with the other Englishman. Christina's shoulder was drooping, and Deacon realised she must have injured it in her fall.

Christina picked up her crossbow, but her attacker pulled it from her hand.

Metal struck metal as Hamish tried to attack him with his sword. Hamish's guard had stabbed his attacker, who fell to the ground. He rushed to help Hamish, but the other attacker had taken the crossbow and fired it directly into Hamish's chest. Hamish slumped back onto Christina and groaned.

She pushed Hamish away so she could get to the English soldier, but he swung his sword, catching Hamish in the side as he fell. The Scottish guard was now behind the English soldier and ran him through from the back. His sword point stopped short of Christina's torso.

Deacon had barely taken a breath as he watched the fight. He pulled his dagger from its sheath and nicked his lip with the tip of the blade. Blood oozed down his chin and started to run down his shirt and cloak.

'That should convince them,' he mumbled.

The Englishmen are dead, and I will now join the winning side.

Just as he climbed back onto the path, the first attacker, who he had thought was dead, seemed to rally and made one last attempt to slash at Christina.

Deacon rushed towards him and stabbed him in the neck. Blood spurted out of the wound as the soldier grabbed his cloak, trying to pull him off his feet. With his last ounce of strength, he pointed at Deacon.

'You traitor.'

His artery had been cut, and a frothy mix of blood and mucus drizzled down his chin as he fell to the ground.

Deacon stood over the man he had just killed as the guard checked Hamish, but it was clear he was dead. Christina pushed him.

'Move away,' she fell to her knees, lifting Hamish's head with her left hand onto her lap. Her right arm lay limp beside her.

'Hamish!' She kissed and then embraced his face.

The moment was solemn. The guard stood in silence as Christina held Hamish, not letting him go.

'Madame, we should go,' the guard pleaded. 'You will be safer in Tarbert Castle, and there may be more of these men around here.' His sword had never left his grip, and Deacon could feel his anxiety. Only Deacon knew that these soldiers had been alone.

'You can take him now.' Christina stood up. Her right shoulder hung limply, but she didn't cry out.

Deacon lifted Hamish onto the horse as the guard checked the two attackers for any belongings before kicking them off the path and down into the steep embankments.

'Do we know who these men are?' the guard asked. His face was splattered with blood and matter, and Deacon thought he looked like the depictions of hell he had seen painted in the church.

'I have no idea,' Deacon said, 'but this was an ambush either for my lady or for Hamish. They are both wanted by the English. It is their agents.' He had little time to think of a story, but it sounded plausible because it was the truth.

'You need to get back to the castle quickly,' the guard replied.

'Help me get onto my horse …' Christina tried to hoist herself onto its back as Deacon watched. He was securing Hamish across the saddle whilst the guard lifted her carefully into the saddle and placed the reins into her left hand.

'We need to get the stores in the barn at the end of this path over to King Robert,' Christina cried.

Deacon knew she was in considerable pain and smiled behind his stony-faced concern. He might not have engineered her kidnapping successfully, but he had managed to create the circumstances for Hamish Campbell's death, and Valence's reward would be handsome. For now, he would have to put up with a grieving mother, Eilidh Robertson, and would have to hide his joy at her misery.

'You never mind about the stores,' the guard said. 'I will see to it. But you must get this lady to safety. I have orders from King Robert to look after her … and you saved me as well. I thought I had killed that man, but he seemed to die twice.' He shook Deacon's hand in gratitude.

'My men are waiting in a birlinn to load and transport the supplies. You can travel back with them and bring the King the tragic news about Hamish.' Christina turned her horse to head back up the path towards the castle.

Deacon grabbed the reins of the horse carrying Hamish's body and followed behind. They would have to hurry, as the tide would flood the castle causeway.

He tried to relax; that was close, and he was nearly discovered. His heart was still pounding, and he struggled to regain his composure. Christina looked straight ahead and said nothing as they led the horse carrying Hamish's body back to the castle.

As they entered the courtyard, Eilidh ran towards them, not yet realising the body face down on the horse was her son. Two servants carefully lifted it down. Only then did she see the face and become hysterical. Christina clumsily slid out of the saddle and bent down to comfort her.

Eilidh was kissing Hamish's pale face. 'What happened?'

Her sobbing resonated around the courtyard. Deacon felt nothing for her sorrow. These were cries of real pain, like he had witnessed when animals were caught in traps, mortally injured but not yet dead. He understood her behaviour and found joy in her anguish. He wanted to tell her about the money he would make from Hamish's death, but that was a pleasure he had to keep to himself. Someday he would take the opportunity.

'Wake up – please, wake up.' She shook Hamish's shoulders and kissed him again.

Christina embraced her whilst Deacon remained on his

horse, watching their pain and grief.

'You need to help the ladies to their rooms whilst we clean up here,' one of the servants said. They were staring at him, as he remained on his horse, making no attempt to help Eilidh. He needed to be above any suspicion.

He dismounted and removed his cloak, placing it under Hamish's head, it was a compassionate gesture he had done for effect. He tried to bring Eilidh to her feet, but she wouldn't budge, she slapped and scratched at him. He waited for Christina to make a move.

'Eilidh, Hamish can't stay here,' Christina said, 'and he wouldn't want you to either. Let's honour him properly and place him in the house of God.' She turned to the servants. 'Remove Hamish from the courtyard and place him in the chapel.'

They carefully picked up his body and placed it on Deacon's cloak, which they used to move it towards the far side of the courtyard where the chapel stood.

'The chapel is decorated with flowers and is a place he can rest at peace,' Christina said. 'You can visit him in private or stay with him – and we both need to be suitably dressed.' Eilidh stood, shaking, as Hamish was carried away.

Eilidh looked at Deacon, and in that moment he knew she believed he was responsible ... and without proof, everyone would put her suspicions down to hysteria. He would grieve tomorrow and fool everyone again.

'Deacon, ask the garrison medic to visit me. I have need of poppy water if I am to reset this shoulder.'

He watched Christina and Eilidh walk away towards their apartments before returning to his rooms below.

Now he had a letter to write telling Lord Valence about all his good news.

Chapter Fifteen

Orkney, September 1306:
Castle Halcro and the Bear

Hugh Halcro was part Scot, part Viking, but mostly bear. He studied the sea below, urging the king's ships to arrive.

'Lord Douglas, you were lucky. Any other boat would have been smashed on the rocks. God smiled on you. The coastline is an exacting one, peppered with ships of all types – friend and foe, warship and fishing boat.'

Halco fought with the banging shutters as the last of the winds battered the tower. They had become loose, and his huge hands clumsily tried to fasten them to the walls.

'The crew was saved but my ship now feeds the castle fires. Your Norwegian boat man used all his skills, but he could save nothing but the mast and keel.' Lord Douglas shook his head convinced there was still sea water trapped within his ears.

The boatman's voice resonated in his head.

Lord Halcro, only reckless or desperate men would risk these waters so late in the season.

The Norwegian loved ships more than people, and Halcro was sure that he had spotted tears in his eyes when he had told him that the birlinn couldn't be repaired and instead would be cut up.

'It is to be hoped King Robert doesn't encounter those same seas – I can't settle.' He paced the room and looked out to sea, where he hoped he would catch the first glimpse of approaching topsails. The mist at this time of year clung to the seawater until late morning. The conditions had saved the castle in the past, but they didn't distinguish between friends and enemies and had almost cost Lord Douglas his life.

In between pacing, he momentarily warmed his huge hands from the heat of the ship timbers that fed the fierce fire. Then, with his back to the fire, he lifted his woollen cloak and heated his rear.

'The Orkney winds blow the rain at a horizontal angle, and my hose is saturated.' Halcro muttered.

'Like the most attractive women, the place certainly has a unique blend of beauty and danger. If the King will be safe I am content,' Douglas replied.

The castle consisted of a two-story stone keep surrounded by a ribbon wall, which enclosed separate stables, workshops, and a kitchen. The tower was crenelated at the top, but apart from the ramparts, the fortress was plain and substantial.

This was a castle built for defence. It was tall, with thick walls and an entrance higher than any siege engine could reach, and it would take an army to breach.

'There are tunnels into the cellar from the shore via caves. When the King arrives, he can be in brought into the castle safely and without being observed. I have made all the preparation for the arrival of all the king's ships – where are you, Robert?'

He could see across the whole of the island where the winds had lifted the sea fog and the sun had burnt through. In September that happened less and less but today was clearer than most.

'My castle may be a simple arrangement, but it will provide for all our needs – protection, transport, weapons, food, and water. There is even a small chapel, "Our Ladie at Halcro", is just outside the inner wall and can cater to the garrison's spiritual needs.'

Douglas didn't respond.

Halcro watched as a few reluctant sheep were being taken to the kitchen. They would soon be smoked and in the larder to feed them over the winter. The fields had been harvested, and bales of hay and barrels of oats and wheat were stacked to stave off any attempt at siege. Chickens strutted and cows mooed, sheltering with the horses in the stables.

'Does the Norwegian King come here at all?' Douglas asked.

'Not at all – South Ronaldsay is an island loyal to Scotland and King Robert, paying but a passing acknowledgement to King Haakon. Haakon is too far away to be a threat or offer us protection, and we look to ourselves. He sits fat, happy and disinterested, in Oslo if we pay his taxes as overlord. When King Robert arrives, we will be ready. The larders are stocked, and we have enough wood to heat the keep over the winter. Your ship will keep many islanders warm this winter.'

Douglas was a pallid colour, tinged with the greenish-blue hue that rough seas gave to anyone but the seasoned sailor. He consumed the ale placed before him like a condemned man washing down his last meal.

'I can see you appreciate the properties of the brewer's ale. It has revived many an Orcadian.' Halcro chortled.

King Robert would have only sent word of his arrival ahead in the hands of his most trusted supporter, yet it was clear Lord Douglas was no sailor.

'I swallowed the ocean, so I have made a contract with God with only one clause.' Douglas had a chronic hacking cough.

'And what would that be?' Halcro asked, already knowing the answer. It was an oath he had heard from many people who had crossed from the Scottish mainland.

'The Almighty can ask anything from me, but when it comes to crossing the Pentland Firth, I will graciously decline.'

Douglas quickly filled his goblet and drained it twice as quickly. The excess drained through his thick black beard, which dangled heavy with drying salt.

'Lord Douglas, it will be hard for you to seal that contract with God, because I am sure you have noticed Castle Halcro is on an island. The sea is the only way out of here.'

Halcro slapped Douglas on the shoulder. Douglas forced a reluctant grin, acknowledging the unpalatable reality.

'This castle will protect the King whilst we plan his return to Scotland – and remember, my lord, that those caves reach all the way through to the crypt of this keep. They are also a way in for our enemies, and they are guarded by my most trusted sentries. Their existence is known to only a handful who remain inside the castle. There are thick iron gates before the crypt, which can be locked if we are attacked.'

Halcro was honoured the King had trusted him with his protection and was alert to any threat and vulnerability. He returned to searching the horizon.

'The King left a day or two behind me. He may have taken a less direct route to Orkney, stopping off at Rathlin Island. The English are obsessed with his capture – his coronation was an affront to their arrogance.'

Douglas sighed and lowered his eyes.

'King Robert has also been indisposed.'

'Lord Douglas, your words are very diplomatic – I heard gossip and your manner suggests these rumours are true.'

'The King doesn't wish his illness to be discussed.'

His furtive demeanour suggested that he was understating its extent and didn't want to talk further. Halcro knew when to change the subject.

'Lord Sinclair understands these waters better than any Englishman and will land the King safely. I hope my praise isn't just flattery.'

Halcro handed Douglas a small flask. Douglas sniffed the contents and smiled.

'I know what this is.' Douglas moistened his lips with its contents.

'A local medicine known to combat any ill effects from near drowning and recommended by my physician for its medicinal effects.' Halcro urged Lord Douglas to drink more.

'Well, if this is on the physician's advice, I cannot in good conscience go against him.' Douglas swallowed most of the contents in one gulp.

'How many ships will the King bring?' Halcro asked as Douglas finished the whiskey.

'There are at least six ships and around one hundred men. Aonghus MacDonald brought twenty to add to the men that escaped Tioram. More men will come when King Robert returns to Scotland – and he will need people like you to lead them, Hugh.'

Halcro slightly inclined his head, acknowledging the compliment, yet he was not complacent. One hundred men were hardly sufficient to take on the English army.

'James, men need battlefield success to bring their swords confidence. King Robert has not won a battle since his coronation.'

'I do not ignore the challenge that we are facing, but we would be fools to try and fight the English on the battlefield again because we would lose. We have a new tactic: making sure they never benefit from any victory. Tioram has barely two stones left on top of one another. The English take their frustrations out on the people when they should be trying to make friends with them. Skirmishes are already taking place all over Scotland, tying down their men and supplies. The English have retaliated in places they haven't been attacked. Their actions are ill-judged and disproportionate, and they ensure that it is only a matter of time before they marginalise the people and they join the Bruce in numbers. The English will lose the country through hubris.' Douglas's passion was convincing.

'It doesn't take too many men like us to build and lead an army,' Halcro added as he filled both their goblets. 'Let's toast King Robert.'

Halcro lifted his goblet, and Douglas followed.

'To the good health of King Robert.' Halcro drank the goblet just as the door opened and his steward ran in, out of breath. The evidence of a muddy ride was splattered all over his cloak.

'Lord Halcro, ships have been sighted on the west of the islands flying the colours of the House of Bruce!'

*

They had disguised MacDougall's horse transporter well. However, whilst it looked like a merchant ship, it smelled of horse shit, and as hard as he tried, Jean de Grailly couldn't erase it from his nostrils.

'So, this is Kirkwall.' Konrad was contemptuous.

They had docked at the jetty near the main thoroughfare.

'Valence's brave Englishmen couldn't desert fast enough. Let's hide behind the wool bales over there.' They snuck off the ship and were now hidden behind a cargo of wool and wine.

'How sure are you that Valence's crew won't say something that gives us away?' Jean understood the limits on the balance of loyalty a conscripted man could have to Valence once drink and a whore were factored in on the other side.

'We were well hidden in the hold beneath the captain's cabin. I would have killed them all if necessary.' Konrad appeared undisturbed by the possibility.

'Wouldn't you jump ship at the first opportunity? Most of Valence's men were Welsh and conscripted. They would prefer to embrace the Scots than kill them,' Jean replied.

'I intend to return here with Bruce in a sack before anyone realises we are here.' Konrad's attention was on his surroundings.

Between each row of inns and shops were the dark recesses of hidden criminality. The two men would wait until there was no one around before they moved again. Jean knew to be patient, to watch and listen, after so many years in his Byzantine prison.

'We will wait an hour until the temperature drops, and the sea fog rolls in before we make our move.' Konrad removed some dried sausage and a flask of wine from his saddlebag before placing it beneath him, concealing his face.

'I am too old to get a fever sitting on a cold, damp floor,' Konrad mumbled as he oriented himself on his makeshift seat and was joined by Jean.

'Ruaidhri Ranald will rendezvous with us here later. Strange that he found excuses not to join us on the journey here, given what Bruce did to his brother. Valence has an agent who will know how to get us into the Halcro castle, if Ranald fails to appear.' Konrad spat sausage skin indiscriminately onto the floor as he spoke.

'Strange – he left before us yet hasn't arrived. Lord Valence wants us to wait for him. I think we should.' Jean was still hopeful he would appear.

Konrad grunted his approval.

They drank, ate, and didn't speak again. Silence was a familiar form of communication for two men who had lived every day for fifteen years in each other's company. The silence meant all was well.

The sea fog had started to roll in as predicted, but it was patchy. At sea level it was deep and enveloping, and they felt hidden and unobserved as they crept out of their hiding place. About twenty feet above, the air was clearer, and shapes could be distinguished.

Kirkwall town was a small settlement stretched out along the seafront. Inns and trading houses were every second or third dwelling, but the town was dominated by the red sandstone edifice that was St. Magnus Cathedral. Its grandeur attracted the eye of anyone arriving. Jean considered its size strange, disproportionate and out of place when everything else was so utilitarian.

'Who would have thought we could find such a place here?' Jean de Grailly had seen many such magnificent cathedral buildings in his life. 'I am astonished to see incredible beauty in such an unexpected place.'

Konrad was disinterested.

The cathedral was directly ahead of their hiding place. Its front arches were lit by large torches subdued by the thickening fog. Next to it was a stone tower, and close by another large building which Jean assumed was the Lord of Orkney's palace.

'There must be money here, see soldiers, expensive weapons and armour.' Jean pointed at two sentries standing at the palace gate.

Konrad appeared unimpressed, he had received an education, but Jean concluded there was nothing classical about it.

'Aren't you the least in wonder?' Jean pointed towards the entrance.

'I am here because I was sent to capture Bruce, and if a chance presents itself, to bring him alive back to Valence and English justice. That's why you are here – not to admire the architecture.'

Jean thought that after so long chained together in different Byzantine prisons, he should have been used to Konrad's lack of appreciation and curiosity. The man lived in a cocoon of ignorance, completely uninterested in the small strands of beauty that made the world wonderful. He wondered how such a shallow character had survived so long.

He had concluded many years ago that von Feuchtwangen's interests were of the more animalistic type and that beauty for him strictly applied to women. When they had been shackled in the Byzantine dungeons, he had never found something to respect about his companion, and their relationship had always been one of mutual survival.

'Lord Valence has advised us to seek out Henry de Stikelaw. His brother Weland is a Bruce supporter. Apparently, there has been a brotherly falling out, and Henry is working for Lord Valence now. It shouldn't be hard to find him. He lives in the first stone house to the left of the main jetty, so it must be a few hundred yards away.'

The evening light was now in constant retreat. Darkness and the fog consumed the houses without torches or fires within to illuminate their outlines. Jean spotted a small one-story house like the one that had been described – a stone building amongst a small row of wooden structures. Smoke was coming out from the roof, and someone was at home.

'I have a letter and some gold to sweeten our arrival.' Konrad threw his saddle and leather sack over his shoulder, and Jean followed.

'I don't think we should run, but neither should we dawdle. This is a wild place without any love for English agents, and if the locals find us, there are a multitude of offences that would guarantee our execution. King Haakon would consider us spies. The Scottish lords who rule under King Haakon have no loyalty to the English or the French and would hang us simply on the suspicion that we are transgressors up to no good.'

'Konrad, you don't need to explain our situation.'

Jean knocked on the door, and a large man answered. It was not what he was expecting. The man looked like a soldier, not a spy. Spies were invariably meek and cunning.

'Come in. I am Henry de Stikelaw. Valence sent word through an English merchant that you would arrive. He only got here two days ago so I have been busy making a map of Halcro Castle, and I have it ready for you. My efficiency will cost you a heavy purse of gold. I hope you are in funds

– there is a great deal of reason not to indulge in pleasantries and to make this as short a meeting as possible, I don't want to know about you or why you are here.'

The house was very dark apart from the peat fire, which was sending smoke up a small fireplace. The house consisted of one main room and a small mezzanine above with two cots on either side where people slept. Jean gently removed the fastening on his sword.

They had never met Stikelaw before, and letters could be intercepted. Konrad strode in as if he had no concerns.

Stikelaw had assembled three chairs next to the fire and urged them to sit. An unfurled parchment lay on a small trestle table.

'Is that our map?' Jean asked.

Stikelaw lit a small whale oil lamp from the fire and placed it on the table, holding one edge of the parchment flat.

The detail was hard to discern, so Stikelaw leaned forward.

'Gentlemen, look.' His hands swept across the document. 'As you can see, the caves are cavernous and open to the sea. You need to find a way onto the shore without being seen. Once on the shore, it is a short walk and climb into the largest cave. There are two caves next to each other, separated by a stone wall that is pitted with flaws. There is then a corridor from the back of the caves running for about four hundred yards that will take you just below the king's apartments one floor above. A stone staircase leads to the keep.'

'How do we know it's genuine?' Konrad asked.

'That's a risk you will have to take, and you are in no position to negotiate, take it or leave it I don't care but Lord Valence might. Now, where is my money?' Stikelaw held out his hand. Jean found his manner overly aggressive. In theory, they were on the same side. However, the map looked genuine, and nothing in this world was free.

Konrad slammed a purse of gold onto the table.

'Now, would you both kindly fuck off before we are all arrested?'

Stikelaw nodded in the direction of the door, and after rolling up the map stuck it in Konrad's shirt. Jean took the hint and bundled Konrad out of the door.

'And he's a diplomat; I should have killed him,' Konrad scoffed. The irony was not lost on Jean as they walked quickly away from the house.

Chapter Sixteen

The Isle of Alderney, Late September 1306:
A Shoddy Crew

'Quickly, throw me a rope and get me on board – and hurry, damn you! I have urgent news. Where is Amerales d'Aunes?'

Aurelian and his companion, Jakob Dedekam, were ten feet away from the side of a majestic painted war galley.

He could see the masts of at least nine others anchored nearby, lined up in a row. This ship flew the emblem of the emperors. This is where the *amerales*, the commander of the flotilla, could be found. However, the announcement of the flagship's location didn't please him.

'That's not like d'Aunes,' he mumbled under his breath, 'Do you normally greet the commander of the Varangian guard with armed crossbows?' he shouted towards the armed sailors.

Two sailors on watch were bent over the side, staring down at him with what he read as vacant disinterest.

The ship was a large galley, about one hundred and fifty feet long. Aurelian could smell the resin from the fresh wood. The single bank of oars was pulled into the keel, and the anchor had been dropped. The wood squealed and croaked as the sea attempted to free it from its restraints.

'Where are the rest of the crew?' He could feel his irritation was a small step from anger.

Singing and laughing from the ship forced him to shout.

'They are eating. Just wait and be patient, and we will fetch the commander,' one of the guys shouted back before he turned and disappeared.

Aurelian could feel his face flush red. Impatience was part of his character, and today it wouldn't be tempered with any of his limited tolerance.

'These sailors need to be taught some manners,' he muttered at Dedekam who was staring silently at the ship. It was a grand vessel and uncommon this far from where it was built in Genoa.

'Axel, we can wait a little while. The journey out here from Honfleur took more than a day of hard rowing. Here, take some wine – the ship is marvellous.'

Dedekam took a liberal glug of wine and then offered the skin to Aurelian, his golden hair was now shorn for concealment. He ran his fingers through the grey-blond stubble in frustration.

'I have had to do much to get here, Jakob. Six months of killing, risking my life pursuing this treasure. I came close to capturing it in Paris for the emperors, and now, when its tantalisingly within our grasp we are kept waiting like beggars – it's like the bureaucrats have taken over … Metochites is behind this.'

The wine landed on an empty stomach and didn't improve his mood.

'Pass me some of the bread and dried sausage while we wait for these idiots.'

Dedekam threw him a small hemp sack, and Aurelian cut several large slices of saucisson, which he washed down with mouthfuls of sweetened wine.

'Where did you get such a fine sword? Looks European.' Dedekam pointed beside Aurelian.

'I retrieved this sword in Padua.' Aurelian had placed a heavy sword by his side engraved with lions and displaying a large citrine on the pommel. He pushed it over to Dedekam.

'Fine workmanship.' Jakob ran his hands over the flat side examining the decoration.

'Came from a man I later learned was called Gaston de Bezier. I came across him on the grounds of Scrovegni's palazzo in Padua, injured and groaning and wearing nothing but boots. He swung his sword at me but he was dying – I had to finish him off to silence him. I really wanted him alive so he could talk – whoever had attacked him first had also been looking for something. Bezier's clothes had been removed, cut up, and scattered around him. I had followed him from The Paris Temple – he was acting for someone hiding amongst the Templars, so it was a serious attempt by a well-armed knight to find the treasure – he had instruction that I needed to find.' Aurelian grabbed the wine skin again.

'What did you find?' Dedekam's curiosity had been piqued.

'Nothing in his clothing, so I gutted him to see if he had swallowed it – the crusades often required messages to be carried internally – I still found nothing. I never did find out who sent him to Padua.'

'So, whomever it was is still out there – are we being followed?' Jakob's language moved from curiosity to one of anxiety.

'Yes, and they have been trailing the treasure and us. I feel their presence – twenty years surviving in the Varangian guards gives you this insight. In a day or so, the Scots will be here, it's close to Honfleur and now they have two ships they stand a better chance of finally escaping France. The Emperors Michael and Andronikos sent these magnificent ships to take the riches back to Byzantium – and we are waiting here drinking wine.'

'Isn't d'Aunes your man, Axel? And who is Metochites?'

'Yes, he is my man which makes this situation perplexing. I have always been treated like a son by emperor Andronikos, and Metochites considers me his rival. He wants to remove, isolate me from the emperors, and make me just another dispensable mercenary working for gold. Real power in

Byzantium is moving from the brave to the bureaucrats; they are taking over. In my absence I have had a sense that I was being removed little by little from my position of influence.'

Aurelian paused, he had said enough to a man he knew but perhaps not well enough. Sitting in a small fishing boat so far from Constantinople had brought these doubts into his mind. For the first time in twenty years, he was thinking about going home. He tried to banish these thoughts and focus on the treasure, but these little slights were building in his mind.

'The Scots have survived in France for several weeks, and we know they have been joined by another Scottish ship. More people to fight for the treasure.'

Aurelian nodded.

'They have had help in evading their pursuers, but they are resourceful. I watched them fight at L'Auberge du Lion, and they fought well; they removed the Wolf Brothers and saved me a task. They have courage, strength and intelligence – they killed the people they had to and swapped the treasure from the barge to a cog. Fooled everyone but me – that's how I know they will be here in a cog, and we can use the navy to catch them without the French or English to get in the way. But we need to act fast before the other fools realise they have been tricked. The English and French may have some ships around their coasts capable of trapping the treasure, we can't risk the cog falling into their hands – those who followed the barge will know by now that it contained nothing but rocks and an ignorant crew.'

Dedekam had provided information on where the Scots were heading, and Aurelian wondered where he got his intelligence. He accepted that Dedekam didn't have an exclusive arrangement with anyone, and his information, though purchased, seemed genuine. Emperor Michael used him to pass intelligence to Byzantine agents, and that was how he had known where to meet d'Aunes and the navy.

'The Scots are bound for Orkney, an archipelago off the north coast of Scotland that I know well. It will be a hard trip, nevertheless. I requested that the crew include some of my Varangian's with knowledge of the waters.'

The Scots had been sent some help, a Scottish boat, but Scotland was occupied. Who could have organised another ship?

'My men would take the ship if I commanded them,' Aurelian said. 'They are all fine sailors, they must be with the Byzantine conscripts, who spend most of their time drunk or in the process of getting drunk. We must get the ships battle-ready. This ship needs to capture the cog and be as far on the way back to Constantinople as the weather will allow. I don't want to be fighting the Scots, English, and French all at the same time – do you see how the ships are assembled? They chose the right place, anchored just off Alderney, but they don't seem prepared.'

'I noticed the look on your face when you saw the pennant,' Dedekam replied.

Aurelian appreciated that he wasn't the only one who understood the stupidity.

'They have announced who they are to the fishermen and any ships that come across them. See? The imperial ensign, the *basilikon phlamoulon*, hangs majestically with the tetragram cross in gold and crimson.'

Aurelian pointed to the mast above them, and his companion nodded.

'This warship carries a crew of two hundred, yet there are only two men on lookout. I hope the commanders have been told the importance of a successful outcome. It looks like they have come with all the grandeur and prestige, I hope they are more prepared to fight?'

Aurelian shook his head. 'This is all too strange, Jakob. Ferran d'Aunes is an efficient commander. They need to take up the crescent formation across the strait to catch the cog, yet they are huddled next to each other. They couldn't outmanoeuvre a brick; the Scots could easily sail around them without them even knowing. The Byzantines still believe in their inherent moral superiority and have forgotten that past glories mean nothing; a flawed sense in their own exceptionalism and entitlement, nurturing an aura of invincibility that dimmed three hundred years ago. The Varangians spent years instilling discipline and making them winners again and in the last six months since I have been away, they have resorted to these old habits – the Byzantine Empire is in terminal decay.'

Aurelian's thoughts had become words that flowed out too easily. The truth was always easier than a lie. He couldn't ignore that the empire was declining and nothing he could do would change that. They no longer had the wealth, learning, or creativity to teach the world anything.

'At least I have my Varangians. Each of them is worth twenty conscripted men, and I can place them amongst each of the other ships to maintain discipline. I only need one good ship to seize the cog; the remaining ships can guard it. There is strength in numbers. The ships might not be fighters, but they can intimidate, and that is half the battle. When are we going to get on board?' Aurelian shouted up again as he started to unravel a grappling hook. These ships were high sided to make boarding difficult, but he was in a mood to try anyway.

The singing grew louder as the two sailors returned.

The ship was high in the water, and the deck was surrounded by a wooden screen to stop attackers from climbing on board – precisely what Aurelian was trying to do. He still held his grappling iron in one hand, and two crossbows were now squarely aimed at his chest as a third man appeared. He had no more sense of urgency than his crew.

'Amerales d'Aunes is still in Constantinople, and I am

in command. I presume you are Aurelian. We have been expecting you.'

'Expecting me with crossbows?' Aurelian said. 'I was clear that d'Aunes was to command the ships for the operation. My request to the emperors was unambiguous. What are you doing on this ship?'

'I am Amerales Andrea Morisco from Genoa. I am on this ship by order of my master, Mesazon Theodore Metochites, and I don't take too kindly to your tone.'

'You don't like my fucking tone? Well, I don't like being left in a rowboat whilst you finish eating. I am here by the emperor's command, and you are here to follow my orders.' Aurelian felt the anger surge through him. It was a good thing Morisco wasn't within arm's reach.

Morisco paused and didn't respond, making Aurelian even angrier. The *amerales* brushed Aurelian's words away like fluff from a sleeve.

'We have heard of an increase in vessels patrolling these waters. My master has sent ten ships out from Constantinople, and he wants ten ships back. The Genoese built them for your emperors and haven't been paid yet, and I am here to ensure no one is reckless with our goods.' Morisco clearly didn't know why he was here.

'So that bureaucrat who would get seasick in the baths now controls the navy?'

Aurelian hated Metochites for being a coward, sitting one thousand miles away behind palace walls. The emperors needed this treasure to save their empire, yet they had devolved its recovery into talk, not action. Aurelian imagined Metochites' political choreography to place himself at the heart of this operation, directing its course yet ensuring any failure would be blamed on Aurelian and Morisco.

'Yes, and he writes to me regularly, reminding me of the cost of each new ship down to the price of the nails. Throw the man a rope!' Morisco ordered.

The sailors lowered their crossbows and threw a heavy rope ladder right in front of Aurelian. The hemp fibres brushed the edge of his nose as it dropped on his feet. He didn't believe its closeness was an accident.

I will deal with them later, and they will learn all about Axel Myhre.

Aurelian had arrived in a small single-masted fishing boat that had taken the whole day to travel the ninety miles. The journey back for one man would be hard. Aurelian chose to speak in Norsk.

'Jakob, steady the boat and then you can leave me. Be careful as you return to Honfleur – the wind is against you, and the French and English will be snooping around. Send word to the emperors of what happened here. There is a merchant ship leaving from Honfleur for Constantinople tomorrow.'

Dedekam held out his hand, which Aurelian shook vigorously.

'I have sailed these waters for over twenty years, and as a final gesture of friendship, warn your *amerales* to avoid L'Raz. It's the strait that runs between La Hague and the south of Alderney; it is treacherous. The waves are high and quick, and combined with the wind, they create sea foam. It is so dense that you can't see your bow. There are hidden rocks all around that island, so it pays to be a mile or so off the coast when you travel west. Complacency has claimed the unwary and the greedy.'

Dedekam prepared the sail to return to Honfleur. He moved the large oar to his right and placed it just above the water, ready to steer the boat away once Aurelian had stepped onto the rope ladder.

Aurelian moved his axe further round his back and pulled a large leather sack over the other shoulder. Despite his considerable strength, the items he carried were heavy. He had to grip hard onto the side of the ladder as the ship swayed from side to side, clashing with the small boat.

'The swell is increasing, and the boats are bouncing off each other. There is an unhealthy ring of splintering wood. There is no contest; I am coming off worse,' Dedekam cried as Aurelian started to clamber up the ladder. Aurelian turned briefly and watched him push away using the large oar before grabbing the other oar and rowing with all his might.

The ladder was coarse, and shards of sharp hemp dug into Aurelian's hands. His boot slipped as the rope was splashed by the heavy squall.

The waves rose several feet, so he had to be careful not to be battered against the side of the warship. If he fell into the sea, he would be pulled under by the weight of the axe, his belongings, and his clothes. Dedekam's boat splashed more water onto his leather shoes and woollen hose, and they were becoming saturated.

If he fell he would drown, so he moved carefully yet quickly. Morisco removed a panel on the side of the ship and held out his hand to pull Aurelian onto the deck.

Aurelian firmly grabbed his sleeve and for a second contemplated pulling him over the side but instead clambered onto the deck turning to watch Dedekam sail away to the southeast towards Honfleur. Dedekam waved back.

'Why did it take so long to get me on board? You knew I was coming!'

'We are to offer you every service, but I issue the orders on this ship. My crew was hungry and thirsty, and we were at anchor after a treacherous journey round Biscay, so I saw no reason to assemble them. I expected you would want a quiet welcome. Your Varangians did not have to be persuaded to join my men. They are all below, enjoying the galley together.'

Morisco was calm yet assertive and as smug and self-righteous as Metochites. There wasn't room for two people on the ship who thought they were in charge.

'I also have orders from Emperor Andronikos, in Metochites' hand.' Morisco removed a scroll from his elaborately embroidered sleeve, and Aurelian recognised the emperor's seal.

He was a little younger than Aurelian and looked as if he had just stepped out of a court banquet. His uncreased gown was crimson silk decorated with horizontal silver threads that sparkled as they caught the low sunlight. Underneath the flamboyant gown was a fine linen undershirt and tied at his waist was a red silk cummerbund. Tucked within the belt was a sword, held in place by a gilded chain that also stretched around his waist. It looked ornamental.

He did have one sign of his position: a metal helmet decorated with mythical gods and creatures of the sea, lined with what Aurelian guessed was sealskin. The fur protected his ears and forehead from the abrasive metal.

'Are you battle-ready?' Aurelian asked.

Aurelian took a step closer to Morisco and removed his belongings from his back. He shook off the excess water, and deliberately splashed water onto Morisco, who took a large step back and brushed the large droplets away from the front of his tunic.

'This is something we shouldn't discuss in front of my crew. Somewhere more private would be better.'

Morisco directed Aurelian to a small, covered area on the starboard side of the deck. A heavy padded couch was pressed against the support for the wooden platform and half deck above.

The half deck was open to the air, and on it was a collection of grenades, ballistae and the large bolts used for ammunition, caltrops, containers of lime, crossbows, and barrels of black tar. Aurelian could see the rims had been leaking, and sticky black gunge had run down the side of each barrel. Ahead of the platform, he caught sight of a golden serpent's head where Greek fire would pour down on ships that came within range.

You aren't so ill prepared for this job as I feared. This is certainly the time and place for a serious conversation.

'Ready for what battle? I am here to capture a barge. Nothing was said about any sea combat.' Morisco was clearly not expecting to fight anyone.

'Why do you think the emperor sent ten ships thousands of miles to capture one ship? And what are all those weapons and barrels of fuel for Greek fire stored on the deck – a fucking coincidence?' Aurelian pointed to the cluttered platform.

'You may think you run things here and that the emperor is in your pocket, but since you have been away gallivanting around France, things have changed in Constantinople. Money is tight, and battles are no longer just the realm of the soldier. Let me share a few things about what is going to happen here. These ships are for show and haven't been paid for yet. Metochites has done a deal with Genoa, and the weapons are to intimidate. Sea battles are not fought so late in the year, as the weather sinks more ships than any battle. These galleys do not handle well in rough seas, despite their size – I have two thousand men on board, the supplies alone require an extra ship, and even in favourable weather, we give battle only when we are assured of numerical superiority and the opposition gives in without a shot being fired.'

Aurelian wanted to grab Morisco by the throat and punch sense into him.

'So, shall I tell the crew carrying the treasure to stay in port until the weather improves next spring?'

'Metochites warned me that you might be difficult. That's why he sent me rather than d'Aunes, who is more … how should we say … reckless? I was a pirate before I became an *amerales* in the imperial navy, so don't let my finery confuse you. I know how to fight at sea and survive. We capture this cog using cautious tactics, our priority is to capture the ship *and* protect the fleet. We have been sent information by many agents on the route, and we were waiting for you to arrive to confirm this intelligence.'

'Metochites sends a pirate at the commander of an imperial fleet – doesn't seem right to me?' Aurelian's question was a statement.

'I am here, so my opinion doesn't matter, and neither does yours – Metochites runs things now – by order of the emperors. You can work with me or go over the side and see if you can catch your friend up'.

Dedekam was now a spot on the horizon.

Aurelian was beginning to consider that Metochites had made such an inappropriate choice because he didn't intend for Aurelian to succeed or return. The man dressed like an aristocrat spoke like a thug. Morisco was provoking him, then he would have an excuse to kill him.

Aurelian knew he had been betrayed and abandoned. The emperors had allowed themselves to be outmanoeuvred. This self-defeating action of making Metochites responsible for the treasure stuck in his craw, and the thought of leaving his well-being to such men convinced him that the Byzantine Empire was a lost cause. He would be returning with the treasure, but it would be to his childhood home in Norway.

'I will be well rewarded – as will you – when we return to Constantinople. I see no difference in our stations. We are both here for the money, so let's stop arguing.'

Morisco produced an untidy roll of mismatched messages from his sleeve and started to unroll them.

'We have many messages, some from the Norwegian and English kings, others in your hand and there is a clear suggestion the barge is heading north, to waters to which we could never venture. This time of the year it would be suicide. The currents in Scottish waters are notorious for delivering downed ships and dead sailors. We have neither experience nor charts to help us, so our work needs to be done here – we capture the ship here!'

Morisco pointed to the messages, and Aurelian ignored him. He knew what was written there, as he had authored most of them.

'How are you proposing to capture the treasure if you don't intend to risk anything? This all assumes the weather is with us, and as you can see, the swell and tides are high.'

Aurelian was going to seize this ship once darkness fell. His frustration was such that he considered killing Morisco on the spot, especially since he now realised Morisco would kill him when the opportunity arose.

'The acquisition of intelligence and the element of surprise, as well as overwhelming numbers, will win this prize. We are anchored off Alderney just a short hop from the shipping lane, so we can capture the barge without any conflict. I already have patrols looking for them, and they will return here when the treasure ship is spotted.'

Morisco was smug, defiant, and inflexible, just like Metochites.

'We won't have a fleet if our plan isn't robust,' Aurelian said. 'I assume you are aware that there are several significant players, all highly motivated to seize the treasure. I have been sending back dispatches to the emperors telling them so. The treasure is in a cog that can outrun you and any of the other colossal in this fleet.'

Morisco put up his hand as if he was stopping his words. 'Metochites *always* keeps me informed.' His tone was matter of fact and dismissive.

'Besides overcoming the Scots, who have evaded numerous attempts to capture them and the treasure, we will certainly encounter French and English ships. None of them will give in without a fight. They aren't going to keep in port because they fear losing a ship or two. This treasure can buy a thousand ships, and yet you are still telling me you won't engage them?'

Morisco was listening to what Aurelian was saying, but he certainly hadn't heard him. However, now that Aurelian had decided Morisco was to die, his frustration subsided. The man had hours to live. He would soon be at the bottom of the sea.

'Once they are spotted, I intend to form the flotilla into a crescent shape so we can support each other. The ships on the flanks will drive the treasure ship into the centre. We will be there with weapons ready, and they will capitulate without a fight. If there are any hostile ships, we have Greek fire and a selection of weapons on show. The French and English tactics will not be any different from ours. They will only engage if there aren't any options, and I don't think they have the numbers to engage. The English take whatever ships they can steal from fishermen and merchants. The French don't have any ships apart from the ones they commandeer from the Templars or their Jewish merchants, and, from what I hear, neither are in port. We are the only flotilla in the area.'

Aurelian knew the Templars were trying to get this treasure as far away from King Phillip as they could. He had watched the treasure escape from underneath the Temple, where it had been stored in a labyrinth for many years. King Phillip had been asleep upstairs when it was moved. It was certain the Templars would not lift a finger to help him seize it.

'The English and French may not have navies to take you on, but that doesn't mean to say they won't use whatever forces they can to attack you and steal the treasure from under your nose.'

Morisco started to pare his nails, obviously irritated and bored with Aurelian's continual challenges. 'If they are heading north from the mouth of the Seine, they will have to come around Cherbourg and north of Alderney,' he snapped back. 'That is why I have sent several of my small landing ships to survey the area. You could join one and see for yourself – but not tonight'.

'Why not?' Aurelian demanded.

'The last ones will be returning within the hour, and it will be dark soon. Not even your brave Scots will venture into these waters at night. We will start again at first light, and you can join them. We have already lost one boat, and you would be astounded with how many people have gone over the side.'

Morisco had no intention of returning to Constantinople with the treasure and Aurelian. That suited Aurelian, because now he had no intention of returning with Morisco.

'You should join your men in the galley and fill your stomach. You might not get another chance.' With a flick of his wrist, Morisco summoned a guard.

'Take Varangian Myhre to join his men downstairs. Don't dawdle. I am sure our guest is hungry and thirsty. And tomorrow, see that he is on the first landing boat.'

The armed sailors looked like a guard rather than an escort. Aurelian was keen to join up with his men, and he would soon put his plans to seize the ship into operation.

Morisco's guards walked to either side of him, so close it felt like they were pushing him to an open hatch that led to a staircase and down to the lower deck, where the galley was situated.

'Oh, I split your men up amongst a few of the ships. Good to share their experience around the fleet, don't you think?'

Morisco left and headed up to the half deck above, where a cabin had been built into a high wooden castle facing the bow so that the *amerales* could survey everything ahead.

Aurelian knew he was in imminent danger; he wondered how many Varangians were on this ship, and estimated that there would be at least one hundred and fifty Byzantine conscripts. He still believed that one Norwegian was worth at least ten of any conscripted force, so if he had twenty men, that would be enough.

Killing Morisco was the key to taking over the fleet, so he would spend the next few hours before the next light finding out from his men who was with Morisco and who was not. He would also learn what ships the Genoese were on, because they would also have to die.

As he entered the galley, it was dark, and his eyes could not adjust from the daylight. He could hear cheers as he was recognised.

'Welcome, sir!'

He felt an arm reach out towards him, and he recognised a cohort captain of the palace guards wearing his distinctive scarlet tunic, hose, and gilded cape. Resting on the galley tables were their iron helmets, also gilded.

On their backs were a scarlet shield and axe. Aurelian counted at least twenty men aligned at either side of the fixed wooden benches. Their daggers were laid in front of them and were being used to cut meat and bread.

They looked like they had been placed in the middle of an overwhelming number of non-Varangian sailors and soldiers, many of whom were slumped over their benches, obviously inebriated.

'*Det er bra.*' Aurelian smiled.

'What was that, sir?' the captain asked.

'Nothing – but I think you can help me. I have a few questions for you; sit with me because I have lots of things I want to discuss.'

Aurelian dropped his belongings on the floor, and they started to talk.

Chapter Seventeen

The Alderney Race, Late September 1306: Dangerous Seas and Drowning Men

'Are you sure this will work? It's only a stone, and I don't believe in magic. Looks more like stained glass than anything else.'

Innes held the sunstone up to the sun, which was becoming increasingly difficult to find due to the thickening fog. Colours cascaded onto his hand.

'And if you stand in a different place and point it at the sun, the colours will be different.' Adam de Irwyne was quick to advise. 'The sun is positioned above the place where the refraction and colours merge.'

Adam had been on the cog only a few days, but Jamie had recognised his traits immediately after spending six months living with his younger brother Will.

He was educated and intelligent. As brothers, they didn't look much like each other apart from across the eyes. It was Hendor who had commented on their identical mannerisms. When they talked one on one with anyone, they rested their chin between their index finger and thumb and adopted a quizzical face. Will was always interested in people, even the ones he didn't care for, and Adam was no different.

Will had never mentioned an older brother, and Jamie assumed it was because he hadn't been sure if Adam was alive or dead. He hadn't wanted to tempt fate or share a secret that could be tortured out of his allies by the English. It was better not to know too much about people.

It was clear the Irwyne's had become radicalised after the English killed their father. Jamie didn't know anyone who hadn't been impacted when the English invaded. They had disregarded their position as leading nobles, lost their lands and thrown in their lot with King Robert like everyone else on this boat. What they all had in common was having nothing to lose.

'As you said, Innes, only a madman would try and sail out of Honfleur harbour today,' Murdie said. 'With the low clouds and rough swell, visibility is no more than a few hundred feet ... but that is exactly what the sunstone is for. We can navigate using the sun, even when we can't see it.'

'You must be careful with that.' Adam took it from Innes's hand, and placed it in a velvet purse. 'The stone is a delicate commodity. If it shatters, we will have to stay in port!'

'It's good to have you here, Murdie. My uncle talked about the MacBeith's with considerable fondness.' Jamie liked to be around Murdie, it made him stronger. He had an incredible ability for calmness combined with an inherent strength that was infectious.

Murdie and Gyrid had arrived in Rouen just at the right time, he knew how to handle the cog and helped them escape. Bishop Wishart had mentioned his agent in the English court to very few men, but Hendor knew Murdie. They had been educated at Glasgow Cathedral as his agents, and they had greeted each other just as warmly as the Irwyne brothers. The shared experience of working under such pressure had brought them together like blood ties.

Of the crew that Queen Isabel had sent, only Murdie, Gyrid, Adam, and four others had remained with her ship, the Norwegian skeid, the rest had perished in the fight with Bretagne and the Wolf Brothers. It was clear that the Scots, with their reduced numbers couldn't take both ships back to Scotland. They had agreed to return to Scotland on the cog.

'Hendor, Innes, and I will follow in the skeid with two

oarsmen and will scuttle her just outside the port, blocking the exit to the Seine basin,' Will said. 'We will hole her just below the waterline. Wait for us beyond the harbour entrance, and we will use the landing boat to get to the cog. Keep us in sight and remember we are behind you. That should stop Madame and anyone else from following us. Murdie, Adam, Jamie, and the two remaining oarsmen will leave first. Gyrid will remain out of sight in the cabin at the stern. We *must* go now before the faithful head to Saint-Etienne and this place is swarming with curious people – some of whom we may have met before. Remember, Madame missed us at Rouen, and she will be raging, and Jamie thinks he saw her last night'.

Innes, Hendor, and Will left the cog and started to make the skeid ready.

Jamie had been on watch last night and his sighting of her had been fleeting. It could have been a slightly built man, yet it was strange to see someone just watching the harbour so late at night.

Hendor and Innes had lifted the anchor on the Norwegian skeid the previous evening, as had Will and Jamie on the cog, and they were ready for a swift departure. Each man tiptoed down the gangplanks and carefully lifted the ropes which were holding them fast.

The ropes were carried back onto the ships, when normally they would be heaved onto the decks. The gangplanks slid quietly onto each deck and both ships drifted silently away from the quay.

People were only beginning to stir as the first bells tolled for the early Sunday morning Mass. Some devoted pilgrims had already started to assemble at the front of Saint-Etienne, which nestled adjacent to the harbour.

The ships moved in and out of the mist.

'Maybe I didn't see her, and I need to be sure.' Jamie was looking for more evidence of Madame. He had learned to look for the unusual, but with the changing visibility he could only distinguish shapes. All the other ships were tied fast, and no one was following them.

Ahead, Jamie could see the open sea, which was no more than half a mile away from their berth. It was patchy, dense, and light all within a few seconds as the wind strengthened, then dropped blowing the clouds one way and then the other.

'I am sure Madame is still out there, even if Les Frères Loups are dead. She will never give up until she is dead – or we are,' Jamie murmured to Murdie.

Jamie was using the large oar to steer the cog as Adam quietly unfurled the triangular sail, which gave him greater dexterity and control of the keel. They had to turn the keel ninety degrees so that they were pointing the bow to the sea.

With the help of Murdie and the other oarsmen, the cog started to float out of the narrow harbour. It lurched and let out a gentle groan as it turned to present its keel towards the exit to the open sea.

Gyrid opened the hatch leading from the hold and her cabin beyond. She looked pale, and her eyes were surrounded with dark circles.

'What can I do?' she shouted, almost falling over as the deck shifted.

Murdie rushed forward.

'Gyrid, it isn't safe, and you are still not recovered. The wound is serious. Stay below!'

Jamie recognised Murdie's abruptness was out of concern. Murdie grabbed her around the waist and steadied her.

'I am not used to sitting on my arse when there is work to be done.' She lifted his hands away from her waist, then grabbed him again as she staggered and nearly fell. He placed her down on some sacks and propped her back against the ship's side.

Gyrid had almost died protecting Murdie. Jamie had not met a woman with such confidence and spirit, and it didn't surprise him that Murdie was in love with her.

Jamie looked back and watched the skeid make the same manoeuvre. It groaned as if it was thankful to be heading out to sea rather than confined in a small harbour.

'The cog will handle better once we are at sea. Even with the lateen sail and four oarsmen, it's moving too slowly,' Murdie added. He had left Gyrid and was looking towards their escape.

More people were arriving at the harbour, and they still weren't clear of the narrow entrance.

'Stop them.' The mist parted as armour and swords clashed and clattered. They were wearing the *fleur de lis* and leading them was a small, slight figure pushing towards the front of the harbour wall, a sword in hand.

'Murdie. Look. That's Madame.' Jamie pointed at the slight figure.

'Adam, we need the mainsail hoisted so we can get more speed,' Murdie ordered. 'I think the harbour watch have been called – Madame and some of the king's men are with them – we must get more speed. Honfleur has a chain that the harbourmaster uses to stop ships – Madame will certainly get them to raise it and stop us. If we try to get over it, the metal will rip our keel apart. Jamie, steer until we get this sail unfurled!' Murdie rushed forward to help Adam.

Madame was running towards the harbourmaster's house at the furthest point of the wall where the opening was at its narrowest, and where the chain was lying.

'Quick, Jamie, use the long oar,' Murdie shouted.

Jamie grabbed the long oar that functioned as a rudder, and using the emerging power from the mainsail and the direction the lateen sail gave them, they darted between the two walls on either side of the harbour and entered a narrow channel into the open sea.

Madame and the men were trying to pull the chain tight, but it was too cumbersome – they had too few men.

Hendor lit a large lamp and attached it to the mast of the skeid. Jamie followed suit and quickly hung two lamps on either side of the cog and one on the mast.

'I can watch the skeid, it's right behind us … Will, hurry and sink her!' Jamie pleaded as he picked up an oar.

More men had joined Madame, and the chain was starting to appear at the end above the surface.

Murdie was now back on the oar, and they were moving to the side and dropping the mainsail as the skeid also rushed through the gap in the walls. Jamie could see the soldiers massing at one side in a vain attempt to pull up the chain.

'They are too late!' Jamie cried.

'We need to wait here whilst they hole the skeid.' Murdie and Adam lowered the mainsail just as quickly as they had raised it. They were three hundred yards from the skeid, which had started to list to the left side.

'They must have holed it before they exited the harbour. It just sneaked through, and it's sinking just beyond the walls. Madame won't be able to stop it sinking or pass either side of it and follow us.'

Jamie and the other oarsmen had stopped rowing away from Honfleur and were steadying the ship, preventing it from straying too far away from the rapidly submerging skeid.

The mist had risen away from the water sufficiently that Jamie could see more clearly. Madame rushed back towards the harbour; several soldiers ran behind her as she tried to find a boat that could get out of the harbour before it fully blocked the exit. She struck one of the soldiers with her sword pommel. Jamie was looking out for Hendor, Innes, and Will.

'Where are you?' Jamie mumbled.

Adam had stopped attending to the sail and rushed over to their port side to watch with increasing horror as the skeid started to turn full over to its left, its mast broke in two, crashing into the water.

'Please, don't be underneath that mast,' Adam cried.

Jamie joined him but it was difficult to see anything clearly except the upturned keel, and the sounds of shattering wood that told him everything he couldn't see.

'If they end up in the water, they won't last long in this swell. Prepare to launch our landing boat. We can't risk getting any closer in the cog, or we will sail right over them.'

Murdie dashed to starboard and prepared to lower the landing vessel. It was held fast, and, in his panic, he struggled to untie the complicated knots. Jamie joined him. Adam appeared frozen to the port side, scrutinising each wave for a trace of his brother.

Jamie couldn't untie the ropes. His fingers appeared stuck together as if he was wearing gloves.

'Fuck this!'

Jamie removed his sword, followed by Murdie, and they started to slice the ropes away, freeing one half of the small craft. Then a familiar voice cried out.

'Stop! We are going to need that secured when we are out in the open sea.' Innes was standing in the stern of the skeid's landing vessel, steering it towards them. They were lying deep in the water.

'We nearly didn't make it. The ship listed quicker than we planned, and the ropes wouldn't let us free. The mast fell, and the wave that followed nearly filled this vessel.'

Innes steered the craft alongside them, and threw a grappling hook up onto the side. Murdie tied its rope to an iron restraint.

'I think we will get on board now and let this wooden death trap sink with the skeid.' Hendor stood in the boat as the water approached his knees. He took a large gulp from his flask. 'Maybe not the time but I need this.'

Jamie and the other oarsmen steadied the cog as best they could.

'I can't hold on, lads.' Hendor couldn't grip the rope like the others. It was straining and beginning to fray. Will grabbed the rope that Murdie had secured.

'Throw me another rope – and get on my back, Hendor. Jamie, pull on the rope, make it tight as I climb.'

Will grabbed the second rope and twisted it around his foot like a stirrup, and with Hendor on his back, he started to slide up the ropes, his arms pulling on one rope and his foot wrapped around the other.

It was a fifteen-foot climb, and Will was using all his strength.

'Grab him!' Jamie pulled Hendor up hard over the side of the cog, followed almost immediately by Will.

Adam rushed to his brother's side. 'I thought I had lost you and I have only just found you – I think we could all do with a drink.'

Hendor passed his flask to Will, who drank more than Jamie could ever remember. He was shaking. Jamie had never seen Will look or act exhausted; he was always a marvel of calm. Adam grabbed the flask and drank it empty.

'Don't worry, I made sure Jakob Dedekam provided a barrel or two for the journey.' Hendor smiled as he slapped Will on the back.

Innes and the two oarsmen followed, and as they fell onto the deck, Jamie watched the landing craft join the skeid at the bottom of the sea.

'Madame was following us in a small posse of ships, but they turned back.' Jamie pointed to the harbour entrance, where there was chaos. Ships were running into each other, and men were ejected overboard. Phillip's soldiers were rowing back towards solid ground.

'They are right to turn back, unless they want to be holed. I steered the skeid where the passage is shallowest. It will take days to salvage what's left of that ship and make the harbour navigable – now, let's get out of here.'

Innes just managed to cough out the words before he vomited seawater all over the deck, followed by the rest of the skeid's crew. Jamie made a silent prayer because they had been lucky.

He had hated the sea since the nightmare voyage from Leith to Rouen, when they had set out on this journey and he felt nauseous when he realised that he was repeating that journey – this time travelling even further. Murdie had brought word that King Robert was in Orkney, and he was waiting there for the treasure. Jamie saw the journey as something he would have to endure. Innes had always comforted him that the sea was something he would grow to love, but his loathing had only gotten worse. Today it had nearly claimed his closest friends.

'Adam, we should get these sails up,' Murdie called out. 'Once we clear the Seine estuary, head west until we reach the toe of England. That's the way back to Scotland. We are going home, boys!'

Adam quickly prepared the main and lateen sails as Murdie steered. There was no need for oars, as the wind was brisk and steady. The skeid's crew took the opportunity to clear their lungs of seawater and recover their strength.

'Good – the sun is totally obscured by clouds and sea foam,' Adam remarked.

'What's so good about that?' Jamie asked.

'No one can follow us unless they too have a sunstone, or they risk grounding themselves in the Seine basin. It is full of sandbanks and shallows. We don't need to see the sun; I just use these marks on the crystal and the changes in the light to tell me where it is. I then use those charts to guide us home.'

Adam pointed to a tatty leather pouch hanging on the mast. Jamie untied the tassel fastening the pouch together and pulled out a parchment.

'These squiggles mean nothing to me. How do we get

from here to Orkney?'

Jamie oriented the charts and still could make no sense of them. He did notice the elaborate drawings of mythical creatures. They were faded, but he had seen similar drawings in Glasgow Cathedral's scriptorium. Bishop Wishart had told him they were from the Norwegian sagas, so he knew they were old.

'That's because you are looking but not seeing.' Adam was still finishing finessing the setup of the sails, yet Jamie could see he wanted to explain, and Jamie wanted to know.

'Let me handle the sails whilst you navigate and at the same time educate the boy.' Innes had recovered quickly and had already changed his sodden clothes.

Adam smiled. 'As I said, if you can find the sun, you know what the hour is, and from that you can use mathematics and charts to work out where you are. The distance travelled can be measured using rope to assess our speed. Each knot can be counted, so we can be pretty accurate on our speed.'

Jamie wanted to understand. Outside of money, knowledge through education was the only thing that could give you power. The Wisharts were a family that valued learning more than money.

'Look at those black circles on the crystal. Even when it is overcast, like it is today – when you point them to the brightest point in the sky and the circles merge above you, there is the position of the sun. It's all about the refraction of light, which comes from the sun and tells us where we are. You must never do this when you can see the sun, or you will never see anything again – only when it is hidden.'

Adam held the crystal above Jamie's eyes.

Jamie was perplexed. He always liked to challenge what he was told. Bishop Wishart had taught him never to readily accept anything if it sounded false. A fact would hold up under challenge.

'It looks like magic, and I don't believe in that. Magic

is just a collection of illusions and made-up facts that allow fairground charlatans to take money from ignorant peasants.'

'Well said, Jamie,' Hendor shouted.

'The Vikings didn't believe it was magic, nor did the Arabs. I will direct you to a fascinating work by Alhazen. The Vikings used the content of his *Book of Optics* to conquer the world and master it for three hundred years. I commend the seven volumes to you.'

'He is just showing off, Jamie. We won't be impressed until you get us home to Scotland,' Will shouted, but Jamie knew he was incredibly proud of his educated brother.

'I won't tell you about Ibn Sahl, then,' Adam replied, as a well-aimed pair of Will's sodden hose was flung at him.

'And the charts?' Jamie had picked up the parchment again and started to study it, trying to understand.

'They came from Queen Isabel Bruce, and show the hazards in these waters, like rocks and currents. They have been collected over many years and cost many people their lives. Together with the sunstone they are awesome, and we can sail the known world. Pass me the chart you are holding.' Adam held out his hand.

'Now could you tell me which way to steer to avoid the hazards?' Murdie had been directing the boat away from Honfleur and was using the long oar to steer. The lateen sail was pushing the boat gradually to the left and westward.

'We will soon move northwest away from the Normandy coast and will pass Cherbourg in about seven hours, as we are moving at about ten knots. Once we pass Cherbourg, we hit the narrowing of the sea between the English and French coasts, and we will anchor off Alderney. The currents there in this weather are a death trap, but we have a chart to help us, and we are off Normandy – Innes grew up there.' Adam held up the parchment Jamie was studying.

Innes nodded. 'The Alderney Race is where the island forces water between its eastern shore and La Hague. Only an idiot or an ignoramus will challenge us there. Even if you try to avoid L'Raz, the tides pull you into it and smash your ship to pieces on rocks concealed below the surface.'

'Then tomorrow we will head north across the channel and around Falmouth,' Adam continued. 'We will sail at full speed off the English coast, and anchor off the Manx Islands. If the winds are favourable, we'll be in Kirkwall in four days – I will take readings with the sunstone every hour to keep us on course.'

Adam grinned. He was a skilled navigator, and Jamie, a most reluctant sailor, grudgingly accepted his infectious confidence.

'Murdie, you can bring the oar up now that I have set the lateen.' Innes tied the rope firmly to a hook on the side of the ship. 'We can use the sail to steer us. Keep an eye on the angle of it, and make sure the ropes don't slacken in these strong winds. I am just going to check that the treasure is secure. Hendor, I need a practical man to help me. Adam, I have angled the sails to take us towards Alderney – just keep the boat straight.' Innes lifted the hatch in the middle of the ship and dropped down, and Hendor followed.

'If we can get to Alderney in six hours, we can be safely anchored before dark,' Murdie added as he grappled with the long oar. 'I will store this away and then check on Gyrid.'

'For what it's worth, I will do the first watch,' Will said. 'It's overcast, but the visibility is only about a mile at best. Then the oarsmen in four-hour shifts.'

Murdie followed Hendor and Innes into the lower deck where the hold and cabins were located.

'Jamie, I am starving. We need food and ale. The whisky has gone straight to my stomach, and it is growling. We might not get an opportunity again.' Will sat at the bow and concentrated on the sea ahead.

Jamie's stomach started to rumble as he searched the crates and barrels.

'We can eat, watch and rest a little. Jakob Dedekam provided us with plentiful supplies.'

Jamie placed two sacks over his shoulder. He pulled out meat, bread, and apples, and placed some in each sack.

'Murdie can take some food down to Gyrid. I will lower it down to him. The poppy juice kills your appetite. She hasn't eaten much since Rouen …' Jamie rummaged around in every chest and box, looking for fruits and sweetmeats.

'Dedekam even provided calvados as well as *uisge beatha*.'

Jamie assembled several barrels that contained ale and two small flagons holding spirits onto an upturned chest.

'We need to keep our wits about us. I think we should stick with ale tonight.' Will placed the flagons back in their wooden boxes. Jamie lifted the hatch to the deck below.

'Murdie, some food for Gyrid,' he shouted into the hold before placing a skin full of ale on top of the bread before lowering it in a bucket to the bottom of the lower deck.

A tiny, enclosed lamp on the stairs provided the only immediate light.

On either side of the hold, chests and barrels were equally distributed along the middle of the open space, creating a small corridor. The treasure chests were held fast by a series of ropes tied to iron rings screwed into the sides and the roof. Every piece of the exposed keel had been used. The crew could only get from one end of the deck to the other by walking along this corridor. Jamie felt the vibrations of chests being pushed and dragged, but it was too dark to see anyone.

'How are you doing?' Jamie shouted.

'Some chests have come loose and slid forward,' Innes replied. 'We need to make sure we aren't too heavy at the front and rear of the keel. We are just securing the last of them. Hendor is just finishing.'

'I have prepared some food.' Jamie replaced the hatch

and immediately Innes appeared.

He set the remains of the food on the chest and was soon joined by the rest of the crew, and Murdie. They started to tear into the food and ale despite the rolling deck. Adam and Innes kept an eye on the direction and tweaked the sail. The watch continued, and several hours escaped them. Everyone welcomed the peace, it didn't feel awkward, it was time for reflection and repair. Jamie relaxed and considered the few days since they had left Gaillard and who they had lost.

'I wonder if Madame has found a ship – her frustration at Honfleur will only be temporary.'

'Of course, Jamie,' Hendor said. 'We stopped her getting out of the harbour there, but she will find a ship to come after us. Her setback at Honfleur will cost her time – enough time for us to be far away before she reaches here. Only Templar ships could catch us, and as Bernard said, they were being sent out to sea.'

Jamie considered her a greater threat than Hendor seemed, she was out there.

'The Templars know how to make ships,' Innes commented.

'Is this a Templar ship?' Adam asked.

'Indeed, it is, sourced from their fleet in La Rochelle,' Will replied. 'In other circumstances, it would be chasing us – the King of France's fleet are the Templar ships.'

'I will drink to that.' Hendor crashed his goblet into Jamie's, and by some miracle they didn't break.

'How is Gyrid?' Jamie asked.

'Gyrid will sleep for now,' Murdie said. 'Her wound is clean and shows no sign of putrefying.'

Murdie had a subtle sadness about him. He was an intelligent combatant, yet when it came to Gyrid, he was caring and compassionate. Jamie had never considered that a woman, and a highborn one at that, would be part of this cabal. He had never experienced love with a stranger, but he recognised it in others. He could see it unfolding in front of him in the least likely one amongst them, the aging and curmudgeonly Murdie. He saw that Murdie cared for Gyrid above everything else, including his own well-being.

'How did you meet Gyrid?' Jamie worked up the courage to ask to embolden by the ale.

'At Longshank's court, we were sent to find someone back in Norway – it was an arrangement neither of us had any choice in making, ordered by King Edward himself. In normal circumstances we would never have entered each other's life. Rebellion has a way of changing social norms, creates the opportunity for love and encourages relationships in the most unusual circumstances – we have a chance of making a good life together, when this is all over, if she will have me – and we survive.' Murdie was interrupted.

'Land!' the watch cried and pointed in front of them. 'I saw land – over there through the clouds.'

'Our anchorage is directly ahead, and it will be night soon, so we should settle to the west of Alderney. That way we will avoid L'Raz.' Adam took a further reading with the sunstone.

Adam took the charts and confirmed their course.

'I am sure I also saw a large mast in the distance on the port side,' the watch added.

'Are you sure it was a ship and not some sea creature or rocks?' Will asked. 'The waves can form unnatural shapes and trick your senses.' His brow furrowed as he scanned the horizon, straining to see anything in the diminishing light.

Jamie and Hendor ran to the bow, scouring to see what was ahead.

'Do you see anything?' Innes asked.

Will and Murdie searched the port side as Innes and Adam dropped the mainsail to reduce speed. The poor visibility had deteriorated further, as the winds had blown sea fog towards the islands to add to the sea foam and onset of dusk.

'If it is rocks on the port side, we don't want to speed towards them. Keep right.' Adam dropped the angle of the lateen sail, which further slowed the ship.

'We can't go too near the shore. This island is surrounded with reefs and outcrops of sharp rocks.' The waves began to bump the keel from the starboard side as the ship pushed quickly to the left, toward the shore.

'That's not right.' Adam barely got the words out.

Suddenly, out of the clouds, fire lit up the heavens. It looked like lightning, but it was coming towards them out of several golden-headed sea serpents. The sky was decked with a sparkling golden veil. Balls of fire whistled and flew across their masts, just missing the sails. Jamie hadn't believed in monsters until he saw this.

'Look, the sea is on fire but that is impossible – it must be sorcery.'

Metal exploded into the air as more flaming missiles hit the water.

This is the end of the world and the start of Judgement Day.

'What are they?' Jamie pointed at fragments of gourd skimming across the waves and exploding just beyond the deck.

'It's black powder encased in shells, more powerful that way – Jamie, keep your head down or one of those missiles will blow it off,' Hendor pushed Jamie down towards the deck.

'These must be the flames of hell – ones that could never be extinguished.'

Shapes darted across the deck as Adam, then Murdie tried to steer the ship away from the flames.

'Innes, Hendor move the sails to take us away from shore.' Murdie shouted.

Some ropes were frayed, and strands fell onto the deck and into the sea, still attached to the mast. They caught on some heavy debris and started to pull the mast and the ship down to port.

Innes stopped adjusting the sails and ran towards the ropes, slashing the fibres with his sword as missiles screeched across the deck and continued to hit the sea around them.

'Innes, just cut the strands that are tight – leave the rest. I need you to help with the sails!' The mast was freed from the ropes as Adam struggled to steer. Hendor joined Adam and Murdie pushing the long oar and the ship away from the flames powered by the mainsail that Innes had now unfurled.

Jamie could see through the foam a heavy wooden bow coming towards them.

'The ship attacking us is a huge war galley – twice our size!'

'What are they doing?' Adam cried. 'If we can't see them clearly, how can they see us? They are trying to get us to surrender by intimidating us, throwing missiles randomly in the hope that one hits us. We are too good a crew for that to work and this ship is too agile, and I know where we are, I don't think they do.' He steered the cog towards the sea foam and denser fog.

'That ship is going to ram us, but we can outrun them,' Innes yelled. He extended the mainsail as full as he could lifting the cog up, it was flying on top of the waves.

'We need more speed – everyone take an oar. Push us to starboard and away from the shore. If they try to follow us, they can't manoeuvre like us and are heading towards those rocks ahead!' They were fighting for their lives.

The cog swerved to the left, but it was now horizontal to the wind, and a huge wave pushed it back to the right. The deck was almost touching the water on the starboard side. The galley had passed them, but it had churned the sea and amplified the sea in its wake, and the waves crashed into the cog as it passed at speed.

The galley, lit up by its own fire weapon, proceeded

straight into a blanket of foam. More gourds were fired at the cog from the rear of the galley, but they fell short. Ahead, the sea was on fire, but the cog travelled faster and faster to the right and away from the galley which carried straight on towards the shore.

Adam and Innes tied the lateen sail to direct the cog further away from the galley. Innes moved the mainsail which pushed them to the right and north out to sea and towards the English coast. The galley was moving south towards Alderney's rocky coast.

Jamie ran and grabbed an oar; he would help the sails steer the boat to the open sea – the heat from the galley hit the side of his face. It felt like someone had opened a bread oven.

'Whatever those flames are, they are close by.' The back of his head started to burn as a blast of intense heat hit him.

The cog lifted into the air as if it had been picked up and shaken and every timber trembled.

'Look out, Hendor,' Jamie shouted as the tip of the mast fractured and crashed onto the deck. Hendor fell and heavy ropes dropped onto his legs. The rest of the mast and sail miraculously stayed in place.

The clouds exploded and everyone turned mesmerised by the inferno. They changed from yellow to orange and then black; tinged red and mixed with black smoke. It tasted like burning wood flavoured with an acrid metal taste that burned the back of Jamie's throat. Droplets of black, sticky sludge dropped from the air.

Everyone started to cough as choking smoke blew across the deck.

The explosion was followed with a chorus of screams. A further, more violent, explosion lifted the cog out of the water again before dropping it back down. Whatever had crashed into the shore had started to burn before it hit, and the force was such that the waves caught up with the cog and pushed it further out to sea and away from the source.

Body parts appeared in the water, and Jamie knew that the black sludge was burnt blood and flesh.

'Let's start rowing – we don't want to know what it was. In any case, it won't be following us now.' Will had grabbed an oar and was pulling it through the water with the strength Jamie had witnessed when he had carried Hendor on his back. Jamie followed his lead and pushed even harder.

The waves seem to calm, but black droplets and incendiary fragments continued to fall out of the sky. Several resonating thuds and bangs hit the keel.

'What was that?' Jamie asked, as large pieces of wood and flesh fell into the sea around them. Some crashed onto the deck, just missing the crew.

'It will be debris caught in those frayed ropes,' Murdie said. 'Let's make sure we are out of range of those flying missiles. The poor aim has protected us from the debris, but let's not tempt fate.'

Another loud explosion could be heard, the explosions became less frequent, but the screams didn't.

'There is a small island northwest of us called Burhou, and there is a small inlet. We can anchor there for the night.'

Adam moved the sails, directing the bow towards a spot Jamie could just recognise as a coast. There were a few fishing vessels burning lamps anchored nearer the shore. He was exhausted, and he could see that everyone else looked flat.

'We will anchor in thirty minutes, just before the last light ebbs away. We can check for damage in the morning – I assume no one is injured?'

The crew didn't answer Adam, and he didn't speak further as he guided the ship to its anchorage. It gently meandered as if its reserves, like the crew, were depleted.

The crew slumped forward, contemplating the day's events.

Adam and Innes were the last to rest. They prepared the ship for an early start, carefully lowering the anchor before making a bed underneath the mast. Everyone was resting on the deck, except Murdie.

Jamie watched Murdie lifting the hatch, lowering himself into the hold. He had slept in the small cabin with Gyrid every night, changing her bandages and preparing poppy water.

The ship was calm, protected by a small spur that reduced the strength and frequency of the waves and tide. The sea spray was a mist, rather than a deluge.

Tomorrow they would sail around the English coast, needing all the strength a good night's sleep provided. They had escaped from a foreign navy, but the English sea offered a special challenge that gave him extra determination. He wanted to be at his best to take on any dangers lurking in those tempestuous waters, so Jamie allowed himself to fall into a deep sleep.

*

Gyrid had slept for many hours. The poppy water numbed the pain of her wound, but it also robbed her of her sense of being. Time seemed to slip away, and days merged. She had not had a proper conversation with Murdie or anyone else since she had been carried away from L'Auberge du Lion. She had no recollection of how she had gotten onto the cog, nor of being stitched, or being cleaned of the blood that must have flowed from her wound.

Her dress had been changed, her hair washed and brushed. She assumed that Murdie had taken care of that. She had visions; everything was in slow motion, and she woke up because she felt a presence, a shadow that she didn't know.

Murdie was fast asleep beside her. He didn't hear the footsteps pressing the wooden deck, the boards squeaking with the touch of furtive steps, or the sound of the hatch closing. Her vision was still blurred, and after five or ten minutes awake, the pain and the poppy water sent her back to sleep. She convinced herself it was a dream and returned to Murdie's arms.

*

Aurelian forced his frame behind several large chests. He reckoned that they had been tied down so well that no one would move the ropes again. He prayed for good weather, or at least no storms. He surveyed other hiding places in the hold just in case. There were numerous places that someone even of his height could remain undiscovered.

He had been lucky that he had left Morisco on the first ship to search for the cog. His Varangians had been unlucky. Morisco had taken the opportunity to slit their throats and throw them over the side. He had been heading back to the flagship when he saw bodies floating in the sea and recognised amongst them the brave men that were to help him take over the Byzantine ships. Attempts had been made to weigh some of them down, but Morisco must have panicked when he saw the cog and simply threw them over the side. He had quickly dispatched his small crew to join them before using the confusion to attach a grappling hook to the cog.

Morisco was eviler than he had considered possible, and now he had combined a wicked act with gross stupidity and lost his ship by running it aground. It had then exploded, fuelled by its own Greek fire and black powder.

Aurelian had taken his clothes from a dead conscript and looked just like any other peasant. They were functional, even if they smelled of fish, and they covered his extensive tattoos of Norsk gods. He wouldn't look out of place in any Orkney hovel.

So, this is home for a few days. I have seen worse. This ship is new, and the caulk hasn't fully set, so I will have to get used to a wet arse for the rest of the journey.

The hold had about six inches of stagnant seawater swirling around its deck. It seeped in between the planks where the black tar had come away.

New ships often leak when they are fresh in the water.

He had found a bucket containing discarded food and a flagon half full of ale.

Good, I have some rats for companionship. What more could a man ask for in such circumstances.

Aurelian smiled, anticipating some fine ale to help him sleep.

He had brought some dried sausage, so food wouldn't be an issue, and he would ration his liquids. That would be hard, for it was hot and sticky in the hold, even in late September.

The voyage from Burhou to Orkney is four maybe five days, and the Scots won't dawdle. They will want to be out of English waters and into the friendlier northern seas off Ireland as soon as they can– I can put up with the lack of comforts until we reach the Orkney Islands.

The islands were under Norwegian overlordship but run by the Scottish Earls of Orkney.

The treasure will be easier to transport back to Norway from there. King Haakon will reward me on the spot and all because of Metochites's treachery.

The Scots were returning his help by getting the treasure past the English. It was a hazard he would have had to overcome if it hadn't been for Morisco's pride and incompetence.

Dedekam had shown him a letter from Haakon indicating that King Robert would be sheltering at Hugh Halcro's castle. He knew Haakon was looking for the treasure like King Phillip.

Haakon has agents in Kirkwall, and I will make sure the Norwegian King captures the treasure.

He had understood the risk of failure in using the

Byzantine ships, but it had all worked out well. He was on the treasure ship, bringing it back to Norway all by himself, and he didn't have to worry about coercing a crew to sail it right into the hands of King Haakon.

Once I reach Orkney, I will get off the ship and head for Halcro's castle, Bruce will be there, it's the only place he would be safe, Dedekam, who knows everything about traitors, told me of an English agent, Henry de Stikelaw, who would give up any secrets if he was paid enough. I need a map of the castle, to know where it is vulnerable, and where King Haakon's fleet could capture the treasure without a fight – I will spend the next few days refining my plan.

Aurelian was amongst elusive friends. The cargo for which he had fought so hard would be his companion for the next few days. He had done it and wanted to shout out in victory.

I wonder if it would hurt to take a peek?

He was itching to open just one of the chests and feed his curiosity, he always prided himself on self-control, but this was torture.

Rats don't break locks, and I have waited months to hold the treasure. A little longer would make no difference.

The next few days would also be one's reflection. He would consider his comrades that had died on Morisco's ship. Although he would mourn, he found himself smiling.

Metochites will have some explaining to do when only nine ships return, and without the treasure.

Lying between the gold and jewels he had so relentlessly pursued, he was sure he would sleep soundly for the first time in many months.

*

Madame had watched the sky light up with fire, and she knew the treasure was connected to the explosions. Large chunks of black and smoking wood were laid out in front of the keel, bumping it from side to side. She had pushed the ship to its maximum, but it looked like her efforts were for nothing. She punched her palm in frustration.

Was the treasure ship sunk again or was it a ship in pursuit ... and you don't know me if you think this is the end.

Her ship was about twenty feet long, broad and flat-bottomed for harvesting crabs and shellfish. It was all she could find, and the soldiers who had crammed onto the unstable ship were determined to go no further. It couldn't cope with the open sea.

This is Valois's fault ... if he had only supplied the ships I had asked for. Guillaume de Nogaret didn't even reply to my letter.

'Captain, we will return immediately to Honfleur and requisition another ship capable of pursuing these bastards.'

'Madame, we can't navigate in these conditions … and the debris, if we hit a piece big enough we will capsize. We need a Templar ship for a voyage in the open sea.' She knew he was right, but she didn't have to like it or his timorous demeanour.

'First light you find me a ship; there were several merchant ships in Honfleur, requisition one, and get Dedekam to empty his stores and provision it. Better still get one of his ships ready to sail – the Scots will be heading home, and we must follow them to the remote islands in Scotland. That's where their king is hiding … and that is where they will go.'

'Will Dedekam just let you take one of his ships?' the captain sounded sceptical.

'I think so, it's a small thing to ask in exchange for your life.'

Chapter Eighteen

Halcro Castle, September 1306:
Family Reunions and Reflections

Innes lay on the bed, still exhausted from the journey. The weather had pushed them through the Irish Sea and across the Pentland Firth to Halcro Castle. King Robert had been surprised yet gladdened by their arrival.

'Rest and recover. We will have time enough to catch up.' The King had briefly greeted them in an exultant mood.

The King was a man of his word, and Innes had been sleeping for more than a day, yet no matter how hard he tried to fully open his eyes, they were so heavy that they remained stuck together. He let out an involuntary grunt as he moved.

My bones ache with every hour. Life is catching up with me, and I haven't slept in days. I never thought we would get this far and sail right past the English coast. We should all be dead – our survival must be the result of sheer luck or divine intervention. I can't even calculate how long it has been since we left Gaillard. Each time I try to do this simple calculation my mind gives me a different answer – I think I will give up because it doesn't really matter now. We have our lives and the treasure, and Jean de Bretagne or should I say Gervase de Bretagne is dead.

It was only now that he could reflect on the events in Rouen and seeing Gervase again, now he was dead. Innes felt avenged for the death of his wife and children. He thought Bretagne's death would null his pain, but it hadn't, and there was still an aching emptiness and sorrow in his stomach.

He could hear the shuffle of feet outside the old, thick door, and reluctantly he pulled himself up and rested his head on the bolster.

'Please come in,' he shouted towards the feet.

The door gently opened, and Will stood there looking half asleep. Innes satisfied himself that he wasn't the only one exhausted by the last few weeks.

'I thought I should come and talk about Rouen. We didn't have time to talk properly. Escaping France exhausted us all.'

'It wasn't the right time. Priorities change and now is better. Have you seen the King? I expect that was a wonderful reunion. I will present myself within the day.' Will had been King Robert's armour bearer and one of his closest confidantes.

'He sent word that we are all to rest, we aren't running anywhere, seems strange, and I like it,' Will said. 'The King is injured; he received a head injury at Methven, so I have not pushed for an audience. I want to shout out being home and finding the king alive and the rebellion alight once again – means the treasure can be put to good use – and I know our success hasn't happened without considerable sacrifice.'

Innes hadn't thought much about the deaths of Guillaume and Bernard. He should have cared more about them and less about Gervase. They had all been dead just ten days, and his lack of consideration made him ashamed. 'I would have done the same in Bernard's situation,' he said. 'He had the right to avenge Guillaume. I only wished I had finished Bretagne – and what about the feisty Gyrid? She saved Murdie. So much tragedy in such a short period of time.'

Innes carried the memories like a burden on his back, and he needed to put them away and look to the future. He thought about the note Jamie had given him in the cave under Gaillard, about his brother and he would use the next few months to find him.

He had known his father had another son; Knox de Mayon had not drawn a veil over him – more like a portcullis. He searched his memory and had a vague feeling about meeting a red-haired stranger who had cared for him, but he couldn't remember where or when. Had he met his brother?

'It was Bretagne who directed the English soldiers in Rouen to attack us back in March – the day you came to the inn.' Innes found that mentioning his name still made him retch.

'I did not know him as Gervase de Bretagne, but as Jean. It doesn't sit easy with me that "Jean" was also betraying Bishop Wishart.' Will had injured his shoulder in the fight and had not complained, rowing the ship had aggravated it and his right arm hung loosely at his side.

Will recounted his memory of Jean de Bretagne.

'Bishop Wishart found him in 1297, after Stirling Bridge, tied to a horse. His face was raw, and he said it was the work of Aymer de Valence, and he joined Wallace. The Bishop warned me he could be cavalier, outspoken when the right course was reticence. Then in March this year, we boarded his ship, and he brought us here to find Geoffroi de Charnay and the treasure. It was only at the tavern the first night in Rouen – when the fight broke out – that I had my first doubts about him. People were waiting for us and it could have only been Bretagne who betrayed us.'

Innes nodded. 'Bretagne remained on the boat. If I had seen him, I would have warned you, and he lied to you after Stirling Bridge. It wasn't Valence that scarred him, but my father Knox a few weeks before. Bretagne subsequently offered his services to Valence to get his revenge on the Scots.'

Will paused – the right words seemed hard to find.

'Will, the Bishop warned you to take care around him because Wishart was using him. Bretagne's vanity and arrogance would make him attractive to the English.

The Bishop recognised that his hubris would make him a dangerous man even for the side using him. The English may have thought he was working for them. The reality was that he wasn't working for anyone but himself. He tried to snatch the treasure at Rouen when the English wanted it out of France and in the open sea.'

'Did you notice the clover birthmark above his left ear?' Innes asked.

'No, I didn't, although when we were on his ship, the *Nantes*, he wore a hat all the time which he pulled down over his ears.'

Innes pushed his hair away from just above his left ear, exposing a clover-shaped birthmark. 'He had one just like this.'

'What are you saying, Innes?'

'Bretagne and I are cousins, related through Geoffrey of Brittany, our great-grandfather. This is the mark of the Plantagenet. You remember Bernard told us that Bretagne spent time praying at Rouen Cathedral – kneeling at the feet of Henry Plantagenet, the young king, and kissing the reliquary containing the heart of King Richard the Lionheart. They were Geoffrey of Brittany's brothers, and our great-uncles. Bretagne is the grandson of one of Geoffrey's numerous mistresses, as am I. My mother, Marguerite, inherited lands from Geoffrey that Bretagne he thought should have been his – and they would have been his, had my mother not married and produced me. He couldn't get to me, so he killed my wife and son instead.'

'And that's why you stared so long at the tapestries in the Temple when we met Pierre de Nogaret. You were studying your ancestors.' Will's eyes widened, and he exhaled hard.

'I was not expecting to see Henry II and his sons Henry, Richard, Geoffrey, and John hanging in front of me with their birthmark so prominent – I just had to acknowledge them and wonder why de Nogaret was in possession of a tapestry

I had last seen in my family home. I still don't understand how it got there. I must conceal the mark – it could make things dangerous for me and for others.'

Innes brushed his thick hair over his ear and smoothed it down.

'What sort of "others" are you talking about?' Will asked.

'There was talk when my father was alive that a legitimate heir to Geoffrey had been born in England to his daughter and spirited away from the clutches of King Henry III and hidden for better times to arrive. My father never wanted to discuss it, because he was the father of that child born of a relationship with Eleanor of Brittany, Geoffrey's daughter. She came before Longshank's father, Henry III so the English wanted to kill Knox to keep this a secret. My connection with Longshanks, even if it is tenuous, is something I would like to remain hidden. The man is a monster – I am genuinely ashamed we are connected – and compelled to keep it secret.' Innes looked at the floor wondering if his confession would change his relationship with Will.

'Valence is said to want you dead even more than King Robert, and I understand why – you are close to the English crown.' Will's bow was ironic.

'Longshanks wants my father's son with Eleanor dead even more. He still lives. There was a note in those papers you were looking at in Galliard. He escaped Acre into the Templar world, and I know I can find him. Now you understand my reluctance to talk about my past and my reasons for keeping my life a secret. I am following Robert Bruce because he is the right man for these times. I have been working to set us free, wandering around Europe seeking support for a country without a king, occupied and without hope, losing count of the doors closed in my face. I don't hide behind false statements of loyalty, I do it because I want to, and I would have done it if my wife was still alive.'

Will nodded, and there was silence. Neither knew what to

say next, and silence felt like the most appropriate epitaph to a difficult conversation.

'I think I will return to my room,' Will said. 'I have a few more years of sleep to catch up on.' He didn't wait for a response as Innes pushed himself down under the skin blankets and closed his eyes. The past few months had been exhausting, exhilarating, and the reality was hard to fathom. He was finding pleasure in things he never considered.

Lord Halcro had found a small bedroom for him to relax. It was the first time he had slept alone and without a dagger under his pillow for years. Like everything in Orkney, his room had been designed to thwart the elements. The walls were thicker than four feet, and the storm that had brought them to Ronaldsay was still howling outside, yet he had never felt so safe.

The fireplace seemed to take up the length and breadth of the entire wall, and the radiant heat made him even more drowsy as he pulled the thick sheep and sealskin blankets over his chest. He pushed his feet outside the bottom of the blanket so they could be warmed by the flames. It was a home comfort he had forgotten from his days in Normandy.

He thought on the past few days. He had guided the cog away from the ravages of L'Raz. The ship was troublesome but fast, the sails awkward, the steering unwilling, and the sea unrelenting. He stretched out his hands and studied the pitted and bruised skin, the swollen fingers. He tried to clench his fist, but the fingers held fast, frozen inwards like a beggar asking for alms.

'I wonder if I will ever be able to grip a sword again,' he murmured before dropping his right hand onto his chest.

The dry air in the room had made him thirsty, and he remembered that to the side of his bed, there was a stand that held a flask of ale. He thought he heard the door open again.

'Is that you, Will?' he asked.

His vision was blurred, and as he leaned to his left, he

could see a grey shadow pushing the goblet towards him. He recoiled, as he didn't recognise the figure. As he focused more closely, he recognised Brother Geoffrey, the old monk who had attended to Lord Sinclair.

'Here.'

The monk didn't form the word properly. He pushed the goblet into Innes's hand before sitting next to him on a low stool, which he pulled away from the side of the bed. He sat nearby, his face turned towards a tall, narrow slit in the wall that was angled to keep the wind out yet still provided a view over the surrounding landscape and sea.

'Thank you.' Innes gulped the ale.

'I see it is light,' he said. The monk nodded.

'What is the hour?' Innes asked, Geoffrey was silent.

Innes respected his diffidence and focused on the ale, which was lifting his mood with every mouthful. The monk was fixated on the land below, sticking his face in between the cut stone – or was he trying to remove his face from Innes's stare?

Innes could see the deep scars on the back of his head and neck and wondered how a monk came to get such traumatic injuries. He had noticed prominent shackle marks on Geoffrey's wrists as he had handed him the goblet. The man was an enigma.

Innes was distracted by the door rattling. He accepted that he wasn't going to be allowed to sleep further.

'Good morning – or should I say afternoon, Lord Mayon.'

Henry Sinclair took a step inside the room. Brother Geoffrey stood and rushed towards him as if he was a long-lost friend.

'How long have I been sleeping?' Innes felt ashamed he had not joined the other lords.

'Didn't young Will tell you that you have both been asleep for more than a day? I met him on the way back to his room. The time is of no consequence, what is important is that you are here, and so is your cargo. We only arrived here a few days ahead of you – your unexpected arrival delighted the king.'

Lord Sinclair grinned, and Innes assumed this was the look of someone who knew the ship was filled with treasure.

'Lord Mayon is a salutation that feels strange to me. I haven't been addressed like that for longer than I can remember.' For a moment, Innes didn't recognise himself.

'I know you have been working for Bishop Wishart in France for many years now. The title is yours by right, and I remember people speak about your father in the Holy Land. He was a loyal Scot and friend; and had a reputation as a man with education and wit who was as familiar with the sword as the pen. I was very young, yet in Acre he went out of his way to make my acquaintance. He said you and I were related.' Sinclair embraced Innes.

'Lord Sinclair, you are well informed, and you showed some fine seamanship in helping us dock. The cave entrance is narrow, and the currents and winds would have pushed us onto the rocks without your guidance. Putting to sea in that small ship was brave.' Innes concentrated on the events of two nights ago. He didn't know how to react to Sinclair's familiarity, and he hadn't known they were connected.

'Innes, you arrived on Monday night, and it is now Wednesday near noon. You are in good company. Will, Hendor, Murdie, and Jamie have taken the same opportunity to rest. Murdie MacBeith also brought news from Queen Isabel. Gyrid is a fine companion for him.'

Sinclair addressed the monk, who had not reacted or spoken, as if he understood nothing. 'Brother Geoffrey, please bring more ale whilst I talk with Lord Mayon.'

Sinclair passed the empty flagon to Geoffrey and then pulled the door shut behind him.

'We saw the looming storm, and King Robert had been waiting for your arrival. We knew you would try and reach us with all speed before the October storms. I saw the blinding rain covering the horizon, and we had word of your ship from fishermen who had arrived from Christina Ranald's lands in the Western Isles. We waited for you, and lookouts were placed all along the northern coast, searching for your masts. Queen Isabel has confirmed King Haakon is in pursuit – we will get the treasure away long before he turns up.'

'The people pursuing this treasure won't give up,' Innes said. 'I have seen the risks they are willing to take, and many people have already died.'

'Murdie met Queen Isabel Bruce, and she provided information on Haakon's intentions and knowledge of your cargo.'

'Is that why you sent the old monk away? So, he wouldn't overhear our planning?'

Innes wondered why the monk had been sent to him in the first place.

'The monk is no risk; he has been under Bishop Wishart's protection for many years now. At Methven, the Bishop asked King Robert to take care of him. You will have noticed from his scars that the world has not treated him well; thus, he has retreated from it into another less complicated place where he wishes to remain. He understands little around him and doesn't want to engage with people.'

'Lord Sinclair, he seems very attached to you,' Innes observed.

'I am an old man, and I know my time left is limited. So, given your known loyalty to Bishop Wishart, would you support the monk, see that no harm comes to him should anything happen to me? That is why he was in your room. He has sat with you most of the last thirty-six hours, just watching and keeping the fire well alight. He wanted to be with you, no one asked him, and it was he who brought you ale in the first place – he only left at Will's request.'

Innes was embarrassed for judging the monk.

'It will be difficult; my life wouldn't be compatible with his needs. It has been several years since I have slept in the same bed for two consecutive nights, and my work requires me to be without dependents or responsibilities outside those I swore to the Bishop.'

'Innes, I am only asking that you protect him should something happen to me, keep a roof over his head until Bishop Wishart returns – and I have no intention of dying yet, despite my creaking bones.'

This wasn't some random request, and despite Sinclair's politeness, it was a veiled order.

'I do not need an answer yet. Please think on it. I wouldn't ask this of you unless it was important.'

'I don't understand why you would have chosen me, but I will support anyone who follows King Robert and Bishop Wishart. I have the means to ensure he is protected, even if I can't attend to him myself.'

Innes would honour his promise somehow whilst hoping that no harm came to Lord Sinclair. He did wonder why he had been asked, rather than Will or Hendor, who were equally able to offer protection.

Just as the conversation paused, Geoffrey returned, carrying a flagon of honeyed ale in each hand. The stems of two extra goblets were sticking out of the large pocket on the front of his habit. The aroma of honey and heather swept through the small room. The feeling of comfort made Innes smile.

Innes addressed the monk. 'It is great to be home. The smells and tastes of Scotland are something you never forget no matter where you are, and Orkney has a purity which enhances this palette.'

'Brother Geoffrey, would you pour us all some ale?' Sinclair said.

The monk bowed and did as he was asked. Innes drank another goblet before he heard Lord Sinclair's voice addressing the monk.

'Geoffrey, wake Lord Mayon in time for supper. For now, I think we should let him return to his rest.'

Geoffrey and Sinclair left, and Innes slid back under the blankets. He had nearly fallen back to sleep when he heard the stool move beside him. Geoffrey had returned to watch over him once again.

*

Murdie had tried to dry his clothes by the fire. His leather jerkin was now hanging on a fossilised tree stump whitened by years in the sun. Damp on one side, the skin had begun to crack on the other.

His drying clothes were ill fitting. The last few weeks since he had met with Bishop Wishart at the Tower of London had seen him travel the sea from England to Norway, and now he was back home.

Halcro had laughed at his shrunken frame and ill-fitting clothes and supplied a new set of clothes. As he had put them on, he recognised that today was the first day of the rest of his life.

He tiptoed around the room and sighed.

'Gyrid, I love watching you sleep,' He murmured softly. Gyrid was curled into a ball and had not moved in several hours. The rumpled linen next to her bore his outline.

He didn't want to wake her, and his reasons were entirely selfish. He wanted to enjoy the smells and colours he had missed for so long. He was back in Scotland as himself. He could speak his own words in his own accent, and he didn't have to pretend with people he despised.

Their room was on the top floor of the tower and had one door to the outside battlement and another that led to the floors below. The tower was crenelated and offered partial protection from the elements to anyone walking outside. He grabbed a cloak, carefully lifted the latch, and nimbly stepped outside.

The sea was dark blue, and unrelenting. The waves bounced off the shoreline and sprayed the land for many yards before reluctantly returning. Even in a storm the land was bright with greens, purples, and browns – the lush grass, the thistles, the heathers, and the lichens that his mother had used to dye wool. He had missed this place for so long. It reminded him of wonderful times in the past before Konrad von Feuchtwangen had plunged his family into despair, ordered by the English King.

The days when Valence had beaten him, when he had bowed and scraped to tyrants – it was all worth it, and there wasn't anywhere he would rather be.

One of Lord Halcro's soldiers was huddled in the corner behind a stone upright.

'My lord, are you ill?'

He looked perplexed as Murdie let the rain drench his face and hair. Murdie looked to the heavens and stretched out his arms.

'God, I have missed this,' he shouted as the rain cascaded down his face.

'Missed what, Lord MacBeith?' The soldier suddenly came to attention.

'This … all *this*. I grew up a few miles from here on the mainland, and I haven't been in these lands for many years. Don't you love being here?' Murdie pointed to the land and sea below.

'Not particularly … not when it is like this.' The soldier looked up to the angry sky and shook his head, perplexed by Murdie's sheer joy.

In the distance the sky lit up as forks of lightning burst from the clouds. The clouds roared and the rain increased. Murdie didn't move, and the soldier took this as an opportunity to return to the safety and relative cover at the corner of the battlement.

The door swung open, and a drowsy, barefoot Gyrid appeared, her cloak wrapped tightly around her face. She put her hand out as if she was measuring the strength of the rain but remained steadfastly just inside the room.

'Lord Douglas is waiting for you inside. Will you let the storm finish the English's work for them and catch your death? Please come inside, Murdie.'

Gyrid smiled, but she was insistent, and reluctantly he left the battlements and the storm behind.

Gyrid stumbled back into the bed and pulled the heavy curtains around her.

'Murdie, wake me up in a few days,' she shouted.

'How many days?' Murdie asked.

'About a hundred.' Gyrid had barely spoken before he heard the steady breathing of a deep sleep.

Lord James Douglas was pacing the room. It was a large space and covered most of the top floor of Halcro's tower. The large bed he shared with Gyrid was at one end, and at the other was a separate reception space filled with a wall-to-ceiling fireplace, a few stout chairs, and a long, padded bench surrounding a single-plank oak table.

'My dear James – how long has it been?' Murdie embraced him.

'Eight years, Douglas Castle I think, just before Stirling Bridge, and just before I became angry. I don't think about time anymore – just castles, battles, and killing those who imprison us.' Douglas had a reputation as dangerous and angry, but these were lines written by his enemies. Murdie found him straightforward and honest, there were no bends in his character or motivations, what you saw was what he was.

'You were young then, and your father was alive and it grieves me to think of him. I can see that you have become so much like Sir William – you are no longer the skinny youth I remember. You have filled out, and you carry a fine sword.'

Murdie had returned in his mind to the reality of rebellion, which the joy of being home had blown away.

'It was my father's, smuggled out of Berwick Castle where the English had imprisoned him. After Stirling Bridge, the English took him to London and slowly starved him to death, chained to the father of Will de Irwyne. Took him three months to die, and for the last two weeks he was tied to the corpse of Alexander de Irwyne. They didn't call him Sir William Douglas the Hardy for nothing. I am doing all this work for King Robert for my father, but mostly for me.'

Murdie recognised how the events of the past few years had impacted him and needed to hear he was not alone.

'James, I am glad you took the time to see me. I understand you are busy making plans for the King's return to the mainland. Do you need my help?' Murdie was curious, James Douglas was not one for small talk.

'King Robert has requested you join him to discuss his plans.' Douglas pulled two chairs together. 'Murdie, please sit with me.' He pointed to the other chair. He moved his head closer to Murdie and lowered his voice. 'King Robert knows you have met with his sister Isabel and that you know about the cargo – but her men know nothing about the cargo and Haakon's intentions.'

Murdie nodded.

'Gyrid knows, but none of Isabel's men were allowed to open any chests or explore the cog's hold except for Adam de Irwyne. Queen Isabel was instrumental in getting me here and her men helped all of us to escape Rouen and evade the Byzantine warships. To the best of my knowledge, they are ignorant of the cargo – and in any case, we can rely on their discretion, if that is your concern – they are Scots just like you and even if they have spent half a lifetime at the Norwegian court, their loyalty to King Robert is solid.'

Murdie understood Douglas's caution. These men were

the only ones in Halcro Castle he didn't know.

'I am not aware of a traitor, but money tempts even the most loyal. We need to know who knows what is in that cog. I am sure you are aware that it is only a matter of time before Haakon arrives, and we need to be sure of these men if it comes to a fight. We hope we never have to test their loyalty and all of us will be gone, but we need to know who is with us.'

'The Norwegians will come here; Queen Isabel has written to tell us so,' Murdie said. 'I think we should be more concerned about the English.'

'Lord Halcro has been making plans and preparing for an attack. The English will be searching for the King on Rathlin Island, but it's a small place, and it won't take them long to understand they've been tricked, and they will appear here eventually. Halcro will remain behind, but we will be gone.'

'Where is the treasure, James? Still in the cog?' Murdie assumed it was in the caves where they had berthed.

'Yes, the cog is below Halcro Castle. The King will send it away from here with Sinclair and Adam de Irwyne, Innes, and Hendor. You are to remain here with Jamie and Will. The King has a task for them in the East. I assume he is sending you as well.'

'James, I promised Gyrid that we would help rescue her son.' Murdie lowered his voice, he didn't want to wake her.

'The King acknowledges the debt he owes to Gyrid, especially after Audenborg and saving your life in Rouen. I don't know anything more other than I am to fetch you for an audience. You need to make yourself presentable.' Lord Douglas grabbed Murdie's tunic and the drying jerkin and tossed them at him. 'Here, put these on, it's a good job the King doesn't stand on ceremony.'

'Yes, it will be better to see the King, the last time we met he was Earl of Carrick, and a fugitive leaving Winchester under threat of arrest. There is much to discuss.'

Murdie had promised that after they had brought the treasure home, his next priority would be Gyrid's son. He didn't want to break that promise.

He hurriedly dressed and they headed towards the king's apartments below.

Chapter Nineteen

Halcro Castle, Orkney, October 1306:
Escape to the Lands of the West

Lord Sinclair burst into the king's apartment. The heavy oak doors crashed into the inner stone surrounds. Two perplexed soldiers recognised him, yet they were so shocked by his bombastic entry that they drew their swords.

Jamie started to draw his sword, for a moment he thought they were under attack.

'Sire, three ships flying the emblem of King Haakon have been spotted taking on supplies at Hjalsmdal. Fisherman crossed the Pentlands risking their lives to get this news to us. There could be more Norwegian ships following and they will be in Orkney in a day – tonight if the winds are in their favour.'

King Robert was recovering well. His mental strength was always remarkable even though he worked longer hours than anyone and seemed to remember every dispatch weeks after he had read them.

Jamie had been asked to wait on the King. Lord Douglas had told him that keeping him close by made him less conscious of the loss of Bishop Wishart. Jamie had not done much waiting, and he soon realised the King just wanted someone to talk to.

He had also noted a measurable improvement in the King's physical strength. He was reading, gathering intelligence, walking on the ramparts and making plans for his return.

The King had been working on these plans for several days. His brothers Alexander and Thomas were to land at Loch Ryan. To do this, he had ordered the construction of many ships. The Bruce lands were adjacent to Loch Ryan, and the locals were just waiting for leaders to remove the imposed English noble, Baron Clifford.

Lord Sinclair was the oldest man in the castle, and he didn't appear to hurry anywhere, despite a real edge in his character. He had lived a very full and exciting life, and Jamie loved to listen to him. His knowledge made him interesting, and his experience made his knowledge believable.

Jamie recognised days like this, where reactions were amplified and measured men became agitated. The consequences were always severe. Haakon's ships were a serious enough threat to burst into the king's apartment.

'My sister wrote that Haakon would pursue the treasure ship regardless of our alliance.' The King pointed to her letter.

'She's right, alliances don't matter at all when this much gold is at stake.' Lord Sinclair's answer was curt.

'Henry, we need to be calm – we knew this day would come and have prepared for it. These lands are Haakon's, and he will claim the treasure belongs to him now, because it is here. I would do the same in his position – are you ready to leave?'

Lord Sinclair nodded. 'Yes, Sire. The treasure was tied down well when it left Alderney. We have secured the hold for our journey, taken on most of our supplies, and prepared the men.'

'I took comfort when I visited the preparations. You have organised affairs well and the men and the treasure are in the best hands.'

The King had stayed a little longer each day watching the cog being scrubbed, the rigging replaced, and a new sail fitted.

'The seas where we are heading will be rough, and normally we wouldn't travel in such times,' Sinclair replied. 'Haakon knows attacking us here would require an army, so I suspect he will be watching and waiting for us to leave. The scouts at Hjalsmdal reported three ships taking on water and supplies.'

'I have met Haakon, and I think I know him. He wants to maintain our alliance, but he wants the treasure more. He is trying to negotiate a very tricky conundrum, and his pride will be more than a little hurt that we are keeping it here under his nose. The only surprise is that he acted a little quicker than I was expecting.'

Jamie assumed monarchs saw life through the same prism, but there was an unspoken code for those anointed by God. He had heard the King discuss other rulers, their weaknesses and strengths, and he believed a fundamental part of a king's role was in manipulating them whilst maintaining alliances.

He concluded that kings overall were an unpleasant but necessary evil. Someone had to rule, and in many cases the merit to do so was determined by the bed they were born in and the confidence that entitlement brought.

They were all several generations away from those who had led through merit but the Bruce was different. He had fought for every piece of his land and was a direct descendant of the first King of Scots, Kenneth MacAlpine. He had the ability and the right.

'Sire, I am reluctant to leave you behind in case there are more of Haakon's ships and a greater army sent against you – including Lord Halcro's men, we are just short of two hundred total defenders.'

'We have talked this through at counsel. Lords Hay and Douglas will remain here as my protection with my brothers until we leave. You are the only man who knows how to navigate across the ocean to the lands beyond Groenland. We can't hide the treasure anymore, eventually enough men will be sent here, and the castle will fall. The treasure must be taken to a place where no one will follow, and I am sending some of my best men to help your crew.'

'Sire, what other men?' Lord Sinclair was also surprised.

'I am sending Adam de Irwyne and Innes, because you need all the experienced sailors given where you are going, and the cargo. Hendor Robertson, because he is one of the most practical men alive, and as a soldier can well command Lord Halcro's rough-hewn men.

You will also take Brother Geoffrey, because he cannot defend himself and Innes shares his protection with you. I intend to retake my realm fighting battles along the way and I can't leave him here for the English to arrive. Staying with you provides the only chance for his long-term survival.'

Jamie noticed when the King struggled with decisions. He stared behind people, avoiding eye contact as if he was looking into the future.

'Sire, there are no safe options. Brother Geoffrey was lucky to survive Methven and Dalrigh. I can take on supplies in Groenland at the Benedictine monastery of Saint Olaf. They could shelter Geoffrey until our return from Skraeling Island.'

The King nodded.

'I know Prior Duncan – he is a good man. Leaving him there will protect him from the most dangerous part of the voyage. Bishop Wishart trusted me with his protection, and my decision to send him with you is difficult – I am planning raids across Ayrshire and Dumfries on Comyn lands and allies. They want to kill me even more than the English, so he will be safer at Saint Olaf's.'

'Anyone else joining us?' Sinclair turned towards Jamie.

Jamie held his breath, hoping he wouldn't be facing another long sea journey.

'I have other plans for young Wishart here, along with Will, Murdie, and Gyrid. Murdie is under an obligation to help Gyrid find her son, so he will leave for England. Will and Jamie will join Domhnall in Norway. My brothers, Thomas and Alexander are headed to Dumfries. Edward and I will join Lords Douglas and Hay in Ayrshire, where we will tackle the Comyns. Now, everyone is tasked to make sure you leave unhindered – the immediate issue is Haakon's ships. He must find the caves below empty.'

Domhnall had already left for Norway and the court of Queen Isabel Bruce, but the reasons had not been revealed. Jamie had assumed it was some sort of diplomacy as the departure had been in secret and hadn't attracted the usual speculation that filled the castle corridors. His curiosity was piqued, and he hoped Sinclair would ask.

Jamie admired Lord Sinclair after he learned he hadn't missed a major battle against the English since he had returned from Acre in 1291.

'Sire, I had not expected the Norwegians to arrive first,' Jamie said, 'They must have known the cog's destination before we left France – how else could they have assembled a fleet?'

'Jamie, I fear you are right, but we must look for the traitor later.'

The King repeatedly fidgeted with a letter he had been reading.

Lord Sinclair took the opportunity to scour the horizon through a window beside the King.

'Henry, in this weather you cannot see anything further than the courtyard – there is nothing to be gained in searching,' the King said. 'The scouts will bring us word. The sea fog has the consistency of gruel, and you can barely see the shore. The weather is safeguarding the treasure better than a thousand men, and it leaves on the next tide. We have a sunstone, and the Norwegians won't reach here until after you have gone – unless you delay.'

The King wanted Sinclair to leave.

'Sire, they are also likely be in possession of a sunstone,' Sinclair argued.

'Probably and if they get here sooner, we will know for sure. My sister told me they have a mine guarded day and night. But the stone only tells you where *you* are, not other ships, and you will be eighty miles or more away from them if you leave on the next tide. You also have your charts for the seas beyond Groenland?'

'Sire, I have made the final preparations for the next tide. Final stores are being loaded.'

'Keep the men safe, and do not reveal your destination until you are out to sea. There could still be traitors, even so far from foreign courts. I ordered the boatbuilder to inspect the ship and make it as secure as it can be. He knows the challenges ships must face in those waters, and the cog was well modified for speed by the Templars. Now he is preparing it to face ice and has thickened the keel, even though he only had a few days to do it.'

Lord Sinclair nodded.

'Sire, by leaving we keep the treasure and use it for the battles to come. In these lands there are vines, berries and seals to sustain us. We will lose ourselves and return in the summer.'

The King removed a cross from around his neck.

'I will pray for your safe return. Take this.'

Jamie didn't know about Groenland, but he knew where to look amongst the sagas. He wanted to absorb all the knowledge he could.

The King admired and trusted Lord Sinclair. His reluctance to send him was clear, he shook his head as if he wished he could change his mind.

Jamie was again alone with the King.

'What can you see below?' the King asked.

'The courtyard is full of men preparing to leave – I am seeing that courage and bravery on the battlefield relies on logistics and supplies.'

'That is a valuable lesson – a soldier fights better with a full stomach,' the King replied.

'Lord Sinclair is below with Brother Geoffrey, assembling men – they are walking to the tunnels. I recognise the voices of Innes and Hendor – but I can't see them, Adam is saying his goodbyes to Will.'

Jamie had seen a big change in the King since the day in February when he had arrived at Glasgow Cathedral seeking absolution, soaked and crusted in blood. He was an impressive man and was known as a formidable knight, but his presence wasn't only a physical thing – it was the confidence of being anointed, being a king.

'Sire, can I ask you a question?'

'You can ask, and I will answer if I can.'

'What skills does it take to be a good king?'

The Bruce was self-assured and commanded everyone around him. Jamie wanted to learn how to lead.

'Jamie, I have a lot to learn and prove – I may be anointed but I am a novice. I have narrowed the key skills down to a few things in order: listening, intelligence, courage, experience and judgement – I think if you have all these things or try to acquire them you can be a great king.'

Many of the king's council had some of these attributes, but none of them had them all.

'I will never be a king, but I will try to model my life to acquire all these skills.'

The King nodded and opened a dispatch.

'Jamie, let me test you. I have word from Carrick. Alexander Seton has written to me. Do you know of him? Please, sit by me.' The King pointed to a small, backed chair opposite him.

'Sire, Alexander Seton – I thought he was still loyal to the English – I have heard little good about him. He swore an oath to defend you "with fortune and blood," and now he is the commander of the English garrison at Berwick – his allegiances shift like sand.'

'Well said, you are quickly learning the morals and affinities of my noble lords. However, the fact he has written to me tells me that his fondness for the English may be wavering. It might have something to do with the English executing his brother. He wants to work for me now. Read this.'

The King handed Jamie a tatty dispatch that had been reread many times. Jamie concluded that the King was agonising about what to do. The King did not know whether he could trust Seton. Jamie was inclined to agree with Lord Hay's view: once a traitor, always a traitor.

However, Alexander Seton was now connected to the King; they shared the grief of Christopher Seton's barbaric execution in Dumfries the previous month.

'Do you think he is a traitor?' the King asked.

'Until six months ago, I was an apprentice mason at Glasgow Cathedral. I have no experience in high politics.'

Jamie was reluctant to answer in case he offended the King or appeared naïve.

'You are the son of a great soldier and the nephew of a brave patriot. Who else has such a pedigree? Don't be modest, Jamie – our Lord was a carpenter, and I wouldn't have asked you if I didn't want to hear your opinion. You will give me an honest answer, which I am at liberty to ignore. I will think no less of you if I disagree.'

A king asking was a king commanding, so he felt compelled to reply.

'Based on the evidence, Sire. When I was a mason's apprentice, we required expensive tools – chisels, hammers – and there were those you would lend your tools and those you wouldn't because they were never returned or were returned broken. You didn't give those people a second chance. If you couldn't work because you had no tools, you and your family starved, and everyone knew that. It was important to judge their character.'

'So, you are telling me you wouldn't lend Seton your tools?' the King asked.

'Yes, Sire. He's the kind of man that wouldn't have a second thought about taking away my livelihood and letting my family starve. He fights with the English and defends their interests. There is too much at stake and it seems conclusive that he is working against you.'

Jamie was learning the court politics. Courtiers needed to understand their king and tell him what they thought he wanted to hear to gain his patronage. But he didn't want to be a courtier, simply restating platitudes and untruths. He thought it corrupt – he couldn't be the man he wanted to be if nothing but lies came out of his mouth, and he judged that King Robert wasn't a typical king. Like any good mason, he found the refuge of honesty lay more comfortably with him.

'You are right, and by any measure, Seton is a traitor, and then so are all the noble families of Scotland. The English forced many to swear an oath of allegiance to their king – some more willingly than others. Many are starting to realise the English King is dying – he has three decades on the Pope, and his heir doesn't have the same preoccupation with Scotland as his father. The tide is turning in our favour. Dynasties change, and so do allegiances. The only way I can win our country back is by welcoming former enemies as friends who temporarily lost their way. I need to grow my friends because I need men. In Sir Alexander Seton's case, he has started looking for the righteous path and hopes I will make it easy for him to come over to our side without holding his previous allegiances against him. I will welcome him back, and in doing so, I must also consider that his family controls lands adjacent to mine and he is the commander of Berwick Castle. He can help me more by staying inside with the English, gathering intelligence, and writing letters that tell me their thoughts and plans.'

The King had considered how Seton could be of greater use, but Jamie wasn't convinced that his duplicity should be rewarded.

'And if he betrays you again, Sire?'

'If he does, I have a good memory, and when the time suits me, I will destroy him, starting with his castles. I will take his land and everything he values away from him. When you are penniless, titles mean nothing, and you soon become friendless. If I don't catch up with him, he will have to flee and live off the King of England, and Edward is a fair-weather friend who keeps a close eye on his exchequer. I will send as many over the border to dip their hands into his purse as I can. Without money, Edward can't fight me, and that's why he wants the treasure hiding in the caves.'

'Sire, I have seen what that treasure does to people. It is ours by right. My father and the Templars found it by accident escaping from Acre. They didn't seek it and God placed it in their laps. We have more right than most to keep it – Geoffroi de Charnay didn't want it to fall into the wrong hands. There is a moral justice in that, and he knew we would try to use it wisely.'

'Well said, Jamie. You listened well to your uncle Robert and remind me of his loss every day.'

The King had remarked many times that he missed the Bishop. He had written to the King of France urging him to use his influence with the Pope to obtain Bishop Wishart's freedom from English captivity.

'I am honoured that you consider this an opinion I would have shared with him.'

The noise outside grew and Jamie returned to the window.

'Jamie, what is the weather doing? Fog can clear in minutes, and Orkney is defined by its changeable weather.'

'Sire, a little. The wind is picking up and making it a little patchy. The sun is trying to burn the fog away.'

The King grunted agreement.

'Has Hamish Campbell returned from Tarbert?' the King asked. 'He is overdue. I would have expected him back by now.'

'He may also be a victim of the weather. I don't see his horse in the courtyard, and the ships that docked before the fog set in didn't come from Argyle.'

'Check with the steward and see if there is any news of him.'

Jamie rushed down the stairs from the king's apartments and bumped into Murdie, almost pushing him over.

'Are you rushing to say your farewells to Innes, Hendor, and Adam? I have just come from the ship; you will need to be quick.'

Murdie put a flask of spirit in his hand.

'Let's toast them off. Will and I need to remove all the boxes of papers and scrolls before the ship leaves, and we might need your help. You have been through a lot with them, and they may be gone for many months. I think they would be pleased to see you before they left.'

Jamie hesitated.

'The King is looking for news of Hamish Campbell, and he is waiting. I don't want to make a speech, only wish them well – and I want to do it in person.'

'I have just come from the steward, and there is a letter from Lady Christina. James has an audience with the King right now. He can tell the King about Hamish.' Murdie pointed behind Jamie.

'Once we have seen the ship leave, then you can return – I think the King will understand.'

Murdie placed his arm around Jamie, and they headed off towards the tunnel.

*

Konrad and his companion Jean were sheltering on a narrow

stone platform overlooking a heavily laden cog and several small birlinns. They were all tied by heavy ropes to thick iron hoops within a narrow inlet. The cave overhang made a perfect secure harbour for a small flotilla like this.

Their part of the cave was hidden from view, and that was where the perfection ended, as far as Konrad was concerned. The cave was also full of gunk and droppings and his hose and cloak were liberally splattered with what he assumed was slime dripping from the bats and seabirds that nested above. They were sitting without any lamp, and the natural light was weak.

'This shit smells of rotting fish.' Konrad's eyes rolled, and his face soured.

'Lower your voice, or we will be discovered,' Jean snapped in response.

This was another uncomfortable humiliation amongst so many Konrad had experienced since he had landed on the islands.

'I hate everything about Orkney, the weather, and the constant wind. Its remoteness harbours barbarians who speak neither English nor French, and finally, everywhere you tread, something new appears on your boots. Its rough charm is lost to me – makes the dungeons in Constantinople appealing.'

Jean rolled his eyes.

'They are seabirds, and they eat fish. What they shit out will smell of fish.'

Konrad noticed the sea had reached its maximum and the water mark on the keel was submerged.

'The tide will be turning soon.'

He wanted to be away, but there was something here he needed to finish. Jean had helped him get to Orkney, soon he would assassinate a target he had been chasing for fifteen years and then Jean would be surplus. However, he would keep him alive until after he had killed Bruce and the competitor prince. He had no intention of returning to Valence with any of them.

Jean was ignorant of his schemes – his knowledge only extended to the Scots King, and in this case he thought they were here to capture him.

For Konrad, the death of the competitor was all-consuming. He had waited for so long that he wouldn't allow Jean to get in the way. So many years in his company, and he had never liked him.

Today would be the last day of this grotesque misalignment.

'How long do you think we will have to wait for the Scots King? You are sure he will come?' Konrad asked, as water continued to drip down the back of his neck.

He really wanted to see the old man he had observed with the King. He was the right age for the competitor and had the red-grey hair of the Plantagenets.

'The Scots King has been inspecting the cog over there most days. Have some faith. If he doesn't come here soon, we will just have to visit him. Sounds like they are preparing the ship to leave, so maybe King Robert is planning a trip.' Jean replied.

The level of activity had increased. Konrad could tell from the number of voices.

Jean placed a small sack by him and produced a flask and two small goblets.

'Drink some of this marvellous *uisge beatha*.'

He handed a goblet to Konrad, who admitted to himself that he enjoyed the local spirit, and that was where the list of good things ran out.

'After all these years together in the stinking dungeons of the Byzantines, you would think you would have learned patience,' Jean said. 'Stikelaw's map shows that these caves are the only spot on this island that can't be seen from Halcro Towers, so we need to stay here and wait until it's quieter.'

Jean rummaged inside the sack and produced a round of hard black bread, some dried meat, and two apples. He threw one straight at Konrad, and it bounced off his chest and fell untidily into his lap.

'I bet you wished that was a spear,' Konrad complained.

'It wouldn't have bounced into your lap if it was,' Jean scoffed.

He tore off a piece of meat and bread, and he threw them at Konrad.

'I will be careful that a bird doesn't shit on this. Let me guess – mutton again.'

Konrad liked mutton, but after having it served at every opportunity since he had arrived here, he had begun to hate it. The only bright spot was that he would soon leave Orkney, and the assassination he had first planned in 1291 would be completed.

'After this is over, I am returning to my lands in Franconia. My family castle in Feuchtwangen nestles peacefully amongst lands where the sun shines, the winds are tolerable, and the soil so rich that it could support any beast or crop – not just mutton.'

He closed his eyes and imagined himself sitting at an open fireplace, enjoying the game meats from the plentiful hunting he had enjoyed in the surrounding forests.

'Be thankful it's mutton. Remember the meat we got only on feast days in the Tower of Belisarius? It was so stringy we used the sinews to tie up our shoes. You can enjoy every meal when you are free, shackles taint everything you eat – and on the days when meat is forbidden the fish from these islands, it's so fresh it trembles when you cook it. This island may be brutal, but it's also idyllic.'

Jean tucked in, filling his cheeks with meat, bread, and spirit.

'That is just another of the many aspects of life on which we disagree.'

Konrad didn't eat but filled his goblet again.

'I will drink to that.' Jean held the goblet in front of him and gulped the contents down. Most of the heavy amber rivulets flowed down his untidy beard onto his lap. He wiped his face with the back of his hand.

'There is only one way for us to get the Scottish King out of here, and that is by one of those small fishing birlinns moored below,' Jean commented.

Jean was no fool, and Konrad suspected he had also concluded that their chances of kidnapping the Scottish King and leaving alive were near zero. This was talk to fill the silence. The crew Valence had sent with them had deserted, the certain outcome of sending conscripted men on an impossible mission. Two men escaping with a live king without challenge was an impossible folly.

However, a lone assassin killing the Scottish King and the competitor amongst entourage was indeed possible. Konrad would keep up the pretence.

He wondered why Jean was still around on such a mission where success was marginal – and he concluded Jean was there to kill him.

'We need to capture the King alone. Find a place or a time when he is unguarded or entice him down here and hope he only brings his servant.' Jean didn't sound convinced by his own plan.

Konrad nodded. He believed Jean was a lesser man, however he was an experienced assassin.

'Valence wants him alive for a show trial and a fancy execution. He doesn't just want Bruce dead; he wants the Scottish rebellion humiliated. Go and see what they are doing. I looked whilst you were sleeping.' Jean pointed below. The spirit was making him bolder.

Konrad wanted him to drink more, as it would make him easier to overcome, but he was spilling more than he was drinking. Was Jean trying to fool him?

The ledge at the end of the platform was only wide enough for one man to lie on. The rest of the platform was hidden and could only be accessed from the level below. The water had dripped down the walls, creating a natural staircase. The ledge allowed them to spy on the ships below, and unless anyone looked up from directly below the entrance to the platform, the hiding place was perfect.

'There have been guards there every day since we started hiding here. It seems strange to have guards attending a ship that is tied up. It must have something important on board. It has crates and barrels on the deck that remind me of the ones we saw on the barge where we met. Now they have removed the mooring ropes, after loading an endless amount of supplies. There are even more guards there, and they have lit all the lamps on board.'

Jean had obviously studied the boat, and Konrad wondered what else he had examined whilst he had been sleeping.

'Let me see.'

Konrad crawled to the end of the ledge and studied the ship closely. It was single masted with a very large mainsail, next to the gangplank were two heavily armed guards carrying crossbows and swords. On the deck he could see several ballistae pointing forward of the bow, and on either side of the keel. The barrels and chests that were tied on the deck looked familiar and lit torches surrounded the ship. He slid back away from the edge.

'You are right. That ship is leaving on the next tide, and they have even taken chickens on board, it's going far. It's not the type of ship you would normally see in Orkney, and it's been in a fight very recently. You can see the raised black scars of fire along the deck like something sticky had attached itself – Greek fire – and damaged planks have been replaced; they're a different colour. I wonder if it's seen battle with the Byzantine navy; they are the only navy that uses that weapon – it took a lot of punishment. If I was a fugitive king who wanted to keep something safe or escape, that's the ship I would use – and you are right, it does remind me of 1291 and Acre. Is it really fifteen years ago that our worlds collided?' Konrad sighed wearily.

He had never imagined it would be here in Orkney that he would fulfil his obligation to King Edward. In 1291 he had been tasked to end the life of a prince and had followed him to a barge escaping Acre – a barge full of Crusaders, Scottish knights, and treasure. He hadn't been there for the treasure; he'd discovered that by accident. He had been there to kill the child of Knox de Mayon and Eleanor of Brittany.

Both the barge and the prince had disappeared … for a while. He wondered, was this confirmation that the prince was here?

Could it really be the treasure below? The ship was different, but if the cargo is here, then Valence's intelligence could be correct, and the competitor is also here?

He tried to determine if Jean was arriving at the same conclusion. He appeared far more relaxed than Konrad as he tucked into even more food.

The years in prison had given him a lot of time to think of how he had gotten there, and he had always wondered why two royal assassins had been on the same barge at the same time.

King Phillip would have put someone in Acre to safeguard the competitor prince and keep him until the time was right to announce him to the world. He would have used the competitor like a tragic player in a theatre, to entertain himself and to humiliate and intimidate King Edward. Phillip wouldn't have been able to resist trying to make the prince his own, and he would have used Jean.

Jean had been just as surprised as he was when they had discovered a dead crew and a treasure. Jean was there for the competitor but not to kill him, to save him, and eliminate

Konrad. Now he had watched Jean's suppliant behaviour, he was sure.

Ruaidhri Ranald had failed to join them. That laid the path open for Jean to remove Konrad without any witnesses.

Valence would never know the truth, and Jean would return to France and live off the money from a grateful king. Jean needed Konrad to find the prince, so he would spoil Jean's plan and conclude his own.

Jean was speaking – his words were unimportant, and he would keep him off guard until he was ready to strike.

'Collided is the right word – a joining together with force and consequences. We can't undo the past. Now we must plan how we are going to kidnap the Scottish King and survive. You are right, Konrad, those birlinns are our way out of here.'

Konrad wasn't listening, he needed to see the old man. The cog was brightly lit, enough to see a face, and he hoped he would soon see a prince.

'Shush.' Jean stopped talking and placed his index finger over his lips and pointed below.

Shoes could be heard crunching and squelching through the grit and detritus on the cave floor. The voices below became louder and then heated. There was some sort of argument, then a scuffle, followed by cries and the swish of swords and axes clashing with rock and metal. The voices increased in number and intensity.

Konrad hesitated to crawl out on the ledge, yet he needed to know if the cog had moved and the prince was escaping him again. He was impatient to complete the job, and his frustration made him reckless, so he slithered to the end of the ledge just in time to see all the guards running off the ship to join the fight below them.

He held his breath. The animals above him, woken by the fight, defecated on him. The smell made his eyes water, and he wanted to sneeze.

The cries and groans grew and then subsided. Whatever it was, it was over quickly, and it had happened ten feet below them. Konrad wondered why no one had tried to escape by climbing up to the platform, as the footholds were visible.

A man was being dragged towards the boat, his arms and hands hung limply to either side of his torso, scraping across the cave floor. He looked dead and made no attempt to resist. Then he saw his hand move.

It took two men to carry him up the gangplank before the hold was opened and the body was taken down; he recognised the figure. It was another reminder of Acre. He would never forget the creature that had found them in the boat in Acre and tortured them. He had taken them to Constantinople and consigned them to fifteen years in a stinking Byzantine dungeon. They had referred to him as 'the golden-haired demon.' He could feel his heart race and there was fury inside of him the likes of which he had never felt. His hands clenched, and he felt his teeth grind.

Now, what is he doing here? That ship must contain the treasure. After fifteen years, he is still hunting his prey. He is tenacious and driven. There are two guards in the hold with him, but where is everyone else? They must still be below.

He gently opened the fastening holding his sword to his belt and reckoned the entrance to the ledge was so narrow that he and Jean could hold off many men before they were taken. Still, no one had made any attempt to climb up to the platform and capture them. He looked back. Jean was also still. They communicated through gestures.

Konrad slid as far as he could until his head extended beyond the furthest point of the ledge. He risked falling off and looked below.

Two men with thick cloaks were beneath him. One was bent kneeling over the other who was sitting, so he couldn't see either face. The man sitting was injured, gasping for breath, and the other comforting him and handing him a flask. He had his head partially in front of the other man, a small lamp was in his hands.

Move back so I can see you.

Konrad turned to check on Jean, who hadn't moved but who now had his dagger in his right hand.

Jean mouthed 'who is there?'

Konrad didn't respond. He had to get a better look at the men. The injured man was trying to stand and the other was helping, but he was unsteady, and the other man could barely lift him. Konrad felt a surge of excitement as he glimpsed their faces. His heart pounded, and he wanted to cheer.

I need to see all your face to be sure.

The men linked arms, then stood up and unsteadily tried to regain their balance. They shuffled forward very slowly. The uninjured man had placed the lamp on the floor as he helped the injured one, then held it in front of him. Konrad could see all their faces, and immediately he recognised one of the men. He swallowed hard, doubting what his eyes were telling him. He cast his mind back so many years to Acre, reliving the weeks when he had followed this man. He remembered his smell, his expression – yes, it was many years ago, and he only doubted his memory for a second.

The red hair was greyer, and he was more stooped, but Konrad had the man's form etched in his memory. It was him, and this was his chance. He had to take it before they reached the boat.

The guards had not returned from the hold. This was his moment to finish the competitor prince.

He slid back to where Jean was sitting.

'Are we discovered?' Jean whispered. He had a dagger in one hand and his sword in the other.

'No, but there is something I need to do.'

Konrad pushed past him and silently slid down onto the cave floor. He knew Jean would come after him, and he was becoming reckless.

He could see the men in front of him, and he trod as quietly as he dared, ready to strike. He had decided to kill them both now and then finish Jean. Then the man holding the lamp turned. He was startled, and the lamp slipped from his hand and fell onto the floor. One of the men was wearing a monk's tunic.

'Help!'

The monk picked up the metal lamp and swung it towards Konrad, who parried it away with his sword. Konrad was ready to strike both when he was caught with a blow to his ribs.

'Bastard!' The word resonated in his ear.

He could feel his presence, his pattern, the frequency of each breath. It was Jean. He could smell his scent without seeing his face. The blade caught him again on his forearm as he defended himself, slicing deep into the muscle.

At the same time, one of the men grabbed his feet. What horrified Konrad most was that he had assumed the fifteen years would have no impact on him, that he could take three men on and come out on top. He had fooled himself; he didn't have the agility or strength.

He was fighting Jean whilst his legs were being pulled away from him. The metal lamp swung again, and it glanced off his back and hit Jean in the face. Jean stumbled back, and the space allowed him to grab his sword, which had fallen onto the ground. He swung it towards Konrad, catching him on the shoulder, but the sword was travelling with such force that it caught one of the two men on the floor.

The man groaned and tried to retaliate. Somehow, he had a dirk in his hand and was stabbing at Jean.

They think Jean is trying to kill them, but he is trying to save them by killing me.

Konrad was bleeding badly and fell; his hands wet with blood. He tried to stand but the floor was wet, bloody and slippery. The ring carrying his family's crest, the von

Feuchtwangen of Franconia, fell to the floor, snapped from his neck, distracting him for a second. He fell next to the man he had observed sitting, clutching his dagger, he was ready to stab the prince.

Jean tried to finish Konrad off, but he deflected the blow with his dagger, and Jean's sword glanced the face of the monk who screamed with pain as the sword split his cheek. Blood dripped down his face.

Out of the shadows, voices emerged as several men ran towards them, their swords drawn. They pulled Jean away, pinning his arms to his back. Konrad heard a crack as one of Jean's arms twisted so far that it gave way, and he cried out. Then another man slapped him across the mouth before he could cry out again.

'Who hurt you?' A voice asked.

'Him.' The prince was hysterical and pointed to Jean.

Jean was still struggling and trying to shout out an explanation. He was still fighting, trying to get at Konrad.

In an instant, he ran Jean through.

Jean groaned and fell next to them, his eyes were staring into Konrad's, yet he felt no pity or sense of loss. He watched as Jean's soul left his body; his eyes were wide open, and blood oozed from his drooping mouth. The warm liquid enveloped the side of Konrad's face; he didn't have the strength to wipe it away – he just wanted to sleep.

'Innes, this man was trying to save us.' The man on the floor pointed to Konrad.

'Are you sure, Lord Sinclair?' The man who had killed Jean was now becoming a blur, but Konrad had heard his name – Innes. Everyone was merging into one featureless body.

'This man saved our lives. Brother Geoffrey was injured, but he is a formidable man when armed with a lamp. I have been injured twice today, once by the English agent who is dying in the hold and a second time by this dead assassin. It is not my time to die.'

'Lord Sinclair, I would agree with that.' Innes replied.

Lord Sinclair tore off a piece of his linen tunic and held it tight against the wound on his leg. He tore off a second piece of cloth and handed it to Brother Geoffrey.

'Place that against the wound. It will bleed, but it looks worse than it is.' Brother Geoffrey held the cloth fast to his cheek.

'Do you know the dead man?' Innes asked, as he cleaned his sword on Jean's cloak.

Brother Geoffrey recoiled as he looked at Jean and Konrad. He was shaking, hiding behind Sinclair.

'I have never seen either of these two men before today.' Innes handed Sinclair a flask of spirit, and Sinclair poured it over his wounds.

'Do you know either of these men, Brother Geoffrey?' Innes asked.

The monk pulled his cowl over his head and looked away, saying nothing.

Konrad was barely conscious; he could feel his life ebbing away. He felt cold and started to shiver. The man called Innes stood above him.

'Who are you? What is your name?' he shouted into his ear.

He couldn't move. With his last ounce of strength, he replied, 'William … William de Beaujeau.'

'We will take the dead man on board and look through his clothing – might tell us who he is before we throw him over the side,' Sinclair said. 'That foreign spy we caught earlier is in the hole and will soon join him. The injured man we can take on board too … the ship's carpenter can look after him. Domhnall taught him some skill, he can stitch together sails, so that slash on the shoulder shouldn't be too difficult.' Sinclair opened the clothes around Konrad's wound.

'That's if he survives the infection.' Innes knelt and

picked up the ring.

'We can clean it up with *uisge beatha*. And thank you for saving us.' Sinclair poured the remaining spirit onto Konrad's wounds.

Konrad couldn't react. The pain was agonising, yet he was paralysed, unable to respond. Then darkness filled his brain, and he closed his eyes. He was being lifted and carried away and he wondered if he was on his last journey to his final resting place. He was in a dark place without any light and he couldn't open his eyes. This must be death.

*

'What has happened?' Jamie asked as he rushed towards Lord Sinclair. Murdie was close behind, his sword drawn.

'Lord Sinclair was attacked, but he has survived. He was lucky that Brother Geoffrey was on hand. I arrived just in time to finish one off. The other is in irons in the hold. If he survives, I will make him talk. I had help from a William Beaujeu, though he is thought mortally injured. We placed him in the hold, perhaps the sailmaker can save him. We don't have time to …' Innes start to remove the blood from his sword of blood with the end of his woollen tunic.

'The Norwegians have been spotted in Hjalsmdal and the King wants you away from here before they arrive, and we came to say goodbye.' Jamie interrupted.

'Innes, you seem to have the men secured, it's best you leave and do your interrogations at sea. These men can't go anywhere out there, and we could be attacked at any moment. We wanted to say goodbye and good luck to you all but I think you can take the message on our behalf.' Murdie replaced his sword in its sheath.

Innes simply nodded and turned to board the ship. Hendor and Adam were making final preparations under Lord Sinclair's command. Sinclair was seated, and looked pale, but his voice had lost none of its authority.

Jamie felt despondent, he wondered if he would ever see his friends again. He had grown up rapidly in the last six months and there would be a void in his life without them.

'You will see them again, young Wishart.' Murdie turned and headed back to the tunnel. Jamie reluctantly followed. He didn't want to look back as tears welled in his eyes.

*

Lord Hay entered the king's chamber.

'I wasn't expecting you, my Lord.' The King was deep at work. Hay was accompanied by one of the men from the garrison.

'Something has happened, and we think you need to know – regarding the cog – tell the King what you told me.'

'Sire, a patrol had reports of a small ship moored below the caves,' the soldier said. 'Lord Innes and our men searched the shore but couldn't find anyone. Then we heard noises inside the cave – what we didn't know was that Lord Sinclair and Brother Geoffrey were being attacked. Lord Sinclair managed to fight off him off – then, just before we got to them a second man attacked them. Lord Sinclair was on the ground and Geoffrey was protecting him – Lord Mayon ran the second murderer through with the help of a knight we had never seen, William Beaujeu. We don't know how he got there but he saved Brother Geoffrey and Lord Sinclair.'

'Is Lord Sinclair badly injured?' The King sat forward. He was vital for the treasure's escape, and he didn't want to delay the departure if he could avoid it.

'Not badly – he is as strong as an ox and twice as stubborn,' the soldier replied.

The soldier amused King Robert in his frankness and forwardness. The Orcadians didn't display the filters of court etiquette.

Lord Hay dismissed the soldier, and the King knew that Hay had more to tell him and didn't want the soldier to know.

'Lord Hay, where is the attacker now, and do we know what he was looking for – and who is this William de Beaujeu?'

'Sire, the attacker is on the boat with Domhnall's assistant, the ship's carpenter, being sewn up. He is a large man – but not much of a fighter, and he is still a bit of a mess. He had a map of the caves in his pocket. We haven't had time to question him, as he is unconscious – I don't know if he will survive.'

Lord Hay placed an engraved sword onto the table. The King picked it up and examined it closely. The pommel had at one time contained a stone. The King suspected he knew who this man was working for.

'I presume this belonged to the attacker?'

'You appear to recognise the sword,' Lord Hay observed.

'I recognise the type, not the sword itself, but it is missing its jewel. He lost it, although it looks like it was removed – you can see where it has been prised out of its setting.' The King handed the sword back to him.

'What does it mean?' Lord Hay examined the pommel and ran his finger around the setting. The metal surround was bent where a dagger or sword had been used.

'The missing stone is a citrine. They are a rare and expensive adornment. Whenever you find people bearing swords with this jewel, the English are behind them. Innes told me such a sword was used in Rouen back in March by someone who was disguised as a French soldier but fought like an Englishman. The costs could only be borne by a king or someone close to him. I saw them at Longshanks' court in Winchester – Bishop Wishart told me a story about such a sword being found on a knight who just happened to be slaughtered on the barge where John Wishart first discovered the treasure. There is never that much coincidence. This man was clever enough to remove the stone from the sword, but not adept enough to avoid Lord Sinclair – a big man, you say?' The King was intrigued.

'Yes – must be well over six feet, greying hair, many injuries and scars … do you think he is working for the English?'

'He either owns the sword or took it from an English agent. Do you know differently?' The King wondered what other secrets this man was carrying.

'No, Sire, just that he was covered with tattoos of Norse gods, which he had tried to hide with his clothing. I don't think an Englishman would want such decoration … unless he is working for more than one master, and he found the sword somehow.' Lord Hay continued to study the setting. 'Innes has him closely confined and in any case his injuries will keep him quiet for a while.'

'I expected Haakon to send people to Orkney to seize it. It was always more likely that it could be stolen by a small band of agents rather than a grand siege – and what about William Beaujeau?'

'Sire, we believe he is a Templar working for Geoffroi de Charnay so we are treating him kindly. He is badly injured and is on the ship receiving attention.'

'I heard of William de Beaujeau from my father, he was a fine crusader and disappeared after the Templars left Acre. If he recovers, he could be a useful addition to the crew, he is a thinker as well as a fighter – see he is cared for.'

The King would have to allow the treasure to leave with these men. He recognised the risk but the ship had to be gone before Castle Halcro was besieged.

'Sire, we placed the tattooed man in the hold with a couple of guards, Beaujeu is safe from him. We have searched the cave, and there is no one else hiding there, but we did find this ring on the floor after the fights.'

Lord Hay handed it to the King who placed it on the table in front of him. He didn't recognise the coat of arms, except that it wasn't Scottish or English.

'It's not an emblem from these islands. Murdie knows all the nobles' coats of arms; I will get him to look.'

The King's eyes were drawn to Lord Hay's hands and the front of his tunic, which were stained with blood.

'It's clear that these killers were here to stop Lord Sinclair and keep the treasure here, so we must frustrate these plans, I expect de Charnay sent Beaujeu to prevent them and has yet to send word. Nevertheless, let Innes know and tell him to watch Beaujeu and the tattooed man,' the King said. 'The ship leaves right away.'

'Yes Sire, and if I have to, I will drag them out the caves myself.'

Lord Hay left the King alone and he returned to his maps planning his return and the recapture of Scotland.

*

Maccabi Tagaris had been submerged in the freezing water for hours. The physicians at Saint Catherine's had provided him with a potion that kept him alive in such temperatures. He had also smeared an inch of seal fat on his torso, and whilst he shivered, he had not passed out due to the cold. He had seen and heard all he needed to.

He had watched the Norwegian strengthen the keel and knew the treasure was heading to the icy waters in the west. Today he had discovered the identity of the English prince.

Konrad von Feuchtwangen had failed to kill the competitor and had somehow engineered the death of Jean de Grailly. Bringing Jean back alive and Konrad's head to Empress Eirene were no longer possible.

He patted the relic of Saint Fillan, which he held in a pouch around his neck. He would go home, back to Saint Catherine's, but only after he had stopped off at Thessaloniki and visited the Empress. She would need ships if she was to seize the treasure and his price would be high if she wanted his help.

It had been hard, and he couldn't imagine a place more utterly different from Sinai than South Ronaldsay.

She would be surprised to know the prince's real name. He wondered what she would do with his news. He didn't really care, except that he would hold her to deliver on her part of the bargain. Once she had the treasure, she would purchase all the relics stolen by the West. That would be his price.

Now I need to get out of here before they set sail and I freeze to death.

He removed himself from the berth and disappeared into the night.

*

Wamrok had anchored his small flotilla a couple of miles off the west coast of South Ronaldsay. He was anxious because the sea was choppy, as it always was off the Scottish coast. Even this far from the shore, the winds were so changeable and unfettered that every ship could be blown aground, and there would be little he could do about it.

He relied on Fjelstad, and his first impressions had been confirmed that the man was an expert sailor but so intense he couldn't communicate on any other subject.

The ships were perilously close, and long ropes had been attached to the side of each ship so they could stay together in the sea fog that had hidden Castle Halcro from view. His ship was in the centre. The anchor ropes strained and groaned to keep the ships stable, and several pairs of oarsmen were using all their strength to keep the ropes from snapping.

'If anyone can get on that treasure ship, it's Axel, and that intelligence King Haakon paid for from Jakob Dedekam on the cog was worth it,' Olav commented.

Wamrok could see from his face that Olav was just as anxious as he was. The journey had been a rough one, and the crew was frightened. It had been a long time since their ancestors had sailed into fogbound seas heading west and guided only by a sunstone.

'Jakob would sell his mother if there was a market. Axel found the ship in the caves underneath Halcro's castle preparing to leave. He took a great risk to row out and tell us and then to return. If he succeeded in killing Sinclair, the Scots will have no one to guide them west. Only a brave man or a crazy one would attempt it.'

Wamrok knew the risk was worth it. The treasure was only two miles away, and if the Scots were prevented from leaving, he and his men would attack the castle via the caves. A small force would never be able to lay siege to Halcro, but one with a copy of the castle plans and a secret route right into the keep stood a chance.

'If the treasure ship doesn't appear by tomorrow, we can make preparations to attack Halcro,' Olav said. 'Fjelstad thinks the only way to escape is to go west.'

Wamrok studied Fjelstad as he noted down more figures on the numerous small scrolls he kept on his person. The haphazard system seemed to work, as he could always find what he was looking for.

'Fjelstad said we are going west?' Wamrok was making conversation. They had been waiting here for almost twelve hours in the strangest of seas, isolated and without a sound apart from the noise of the sea and the groaning of the ships. The men were subdued, busying themselves with drinking and eating.

'Where else could they go? If the Scots went east, they would be sailing into Norwegian waters, and if they went south, they would head into the grasp of the English. North is a cold wasteland. Axel also said they would go west, because there is nowhere else.'

'I wonder how Axel will let us know he is on board,' Wamrok mused.

'Fjelstad is convinced any ship leaving Orkney will

travel just north of our position. The current will pick you up and push you out to the west faster than a sling shot. He said anyone who knows these waters and wants to be west as quickly as possible will do that. Axel will find a way on board and a way to help us follow. We must hope that the weather clears.'

'Your knowledge of the sea is commendable, Olav. But I assume that whenever you have a conversation with Fjelstad, it's never two-way – he talks at you.'

'And I turned to this wonderful elixir as a result. The Scots were blessed when God gave them the recipe for *uisge beatha*.'

Olav produced a flask and handed it to Wamrok. He hesitated and only moistened his lips.

'Olav, I am worried about the journey west. The crew are frightened.' Wamrok had used all his skills to stop a mutiny.

Olav seemed less concerned. 'Their heads are full of sagas and sea creatures. Gossip of ships disappearing and crews consumed. If you don't have facts, then you make up for any gaps with such tales. There haven't been any ships sent further than Groenland for centuries. Fear of the unknown is a powerful conspirator. Once they have a few battles under their belt, they will be fine.' He pointed to the flask Wamrok was holding. 'Drink this. It always helps. I need to return to my ship.' Olav stood up and wobbled as Wamrok steadied him.

'Be careful. I need you more than ever. There is another big adventure about to happen. Despite the risks, capturing this treasure is an obsession now. I can't stop.'

Olav smiled. 'With *uisge beatha,* we can capture this ship and then go on to conquer the world.'

Wamrok took a large glug from the flask and was sure he was right.

Epilogue

Kolossi Castle, Cyprus, September 1306: Molay's Return

Jacques de Molay loved Kolossi Castle. It reminded him of his years on crusade. It was built of the same sandstone the Order had used for their fortresses in the Holy Land, with thick walls that would withstand even the most determined attacks. The Vexillum Belli, the battle flag of the Order, flew proudly from the battlement. The white banner and red cross displayed to everyone that the Grand Master was in residence and that the Order had been doing what they did best – fighting a tyrant.

The interior smelt of the sea and was filled with the collection of knights, apprentices, clerics, and people on the make that reminded him of Acre.

Molay had good reason to be pleased with himself.

'We did the right thing in removing the inept King Henry from Cyprus – his brother Amalric is far more amenable. It felt just like the old crusading days, when we raised sieges and removed unfriendly rulers.'

Molay was in his mid-sixties, yet he was still a marvel of a man, over six feet tall and not pronc to the illnesses of his age and profession. His back was still straight, and he could wield a sword with the power of a man half his age, though lately he had reflected on his inactivity due to his more political role. The Order was under attack, and he was less reliant on his sword arm and more on his intellect, which was considerable.

He was in his audience room with Hugues de Peraud, his deputy, who was of a comparable age and state of health. He shadowed Molay in all his offices, and together with Godefroi de Gonneville, he acted as the Grand Master's eyes and ears as well as his bodyguard.

Molay wondered if they had been blessed by God or if it was the good life and wealth the Order had provided for them. They might be rich, but every knight had placed his life at risk in this coup they had engineered. Protecting their interests and then benefiting from them was not pleasure without pain.

'King Henry's biggest mistake was playing the Order. He regrets stealing from us and murdering our brothers as he languishes in Armenia in exile under the watchful eye of Amalric's brother-in-law,' Jacques continued

Molay was defending the Order in other places as well, and trouble was brewing. He removed two letters from his sleeve and read them again.

The door rattled and Godefroi appeared. He was twenty years younger than Molay and de Peraud, yet was well into middle age. His hair was grey speckled with black, whereas the others already had the blanket of grey that all men in their sixties surrendered to.

'I am glad you are both here, as I need to show you a couple of dispatches.'

Godefroi bowed in respect. 'Master, who are they from?'

'The first is from Pope Clement, politely ordering me to meet him at the papal court in Poitiers.' Molay handed the letter to Hugues.

'And the second?' Hugues's scanned the papal note.

'That is from an anonymous Templar warning me the Order is in extreme danger and, I quote, "under threat from kings". I am asked to return to the Temple as quickly as possible. It has the Templar seal but remains unsigned and was dated in August. This note arrived along with several from Gerard de Villiers reporting on King Phillip's Temple visit to escape a rioting mob. The mob wanted to rid the country of the king and string Guillaume de Nogaret from the nearest scaffold.'

'The mob and I are in agreement,' Godefroi commented as Molay handed him the other note.

'Can we assume that when he mentions kings, our anonymous Templar is referring to King Phillip?' He swapped notes with Hugues.

'Certainly, we know Phillip has his avaricious eyes on anyone he thinks will fund his wars with the English and the Flemish. He was at the Temple hiding whilst at the same time valuing and stealing whatever wasn't nailed down. I deliberately removed all the valuable furniture from my rooms, knowing that if he stayed there he would clear the place. There are rumours that he will exile the Lombards and accuse them of heresy. We all know he can't be trusted, and I am godfather to his daughter! He only did that because he needed a loan when she was born. I wouldn't put the Order out of his purview for duplicity.'

Molay understood the King's position, but he didn't like it.

'I want to support our King but even the Templar pockets aren't deep enough for his excesses. Kings only remain powerful with money, and Phillip likes to take loans and find an excuse not to pay them back. Money seems to drain through Phillip's hands like water.'

'Master, Gerard de Villiers is an old gossip and values his charm over good sense. Do you think these threats are real? There are many Templars who would like to create division between the Order and the king. Some believe we are bigger than the realm, and that level of arrogance is dangerous. This sort of conspiracy will always appeal to a faction, and the situation viewed straight on is rarely how it is portrayed. We all know that Phillip is imperfect and is driven by the foibles of man, but he is the king, and we need to live alongside him, not in conflict. If we are in such danger, you would think Geoffroi de Charnay would have sent word to Cyprus to alert us. I am sceptical about the motivations of this nameless knight – it's probably Gerard but he doesn't have the courage to put his name to his suspicions.'

Hugues was calm and measured, and Molay always considered his advice, which included patience, thought, and long-term planning. He was the supreme pragmatist, and he had often been in battle, so he was no coward. It had been many years since the last Crusade, and some of the new Templar hierarchy had no experiences of battle. Hugues was a veteran, and a man of many talents. His strategic thinking had also helped make the Templars the biggest bankers in the world.

Molay wondered if his reluctance to act was driven by age, as he had played a small part in the fighting in Cyprus, unlike de Gonneville, who had been at the heart of the fighting against King Henry.

Molay trusted them both, and he understood they had different strengths.

'And Clement? What will you do about him? His note is from June, and this is the first time you have shared its contents with us.' Godefroi sounded hurt, as if Molay had deliberately kept this a secret from his advisors.

'You were both busy dealing with this coup, and I wanted time to consider it. He is, after all, the only temporal authority we recognise, and we may need his protection. You can see that he is planning a new Crusade and wants the Holy Order of Knights Templar and Hospitallers to merge, believing we are stronger together. He thinks we can win against the Mamluks if we assemble an overwhelming force of holy knights and Christian kings. He also mentions involving the Orthodox Greeks. And there is talk again of mending the schism between the two Churches. I am attracted to any new venture that protects our religion but the world is changing.'

For a little while the hero within him looked forward to a new crusade, but deep down, he recognised the era was gone. There were no Christian cities in the Holy Land. Money was more powerful.

'There has been talk of that for as long as I remember, and knowing the characters involved, Patriarch Athanasius and Pope Clement are more likely to smash what is already broken. It's only talk, and Clement knows it. The Greeks even exiled their Empress Eirene and Patriarch Gregory for suggesting it. The winds of this front are blowing in a different direction. Master, it is a trick.' Hugues's analysis was correct. Molay believed Clement was lying.

Molay wasn't going to try and convince his advisors that the Order was suddenly going to be at the heart of the unification of the Christian world. That sounded great on paper, and Clement was appealing to their vanity, but after over two hundred and fifty years since the break of communion, there wasn't going to be an idealistic rapprochement. Clement and Athanasius each considered the other inferior, and if they thought they could use force to master the other, they would. Either side had the capability to make any confrontation intolerant and bloody.

Molay decided to look for another way of persuading his colleagues to return to the Temple.

'In my other dispatches, there is talk of great wealth hidden by the Order. Clement is under Phillip's control and talk of Templar treasure has ignited their mutual greed. I am sure they are counting the money already.'

Molay smiled as he imagined the greedy duo wallowing in a river of gold, though he was more wary of King Phillip. He had been pleading with the Templars for more loans – loans Molay knew he would struggle to repay.

'I have heard those rumours too – a fabled treasure hidden by the Templars reemerges,' Godefroi said. 'I heard some rumours from the Varangian mercenaries. They acted as bodyguards to the Byzantines emperors, and they described them as being obsessed with its recovery, which isn't unusual, since it belonged to them. It was reported that it had been hidden in Acre in an underground cavern after being stolen from them by the Venetians. Then after Acre fell, it disappeared again. It was said to be in Italy and then in France, but it sounded like a tale told by dreamers. I was in Acre, and if there had been a treasure there, we would have known about it. Master Beaujeau would have used it to buy an army and defeated the Mamluks.'

Godefroi sounded dismissive, and he had been in Acre at the time. Molay thought if Beaujeau trusted anyone, it would have been Godefroi and if he said there was no treasure then there probably wasn't.

Molay had always believed that William Beaujeau, the Templar commander at Acre in 1291, had kept many secrets, and he wondered if the secrets that weighed so heavy upon him had included this legendary treasure.

'Master Beaujeau was my immediate superior,' Godefroi continued. 'I knew him well, and he would have understood the treasure's power for good. He would also have considered how such wealth would have corrupted those that remained. The Crusader armies had more battles fighting against each other than they had with the Mamluks. It was a struggle just to keep everyone together. The politics of desperation don't bring out the best in people when they are isolated and know that death is only a small step away. It would have been stolen for sure, taken away by those that left before the siege ended. The rats left with the thieves.'

Hugues interrupted. 'Master, we must act with caution if the pope is looking for us to provide information about this treasure.'

'I have considered refusing Clement's "invitation" because he is duplicitous. However, timing is on his side.

It is time we went home. I have been away for too long from the heart of the Order, leaving de Charnay on his own unchecked. He is charismatic and clever, but he is also self-righteous and reckless. I hear nothing but complaints from Pierre de Nogaret.'

Godefroi rolled his eyes at de Nogaret's name. 'Pierre is a bureaucrat – an overly ambitious weasel who would struggle to know which end of a sword to hold. At least Geoffroi is a fighter.'

'We need a few pen-wielding weasels,' Hugues said. 'I am not ignorant of Pierre's shortcomings, but we need men of details just as much as we need men with charm.'

Molay had no liking for de Nogaret, but he would always defend someone with talent. 'And we need to be nurturing Clement's friendship, not inflaming it. I haven't met with him since he became pope, and that was over a year ago. There are many reasons for returning, including the anonymous letter. Even if there is nothing in these threats, it is time, and I want to see my home in Burgundy before I die.'

Godefroi nodded and gave the reluctant smile that Molay needed. He agreed with his decision and would now support the Grand Master. Hugues sat with his arms folded in silence. He didn't nod or shake his head, and that showed Molay he needed a little more enticement.

Godefroi stepped in. His smile had broadened, and he offered Hugues a goblet filled to the brim with Commanderie wine.

'It's time to go home, Hugues. As Templar knights over forty, we are lucky to still be alive, and we should take this opportunity. The garrison at Kolossi has a friendly benefactor in Amalric, and he is grateful for our support in getting rid of King Henry. We can return to France well-armed and in force with battle-hardened men. We have sufficient ships filled with good wine and gold from the new King of Cyprus.'

Hugues drank the wine and displayed a quiet acceptance,

even if it amounted to a nod. Molay understood his caution, but he had made up his mind.

'I will instruct the sergeants to prepare to leave. I will also write to Geoffroi and let him know that we are returning, and I will ask him for a full report on events at the Temple and the King's visit the moment I return. Sergeant!'

The door snapped open, and a dark-robed Templar stepped inside.

The Templar sergeants did most of the work and the dying in the Order. They were from the lower classes, and the distinction was emphasised in the robes they wore. Unlike the aristocratic Templar knights, who dressed in a surcoat of white marked by a red cross, their darker robes were indicative of the dirtier work they were required to conduct.

Molay appreciated them and understood how reliant he was upon them. He treated them with respect, but not equality; that was restricted to the noble Templar knights.

'Sergeant Florent, make preparation to leave.'

'Master, where are you going? Shall I get your horse and escort ready?' Florent was expecting something quite ordinary and today was extraordinary.

'We are going home, back to France, and we are taking a thousand men.'

The sergeant took a step back.

'Master, I want to return home more than you know, but that will take some time to organise. Our hospital is still full of men injured from battle, and our stores need replenishing.'

'It's September, the harvest is available to restock. Once the men hear they are going home, you will be amazed how quickly they will heal. Get things ready as quickly as you can, though I understand the preparations will take several weeks. We will travel by sea.'

Molay knew his decision would be unexpected after five years away, and there would be much to do in organising the transport and food for a thousand men and their horses. The ships would need to be assembled in the harbour nearby at Limassol.

'Yes, Master – immediately.'

The sergeant bowed, struggling to contain his excitement as he left with obvious enthusiasm. Molay was sure he heard him bound down the stairs before running across the courtyard, shouting in delight.

'Well, it appears we have pleased two people I never thought I would mention in the same sentence – Sergeant Florent and Pope Clement.'

Molay poured three goblets of Commanderie wine and handed them to Hugues and Godefroi.

'Let's drink to that.'

List of Characters

The Scots

Adam de Irwyne	Older brother of Will de Irwyne, bodyguard of Isabel Bruce, navigator and soldier. Aged 38
Alain d'Orthez	Alias of Murdi MacBeith
Alexander Bruce	Brother of King Robert Bruce. Aged 21
Aonghus Og Macdonald	Bruce supporter and Clan Chief of the MacDonald. Aged 30
Bernard du Gascon	Owner of L'Auberge du Lion and ally of Geoffroi de Charnay. Aged 40
Christina Ranald	Lord of the Isles and cousin of Robert Bruce King of Scots. Aged 25
Deacon Harrison	Chief steward to Ailean and Christina Ranald and Gascon Monk. Aged 28
Domhnall MacBeith	Brother of Murdi & son of Hector. Priest, physician and alchemist. Aged 38
Edward Balliol	Son of John Balliol and chief competitor for the Scottish crown. Aged 23
Edward Bruce	Brother of King Robert Bruce. Aged 25
Eilidh Robertson	Chief maid to Christina Ranald and wife of Hendor Robertson. Aged 38

Elisabeth de Burgh Queen of Scots	Second wife of King Robert of Scotland and daughter of Richard. Aged 21
Geoffrey of Brittany	Son of Knox de Mayon and Eleanor of Brittany. True heir to the English throne
Gilbert de la Hay	Head of King Robert's personal bodyguards. Aged 30
Hamish Campbell	Head of Christina Ranald's guards. Son of Eilidh Robertson. Aged 20
Hector MacKeown	Knight and head of Queen Isabel's Scottish Guards. Aged 40
Hendor Robertson	Loyal servant of Bishop Wishart. Veteran of Battle of Falkirk and Stirling Bridge. Aged 38
Hugh Halcro	Earl of Orkney. Aged 28
Innes de Mayon	Agent in France for Bishop Wishart. Son of Knox de Mayon and a French mother. Aged 35
Isabel Bruce Dowager Queen of Norway	Sister of King Robert, widow of King Eirik of Norway (died 1299). Aged 34
James Douglas	Chief Commander of King Robert and son of Sir William Douglas who died in the Tower. Aged 22
James Stewart	High Steward to King Robert. Aged 46
Jamie Wishart	Apprentice Mason. Nephew of Bishop Wishart and son of his missing brother John de Wishart. Aged 19
John de Wishart	Father of Jamie brother of the Bishop. Missing since 1301
John Lorn MacDougall	Lord of Argyle and Chief of Clan MacDougall. Aged 36

Murdi MacBeith	Spy for Bishop Wishart in the English Court. Aged 35
Robert the Bruce King of Scotland	King of Scotland (crowned 1306). Aged 32
Robert Wishart Archbishop of Glasgow	Bishop of Glasgow and former Guardian of Scotland. Leader of the Independence Movement. Uncle of Jamie Wishart and brother of John. Aged 65
Ruaidhri Ranald	Illegitimate brother of Catriona Ranald. Aged 24
Thomas Bruce	Brother of King Robert Bruce. Aged 22
Will de Irwyne	Armour Bearer of Robert the Bruce. Aged 30
William Lamberton	Bishop of St Andrews. Aged 56
William the Lion King of Scots	Grandfather of King Alexander III of Scotland. King from 1165-1214
William Wallace	Patriot and Guardian of Scotland. Died 1305

The Byzantines

Andrea Morisco	Admiral of the Byzantine navy. Native of Genoa. Aged 35
Andronikos II Palaiologos's	Byzantine Emperor and father of joint Emperor Michael. Aged 47
Axel Myhre (Aurelian)	Commander of the Byzantine Varangian guard, the Emperor's personal bodyguard. Byzantine assassin and spymaster. Aged 35
Christiana Bruce	Sister of King Robert, and wife of Sir Christopher Seton. Aged 28
Christina Ranald	King Robert's cousin and Chief of Clan Ranald. Aged 23

Eirene Palaiologos Empress of Byzantium	Second wife of Emperor Andronikos II. Aged 32 and exiled
Ferran d'Aunes	Admiral of the Byzantine navy. Aged 35. Native of Gascony
Maccabi Tagaris	Orthodox monk from St Catherine's Monastery in Sinai. Aged 35
Michael IX Palaiologos's	Byzantine Emperor and son of joint Emperor Andronikos II. Aged 28
Patriarch Athanasius I	The Patriarch of Constantinople appointed by Emperor Andronikos. Aged 76
Patriarch Gregory	Patriarch of the Orthodox exiled to Greece. Aged around 45
Theodore Metochites	Personal advisor to the joint Emperors. Aged 40

The English

Aymer de Valence	2nd Earl of Pembroke and King Edward I 2nd cousin. Aged 36
Edward I King of England	King of England (Longshanks). Aged 67
Edward Plantagenet Prince of Wales	Son of King Edward of England and Prince of Wales. Aged 19
Henry Stikelaw	Brother of Weland Stikelaw and English Spy working for Valence. Aged 40
Konrad von Feuchtwangen	German assassin working for King Edward I. Aged 45
Jean or Gervase de Bretagne	French double agent working for the English king. Aged 40
Ralph de Sandwich	Chief Justice of the Common Pleas in King Edward's court. Aged 71

Robert De Clifford - Baron Clifford	Soldier and English noble. Aged 32

The Italians

Brother Albertus	Dominican friar, alchemist and scientist. Aged 30
Bishop Padano della Torre	Bishop of Padua. Aged 30
Cardinal Francesco Napoleone Orsini	Papal legate to King Edward's court. Aged 70
Enrico della Scrovegni	Italian banker and relic maker. Friend of John de Wishart and Geoffroi de Charnay. Aged 36
Geraldo della Procacci	Servant to Enrico Scrovegni. Aged 19
Giovanni della Giordanno	Head of Enrico Scrovegni's guards. Aged 35

The French

Baldwin du Toulon 'Les Frères Loup'	Mercenary attached to Madame of France and in the pay of Charles de Valois. Aged 30
Bernard du Gascon	Owner of L'Auberge du Lion and ally of Geoffroi de Charnay. Aged 40
Bernard Ferrers	Member of the Catalan company and mercenary ex Templar. Aged 35
Betrand du Toulon, 'Les Frères Loup'	Mercenary attached to Madame of France and in the pay of Charles de Valois. Aged 32
Charles de Valois	Full brother of King Phillip IV. Count of Valois and Latin Emperor of Constantinople. Aged 36
Esquieu de Floyran	Head of the Temple guard. Aged 28

Geoffroi de Charnay	Preceptor of Normandy. 2nd in command of the Knights Templars. Aged 50
Gerard de Villiers	Templar dignitary and leader. Aged 36
Godefroi de Gonville	Bodyguard of Jacque du Molay. Aged 45
Guillaume de Nogaret	Chief advisor to King Phillip IV. Aged 46
Guillaume du Gascon	Son of Bernard du Gascon. Aged 18
Guy de Nogaret	Nephew of Guillaume and Pierre de Nogaret. Templar squire. Aged 17
Hugh de Verneuil	Templar knight commander and close friend of Geoffroi de Charnay. Aged 35
Hugues de Peraud	Second in command of the Templar order after Jacque du Molay. Aged 65
Jacques du Molay	Grandmaster of the Templar Order and aged about 66
Jean de Grailliy	French assassin working for King Phillip IV. Aged 45
Jean the Leper	Friend of Bernard du Gascon. Aged 40
Madame de France (Fallone)	Female French assassin working for King Phillip IV. Phillip's illegitimate daughter. Aged 21
Phillip IV King of France	King of France. Aged 38
Pierre de Nogaret	Templar administrator, banker and Cathar. Brother of Guillaume de Nogaret and uncle of Guy. Aged 44
Raimund de Braose	Prominent Anglo Norman family. His great grandfather was implicated in the disappearance of Arthur of Brittany
Raoul du Bec	Templar apprentice and ally of Geoffroi de Charnay. Aged 25

The Norwegians

Audun Hugleikkson Hestakorn	Former advisor to Kings Eirik and Haakon of Norway. Executed in 1303
Cnut Myhre	Older brother of Axel Myhre and servant of Audun Hugleikkson
Gyrid Hugleikkson	Wife of Audun Hugleikkson. Aged 36
Haakon v of Norway	King of Norway (crowned 1299). Ally of King Robert. Brother in law of Isabel Bruce. Uncle of the Maid of Norway. Aged 36
Jakob Dedekam	Ivory Merchant, spy and ex lover of Isabel Bruce. Aged 35
Jonas Fjelstad	Navigator and Dominican friar. Aged 30
Olaf Nielsen	Ex Varangian guard, master builder. Aged 42
Rolf Steen	Dominican monk and ex soldier in King Haakon's army. Aged 40
Wamrok Skjelden	Ex Varangian guard and master of King Haakon's bodyguard. Aged 42

Other Characters

Ailean Ranald Lord of the Isles	Father of Christina Ranald. Died pre 1306
Alessandro della Spina	Dominican friar and inventor of spectacles. Aged 56
Alexander II King of Scots	King of Scotland and father of Alexander III 1214-1249.
Alexander III King of Scots	King of Scotland 1249 - 1286 grandfather of The Maid of Norway.
Alexander Seton	Brother of Sir Christopher. New follower of King Robert. Aged 26
Amalric of Cyprus	Ruler of Cyprus 1306-1310

Andrew de Moray	Joint Commander of Scottish forces at the Battle of Stirling Bridge with William Wallace. Died 1297
Arthur of Brittany	Son of Geoffrey of Brittany. Disappeared in 1203 and brother of Eleanor of Brittany
Baldred Bisset	Scottish Lawyer and diplomat. Aged 46. Submitted evidences on Scottish independence to the Pope in 1301
Constance of Brittany	Wife of Geoffrey of Brittany and mother of Arthur and Eleanor of Brittany. Died 1201
Davie Munro	Chief of Clan Munro. Aged 36
Eleanor of Aquitaine	Wife of King Henry II, mother of King John and the Young King Henry. Died 1204
Eleanor of Brittany	Daughter of Geoffrey of Brittany, son of King Henry II of England
Erik King of Denmark	King of Denmark since 1294 and chief rival of King Haakon. Aged 32
Geoffrey of Brittany	Son of King Henry II of England and Eleanor of Aquitaine died 1186. Father of Eleanor of Brittany
Hugh Halcro	Earl of Orkney. Aged 28
Henry of Cyprus	Last crowned king of Jerusalem. Fled to Cyprus after the fall of Acre ruled 1291 to 1306
Henry II King of England	Great grandfather of King Edward I
Henry III King of England	Father of King Edward 1 reigned 1217 to 1273
Henry Plantagenet	Known as the 'Young King' son of King Henry II. Died 1183

Hubert de Lacy	English Ambassador to the French court. Aged 45
Hugh de Percy - Baron	English soldier and noble. Aged 33
Hector MacBeith	Father of Murdie and Domhnall. Died before 1306
Hugleik Hugleikkson	Son of Audun and Gyrid, Prisoner in the Tower of London and lover of Prince Edward of England. Aged 19
Ibn al-Haytham	Author of the Book of Optics 965-1240. Iraqi mathematician, physicist and philosopher
Ibn Sahl	Persian mathematician and physicist 940-1000
Isabella MacDuff	Countess of Buchan Hereditary noble of the House of MacDuff entrusted with crowing of all Scottish kings. Aged 30
John King of England	Grandfather of King Edward I. King from 1199-1216
John Baliol	King Edward's nominee as King of Scotland. Abdicated and exiled 1296. Aged 56
John Palaiologos	First born son of Empress Eirene and Emperor Andronikos. Aged 20
Knox de Mayon	Father of Innes and lover of Eleanor of Brittany heir to the English throne. Deceased
Lachlann Ranald	Illegitimate brother of Catriona Ranald. Aged 26
Laurent d'Aumale	Templar knight commander and close friend of Geoffroi de Charnay. Aged 35
Malcolm MacQuillan Lord	Nobleman and follower of King Robert

Margaret the Maid of Norway	Granddaughter of King Alexander III. Last surviving grandchild and heir to the throne of Scotland. Grand Niece of Edward I
Marguerite de Mayon	Mother of Innes de Mayon. Dead by 1306
Marjorie Bruce	Daughter of King Robert Bruce. Aged 11
Mary Bruce	Sister of King Robert, and wife of Sir Christopher Seton. Aged 26
Niall Bruce	Brother of King Robert Bruce. Aged 27
Niccolo	Italian seaman and mercenary. Works for Jean de Bretagne. Aged 28
Olivier de Pau	Cathar and physician. Proprietor of the Moors Head Tavern. Aged 40
Otto de Grandison	Crusader Knight killed in 1291 at acre. Alias of Konrad von Feuchtwangen
Pagano della Tore Bishop of Padua	Bishop of Padua. Aged 30
Pope Clement V	Pope from 1305. Resident in Poitier. Aged 42
Prefect Belibaste	Last leader of the Cathars. Aged 45
Prior Duncan	Dominican Prior of St Olaf's in Groenland
Reginald Crawford	Knight and leader of the Galloway rebellion
Richard de Burgh	Father of Queen Elisabeth and father in law of King Robert. Aged 66
Roger de Flor	Soldier of fortune and head of the Catalan mercenaries. Killed in 1305 by Emperor Michael

Saint Helena	Mother of Constantine the Great Emperor of Rome
Talbot Armstrong	Minor Scottish noble working for King Edward
Trulls	Norwegian boatbuilder to Sir Hugh Halcro
Weland de Stikelaw	Bruce loyalist and brother of Henry

Acknowledgements

I would like to thank Isobel Freeman, David Webster, Sandy Jamieson, Efa Walker, Meillidy Campbell, Anna McClelland, Benedetta Campoleoni, Martyna Przybolewska, Maisie Raven, Émile Steinbach and everyone at Ringwood Publishing Ltd and Ringwood AMC who encouraged and gave their time freely and without condition so this book could be published.

Particular thanks to Gabriele Jaceviciute for her marvellous front cover presenting the contents with her amazing skills and artistry.

I would also like to thank Aaron Redfern and Jenny Quinlan at Historical Editorial for making a draft something worth reading, and Ralph and Lynnette Appelby for their boundless enthusiasm and encouragement when I wanted to give up writing.

About the Author

Born and bred in Glasgow, author L.A. Kristiansen discovered a passion for Scottish History through her enthusiasm for genealogy. In her research, she uncovered close family ties with many of the leaders of the wars of Scottish Independence – the likes of Bishop Wishart, Robert the Bruce, and the fearsome William Wallace are, in fact, woven into her own ancestral tapestry.

During further research and exploration, she discovered how their bravery and courage played a significant part in influencing the events of the 13th and 14th century, and she decided to write about them, interlacing fact and fiction in the lead up to the acknowledgement of Scotland's sovereignty in 1328, and Bruce's death in 1329.

She is a writer, and dabbles in IT whilst spending her time in Scotland, France, and Norway, researching the new adventures of the characters first found in this book.

Books by this Author

If you enjoyed *The Bruce's Treasure*, you will most certainly like the other books in the series:

Raise Dragon
L.A. Kristiansen

In the year of 1306, Scotland is in turmoil. Robert the Bruce and the fighting Bishop Wishart's plans for rebellion put the Scottish kingdom at risk, whilst the hostile kingdom of England seems more invincible than ever. But Bishop Wishart has got a final card left to play: four brave Scottish knights set off in search of a mysterious ancient treasure that will bring Scotland to the centre of an international plot, changing the course of history forever.

ISBN: 978-1-901514-76-6
£9.99

Revenge of the Tyrants
L.A. Kristiansen

The fight for the nation's soul has begun, and nothing will ever be the same. While the King of Scots wages a desperate, bloody war for Scotland's independence, four intrepid Scottish knights embark on a treasure barge. What follows is a journey directly to the heart of the conflict, and a vivid depiction of the scheming, treachery and violence it entailed. Meanwhile, Kings Edward the first of England, Philip the fourth of France, and Haakon the fifth of Norway have their own reasons to thwart the Scots, and each will stop at nothing to gain their victory.

ISBN: 978-1-901514-89-6
£12.99